Fiona O'Brien left an award-winning career in advertising to write fiction. She lives in Sandymount, Dublin.

Praise for NONE OF MY AFFAIR:

'Long lunches, hot evenings and plenty of sex – O'Brien never puts a foot wrong'   *Irish Independent*

'A delicious novel, full of warmth, glamour and excitement'
Cathy Kelly

'The right mix of heartfelt emotion and upbeat humour' *Image*

Fiona O'Brien

NONE OF MY AFFAIR

HODDER

First published in Great Britain in 2008 by Hodder & Stoughton
An Hachette Livre UK company

First published in paperback in 2009

I

Copyright © Fiona O'Brien 2008

A CIP catalogue record for this title is available from the British Library

ISBN 978 0 340 96231 2

Typeset in Plantin Light by Palimpsest Book Production Limited,
Grangemouth, Stirlingshire

Printed and bound by Clays Ltd, St Ives plc

Hodder & Stoughton policy is to use papers that are natural,
renewable and recyclable products and made from wood grown in
sustainable forests. The logging and manufacturing processes are
expected to conform to the environmental regulations of
the country of origin.

Hodder & Stoughton Ltd
338 Euston Road
London NW1 3BH

www.hodder.co.uk

Dedication

To every woman, struggling in a soul-destroying relationship.
For having the courage to try,
the strength to survive and, hopefully,
ultimately, the bravery to walk away.

Prologue

The day was perfect. Just as she had known it would be. From her window in the Armstrongs' villa, Babs inspected the clear blue sky without a cloud on the horizon and noted, with satisfaction, the wisp of a breeze that would temper the already building heat. Before her, the deep, settled blue of the Mediterranean stretched as far as the eye could see.

It was simply a perfect day for a wedding, although for added certainty, she had put the Child of Prague statue out on the windowsill last thing before going to bed. The old Irish custom of putting the much-loved statue of the baby Jesus outside the night before a wedding warded off all manner of inclement weather, it was held, never mind global warming. This might be sunny Spain, but weather conditions were changing everywhere and it didn't do to take anything for granted.

Despite her seventy-five years, at seven o'clock in the morning Babs was up, dressed and ready for action. Not in her wedding outfit, of course: that would come later.

Looking at the delicate ensemble of coffee-and-cream chiffon hanging regally on the front of the wardrobe door, she felt a sudden rush of emotion.

Only nine hours to go, and they would fly. Nine hours until the wedding of any girl's dreams. It was going to be magnificent. Well, it was going to be, fullstop, and that in itself was a blessed relief.

Little Ali, she mused, the minx of the family, the first of the girls to be married. The three Armstrong girls were like her own. She'd been a part of their lives for twenty-three years, after all.

Feeling suddenly tearful, Babs sat down on the bed and allowed herself a trip down memory lane. It genuinely seemed like only yesterday she had come into their lives.

'I've come about the ad.' Babs was still slightly out of breath after her cycle up the rather steep road to the Armstrongs' semi-detached house in the newly built development.

'And I hope you don't mind, but I like to wear trousers when I work. I cycle, you see.' There, she had said it. Better to get it out in the open straight away. Some of those snooty society women she'd worked for in the past had actually told her they would prefer if she wore a dress or skirt while she was working for them. A maid's uniform and lots of curtsey-ing was what they'd really been dreaming about. Mind you, that had been a good few years ago, back in the old days.

But though Babs hadn't worked outside the home in a while because she'd been raising her own children, she had learned a thing or two in her time, and one of them was to get things straight with a prospective employer right from the start. Babs Buckley, mother of five, oldest of ten and who'd grown up the hard way, was nobody's fool.

'Oh, you'd like to wear trousers,' said the rather startled-looking young mother who opened the door. 'Of course, that's perfectly fine. Wear whatever you'd like. It's that, I, um, wasn't expecting anyone so soon, but please, do come in. You've caught me on the hop, I'm afraid.' She wiped her hands hurriedly on the tea towel slung over her shoulder.

Babs relaxed. This attractive young woman with her chestnut curls and wide, welcoming smile was clearly not a society matron with notions of grandeur.

'I know I should have rung to say I was calling,' Babs checked to make sure her bike was parked safely against the wall, 'but I saw the ad in the newsagent's and seeing as I only live around the corner, I thought I'd just come straight up. Strike while the iron's hot, you know, that's my motto. If it's inconvenient, I can always come back later.'

'No, no, not at all, please, come in,' the woman said eagerly. 'I was just about to make a cup of tea before I feed the baby, would you like one?'

'I'd murder one.'

'I'm Carrie, by the way, Carrie Armstrong.' She held out a hand that Babs shook firmly.

'Nice to meet you, Mrs Armstrong. I'm Annie Buckley, but I've been called Babs for so long now it's all I answer to.'

Babs followed Carrie across the hall and into the cosy kitchen, where a small girl sat at the scrubbed pine table wielding a crayon across a brightly coloured page, her tongue poking out of the side of her mouth in concentration. Looking up, she fixed Babs with big solemn brown eyes, smiled shyly, and went back to her drawing.

'Well who have we here?' said Babs, sitting down at the table opposite her.

'This is Hope,' said Carrie, smiling over at her little girl as she turned on the kettle and reached into the overhead cupboard for two cups. 'She's our eldest. Say hello to Mrs Buckley, Hope,'

'Hello.'

'And an artist, too, so I see.' Babs peered over at the drawing, making noises of appreciation. 'What a lovely picture. What is it? I'm not very good without my glasses.'

'It's a car. My daddy's getting a new car today, so I drew a picture for him when he gets home.'

'Well isn't that a lovely thing to do. And how old are you, Hope?'

'I'm going to be seven next week.' She looked up at Babs with a serious expression. 'How old are you?'

Babs grinned. 'Oh, I'm very old, very old indeed.'

The crayon paused in mid-air as Hope studied her.

'Hope!' Carrie protested, laughing. 'I'm sorry,' she said to Babs. 'Hope, you mustn't ask grown-up people how old they are. It's not polite.'

'Why not?' Hope asked curiously.

'Why not indeed,' said Babs, chuckling. 'I'm fifty-two, love, and I don't mind telling you or anybody. Age is only a number, you know.'

Hope continued her study of Babs, her head tilting to one side as she regarded her from across the table. 'You have funny hair.'

Babs snorted with laughter, as Carrie, looking alarmed, placed two cups of tea and a plate of biscuits on the table. 'That's enough, Hope.'

'Funny is the right word for it, young lady. It has a sense of humour all its own, my hair.' Babs ran a hand through the wiry shock of grey hair that stood up relentlessly. It had once been a fiery red and then, overnight almost, decided to turn grey, not that Babs had minded. She'd never bothered much with looks or worrying over her hair, and Larry, her late husband, had always said he loved her just the way she was. 'I gave up fighting it years ago.'

'Come along, darling, into the playroom. Mummy wants to talk to Mrs Buckley—'

'Babs,' interjected Babs.

'Er, to Babs. Take your drawing into the playroom like a good girl, and I'll come and see it in few minutes.'

'Okay, I'm nearly finished anyway.'

'Good girl,' said Carrie as Hope gathered her crayons and paper and slipped off the chair, walking quietly from the kitchen through a glass door that led to another room where a big television had pride of place and a lot of toys were scattered.

'We built the playroom on last year,' explained Carrie. 'It's been a lifesaver.'

'Now,' said Babs, 'let's get down to business. I've worked as a cook and a housekeeper all my life, and I'm good at it, if I say so myself. The references say the rest and I have them with me.' She pushed a collection of papers across to Carrie. 'My last position was in an embassy, but that was ten years ago. I have my own family, all grown up now of course and on their way, but I wanted to be at home for them when school got tough and they were doing the exams and so on, so I gave up working. Of course, Larry was out working then too, my husband, one of the head gardeners he was, up in the Botanic Gardens. He died just over a year ago and—'

'Oh, I'm so sorry,' Carrie interjected awkwardly, her eyes full of sympathy.

'Thank you love, it was sad. He was young, you know, two years younger than me, so it came out of the blue, but then cancer does that. But we had a great life together and a great marriage, and five lovely children, and he spent his days doing what he loved best, out in the fresh air, foostering with his old plants and flowers.' Babs sniffed and took out a tissue to blow her nose before continuing. 'The children, as I said, are all grown up, three in Canada, one in America and then my youngest, Annie, had to go and marry a Guard who's been posted up to Donegal.' Babs paused. 'I was finding it a bit lonely in the house on my own, and I'm not about to go galivanting off to America or Canada to live at my age, although the invitation's offered regularly, so I thought I'd go back to work, get a bit of routine going again. I'm a great believer in routine.' She took a drink of her tea. 'Now the ad said you were looking for a home help, but that can cover a multitude. What exactly is it that you are looking for?' She fixed Carrie with a direct gaze.

'Oh, well, I, um, that is, my husband and I, well, we have three young children now, and Rob, that's my husband,' Carrie explained, 'well, he's working all the hours God sends these days, and suddenly, well, that seems to involve a lot of entertaining, you know, bosses, prospective clients, that sort of thing, and trips away at short notice, everything has to be ship shape . . .'

'Don't I know it well,' said Babs, nodding.

'I thought I could cope with it all, but with the girls, and the new baby, well, it's just that Rob said that we, I mean, I, could do with an extra pair of hands.'

'And what ages are the other two?'

'Hope, who you met, is seven next week, Ali, her younger sister, is five, and the baby, Stephanie, is three months old tomorrow.'

'And what about you?' Babs looked at her keenly. 'What do you think about all this needing a pair of extra hands?'

Carrie let out a deep sigh. 'Well, it would be lovely in theory, but,' she bit her lip, 'I feel, I suppose I feel that I shouldn't need help. I should be able to cope on my own. It's just that . . .'

'Just that what?' Babs probed, listening attentively.

'Well, my own mother stayed at home with six of us, and she managed perfectly, and I only have three and already I'm finding it difficult, and, and . . .' her voice wavered, 'well, she died, too, just six months ago, and I thought I'd be able to cope without her, but she was brilliant with the girls, and always ready to step in for me, but now I'm finding it so hard, all the sleepless nights, and Rob's always working and I, I feel that I'm just not making a good job of it any more.'

'There, there, now, don't go getting yourself all upset,' Babs said kindly, patting Carrie's hand. 'Don't I know well what having three young children is all about, and easy it's not. It's just that nobody ever tells you that. And things today are different. Oh I know, it may be the 1980s and all that, but there's pressures now on young families that we never had to cope with in the old days. I blame it on the breakdown of community, myself. But you know, nothing can ever make up for the loss of a mother, and why should you be expected to cope with that because you have a young family of your own? Is your father alive?'

'No, heart attack.'

'Ah, I understand more now. You see, you're nobody's daughter any more, and that's quite a wrench to come to terms with,' Babs nodded to herself. 'Especially when you have your own young family.'

Carrie looked surprised. 'Yes, yes, that's it exactly. I could never quite put it into words, but now you say it, that's exactly how I feel. And Rob, well, men aren't good at that sort of thing, everyone's been very sympathetic and everything, but it's hard to explain, and I feel I'm not being good enough for Rob, or my children.'

'It sounds to me like you could do with some help. How many days a week were you thinking of?'

'Oh, well, I hadn't really thought it through, to be honest, Rob thought—'

'Never mind Rob for a moment, it's you who has to deal with another body in your house and under your feet. What feels right to you?'

'Twice a week, mornings?' Carrie ventured.

'How about Monday and Friday, that way you have a nice clean house for the weekend and a clean-up after it, and I can help out with the entertaining when you need it. Then we can see how it goes from there?'

'That sounds great,' said Carrie, smiling.

'Now you have my references, you can give them a call, and let me know when you've interviewed any other applicants and had a bit of a think about it.' Babs drained her tea.

'Oh, that won't be necessary,' Carrie said, 'I think we'll get along perfectly. Would you like me to show you around the house?'

'That would be lovely, but what I'd really like is to see the baby. I know she's sleeping, but just a peek maybe?'

'Of course.' Carrie's face lit up. 'Come on, I'll show you around.'

Babs followed Carrie out of the kitchen and upstairs, noting how clean and well-kept the house was, if a bit untidy. She liked that, liked knowing that a house was a home and somewhere to be lived in, where life with all its ups and downs and untidiness unfolded, and not just a showpiece.

Along the way through the typical, if luxurious, three-bedroom semi-d, Carrie pointed out the bedrooms. The larger, of course, was hers and Rob's, and the second, done up in pinks and purples with two twin beds, was Hope and Ali's. Babs chuckled when she saw the makeshift wicker fence between the beds separating the room into two halves.

Carrie shook her head and laughed. 'Honestly, you wouldn't believe the pair of them. Ali's a tearaway and throws her clothes everywhere and Hope is a neat freak. The only way of keeping the peace was for their father to put up this "fence". If they hadn't pestered him so much, I wouldn't have believed he'd do it myself.' Carrie laughed at the memory of Rob putting it up. 'But for the moment, it keeps them quiet.'

'Everyone needs their own space and a place to express themselves. I think it's a great idea.'

Then they came to the smallest room, where the door stood slightly ajar and a faint night light shone dimly. Carrie gently opened the door and Babs followed her quietly, almost tip-toeing behind her. Beside the window stood a large cot with white wooden bars and a colourful mobile of birds and stars floating above it.

'This is Stephanie,' Carrie whispered. 'This is our baby.' She moved over so that Babs could get a good look at the sleeping child.

Babs took out her glasses, placed them firmly on her nose and looked over the cot at the loveliest little face she had seen in a long time.

Lying on her back, arms thrown out to the sides, and buttoned up to the chin in a sweetly patterned babygro, the baby lay with her head turned to one side, breathing softly, dark wisps of hair framing her face, and the longest eyelashes Babs had ever seen making a perfect fan on her lightly flushed cheeks. Looking at her, Babs thought the child was the nearest thing to a living doll she had ever seen.

'Isn't she precious?' Babs murmured. 'You know, it doesn't seem so long ago my own were all that age. You have to enjoy them while you can, they grow up so quickly.'

Just then the doorbell rang loudly and little Stephanie stirred and began to whimper. 'I'd better get that,' said Carrie, sounding flustered. 'It must be Ali, she's being dropped back from ballet lessons. Would you keep an eye on Stephanie for a minute?'

Babs nodded. 'Of course I will, take your time.'

Seconds later, footsteps tore up the stairs and a pink flash raced by and then doubled back, peering around the door at Babs, who by now had picked up a crying Stephanie and was rocking her gently in her arms.

'Who are you?' demanded the small ballerina in a pink tutu, entering the room, 'and why are you holding our baby?'

'I'm Babs, and she was crying. You must be Ali.'

'How did you know that?' Ali looked perplexed and not altogether pleased.

Before Babs could answer, Ali yelled out in a piercing voice, 'Mummy, baby's crying again.'

'I'm coming, I'm coming,' Carrie called from downstairs.

'Stupid baby,' Ali said scornfully, 'she's always crying.'

'Well,' said Babs, 'that's what babies do a lot of the time. You probably did a lot of it yourself, I don't doubt.'

'Sorry about that,' Carrie said breathlessly as she came back into the room. 'Now Ali, go and get changed and put your tutu on the bed nicely so I can hang it up.'

'Won't,' Ali proclaimed defiantly. 'I'm keeping it on for Daddy. Daddy hasn't seen it yet and he promised he'd be home in time to see me twirl. See?' Ali performed a series of rather enthusiastic

twirls, nearly hurtling into Babs, who handed little Stephanie
hurriedly over to her mother. The baby had stopped crying
now and was regarding her unsteady sister with interest.

'Ali, please. Be careful! You're going hurt somebody, and
you'll ruin that tutu if you don't take it off.' Carrie raised her
eyes to heaven and looked helplessly at Babs. 'Everything's
a battle with that child and she's only five. I dread to think
what she'll be like at fifteen, and she is such a daddy's girl.'

'Aren't they all at that age, bless her. She's certainly high
spirited.'

'That's one way of putting it. Gosh, look at the time, Rob
will be home any minute and I haven't even fed Stephanie.
I'm so sorry, I've kept you far too long.'

'Not at all, it's been a pleasure,' said Babs as they made
their way downstairs. 'I can see you have your hands full.
Give me a call when you've checked my references and I'll
see you on Monday.' She held out her hand to take Carrie's.

The sound of a car door slamming and a key in the door
was followed by a triumphant shriek from Ali, who hurtled
down the stairs behind them. 'Daddeeee, daddeeee.'

Babs smiled as Ali flung herself at the tall, attractive young
man who came in the door, and noted fondly that Carrie's
face lit up at the sight of her husband.

'Well, well, well, what have we here, it's my prima ballerina!' Rob picked Ali up and swung her around to more
delighted shrieks.

Babs stood back and watched the exchange with interest.
The girls and Carrie were hanging on his every word and
glance. Rob Armstrong was one of those people who brought
a sudden sense of energy with him when he entered a room,
the kind that made people light up and feel they had something to look forward to. This was a man who oozed self-
confidence, unlike his wife, Babs noticed, who was considerably
less self-assured. She wouldn't, she mused, have put them

together as a couple, although God knows people claimed opposites attract. Personally, Babs wasn't so sure about that.

'Hi,' Rob leaned over and kissed Carrie on the cheek before turning quizzically to Babs.

'Rob, this is Mrs, er, I mean, Babs,' explained Carrie. 'She's going to be starting with us next week.'

'Pleased to meet you,' said Babs, shaking the hand that Rob wrested away from Ali.

'That's great! Welcome to the madhouse, Babs. I see you've met the family.' He grinned wickedly at her. And Babs grinned right back. You couldn't help grinning at a man who looked at you like that – whatever age you were. Rob was a charmer and no mistake, although Babs wasn't so sure she'd have relished being married to one. In her experience, they were trouble.

'I have, and they're lovely.'

'Hope you still think so this time next week.'

'Daddy,' Hope tugged at his sleeve, proffering her picture. 'Look, I've done a picture for you.'

'What? Oh hello, darling.' He ruffled her hair. 'That's lovely, I'll look at it properly later, Daddy has to go out again. Sorry,' he mouthed at Carrie. 'I just came back to drop the new car off, Frank's picking me up in twenty minutes, we have to go back into town to meet the English guys, I've got to shower and change.'

'But Daddy,' Hope protested, when suddenly Ali snatched the picture from her hands and pushed Hope roughly away from Rob.

'Ali, stop that, or it's bed immediately,' Carrie protested as Hope almost fell over and Ali burst into noisy sobs, flinging Hope's picture on the floor. 'Want to see Daddy's new car, want to go in Daddy's new car,' she wailed.

'Tomorrow, darling, I promise,' said Rob, making his escape up the stairs.

'I'd better be on my way,' said Babs, throwing Carrie a sympathetic look. 'I'll let myself out, see you Monday.'

'Oh, would you?' Carrie smiled gratefully, 'and thanks again for coming by.' Carrie reached for Ali's hand with her free one, 'Come on girls, bath time, and then if you're very good, we might have a *Barney* video before bed.'

'Not at all,' said Babs, closing the door behind her.

Outside the front door, Babs reclaimed her bicycle, and mounting it, set off along the downhill ride to her little home in the council estate around the other side of the village. What a lovely family, she thought to herself. It would do her good to be in the company of other people again. The young mother was a lovely person, she could tell. Babs always prided herself on being a good judge of character. And the husband seemed a nice man too, and good-looking, in that offbeat sort of way that was so attractive to women. It was plain they all adored him, although she'd bet he could be a real character. Why, if she hadn't known better, she'd have said he was flirting with her, even if she was old enough to be his mother.

But try as she could, even much later that night when she was making a cup of cocoa to take up to bed with her, she couldn't forget the image of the eldest little one, Hope, picking up her picture from the floor, and carefully folding it into four, and the forlorn look on her face as she followed her mother slowly upstairs.

Babs shook herself back to the present.

The Spanish morning sun was heating up and there was work to be done. The day was going to fly by before they knew it, and whatever any of the family said, she wasn't having anyone setting out for a wedding without a good breakfast inside them. It would be no time at all before hairdressers and make-up people were descending on them, not to mention photographers, and then there would be pandemonium.

Thank God she had brought all the makings of a real Irish out with her – bacon, sausages, black pudding, proper butter and brown bread – the works. She was prepared to relent and use the Spanish eggs that were stocked neatly in the fridge and those nice big sunny tomatoes that fried up so well, but that was it.

And whatever notions Ali had of not eating would be firmly quashed. Supermodel or no supermodel nonsense, there was nothing like the smell of sizzling bacon to get those girls, and indeed their parents, up and out of bed. God knows what time it would be before they all ate again.

And then it would be on the yacht, which, from what she had seen of it, looked more like a ship. Babs desperately hoped she wouldn't feel seasick or anything dreadful like that. She knew the yacht would be moored and not careering off on the high seas, but all the same, things could be unsteady. Babs had sailed only once before when she and Larry had taken the ferry to Holyhead and a gale force storm had ensued. She had there and then vowed never to set foot on a boat again as long as she lived.

Why they couldn't have had the whole thing on dry land like normal people was beyond her. Although, she reflected, there was precious little normal about the Armstrong family these days. Still, a wedding reception on board the *Excalibur* would be a once-in-a-lifetime experience and there was no way she would miss it. Why, real live movie stars and royalty had sailed on her in her heyday. And Ali would make the most beautiful bride of any of them. It would all be like a wonderful fairytale. But just to make sure, she would bring her seasickness tablets in her handbag, along with the Alka Seltzer and the safety pins. After all, she might not be the only one who needed them. Babs didn't believe in leaving anything to chance, and weddings could be unpredictable affairs at the best of times.

She checked her watch. It was seven thirty on the dot, time to make for the kitchen. The day had been planned out with military precision. The countdown had begun.

I

(Four months earlier)

Carrie Armstrong awoke to the crisp brightness of a perfect February day and for a moment lay perfectly still. Allowing her eyes to wander around the room, she carefully took in the unmistakable luxury of her surroundings: the silk moiré wallpaper, the huge gilt framed mirrors, the Italian marble mantelpiece, the lavishly draped windows through which the sun now streamed, casting a pool of light onto the Persian carpet, beneath which the jewelled colours seemed to glow.

The exquisite trappings of luxury, the thought came to her, but not for the first time. Sitting up slowly, she noted the barely disturbed sheets and the vast expanse of the otherwise empty bed.

Today, she thought suddenly. Today I am going to do it. She got up quickly, fuelled by the momentum and purpose of her decision.

In the bathroom, she regarded her reflection critically, but not without kindness. She was still in good shape. She had worked hard at that, and it showed. Her breasts were full and shapely, thanks to the implants, and constant sessions with her personal trainer kept everything else reasonably where it should be. But after three children, gravity had taken its toll, workouts or not. Nonetheless, she looked good for her forty-eight years. Or rather, forty-nine. It was her birthday and she had almost forgotten, despite herself. She smiled.

Her face, she still thought, was a nice face, slightly long in the nose, above a generous mouth, although she would have liked fuller lips. Her teeth were straight and white, her skin clear and well maintained and her chestnut curls groomed and shaped regularly every six weeks in a style her hairdresser reliably informed her softened her features. Only her soulful, big green eyes hinted that there was any pain behind Carrie Armstrong's smile.

She showered quickly, pausing only to dip her head, allowing the steaming hot jets of water to ease the tension that lately seemed to hold her shoulder blades together in a vice-like grip. She didn't bother to dress, just wrapped the white towel robe around her and applied a modicum of make-up. Passing the dressing room, the wall-to-wall wardrobes on her side remained steadfastly shut.

On Rob's side, a door stood ajar and a faint smell of aftershave hinted at his obviously recent departure. She must hurry if she was to catch him. Down the stairs she went, barefoot, feeling the softness of the carpet beneath her. She remembered, with sudden vividness, the three threadbare stairs at the top of the flight in the four-bed semi where she had grown up. The mad race between her and her five brothers and sisters to be the first to get to the bathroom used to drive her poor mother demented. Back then, Carrie would have killed to have a soft-as-silk pure wool carpet, never mind a choice of bathrooms. Now she had them, and where had it got her?

Strange, she thought, how the most trivial of things crept into your mind when you were facing a life-changing moment.

The aroma of fresh coffee wafted towards her, and taking a deep breath, she walked into the kitchen.

Rob was sitting there, calmly reading the paper.

For a split second, she almost lost her nerve – was almost overpowered by the ever familiar wave of love that enveloped her whenever she saw him.

By any standards, Rob Armstrong had always been a good-looking man. But now, at fifty, the combination of maturity and acquired confidence made him more lethally attractive than ever. The slightly unruly hair, now streaked with grey, the frown of concentration that creased between the eyes that were by turns hazel, or as she had often mused, treacle coloured, shaded now by the half-moon reading glasses. She felt the urge, which still took her by surprise, to reach out and gently stroke his face.

Hearing her come in, he looked up from his paper.

'You're up early.' It was a statement, not a query, and he returned his attention to the morning's news.

For a moment, rage threatened as Carrie swallowed back a tart response. What the hell time would he know that she got up at? He was never there. Never mind the separate bedrooms they had occupied now for several months; their lives had become as diverse as the many beds she knew he had shared over the years, with many other women.

But recriminations would get her nowhere now. Enough had been said. Now it was time to act.

She sat down opposite him at the table, rested her chin in her hands and looked at him, willing him to see her – really see her.

'What?' The slight edge of irritation was audible as he looked up.

'I want a divorce, Rob.'

The words, slowly enunciated, seemed to come from another person, another reality. So often rehearsed, so often threatened, their very utterance now seemed to her unreal. Only the slight trembling of her hands, her fingers still firmly linked together under her chin, indicated how very much she meant them.

Her husband of twenty-nine years sighed a long, exasperated sigh. The corner of his mouth slid downwards, in that mildly amused way, as if he was talking to a recalcitrant teenager.

'What is it?'

For a split second, his eyes flickered from irritation to wary.

'What's upset you this time, Carrie?' He folded the paper and set it down on the table, then checked his watch and stood up.

With immense effort, Carrie held her temper and said nothing. There was nothing more to say, nothing that hadn't been said a thousand times before.

'Look, whatever it is, we'll talk about it tonight.' His eyes lingered on hers as a note of warmth crept into his voice.

For moment, she almost wavered. It was the warmth that did it, just as he knew it would. When he would sound like the old Rob, the one who'd loved her, made her feel beautiful, desirable, as only he could. He could play her like a cat plays with a mouse.

No, she screamed inside, don't weaken, not now, not again. Those eyes, that voice, they did such terrible things to her. Made her believe the tantalising promise they held that hinted I still care for you, I still come home to you, it's you I've stayed with, isn't it?

And it was that very thing that was destroying her, his staying with her despite everything.

She remained silent. She simply didn't trust herself to speak.

'I have to go now,' he said. 'Oh shit, I forgot, I'm in London tonight. Meetings with the new tax guys, I won't be back 'til tomorrow. It'll have to wait 'til then, okay?' His voice was apologetic, placating, but she recognised the impatient twitch of his mouth. He was eager to be gone, to be away from this uncomfortable, accountable situation. Rob, she had learned long ago, didn't do accountability. 'I promise, whatever it is, we'll sort it out then.' He grabbed his briefcase and mobile and made for the door. 'Gotta go, love.'

Love, she almost laughed aloud. That was pushing it, even for Rob. She hadn't been his 'love' for a long time. He had dispensed with endearments as easily as he had fidelity, unless, of course, he wanted something, and wanted it badly.

She listened, immobilised, as the front door closed behind

him, as he revved the engine of the Aston Martin and drove out the gates as if nothing at all had happened, as if it was a perfectly normal way to start the day.

Carrie knew she had done the right thing, without a doubt. She had been thinking of nothing else for the last two years, ever since, well, ever since . . .

Still, thirty years, loving, living with the man she had given her heart to, her hopes, her dreams . . . *Stop*, screamed the voice, don't think about it, don't go there.

Of course she was doing the right thing. Why, he hadn't even remembered that today was her birthday. Not that that mattered anymore, one of the kids always reminded him, or his secretary, and there would be the usual perfunctory present and, if things weren't too volatile, even a family dinner in the latest hip restaurant in town. It meant nothing.

She had done the right thing, of course she had. It was just that, why then, she wondered, if she had done the right thing, was she fighting for breath? Why was she crying?

Jay Farrelly manoeuvred her brand new Mercedes McLaren out of the car park and onto the road. She had just spent a very enjoyable and expensive morning in one of Dublin's most exclusive boutiques and was heading home with her spoils. Beside her on the passenger seat were bags bearing Cavalli dresses and a YSL shirt, heart-stoppingly expensive all. She'd also bought some new underwear. When you were heading for fifty and everything was heading south, you needed serious help in the sucking-in department. Petite and curvaceous, Jay's figure would, if allowed, develop a mind of its own unless it was very definitely rerouted.

Driving slowly along a narrow street, she turned left and hit the main road, grinning as the accelerator responded eagerly to the tentative pressure she applied. The car had been delivered to her only yesterday, and she was still unfamiliar enough with it to tame her usual recklessness on the road for at least a day or two.

Not that it would matter if she wrote it off – she would just go straight out and order another one. It was the first of many items she – or rather, her husband, Frank – was going to treat her to. He just didn't know it yet.

Thinking of Frank made Jay's stomach clench in a manner that was becoming all too regular of late. This time he was overstepping the mark big time. This time he was being beyond stupid. And Jay was going to put a stop to it all right now. Regardless of his enviably blithe disposition towards their marriage, even Frank would have to acknowledge the unmistakable message she would be sending him loud and clear through her avenging lawyers if he continued with this latest dalliance. After all, she could ruin him – that's all there was to it. It wouldn't come to that, of course. Jay had been preparing all her married life for a moment such as this.

Frank needed to be pulled up in his tracks, and the sooner the better. He wouldn't put up much of a fight – he never did. He couldn't afford to, not taking into account all that was at stake. That was another one of the nice things about being married to a mega rich husband, reflected Jay. There was so much more for him to lose.

It was ironic, really. You would think that the more money a man made, the more he could afford to part with some, but it didn't seem to work that way. Whether they were worth two million or two hundred million, they all seemed to want to cling to every last cent of it. Well, that suited her just fine.

Whatever thoughts this avaricious little hussy had put into his head would soon be put out of it. After all, whoever the foreign floosie was (Jay made a mental note to meet next week with the private detective), she had no idea who she was dealing with. Because if there was one thing Mrs Jay Farrelly had no intention of tolerating in her marriage, it was the 'D' word. Divorce.

However, extreme situations called for extreme measures, and this was as extreme as it got. Not so long ago, Jay reflected – well, it felt like not that long ago – she would have been consumed with guilt at the idea of hiring a private detective to spy on her own husband. But she and Frank had come a long way since their early, innocent beginnings, and if hiring a detective was what she had to do to get to grips with the current situation, then there was no point berating herself about it.

'Golf at the K Club' had been Frank's code for a night away with a woman, Jay had discovered for the first time ten years ago, when a well-intentioned 'friend' had informed her she had seen Frank and another woman enjoying a very cosy dinner in the exclusive club. Jay had confronted him and after a few unsuccessful attempts to evade and deny any accusations, Frank had come clean and confessed – even to the fact that they had stayed overnight, which Jay hadn't realised. That was the trouble with Frank, she thought. He never knew when to stop.

Then she had been shocked. Shocked and hurt. After everything they had been through together, she'd sobbed, crouched on the floor in her mirrored dressing room, surrounded by everything and having nothing.

'How could he?' she'd sobbed, Estée Lauder cried off, her face raw. But Jay Farrelly was made of strong stuff. Somehow, she'd picked herself up off the floor. She and Frank were meant to stay together. It was that simple. She needed to know what he was up to in order to stay in control. Because control was what it was all about for Jay. Sheer drive had dragged her out of Ballybonane and transformed her into a considerable force to be reckoned with in the upper echelons of the society circuit.

Pulling up outside the imperious Tudor-style mansion nestling in one of Dublin's most exclusive suburbs, Jay waited as the imposing set of electric gates slid obediently open for her. She parked the car, gathered her parcels and let herself in the front door. She would just have time for a quick shower and change of outfit and then she'd make her way to the charity lunch.

Stomping up the stairs and into her bedroom, she dropped the bags to the floor before stretching to ease the ache in her back and kicked off her shoes. Four-inch heels, she thought grimly, were definitely not the ideal footwear for a shopping spree, but Jay had worn high heels ever since she had had to smuggle them out of the house as a teenager, hidden in a handbag, away from her mother's razor-sharp eyes. If she stopped wearing them now, she rationalised, not only would she concede the vital inches added to her petite five-foot frame, but her calves would probably fall off.

She showered quickly, making sure the jets of water avoided her from the neck up in order to protect her professionally applied make-up and just blow-dried feathered bob. Afterwards, she slipped quickly into the charcoal suit which hung obediently on one of the mirrored doors of her dressing room. Drawing herself up to her full height – five feet, five inches in five inch heeled new boots – she regarded her reflection appraisingly. The couture suit clung to her curvaceous figure from every angle, and she had to agree with the personal shopper in the store who'd advised her that dressing in monochromatic shades, including, of course, your chosen tights or stockings, made one seem instantly streamlined and taller.

She wondered fleetingly if anyone would have heard of Frank's latest exploits. The city was such a hotbed of gossip these days.

With determination born of experience, she immediately put the thought out of her head. Who the hell cared? She was Mrs Frank Farrelly, wife of arguably Ireland's richest businessman. That was all that mattered. And she was going to make sure that was the way it stayed.

Whatever rumblings might be doing the rounds on the subject of their marriage would be easily deflected. Nothing like a brand new Mercedes and an obscenely large, emerald-cut diamond ring to take the eyes out of any malicious women who might be sitting at her table.

Jay's jewellery collection was notorious and expanded randomly according to Frank's peccadilloes, and indeed her own voracious appetite for all that glittered. If she had to go and do battle at a ladies' charity lunch today, she was going to do it in full body armour. Boadicea had a metal breastplate and warrior bodyguards – Jay Farrelly had YSL, Glanz knickers that held her stomach in and jewels to make Harry Winston drool.

Twenty minutes later, Jay pulled up outside the Four Seasons Hotel, handed her keys to the parking valet and marched as fast as five-inch heels would allow into the lobby. Turning left at reception, she headed for the ladies' room for a last minute once-over.

Inside, it was empty. Most of the women, she correctly deduced, would already be at the champagne reception prior to the lunch, swigging back a few glasses of bubbly, catching up on who was wearing what and checking out the table list. She needed to do neither. That's how it was when you were an A-lister on the circuit.

Besides, Jay was very careful about drinking alcohol at these types of lunches. She prided herself on her self-disciplined approach to life and couldn't bear any kind of 'sloppy' behaviour. That's how she had got to be where she was today, and God knows, with the amount of predatory young women on the prowl, a woman such as she, with so much to hold onto, so much at stake, had to keep her wits about her. Today would be no exception. Nobody was going to see Jay tripping up or weaving around the Four Seasons hallways.

She popped into a vacant cubicle, opened her handbag and pulled out a one hundred euro note. Then, slipping the small packet from the inside leg of her silk stocking, she emptied just the right amount of white powder onto the toilet cistern, rolled the note and deftly hoovered up the magic powder. It hit her, as she knew it would, that lovely feeling when the fear evaporated and everything was just as it should be.

Outside, she checked her reflection for any tell-tale signs and smiled prettily at the mirror. Everything was perfect, from the top of her immaculately blow-dried hair to the tips of her softest suede, high-heeled boots. She looked amazing and felt invincible, which, of course, she was.

She made a late, perfectly timed, and much-noted entrance into the large ballroom and graciously acknowledged the flurry of greetings that ensued as she wove her way through the maze of tables until she reached her own.

One of her closest friends, Carrie, was already seated across the table from her. Jay smiled hello at everybody, but the smile reached her eyes for Carrie. She hadn't seen her friend in a while and had hoped to sit next to her, but they would catch up once the meal was finished. It was hard to believe it was almost twenty years since they had first met, since she and Carrie had formed an unlikely friendship that, in the intervening years, had developed into a very important mutual support system.

Jay could still vividly recall the day that she had rushed into class late, as usual. 'So sorry I'm late!' She had breezed into the room, a small powerhouse of energy, in such a way that everybody knew she wasn't sorry at all. Carrie, along with the rest of the class of post-baby-flab-fighting mums, had watched in admiration as Jay strode to the front, unrolled her mat, twisted her hair into a chignon and pinned it up while simultaneously sliding into a textbook-perfect leg stretch. Everyone, including the teacher, sat up a little bit straighter and focused that little bit harder. Jay knew she just had that effect on people.

Jay, for all her carefully cultivated bravado, was no stranger to feelings of inadequacy, particularly in light of having been recently thrown in at the deep end of nouveau riche Dublin society, thanks to the burgeoning success of her husband Frank's electrical wholesale company; she was just better at hiding it. *Act as if* had become her mantra. And she did. So much so that sometimes she even fooled herself. When she had literally bumped into Carrie one day as they both made for the door after class, causing Carrie to drop her bag and stammer an apology to Jay, Jay had looked at her strangely.

'You shouldn't apologise,' she said coolly, bending down to help Carrie gather the spilled contents of her bag. 'It was my fault, I wasn't looking where I was going, as usual.'

She appraised Carrie thoughtfully as the two women stood up and Carrie smiled nervously and proffered a hand.

'I'm Carrie,' she said, shyly. 'I never look where I'm going either.'

'Fancy a coffee, or are you rushing?' Jay suddenly asked. 'I'd like that.'

The coffee after class had become lunch once a week, both women finding solace in the total opposite of each other's character. Where Jay was assertive and tended to adopt a sledgehammer approach to life, Carrie was reserved and intuitive. Both learned much from their differences. Soon the friendship extended to include their respective 'others' and Frank and Rob made up the foursome. Neither one slow to miss an opportunity, the two men were soon putting deals together, Rob's charm and ruthless ambition happily marrying with Frank's unerring nose for a deal and peerless business acumen. But Jay knew her friendship with Carrie was the real thing, while Frank and Rob's was merely a mutually beneficial business arrangement.

Now, observing her friend from the opposite side of the table, Jay thought she wasn't looking her best. Oh, she was beautifully turned out, as always – slender in a black and white trouser suit with her chestnut hair in a sleek knot – but Carrie's face was pinched and drawn looking. Athough she was smiling and chatting to the woman next to her, Jay noticed that Carrie was throwing the champagne back as if it was going out of fashion.

Hmmm, she thought, I wonder what that's all about? Husband trouble, no doubt, Jay hazarded a shrewd guess.

Jay and Carrie moved in the same circles, wealthy circles, where having your own helicopter or 'timeshare hours' in a private jet was as natural as going to Royal Ascot for the racing or Cowes for the sailing. Although Jay, and indeed Carrie too, preferred to keep a lower profile. It was the boys who insisted on flashing the cash. Why, look at her Frank, Jay thought now with exasperation. The man had bought the biggest yacht in the Med – and he couldn't even swim! Not a lot of people knew that, she mused, grinning inwardly. And to christen that same yacht *Excalibur*, after the magical sword in the Arthurian legends – well, the irony of that had surely escaped him. Although she had been warned by a friend of hers who sailed that it was considered very bad luck to rename a boat, a superstition that went back to the ancient mariners' times. Jay hadn't paid much attention. She didn't hold with luck – in her opinion, you made your own.

Rob, Carrie's husband, was a player, and a very charming one. The trouble with being married to a man like that was that you couldn't help wondering how many of the women at your table – no, make that the entire room – they had slept with, including your so-called friends.

Jay had long since stopped letting it get to her. After all, she was holding the reins of her marriage very firmly within her grasp and fully intended to continue doing so. But Carrie, she knew, was softer and took it all far too much to heart. Despite Jay's in-depth coaching over the years on the subject, Carrie was a gentler soul.

Mind you, Jay conceded, it was hard for Carrie: Rob was very attractive, not to mention sexy, and had that uncanny talent of making any woman he spoke to feel as if she was utterly unique in the entire universe. And Carrie, of course, was still madly in love with him. Frank, on the other hand, had not improved with age, but his appetite for extracurricular activities, coupled with his ever-growing business empire, made him a perennial prospect for marital disturbances.

It wasn't that she was still in love with him, Jay mused, although she must have been, she supposed, at some stage. But all that was so long ago – they were just kids then, the pair of them – gawky, insecure sixteen-year-olds, from the wrong side of the tracks. Looks had never been Frank's strong point. In fact, before he had become insanely rich, he had been the one who felt grateful to have her around. But they got along well, they were a good team, and Frank, she acknowledged, had been a good provider and a generous husband, if not an ideal one. The money more than made up for any other shortcomings. All the same, you had to be tough. But coming from a small town in the hinterland of Ireland, long before anyone had ever heard of Celtic Tigers or the like, was a good exercise in character formation.

She and Frank had met when they were teenagers. She'd lived in a small town outside Portlaoise, while he came from thirty miles away. His parents had a tiny, down-at-heel farm. He'd whistled at her from the old stone wall beside the pub where all the local lads would gather of an evening to watch the girls go by. This had been followed up by a lewd, if appreciative comment.

'Will ya look at the arse on the small one!' Frank had yelled. 'I wouldn't mind parking me bike there, lads!'

Jay had promptly clocked him with her handbag and a mutual, if grudging respect had developed into an unimaginative courtship and predictable marriage three years later. It was then, with a baby at home and Frank spending too much time on the road driving his truck, delivering his electrical gadgets, that Jay had insisted on moving to Dublin and chasing her dream of prosperity. The rest was history.

Although even Jay wouldn't have believed it could happen so quickly. Frank's old pick-up truck had been exchanged for a series of bigger and faster Mercedes ·and they had moved house five times in as many years. And that was before they'd made the really big time.

Prosperity had been attained, but not without a price, Jay reflected, albeit one which she had been happy to pay and would do so again. Some things, however, were non-negotiable, and having stuck with Frank through the lean times, Jay was not, in any manner, shape or form, going to relinquish her marriage just as she was enjoying reaping the financial rewards of her hard work. After all, she'd seen what it had done to her own mother, struggling and scrimping to bring up a family on her own.

Never rely on your looks or a man, her mother had often said to her wearily. They can both run out on you when you least expect it. And Jay hadn't, vowing there and then to hold on to both as if her life depended on it. Looks were easy: why, she was a walking testimony to the miracle of modern science. But the man thing – well, that was another kettle of fish.

Single parenthood had turned her mother into an old woman and heralded, Jay felt sure, her sudden and untimely death, leaving Jay to step into the role of caring for and rearing her younger brother and sister. And she had done it, and made a good job of it too. Responsibility didn't frighten Jay; losing it did.

It was terrifying really, how little marriage counted for these days, she often thought, and husbands, especially rich ones, were not to be treated lightly. They simply had too much going for them, and if you didn't watch it, they walked all over you. Well that wasn't going to happen on her watch, Jay thought as she dabbed her mouth with her napkin.

As soon as the meal was over and people began to table-hop or slip outside for a cigarette, Jay slipped into the seat next to Carrie. 'What's up? You're not in good form, are you?'

'You could say that, I suppose.' Carrie looked slowly around the room. 'I've come to the conclusion,' she took a swig from her glass and signalled for a waiter to refill it, 'that I don't really like these lunches – these armies of women. In fact, I'm sick to the bloody gills of them. This is officially the last one I will ever attend – you heard it here first.'

'How's Rob?' Jay ignored the former comment.

'How would I know?'

'Keep your voice down,' Jay warned, smiling in case anyone should overhear, or God forbid, lip read. 'What's going on, Carrie?'

'I've told him I want a divorce. I've had enough, Jay. I can't do it any more.'

'Are you out of your mind?' Jay was incredulous.

'On the contrary, I'm trying to reclaim a small part of it.'

'Come on, Carrie, I'm getting you out of here. You're drunk. I don't know what's going on with you and Rob, but I do know you'll regret it if you make any decision in the state you're in now. Come out with me to my car and we'll drive somewhere and talk.'

'You won't make me change my mind.'

Jay ignored her. 'Come on.'

Once the car had been delivered to them by the parking valet, Carrie obediently slid into the passenger seat and Jay drove away from the hotel, taking the sea road. 'Now,' she said briskly, 'what's all this nonsense about a divorce?'

'I told you. I've had enough, that's all there is to it.'

'What's he done this time?' Jay glanced at her friend, who was gazing steadily out of the passenger window. 'He's messing around again, isn't he?'

'Yes, but this time he's in love.'

'Oh for God's sake, Carrie!' Jay almost laughed with relief. 'What the hell has love got to do with it? Haven't you listened to anything I've said to you over the years? You must know the drill by now, why—'

'Shut up, Jay,' Carrie's voice was steady. 'This is about me, not Rob, and love happens to have everything to do with it.' She took a deep breath. 'You see, I love him, I always have, despite everything, all the infidelities, all the hurt. I could tell myself the others didn't matter, that they were passing flings, but not this time. This time he's in love and I can't . . .' Her voice was breaking. 'I can't bear the pretence any more, the hypocrisy. I suppose, too, I can't stand knowing he's as unhappy as I am. We're both locked in this ludicrous façade of a marriage, a marriage that's run out of reasons or excuses to exist.'

Carrie bit her lip as the memories flooded back, all thirty-odd years of them. It had always been her and Rob. There seemed to be so few memories that didn't contain him. From the moment she'd first set eyes on him, hanging out with the cool crowd, lounging on his motorbike, one long leather-clad leg steadying it as he leaned in to take a light from a mate, and looked up to catch her gazing at him and smiled that lazy smile that would enslave her for ever. She couldn't help it, could never help herself always wanting him.

'Fancy a ride?' he'd said that first night.

Carrie had flicked back the long chestnut curls that brushed her shoulder blades and said primly, 'I don't ride with strange men,' her heart thudding alarmingly.

'Maybe you should make an exception then,' Rob had replied, still smiling.

And she had.

After that she hadn't heard from him, despite giving him her phone number, and had been at first desolate, then furious. Until a month later, when he showed up again and she had been determined to ignore him, chatting animatedly with her best friend Clara, who, much to Carrie's annoyance, went all fluttery when Rob strolled up to talk to them.

'Don't I know you from somewhere?' he'd said to Carrie, grinning infuriatingly. And despite herself, she had laughed.

It had begun as it would continue: Carrie always wanting Rob, cajoling Rob, pleading with Rob. He had never wanted her in the same way. In her heart she had always known it, but somehow she had believed if she held on long enough, if she could make him see that she loved him more than anyone else ever would, if she was always there for him when other girls refused to put up with his casual, non-committal attitude, she would eventually win out.

Getting pregnant hadn't been deliberate, although Carrie had been thrilled to bits. But she had never forgotten the look on Rob's face when she'd told him. A shadow had passed across his eyes, taking with it the light of freedom that was as much a part of him as living and breathing. Bottles and nappies weren't part and parcel of roaring around on a sleek Kawasaki motorbike. He'd never wanted a baby, she knew, of course she knew. She had, but he hadn't. Carrie had got what she wanted, but she had also made her first mistake of their partnership.

Seeing the look of despair on her friend's face, Jay pulled off the road and parked in a quiet spot that overlooked the sea. She sighed as tears rolled silently down Carrie's face.

'Look,' Jay said with as much patience as she could muster, 'I know this is tough, believe me, I do, but you can't, you mustn't think like this, Carrie.'

'So what am I supposed to do? Go on turning a blind eye? Sleeping on my own? Lying awake at four in the morning wondering if he's with her? And worse, knowing that when he isn't, he's wishing he was?'

'Have you been going to counselling?' Jay asked.

'No.'

'Good. For a minute you had me worried.' Jay didn't approve of counselling. Why talk when you can act was her motto. 'Carrie,' she went on, 'this is no time for victim talk. You've got to get tough and deal with this. Rob's an idiot – they're all fecking idiots – but there's nothing we can't sort out, including Rob and his latest inamorata. Speaking of which, who is she? Tell me everything you know.'

'You're not listening to me, Jay,' said Carrie. 'It doesn't matter who she is. The point is, I can't do this any more. I can't fight to make someone love me who never will and probably never did. I realise that now.'

'Tell me anyway,' Jay said softly, deciding to back off a bit. Clearly Carrie was too upset to think for herself, so in the meantime, Jay would have to do it for her. Otherwise God only knew what would happen. Why, if Carrie allowed Rob to just walk off into the sunset after twenty-five-plus years of marriage, and far too many millions, it would make serious ripples for others – herself included. Imagine Frank thinking that leaving was an option! Jay shuddered. But Frank was an old softie at heart, an easily led softie, mind you, but whatever he was up to, he wouldn't seriously consider leaving. Besides, Jay couldn't and wouldn't let that happen.

'What do you know about her?'

'Well,' Carrie began listlessly, 'she's a journalist and looks like a supermodel. What else do you want to know?'

'Typical,' snorted Jay. 'A career woman who forgot to get a man so she's after one of ours – a money-grubbing gold digger.'

'Actually, she's not. I wish it were that simple. It would make it easier for me.'

'What do you mean?'

'I suppose you could say I'd have liked her if we'd met under different circumstances. Actually,' Carrie went on, 'I admired her, until I found out she'd been sleeping with my husband.'

'You've met her?' Jay stared at Carrie as if she was on drugs. Thinking of which, she could have done with another line of coke if she had known she'd have to listen to this extraordinary account of events. Something to settle her nerves would have helped.

'Let's just say I know all about her,' Carrie said with a grim smile. 'She's divorced, has no children, lives in a beautiful house and drives a sports car. She also has her own television show. They call her the thinking man's sex symbol,' she added, sounding as if she almost enjoyed dropping the bombshell.

'You're talking about Olwen Slater?'

'Yes, it's her.'

For once, Jay was stumped for words. No wonder Carrie was sounding defeated. Olwen Slater was the television poster-girl for intelligent beauty. A political commentator, she'd worked in America and London and was a respected journalist, a celebrity, albeit a reclusive one. In other words, your basic nightmare.

Seeing Jay's face, Carrie allowed herself a small sad smile. 'Now do you understand? I can't compete against that. I never could have.'

'Don't be ridiculous,' Jay snapped. This was worse than she'd thought. 'Of course you can. What about the children?'

'The children, as you so charmingly refer to them, are no longer that. Stephanie was twenty-three this year and they've all got their own lives now. That's perhaps why I've made this decision. Now I only have myself to think about.'

'You know what I mean,' Jay pushed on. 'That's not the issue. It's the family that's at stake here, you know they'll side with you. The girls are not going to stand by and see their mother made a fool of.'

'Oh really?' Carrie's face tightened. 'And what exactly do you think I'll look like if I sit back and take all this? Do you know one of my own daughters has even told me to sort out my marriage? Do you know what that feels like? To realise my own girls have more self-respect than I have?'

'Oh, for God's sake, Carrie! They're all self-righteous little prats at that age. Give them a few years and a marriage of their own to deal with and you'll see them change their tune.' Jay didn't have daughters, but she knew enough from her own four boys and their ever-changing rota of girlfriends to see that young people today were not interested in putting in the hard work that was undoubtedly required in a long-term relationship.

'That's just it, Jay. I don't want them to change their tune. I don't want them to ever have to go through a marriage or relationship where they feel they have to hang on for dear life, where they feel second best, inadequate, as though they never quite measure up. I sometimes think that over the years the only thing I've been qualified to be is Rob's pimp.'

'I beg your pardon?' Jay blinked. She'd never heard Carrie speak like that before.

'I can go into any room, walk down any street, and mentally pick out the girls he'll go for, the ones he'll find attractive. Have you any idea how soul destroying that is? Probably not. I wouldn't wish it on my worst enemy.'

Jay wondered if Carrie was having a nervous breakdown. She had read about situations like this, but now, as she listened to her friend, she became seriously concerned. This wasn't the Carrie she'd known all these years: this was a woman falling apart.

'Look Carrie, I know you're upset, but you're talking complete rot! You and Rob have just hit a bad patch, and you'll get through this, but not if you're going to take that attitude. Why, financially alone you could ruin him. You have to go on the offensive here.'

'That's where you're very wrong, Jay.' Carrie was looking at her strangely. 'I may have taken a lot of wrong turns along the way, but I am not going to descend to that level.'

'Who's talking about descending, for God's sake?' Jay cried indignantly. 'We're talking about winning.'

'I am not going to descend to the level of using my own children to pressurise a man who doesn't love me to stay with me.' Carrie was adamant. She wasn't a greedy, manipulative monster and wasn't going to become one. Why, she thought angrily, did everything have to be about money? 'Why should I have to threaten him with financial disruption? Do I have to pay him to stay? What sort of a victory would that be? It sounds even more hollow than the empty charade we're playing at now.'

'You can't just hand him over to this woman, Carrie. You have to have tactics, we all do. You have to fight back.'

'For what? Some chance of happiness? I don't think so. The girls have their own lives now, it would just be me and Rob avoiding each other except for the usual dinner parties and functions we have to go to – and quite frankly, I've had enough of those to last me a lifetime.'

'You can't just sit back and let this woman win.'

'She already has.'

'What? He's left already?' Jay held her breath.

'No. It's over. She ended it.'

Jay almost fainted with relief. 'For heaven's sake, Carrie! You had me seriously worried there for a minute. You see? I told you there's nothing to worry about.'

'You just don't get it do you Jay?' Carrie shook her head and smiled. She felt a rush of affection for her friend. Jay was tough and tenacious, the sort of person who'd stick with you through thick and thin, but would never in a million years understand that sometimes letting go, instead of holding on for dear life, could be a real emotional breakthrough. 'You're really quite remarkable.'

'What?' Jay blinked.

'That was the final nail in the coffin for me. He's so, so miserable.'

'He'll get over it.'

'That's not the point. He's so miserable I can't stand to watch it. He's so miserable, he's being nice to me, kind even.'

'Typical.' Jay sniffed. 'He's been dumped and he's terrified you'll kick him out too. That's exactly what this Olwen wants. Can't you see that? You're playing into her hands, Carrie.'

'No, Jay, you're wrong.' Carrie was quietly insistent. 'That's what I thought too, at first. He's being nice to me because I genuinely think he understands for the first time now what it's been like for me all these years. He understands what it's like to lose someone you really love, and he's feeling the pain. That's what I can't bear. I even feel sorry for him. I've never seen him so sad, so . . . stricken. And I want to reach out to him, to tell him I understand what he's going through – and I can't. I know that's the last thing in the world he'd want. So we're both there, both tiptoeing around our respective misery, and it's the loneliest place I've ever been to in my life.' Carrie resumed her gaze out the window, where a young woman with a pushchair was walking by, laughing as she stopped and bent down to do up the shoe of her little boy, who stood unsteadily holding onto her shoulder. The touching innocence of the scene made Carrie want to cry all over again. It didn't seem so long ago since she had done the very same thing with her girls. Although she knew Rob would have loved to have had a son, for Carrie, her girls were everything she had ever dreamed of.

'So you see, Jay, I really do mean it when I say I'm getting a divorce, and I don't want to talk about it any more. So please, just take me home, will you? I'll pick up my car from the Four Seasons in the morning.'

Jay reluctantly decided not to push it, realising that for now, certainly, there was nothing more she could say.

They drove back in relative silence until she turned into the curving gravelled driveway leading to Carrie's house, just a mile or so from her own. The unashamedly affluent suburb where they lived was full of such statuesque homes built or lavishly remodelled during the current property boom that had swept in with the Celtic Tiger.

Carrie patted Jay's arm and opened her door. 'I know you mean well Jay, really I do, and I appreciate your support, but I've made up my mind.'

Jay took a deep breath. 'We won't say any more for the moment Carrie, but believe me, you'll feel differently after a good night's sleep. I'll ring you tomorrow.'

Carrie smiled at her friend before closing the car door. 'You still don't believe me, do you? Any more than he does, but you're both wrong. I'm through with living a lie. This time it's over.' And with that, she walked slowly up the steps and into the magnificent house that had long since ceased to be a home.

2

Carrie watched Jay roar down the drive. She had been sure that telling someone, especially Jay, would make it all real, but now she felt more than ever as if she was sleep-walking through a strange and frightening landscape.

Rob was so in love with another woman that he couldn't even try to hide his pain – it was palpable. God knows, Carrie knew the feeling. She had gone through it many times herself – over him. But when it had been her, well, she could cope, knowing how much she loved him, needed him. But this was different. If ever there had been a death knell for a marriage, this was it – and it was ringing now, loud and ominously in her ears.

Inserting her key in the lock, the heavy oak door obligingly swung open. The door and hallway of Fairways were impressive. People always said so at parties, and Rob loved that. They had moved here five years ago to the old, imposing manor house and, after eighteen months of gruelling refurbishing and extending, had finally created the home of anyone's dreams. Carrie had hoped it would be their last move.

In the smaller, inner hall, she paused to rifle half-heartedly through the morning's post. It was laid out, as always, on the heavy silver tray that took pride of place on the Victorian rosewood table, the only piece of furniture her late parents had given them to survive the most recent redecorating venture carried out by a London interiors firm recommended by Rob's current pet architect. Rob's parents, she remembered affectionately, not being quite as affluent as her own, had given them a particularly florid china tea service. It had embarrassed him acutely at the time, although Carrie had loyally used it at every opportunity. Carrie's parents hadn't been wealthy, but they had been comfortable and had instilled in her a strong sense of decency and the importance of treating other people as you would like to be treated yourself. Now that they were both gone, she missed them dreadfully. Particularly lately, although God knew what they'd have made of the situation she was in. What would she have said? 'Mum, Dad, I know you were never that keen on Rob and he's having another affair, but this time he's in love and I'm scared witless.'

The post held no surprises. There were the usual official envelopes, a couple of direct mail hits, a postcard addressed to Stephanie who was just finishing a cookery course in London. Nothing for her. Rob's mail was sent to his personal secretary at the office.

The grandeur of the circular main hall, from which the four reception rooms and kitchen area led, had long been lost on Carrie, who now heard her footsteps echoing through its cavernous depths. Now matter how hard she pretended, she would never get used to coming home to an empty house. Growing up as one of six, her own family home had been a constant hive of activity from which she had longed to escape to set up house (or basement flat, as it had turned out) with Rob. Until recently, Stephanie had been at home, but now it was just her and Rob, punctuated by the daily visits of Babs, their long-time housekeeper, who was now a bone fide family member. As usual, Babs had done a sterling job and the house was immaculate. Carrie often wondered how she would have managed without her. Over the years she had come to depend on her and, indeed, confide in her in the absence of her own dear mother. Lately, though, if she was honest, Carrie had avoided her usual chats over a cup of tea with Babs. She was afraid of what she might say – of what Babs, more accurately, might guess – if she hadn't already, Carrie acknowledged. Part of her desperately wanted to tell Babs, to ask for the advice that would so readily and sympathetically have been forth-coming, but another part of her knew it would deeply upset her – and Babs wasn't getting any younger. It wouldn't be fair to confide in her – it would be like asking her to take sides.

Although she knew as much about them as a family as it was possible to know, Babs was the soul of discretion and ever respectful of her 'position', as she always referred to it, despite Carrie's constant protestations.

Carrie walked quickly now through the hall, hardly trusting herself to reach the bottom of the curving stairway without turning on her heels and fleeing the emptiness. Not stopping to switch on the lights, she ran lightly up the stairs to her bedroom. She was emotionally and physically wrung out, and the champagne, she reflected, hadn't been such a good idea. She had been drinking too much lately, but sometimes it seemed to be the only thing that helped abate the loneliness. She would lie down, have a nap, and try to forget that she was another year older and her life seemed to be taking a very scary detour.

She drew the curtains, undressed quickly, threw her clothes on a chair and sank into bed between the cool linen sheets. It was only five o'clock. Turning off the bedside light, she curled up, longing for the escape that sleep might bring. She couldn't remember the last time she had slept the whole night through. No mater how late she read or watched TV, she would find herself wide awake at three a.m. on the dot, then toss and turn until she fell into an exhausted but un-refreshing sleep at six thirty. She was lucky, she supposed, that she didn't have to face a working day in some office. At least she had the luxury of staying in bed later if she needed to, but what-ever time she got up at, it still meant having to face another gruelling day, and she was always, always tired.

'Hello-ooo?' The breathless voice of her youngest daughter, Stephanie, floated up from below, just as Carrie was drifting off. 'Anybody home?' She heard footsteps as Stephanie ran up the stairs two at a time.

Carrie quickly sat up, turned on the light and grabbed the book that lay on her bed beside her.

'In here, darling,' she called, smoothing her hair and hoping she looked better than she felt.

The door flew open and Stephanie hurled herself into her mother's arms.

Carrie gasped, laughing, as she hugged her back. 'Sweetheart, I thought you were in London – what are you doing home?' She breathed in the delicious scent of something citrusy and, knowing Stephanie, unmistakably expensive. 'Mmm, you look wonderful.' She pulled back to take in the welcoming sight of what she had always thought of as a prettier version of herself.

Stephanie had done well out of the combined gene pool, although it was her elder sister, Ali, currently enjoying a successful career in modelling, who'd really lucked out.

Stephanie had inherited her mother's colouring, contrasting with a pair of ice-blue eyes courtesy of her maternal grandmother. She had a turned up, smaller nose that Carrie would have killed for, an hourglass figure and a swagger that was all her own. Not a lot got Stephanie down, but if something did, she eradicated the offending matter swiftly, moving on seemingly unscathed. It was, thought Carrie, an enviable disposition to be in possession of. And she thanked God daily that her youngest daughter, who looked so like her, was stronger and less vulnerable. She would have hated her darling Steph to be plagued by her own insecurities.

'Happy birthday, Mum,' Stephanie grinned. 'You didn't think I'd miss it, did you?' She wagged an admonishing finger. 'And you better not have any plans for this evening, 'cos we're all going to dinner. It's a surprise. Dad's booked

Guilbaud's. We're to be there for eight thirty. He'll meet us there. Hope can't come, she's got a deadline or something.'

Hope was thirty and Stephanie was still slightly in awe of her. Not only was she beautiful, but she very definitely had the brains in the family. She was kind too, and calm, and Stephanie missed her more than she let on, now that she was living in Spain.

She paused to draw breath. 'Pity Ali's still in Paris, but,' she went on, 'she's stuck on some mega-modelling assignment – couldn't get a flight.' Stephanie knew her other sister was doing her best to turn up for the dinner, although Ali had warned her not to say anything, as she was having trouble getting a flight in time to join them at the restaurant, but had assured her she would definitely be showing up at some stage.

'Well,' Carrie smiled, 'I don't know what to say, except what a lovely surprise, I had no idea . . . although I did speak to Hope this morning to thank her for her lovely card and gift and she didn't let on a thing.' And neither, thought Carrie, had she, although finding the right time to tell the girls about the momentous decision she had made regarding their father was weighing heavily on her mind.

Stephanie suddenly looked concerned. 'Mum, what on earth are you doing in bed at this time of the day?' She glanced at her watch. 'It's only six o'clock. Are you sick?'

A worried frown made her wide, heavily fringed blue eyes seem even bigger.

Carrie did her best not to look sheepish. 'No such excuse,' she said, making a face. 'I had a long lunch and drank far too much champagne, I'm afraid. I thought I'd just have a little lie-down, and then I ended up reading this old thing.'

'Really?' said Stephanie, glancing at the book in her mother's hands. 'Good, is it?'

'Brilliant,' Carrie lied.

Stephanie looked at her quizzically. 'You're bluffing, Mum.'

'What do you mean?'

'Can't be much good if you're reading it upside-down,' she observed. 'It's all right though, Mum, your secret's safe with me. I do that all the time.'

'What? Read upside-down?' Carrie laughed.

'No, bluff,' she grinned as she took Carrie's hand. 'Come downstairs, I've got a present for you and I'm sure as hell not lugging it all the way up here. It's way too awkward.'

'Must be some present.' Carrie swung her legs out of bed, grabbed her robe and tied it round her.

'It is,' said Stephanie, smiling mysteriously. 'I just hope you'll like it – no, that you'll love it. I think you will.'

Carrie followed her downstairs and Stephanie switched on the lights, illuminating the spectacular hall. For a moment Carrie blinked, and then her eyes focused on what appeared to be a large square box, covered with a brightly coloured blanket, standing in the middle of the floor.

Stephanie grinned. 'Are you ready?'

'What on earth?'

'Ta-da.' Stephanie pulled off the blanket with a flourish and bent down to open the door of what appeared to be a cage. She stood back and coaxed out what transpired to be the most unusual dog Carrie had ever seen. 'Mum,' said Stephanie proudly, 'meet Toby.'

As Carrie looked from Stephanie's delighted face to Toby's bewildered one, she felt as if – no, wished – she was hallucinating. Valiantly trying to summon a smile, she held onto the banisters and tried wildly to think of something positive to say. The nightmare day was heading for horror territory, but she had to try to keep it together for Stephanie's sake.

'Oh, Steph.' Her hand flew to her mouth.

Her daughter mistook her shock for joy. 'Isn't he just gorgeous? I know it's probably a bit of a surprise, but I was thinking about how you said the house is so empty now without us all, and how you have so much time on your hands – and he's a rescued dog, Mum, he just needs loads of love and attention – and – well – that's what you're good at, isn't it?' Stephanie looked thrilled with herself. 'Come on, just say hello to him.' She attempted to drag Toby over to Carrie, but he dug his heels in and refused to budge. Then they watched, mesmerised, as a powerful stream of urine hit the floor and spread in ominous rivulets towards several valuable Persian rugs.

'Oh God, Steph, he's peeing.' Carrie ran to the kitchen to fetch a cloth.

'Poor thing, there, there, darling,' Stephanie was murmuring as Carrie flung the kitchen roll down just in time to stop the rugs being drenched. 'He's just frightened, Mum, that's all. He's not used to a house, or people, but the woman at the rescue centre said they're easily house-trained, and then he'll be fine.'

'They?' Carrie got up breathlessly and eyed the dog.

'He's a lurcher – a greyhound cross. They make wonderful pets. They just like lying around. They don't even need much exercise, just the odd run . . .' Stephanie trailed off. 'Don't you like him, Mum?'

'Oh, Steph.' Carrie shook her head. 'I don't know what to say. I know you mean well, but a dog, well, it's just not a good time. There's no one to look after him,' Carrie blurted, suddenly reduced to helplessness. How could she possibly tell Stephanie that her family and her home were about to change irrevocably? She tried again: 'I mean, now that you're all gone – and your father, well, he's not keen on dogs, you know that—'

'Dad's hardly ever here,' Stephanie retorted – a little sharply, Carrie thought, although she wouldn't meet her mother's eyes. 'And there's loads of people to look after him. You're here, and Babs is here during the day, and—'

'It is not up to Babs to look after a dog, Stephanie.'

'She loves dogs, she told me so – and he'll have a ginormous garden to run around in, won't you, Toby?'

Carrie paled at the thought of the designer garden. 'That's another thing! He'll destroy it.'

'So? You've got two gardeners looking after it. It'll give them something to do for a change.'

'Stephanie,' Carrie's voice was rising, 'that really isn't the issue.'

'Oh, please, Mum, please! Just let him stay for a week. Then, if you don't want him, I can send him back to the rescue centre,' she begged. 'But he's been there for eight months already – no one wanted you, did they, darling?' She stroked the glossy head. 'And he's lovely and clean, Mum, I had him washed and blow-dried specially at the dog-grooming parlour. He loved it, didn't you?'

Toby stared blankly at her.

Carrie was all out of fight. She looked at her daughter and then at the dog, who, she had to admit, was rather handsome. As if reading her thoughts, Toby watched her as she sat down on the stairs and sighed. Slowly, the long tail, feathered at the tip, began to rotate, in a wide, happy circle.

'Here, boy,' she ventured, smiling despite herself as she held out a hand to him. 'Come here, Toby.' He trotted over, sniffed her, then laid his head on her shoulder.

'See?' Stephanie said triumphantly. 'He loves you, Mum. How could you not love him back?'

'Let's not get carried away, Stephanie. One week, that's all I'm promising, and your father is not going to be happy about this – and, oh God, what about tonight? We're out! What'll we do with him?'

'We'll leave him in the kitchen. I've got a special bed for him so he can stretch out. They don't like baskets. He'll be fine.' Stephanie spoke with confidence. 'What harm can he possibly do in the kitchen?'

Carrie was too weary to contemplate. 'Fine. You get him

settled in there now. Gosh, look at the time, I have to go up and get ready.'

'Me too,' said Stephanie, ushering the dog into the kitchen.

Twenty minutes later, not even the roar of the power shower was enough to drown the plaintive howls that issued from the kitchen when Toby was parted from his new friend. As Carrie listened helplessly, putting her hands over her ears, she felt she could not only have matched him, but outdone him.

After her shower, Carrie sat on the bed, feeling fresher, but nonetheless overwhelmed. Her mind was racing in a most unsettling way. It had come as a shock to hear from Stephanie that her father had organised dinner in Guilbaud's. Clearly Rob was making an effort, but it wouldn't change anything. She had made up her mind.

On the one hand, she was dreading the night ahead, the false gaiety, the strain of the ever-present undercurrent that ran between them. So he had remembered her birthday – so what? It didn't make up for anything, did it?

And then she remembered Stephanie's excited face and felt immediately remorseful. It would be lovely to go out together again. Surely for tonight, for Stephanie's sake, she could put aside recent events? She hated the person she had become lately, cynical, bitter. It wasn't her, wasn't in her nature. It never had been. But the constant strain of trying to maintain the façade had taken its toll on her – of all of them, probably, Carrie realised with a jolt. She always pushed the thought to the back of her mind whenever it surfaced, but there was no denying that whatever she said or did, the girls probably knew much more than they let on.

It was funny how she still thought of them as kids, but of course they were all grown now. Why, she had been married at Stephanie's age.

And Ali, her middle daughter, certainly pulled no punches. Carrie smiled thinking of her. With Ali, what you saw was what you got. She called a spade a shovel, and had mentioned on one of her previous visits home that she felt her father's behaviour left a lot to be desired. Taken by surprise, Carrie found herself defending Rob to his overly observant daughter. 'Of course Dad and I love each other,' she had protested. 'Your father can just be, well, thoughtless sometimes. All couples row occasionally, sweetheart.'

But there was no point in dwelling on any of that now, Carrie thought as she ran a comb through her damp hair.

She paused, now thinking of her eldest daughter, Hope. She worried about her, always had, from the moment she had entered the world. Carrie had longed for a baby, but she couldn't help feeling hugely guilty about presenting Rob with a *fait accompli*, and had determined, from the moment little Hope was born, to over-compensate both father and daughter simultaneously.

If Rob had felt compromised, he never showed it – at least, never to Hope. He adored her, just as Carrie did, falling instantly in love with her tiny scrunched-up face, her rosebud mouth and the little fingers that clutched his own with a ferocity that both terrified and enslaved him.

'Isn't she beautiful?' Carrie had murmured, stroking Hope's velvety cheek as Rob held his baby girl for the first time in the hospital, gazing at her in wonder. He had looked up at Carrie, still flushed and glowing with happiness, and said, 'Of course she is, Carrie, she's the image of you.' Carrie had thought she would die of joy.

As it turned out, Carrie's worry had been futile. Hope – Carrie had chosen the name because she had hoped so much that everything would turn out for the best – had been an easy child in every way, calmly amusing herself as a young-ster, and later keeping peace between her constantly warring younger sisters. Clever and popular, she went through school collecting friends and academic accolades easily. And now,

Carrie marvelled, Hope was a respected photojournalist, Ali a supermodel, and Stephanie – well, darling, flighty, giddy Stephanie was still a work in progress. But Carrie didn't care what she ended up doing as long as it made her happy.

Thinking of her youngest daughter, Carrie was brought smartly back to the present. She resolved to enjoy the evening ahead. It was the least she could do. One day at a time and all that. She and Rob would break the news of their divorce to the children together. When the time was right. After all, it wouldn't exactly come as a huge surprise to them. They were well aware their parents had been having 'problems' for quite some time now.

But for tonight, she would put the matter of divorce firmly off the menu and firmly out of her mind. It was her birthday. She didn't need it to become the annual reminder of her marital misery and the pain she was going through.

She blow dried her hair quickly, running the straightening irons through it, deftly flicking the ends out, just as her hairdresser had shown her.

Then she applied her make-up artfully, playing down her nose with clever shading and enhancing her eyes, which she had always felt were her best feature, ever since, she supposed, Rob had told her all those years ago on their honeymoon – a cheap package holiday to southern Spain. Although she'd had to contend with morning sickness in the searing heat, Carrie had never been happier. 'You have beautiful eyes, do you know that?' Rob had said sleepily as she nursed him through three days of sunstroke. Carrie, naturally sallow skinned, had tanned easily, while Rob, ignoring her warnings, had roasted himself into an all-over body blister that had confined him to bed and required constant applications of calamine lotion.

There had been such happy times, back then, but now . . . Carrie pulled herself together. Perhaps this evening could be pleasant at least. She would do her very best to make it so. She looked through her selection of evening wear and decided on a silk scarlet wraparound dress and matching high heeled satin slingbacks.

Taking a critical look in the mirror, she smiled at her reflection. Red had always been her best colour. It always gave her a boost of confidence when she needed it. She pulled out a drawer in her wardrobe, opened a velvet-lined box and lifted out the ruby and diamond pendant Rob had given her several years ago. She held it up to her neck, where it sparkled prettily in the mirror, accentuating the neckline and colour of the dress perfectly. Then she put it back in favour of a pair of gold hoop earrings.

'Mum!' she heard Stephanie call from downstairs. 'Are you ready?'

'Coming, sweetie.' She picked up the matching clutch bag and walked downstairs.

'Wow!' breathed Stephanie, 'you look amazing.' She linked her arm through Carrie's. 'You could stop traffic in that dress. I've always loved it on you.'

'You're looking pretty hot yourself.' Carrie gestured at the confection of vintage and high-street clothing put together as only Stephanie could.

'These arrived when you were upstairs – pretty spectacular, huh?'

Carrie followed her gaze and saw a vast array of at least three dozen red roses arranged in a beautifully designed bouquet sitting on the hall table. Attached to it was a small envelope.

'Well, go on, open it,' Stephanie urged. 'Perhaps you have a secret admirer.'

Carrie walked over to the roses and picked up the envelope, opening it with a feeling of – what? Uncertainty? Trepidation? Taking out the small card inside, her eyes followed the familiar, sloping, writing:

For my birthday girl,
love always,
Rob.
p.s. Bring your wallet and laughing gear, we're going for dinner!

Carrie smiled. But then, Rob could always make her smile when he put his mind to it.

'They're from Dad, aren't they?' Stephanie grinned. 'Wow, I hope someone loves me enough to send me masses of roses – when I'm your age,' she added wickedly.

Carrie blinked back the tears that suddenly threatened.

'Oh, Mum!' Stephanie smiled. 'You thought he'd forgotten, didn't you? You really are silly sometimes!'

Oh God, thought Carrie, she doesn't know the half of it. Instead she smiled and said, 'I'm sorry, Stephanie. I'm just feeling a bit emotional, that's all.'

'Good. It's ages since we've all been out together, well, almost together – but we'll manage without Ali and Hope, won't we?' She added quickly, almost blowing the surprise.

'Of course we will, darling.' Carrie brushed a stray lock of hair from her daughter's eyes.

'If Ali can't make it home, we'll go and surprise her with a visit soon, a girls' weekend in Paris. How about that?'

'Brilliant! Come on, let's go. The car's outside, Toby's been fed and I've left the TV on for him so he doesn't feel lonely.' Stephanie headed for the door.

'I thought he was being suspiciously quiet.' Carrie didn't dare think about the possibilities.

Her daughter held the front door open for her. 'I hope they're ready for us, Mum, 'cos we're gonna knock 'em dead!'

Carrie wished she had her daughter's seemingly endless supply of confidence. She was feeling decidedly wobbly, but she wouldn't spoil Stephanie's obvious excitement. One step at a time, she reminded herself. It was only an evening, only one evening to get through. She could do that, despite everything, couldn't she?

At Paddington, Ali Armstrong wrenched a one-way ticket for the Heathrow Express from the dispenser after queuing behind a particularly slow woman who had stood regarding the machine as if it was going to converse with her.

'Excuse me,' she said breathlessly, dodging around a group of businessmen who were ogling her. She slung her suit carrier over her shoulder and, dragging her wheelie case behind her, broke into a practiced run. If nothing else, modelling taught you how to move quickly and adroitly with varying amounts of luggage – even in heels. That was perhaps the only perk of years spent running between bookings. If you didn't get there first, somebody else would. Now, of course, she was beyond all that, one of the elite group of models entitled to the 'super' tag, and those days were behind her.

She made it just in time. No sooner had she stowed her case and collapsed into a seat than the train pulled out.

Fishing in her slouchy oversized handbag, she found her book, which she opened quickly. She pulled the brim of her seventies-style floppy hat over her face and tried to ignore the two American men in the opposite aisle who were gazing at her with open admiration. Staring intently at the pages of her novel, she tried very hard to resist scowling at them. In Ali's experience, if you made eye contact at all, even to glare, it only made them gaze even more wistfully in your direction.

She sighed, not so much in irritation – she was used to people staring at her – but because she was tired. It had been a long, gruelling day and it wasn't over yet.

Leaning back against her first-class seat, she closed her eyes, enjoying the soothing motion of the train, and thought about what Sandi, her agent, had said when she had phoned her first thing, breathless with excitement.

'It's almost certainly yours, Ali. I know you don't do go-sees any more, but, strictly, this isn't one. It's just a chemistry meeting at the ad agency. A courtesy thing. Stay Tru is the biggest contract to come on the market in years. If they like you, and we know they already do, you'll be the highest-paid model in the world – bigger even than Kate!'

Ali smiled wryly. It wasn't quite that simple, but she was in with a good chance. Stay Tru was a huge worldwide brand, based in the US. They represented clean, fresh, wholesome, girl-next-door beauty and were prepared to pay handsomely for the right face. There was only one hurdle to clear. The president of the company was a seventy-odd-year-old Bible basher, your genuine grass-roots evangelist who ruled his empire with a rod of iron and a will of steel. More than one girl had come a cropper when some less-than-savoury aspect of her lifestyle had been gleefully unveiled by the press or a jealous colleague. Gerald J. Simmington took instant likes and dislikes, and once he had made up his mind about a model, there was no dissuading him. So far, her agent told her, she was wowing him.

'He loves you, Ali,' Sandi had said. 'We sent your latest DVD over, of course, with the Milan runway shows and New York fashion week, and the Stay Tru people viewed it in Paris. Apparently he was bowled over – said you had a particular brand of integrity that shone through your beauty. His exact words. How about that?' Sandi chuckled. 'Anyway, I set up the meeting for next Thursday. You'll be back from the Bahamas shoot by then and, of course, I'll be with you at the meeting. They'll have the big guns out, you know. The ad agency's terrified of losing the account, so everyone's going to be a bit jittery. It's not often Muhammad comes to the mountain. So far as I know, this is the first time Gerald J. has deigned to visit the London agency – it's a big deal for them.'

Yeah, right, thought Ali, of course it is – for everybody. Everybody wants a piece of the action. That's what you got paid for. She wondered briefly if any sane human being had any idea at all of the unbelievably hard work that went into constructing the meticulously crafted images that sold everything the world over from washing powder to make-up to cars and, if you weren't careful, your soul. That was the hard bit: to keep a part of yourself back. So far she had succeeded. It kept them wanting more. And everyone always wanted more. People often said models were treated like meat – everyone wanted another slice, cut just another way. Even at the top it was the same, the stakes just got higher. Same meat, more expensive cut. The trick was to get out while you were still ahead, and as far as Ali was concerned, she was ready to go. With the Stay Tru contract, she would make her exit in style.

Word on the street supported her agent's theory. Earlier that day, during a break from an exclusive fashion shoot she was doing for *Vibe* magazine, her favourite make-up artist had echoed her words. Dusting Ali's face with powder, Ronnie had kept up a running chatter.

'Word on the grapevine is you're gonna be the next Stay Tru girl, Ali. It's down to you and two others – a Ukrainian girl who I know for a fact is bi-sexual, and a gorgeous Texan kid with a cocaine habit and a sugar daddy – I know who my money's on.' Ronnie grinned as she went about her work, meticulously scrutinising Ali's perfect features.

'Hey, the fat lady hasn't sung yet,' cautioned Ali. 'I never count my chickens.' She crossed her fingers for extra measure.

'No contest, hon,' Ronnie said loyally, and then, 'there. Hold on a sec, just a teeny bit of filler.' She deftly applied a smear of light-reflective cream round Ali's eyes. 'See? Perfect! Not a trace of those little lines. All gone.' Ronnie stood back to admire her handiwork. 'If I say so myself, nobody does it better, although I must admit you're an easy canvas to work on! Here, what do you think?' Ronnie held up the magnifying mirror so Ali could inspect herself.

'Great,' she said, trying not to peer too hard at the lines. She couldn't see them – but that didn't mean the camera wouldn't, or, indeed, the client, in this case the most difficult fashion editor in the business. After all, she was twenty-eight now, pretty ancient when you considered that sixteen-year-olds were being made up to project thirty-five-year-old glamour. Yes, it was definitely time to go, Ali thought, an uncharacteristic wave of panic washing over her, before the fashion world tired of her and she was unceremoniously dumped.

The bleeping of her phone startled her from her musings. Checking her messages, she saw one from Stuart, her boyfriend, to confirm he'd be at the airport to pick her up and take her home. From there they'd go to the restaurant for Mum's birthday dinner. Thinking about the night ahead, Ali frowned. She hoped there wouldn't be any tension and that her father in particular would be on his best behaviour. Mum had no idea she was arriving for a couple of days and it would be a lovely surprise for her – that, of course, and the news she had to tell them. Ali smiled as the train pulled into Heathrow's underground. Whatever was going on with her parents, this would redirect their attention to more appropriate family matters, which was just as it should be.

Hurrying to Terminal One, Ali walked purposefully to her gate and onto the plane, where the air hostess greeted her warmly. 'Welcome on board, Miss Armstrong,' she said, taking Ali's case as she showed her to her seat in Premier. 'Nice to see you again.' There was a flurry of interest as people recognised a famous face. 'Enjoy your flight. If there's anything I can get you, let me know.'

'Thank you,' said Ali, smiling at her as she slipped into the aisle seat. 'It's good to be going home.'

3

The private jet came in to land, taxied briefly along the runway and came to a standstill. Rob Armstrong gathered his coat and briefcase then thanked the two-man crew who were presently opening the door and lowering the steps. Outside, the cold evening air revived him, and he walked quickly to the waiting car. Thank God he didn't have to negotiate the hordes in Arrivals. Rob's days of flying commercial were long gone. Flying by private jet was the only way to travel in his opinion, and he loved it.

'The Merrion Hotel, quick as you can,' he told the driver.

'Yes, Mr Armstrong. Should make it in twenty, the worst of the traffic's over.' The man manoeuvred the sleek car out of the private zone, then swung out of the airport and onto the M1.

Rob sat back and switched on his mobile. God, he was bone bloody tired, and no wonder: he'd been on the go constantly for practically the last twenty-four hours. And tomorrow it would start all over again. London, Europe, the US, there was no rest for the wicked empire builders. He rubbed his eyes and flicked through his messages: about twenty from his secretary, which he ignored – he knew she'd been trying to get hold of him all day but he'd talk to her tomorrow – one from his daughter Stephanie, confirming that she'd be at the restaurant with her mother at eight thirty, and one from Ali, saying she'd got a flight, but would probably be late. She and Stuart would get there as soon as they possibly could.

Rob ran a hand through his hair and sighed. That was it, nothing else, zilch, *nada*, no sign whatsoever of the number he'd so desperately wanted to see.

With a sinking feeling in the pit of his stomach, he returned the phone to his pocket. Well, what had he expected? She'd finished with him. Said she wouldn't be contacting him and asked that he no longer contact her.

'I can't do this any more, Rob,' she had said, tears in her eyes, that last day in her house. 'All this deceit, it's turning me into someone I don't know. I'm beginning to hate myself.'

'I know, darling, I know.' Rob held her tightly, trying to reassure her. 'It's hard for me too. I just need a little more time, Olwen, to sort things out.'

But she had been adamant.

He had been shocked, but, of course, he had agreed to respect her wishes. He'd just never thought she'd stick to her guns. And now he was in an awful state. He'd heard about this sort of stuff, but he'd never in a million years believed it would happen to him.

He would never have believed either that he could miss someone so much, but Olwen wasn't just someone. She was amazing. 'Missing her' didn't begin to describe the empty, hollow ache he felt when he thought of her – which was all the time. He missed her voice, her touch, her smell and, most of all, her megawatt smile that could light up a room, not to mention his life. At times the longing he felt for her was unbearable.

He smiled ruefully, remembering their first meeting, two and a half years ago. It was indelibly imprinted on his mind.

It was strange, he reflected now, he couldn't remember meeting Carrie for the first time. She just seemed always to have been around, one of the crowd. But Olwen . . .

* * *

Political fund-raising events were always predictably tedious, Rob thought as he worked the room methodically, chatting with fellow businessmen and doing the hail-fellow-well-met thing *ad nauseam*. Today's was for Trade and Industry and it was being held in the newly refurbished Shelbourne Hotel in the heart of town. He'd planned to drop in for five minutes, check in with a few colleagues, then make his escape.

As he turned away to dodge the matronly wife of a local politician who was about to descend on him, Rob's breath caught in his chest. Across the room, the most beautiful woman he had ever laid eyes on was chatting animatedly to a group of admiring men. 'Close your mouth, Armstrong!' a mate of his had nudged him, laughing. 'You'll be catching flies.'

'Who *is* that?' Rob asked, still fixed on the blonde vision with the chiselled profile, laughing now at something one of the group had said.

'That's Olwen Slater, the media babe, back from London. She's just got her own current-affairs show on TV 2000.' Of course, now he knew who she was. It was just that on television she didn't have that luminous glow, didn't exude such warmth, such sex appeal.

Twenty minutes later, Rob joined the group of admirers, a few of whom he knew, and waited hopefully for an introduction, which was not forthcoming. He had to say something – but what? 'I love your boots,' he heard himself blurt. 'They're great.'

Olwen looked at him quizzically, then smilingly quipped, 'Like the song says, they're made for walking. Excuse me, gentlemen.' She turned on her heel and moved away. Rob felt as if he'd been hit by a train. He *had* to talk to her again, get a blast of that incredible smile – but how?

He risked approaching her as the party was thinning out.

'Will you give me your phone number, please?' Rob never begged anyone for anything, but now, today, he had to.

'No,' she said pleasantly and smiled that infuriatingly beautiful smile again.

'Then how am I going to contact you?' he asked.

'You'll find a way – if you want to.' She looked at him mischievously.

And, of course, he had.

She hadn't been hard to track down. She worked in television and Rob had enough contacts in the media to wangle her phone number from a man who owed him more than one favour. That had been the easy bit. Persuading her to meet him was another matter. It had begun with a lunch, which had taken him four weeks and eight phone calls to persuade her to agree to.

He had chosen a highly acclaimed double-Michelin-starred restaurant, a common meeting-ground for movers and shakers and public enough not to arouse suspicion in prying onlookers.

Rob had watched her walk into the restaurant that first day and had known that from that moment on, no other woman existed for him. He stood up to greet her and she waved as she handed her coat to the maître d'. She looked divine, he thought, although he couldn't say for sure what she was wearing. It was soft and black, with a deep V-neck, moulded to her willowy figure. She sat down gracefully, seemingly unaware of the glances that followed her.

'Thank you for coming,' he said. 'I appreciate you agreeing to meet me.'

'Not at all,' Olwen said and sipped some water. 'So,' she said directly, 'how can I help you? Is it something to do with the takeover bid you mentioned?'

Rob cleared his throat, unusually reticent. It was true he was engaged in a takeover bid involving an angle that might be misconstrued if it attracted an unfavourable media spin and his people had not yet come up with a satisfactory resolution. But he had used it as an excuse to meet her, talk to her. All the same, he was interested to hear her view.

She didn't disappoint. Her analytical skills were first rate, and she grasped the awkwardness of the potential fallout instantly.

'Having said that,' she continued, 'I know someone whose expertise would be far more useful than anything I can offer. You should talk to him.' She had given him the name and contact details of a well-known UK spin-doctor. 'Tell him I recommended him. He's a good friend. We worked together in London. He'll deal with it for you.'

Rob was impressed. He knew of the man she'd mentioned, had seen him often on television, sorting out the lives of the rich and famous.

Gradually they fell to discussing and exploring their lives, savouring every detail.

'You're married.' Olwen looked him straight in the eye. It was a statement as much as a question. Rob felt somewhat relieved that she'd guessed. He had been loath to bring it up, although he'd had no intention of deceiving her. In fact, he had begun to wonder exactly what he was doing there. Asking her for advice was genuine, but it had been an excuse. One, he suspected, that Olwen had very probably guessed. This woman wasn't material for a fling, he could see that. She was special.

'Does it show?' he smiled wryly. 'Yes, I am, although . . .' He shrugged. 'Well, it's a rather strange situation.' Olwen merely raised an eyebrow in response. 'You?'

'Divorced. It wasn't a good marriage, but we didn't have kids so we're both free to make a clean start. That's partly why I came back to Dublin.'

'To new beginnings, then.' Rob held up his glass.

'To new beginnings,' she murmured, then shook her head.

'What?' Rob asked.

'Nothing.' She smiled enigmatically. 'It's just that, well . . .'

'Go on,' Rob urged.

'Don't take this the wrong way, but I didn't think I'd enjoy this meeting as much as I am.'

'I won't.' Rob's heart had lifted. 'Take it the wrong way, that is.'

Three hours later, they were still deep in conversation. They'd discussed favourite novels, films, how they both loved Rome. A sense of mutual fascination was building between them. When Olwen checked her watch – 'Gosh, look at the time! I really must go – it's been lovely' – Rob was loath to leave her.

She accepted his offer of a lift, but when he dropped her home, she didn't invite him in.

'Thank you again for lunch. I hope the takeover goes well for you.' With that, she disappeared into her house.

Reluctantly, he forced himself to drive away, wanting with every fibre in his body to run after her.

Instead he went home. He listened absently to what Carrie was telling him about Stephanie's latest phone call from London and tried to stifle the grin that kept trying to spread across his face.

He had to see her again – *had* to.

Their second meeting was different. Lunch, again, but in a more intimate restaurant, overlooking the canal. Olwen had agreed hesitantly, but sitting across the table from him she was wary. They chatted about the spin-doctor, whom he had met and subsequently hired as a consultant, but her conversation was non-committal and her manner elusive. As he sat there, drinking her in, he knew he wanted her, knew it without a shadow of a doubt. But he didn't know what to do – what to say. Here he was, Rob Armstrong, boardroom barracuda, as bashful and intimidated as a teenager on his first date. He knew she knew – they both knew – without saying a word. And she wasn't playing with him. They were both aware of the intensity that enveloped them the minute they came close to each other.

They met infrequently at first, then increasingly often. He found her enchanting: she was quick, intelligent, witty and compassionate. She could listen and analyse without being the slightest bit judgmental, and despite the tough veneer she was endearingly vulnerable. Olwen Slater, he learned rapidly, was a beguiling mixture.

She lived alone, which was a huge bonus as far as Rob was concerned, and since she hadn't been long back in Dublin, after ten years in London and New York, she wasn't yet surrounded by hordes of friends. In fact, Rob found, Olwen tended to keep pretty much to herself. Her two best girlfriends lived abroad, she told him, one in Australia and the other in Spain, and there didn't appear to be anyone special in her life. When he asked her casually one day, she was vague.

'Going through a divorce makes you question a lot of things,' she said. 'I found I needed time to myself, to re-establish things. Not everyone was as loyal as I'd hoped, which has made me cautious of people, to be honest.'

The sadness that flitted across her face was heartbreaking, and Rob realised, with a shock, as he struggled with a feeling that was totally unfamiliar to him, that he wanted to protect her.

Eventually, out of the blue, she suggested he come round one evening for a bite to eat. He felt strangely apprehensive when, punctually, he arrived with a bunch of spring flowers and a bottle of champagne. He stood on her doorstep, nervously, but once inside he felt instantly comfortable. Her house was stylish and uncluttered, open-plan downstairs and decorated in cool, muted shades. The front and back walls were built entirely of glass, hung with swathes of smoky silk curtains. A bold painting dominated one wall, with smaller ones grouped on the other, and Rob noticed some beautiful pieces of sculpture. The only sign of excess was the wall of bookshelves that went up the stairs, filled with every kind of literature.

In her home, away from prying eyes, Olwen seemed relaxed and happy as she cooked their steaks and chatted about her day.

It had involved, among other things, an interview with the deputy prime minister, a man who was revered, respected and notoriously non-verbal. Olwen, however, had got him to talk. He had enthused about the political situation and she had even grilled him on a planning issue he had sworn he wouldn't be drawn on. Listening to her, Rob almost felt sorry for the guy. Who could possibly be immune to her charms?

Now though, like him, he could tell she was feeling shy.

'Why don't you leave that?' he said as she began to clear away their plates.

'What? Oh, no, it's no trouble.' She was flustered, busying herself with the dishwasher.

He got up slowly, walked over to her and slipped his arms round her, breathing in her scent. He held her for a moment that seemed to go on for ever. Then she turned, wound her arms round his neck and they kissed, tentatively at first, then with the certainty of the lovers they were about to become.

Her body was so lovely, with firm high breasts, soft, silky skin, and she was different – even from what he had expected. Tender, yet sure of herself, subtly demanding, passionate and fiery. Rob didn't think he'd ever felt so aroused.

Later, they lay in her bed under Egyptian cotton sheets, hot and sated. Rob thought he'd never move again, until . . .

She was as eager as he was. Rob knew that in their love-making they had made a connection he'd never experienced before. For the first time in his life, he suspected he was finally falling in love.

He stayed late into the night, making love to her, talking to her, holding her, wanting never to let her go. From that moment on he knew he couldn't have enough of her. He would never give her up.

Soon her home became his haven. At every possible opportunity, he went to her there, and he lived for those moments. In a good week, he might see her twice, three times, but sometimes his life was so hectic, with business and family matters, that several days might pass before they could meet. Then he would text and talk to her constantly, always mindful of the risk he took in leaving her alone for any length of time, although she never once complained or berated him for it. 'Of course I'd love to see more of you,' she had said on occasion, 'but what we have is so special we should be grateful for whatever time we have. Some people never get to share what we have.'

As they both had a high profile, he in business, she in the media, their affair had to be clandestine, it was the only way it could work. Both had busy, demanding careers and, of course, there was his marriage.

He had had other affairs over the years, even one or two he'd considered quite serious, but nothing had prepared him for the suddenly savage intensity of his feelings for Olwen. The other flings he'd had were just that, diversions, distractions, but this was the real thing. It terrified him.

However many women had been before her, he knew that Olwen Slater had found her way into his heart – and she would be the last.

And now he was stuck in the middle of this *nightmare*. He was going to pieces. He couldn't sleep, he'd lost weight, and although he was desperately throwing himself into his work, he couldn't shake the desolation that, God forbid, she would meet someone else and he would lose her for good. *Oh, like you haven't lost her already?* a nagging voice taunted him. He pushed aside the monstrous possibility. He wouldn't, couldn't, let it happen. He just needed time to sort things out in his head.

It wasn't that he hadn't thought of leaving Carrie. He'd come close on more than one occasion over the years, when it had become obvious to him that he'd made a mistake. A big one. He loved her, in his own way, was deeply fond of her, but she didn't do it for him. Somehow, though, the time had never seemed right: the children had been too young, his business too demanding. He would ride out a storm – at least for a time – and mostly, he reflected, he had taken the right course. Until now.

Olwen had never pressured or asked him to leave – quite the contrary.

'You must be careful, Rob,' she said with sadness in her voice. 'Surprisingly few affairs survive a marriage break-up, however bad that marriage is.' If anything, she had seemed fearful of the consequences.

'But I want – no, I need and *long* to be with you,' he was adamant.

'Darling, you know I love you,' she said, taking his hand, 'but I couldn't bear to break up a marriage. It would ruin everything, I know it would.' It was then that he cursed himself for not having left Carrie years ago. How ironic was it to have a mistress who didn't want you to leave your wife?

Then Carrie had asked him for a divorce. He had to admit it had hardly come as a surprise, casting his mind back to yesterday morning. Did she know about Olwen? He wasn't sure he cared. He was just too damn miserable. For the first time in his life, he had found love. He was obsessed with Olwen, he couldn't help himself, even though he knew he was putting the stability of his family at risk.

But now, so many arguments raged in his mind that his head spun. The money, the guilt, the publicity, the sheer horror of it all. Of course, they were excuses he made to himself to avoid confronting his own weakness. But however he dealt with the situation, the price he would pay would be enormous.

If he left, he would be the Bad Guy. His children would freeze him out, mutual friends would be forced to take sides – and financially . . . Jesus! It wasn't that he couldn't afford it, but what would it do to his current expansion plans, never mind the investments both here and overseas? Greedy accountants and lawyers would go through his deals with a fine-tooth comb, his assets would be frozen. Hell, it just didn't bear thinking about. His business partners, never mind the banks, would *not* thank him for it. Others have done it, the small voice pointed out.

And if he stayed? If he managed, yet again, to salvage the situation, what then?

A happy, loving relationship with Carrie? Not a chance. The damage had been long since done. It would be a case of far too little far too late.

How the hell had it all turned out to be such a mistake? Carrie had bent over backwards to make their marriage work, no matter what . . . maybe that *had* been the problem.

They'd only been kids, for heaven's sake, when they'd got married. But at the time, well, it had been – or, rather, seemed – the only option. Anyway, all their friends had been doing it. Carrie and he had been an on-and-off item since they were sixteen and seventeen, respectively, so Carrie getting pregnant had merely hastened what would probably have happened anyway.

'I know this is a shock for you, Rob,' she had said tremulously. 'It's a shock for me too, but I'm scared. I don't know what to do . . .'

Looking into her wide, fearful eyes, Rob couldn't bring himself to heed the warning voice that whispered to him with increasing urgency.

In the event, everyone had been thrilled for them, including their families. Carrie's father had provided them with a basement flat in town, for which Rob paid a meagre rent and, sure, they'd had good times in the early days, but he had never thought the situation through. Never considered its implications. That was the trouble, he thought with a twisted smile. He never thought anything through. In business, it made him a risk-taker, which had paid off admirably, but in his personal life, it had proved a disaster.

Two more children came, and they had bought their first house. Rob had knuckled down and started making money, more money, and then even more, but had spent less and less time at home. The affairs had begun soon enough. Probably, Rob acknowledged, because he was bored. He had hated being tied down, hated having to account to someone. He craved excitement, the adrenalin rush of tasting forbidden fruit. He had first strayed about two years into the marriage when Hope was three, Ali just a baby, and Carrie was relishing motherhood. It wasn't that she didn't have time for him, Rob simply felt claustrophobic. His business was beginning to do well and he was spending more and more time at the office. His PA, a small, determined blonde called Emily, was attractive and available. Of course, he led her on, it was part of the fun, and she was a willing participant. At the office party at Christmas, they had danced together all evening and Rob didn't care who noticed. He was just having a good time. When the party broke up, it seemed natural to take her up on her invitation to go back to her flat where Emily, so cool, collected and professional at work, surprised him with the intensity of her need. She ripped off his clothes the minute she'd got him through the door.

'Hey,' Rob laughed, 'hang on a minute! Isn't it me who's supposed to pin you up against the wall?'

'Sorry, Rob,' she whispered and bit his earlobe, 'but back here *I'm* the boss.' He had to admit he'd found her aggressive sexuality a huge turn-on – for a while. After a year or so, she had moved on to another job and, presumably, another man. And Rob had been secretly and guiltily relieved.

And all the while, Carrie had gone on loving him, even when she had found out about one or two of his infidelities. Of course there had been rows, vicious ones, but in the end they had always agreed to give it another go. And the years had gone by.

Perhaps if she had done something with her life – Rob suppressed a flash of irritation – it might have made a difference, might have made him respect her more. Of course she was the mother of his children and she had always made a wonderful home for them all, but even now, when the girls were grown up, Carrie seemed reluctant to do *anything*.

She had never shown any interest in pursuing a career or getting a job or even going to university, as he had suggested, to do a course and broaden her horizons.

He knew some men got off on having a stay-at-home wife as if it were some sort of status symbol – but he wasn't one of them. There was only so much discussing of children that any couple could do.

And it didn't work like that any more. These days women were dynamic, doing their own thing, giving men a run for their money – literally. And he thought it was fantastic. There was nothing more interesting and attractive than a *happening* woman with a life of her own. Which was more than he had these days, he thought bitterly. It brought him back to the crux of his current dilemma. If he stayed with Carrie, he would lose Olwen for good. The idea filled him with dread. Life without her was unthinkable. Hearing about her – seeing her – with someone else . . . he couldn't stand it. And yet . . .

Oh, God, nothing made sense. It was such a fucking awful mess.

'Here we are, Mr Armstrong.' The driver pulled up outside the Merrion Hotel, which housed the famous double Michelin-starred restaurant, interrupting his thoughts.

'Great. Thanks.' Rob tipped him generously and got out. 'I'll call you when we need to be picked up.'

He stood outside the hotel and took a deep breath. It would require quite a performance, but he could pull it off. There was nothing he couldn't achieve once he put his mind to it. He simply had to play for time. Just until he was sure what to do. Just until things were calmer. Then all would become clear. He glanced at his phone one more time before he went in. Still nothing. He felt the by now familiar sinking feeling. Maybe he'd call her tonight, or text. Just to let her know he still loved her. It couldn't do any harm. With a heavy heart, he walked up the steps of the hotel, bracing himself for an evening with his family. He was looking forward to seeing Ali and Stephanie but he couldn't kick back and relax as he used to with Olwen: he had to be on his guard, watching every word he said, in case he let something slip or tripped himself up.

Still, it was only one evening. At least Carrie had agreed to the dinner. For a while he'd thought she might refuse to come, insisted they tell the girls tonight – on her birthday, for Christ's sake! How awful would that have been? He really would have been in the doghouse. Things, thought Rob, could be decidedly worse. Carrie and he had got through plenty of difficult evenings before and tonight was just another. He'd make sure he gave it his best shot. He could perform again for one evening, couldn't he?

4

The evening had started well, thought Stephanie, observing her parents as she sipped her drink. She had been anxious about the dinner, particularly for her mother. She'd seemed so out of sorts lately. Now, though, Carrie was smiling and visibly relaxing as Rob chatted effortlessly.

'You look great,' he said warmly, his eyes flicking appreciatively over his wife. 'Doesn't she, Steph?' He raised his glass to Carrie. 'I've always loved that dress on you. Here's to the birthday girl.'

'To the birthday girl.' Stephanie smiled as Carrie held Rob's warm gaze. Taking advantage of the moment, she sneaked a covert glance at her mobile – although restaurant rules required it to be turned off.

Ali hadn't made an appearance yet, although she had texted Stephanie to say she had landed, that Stuart would pick her up and they would be there as quickly as they could. Stephanie hid a smile. It would be the icing on the cake for Mum – she had no idea Ali was coming tonight and staying for the weekend.

Known as Ireland's only genuine supermodel, Ali Armstrong was making quite a name for herself around the globe. And it had all happened quite by chance, as most things in Ali's life seemed to, Stephanie thought wryly. Ali's rise to modelling had been a glorious accident. She'd just finished a degree in French and business studies and was spending the summer in Provence when she had been spotted by an Italian designer staying at a neighbouring château. He had insisted she come to Paris for a photographer friend to take some shots and before she knew it, she had been taken on by the celebrated Elite model agency in Paris. She had débuted in her first runway collections that autumn in New York and had taken the fashion world by storm.

It was the supermodel fairy story. At five foot nine, she wasn't particularly tall for a model, but Ali's couldn't-care-less, insouciant manner, combined with her edgy but undeniably stunning good looks, had made her the darling of the runways. Her timing had been perfect. The US had had its fill of temperamental girls from newly liberated Eastern Europe and the ever-fickle fashion world had been ready for something new. In Ali Armstrong they got the whole enchilada.

Bright, educated, from a wealthy, privileged background, Ali was as well-known for her one-liners as she was for her smouldering looks. She was a modern-day Grace Kelly – on speed – and she had taken to the limelight like a duck to water. Never shy, she was soon gracing the covers of the international glossies and every party on both sides of the Atlantic.

At first, Stephanie remembered, her parents had been concerned – after all, Ali had been just twenty-one when she'd hit the big time. But they needn't have worried. Ali was smart. She knew her career would be short-lived and she milked it for all it was worth. Her father had made sure she hired a reputable financial adviser and accountants, and Ali was now the proud owner of three properties: a beautiful *fin-de-siècle* apartment in the Saint-Germain-des-Prés area of Paris, a loft in SoHo, New York, and an elegant town-house in Dublin.

'Penny for them?' Dad's voice brought Stephanie back from her reverie.

'Just wondering when the prodigal sister will show up,'

Stephanie murmured, safe in the knowledge that, across the table, her mother was talking to a passing friend. 'She should be here any minute.'

'What's happening with *you*?' her dad looked at her enquiringly. 'We haven't had time to talk much lately, have we? Are you still okay about Colin?' He was referring to her erstwhile boyfriend. 'I thought you said he was a keeper.' He eyed her keenly.

'Yeah? Well, I guess I got that one wrong,' Stephanie retorted darkly, remembering the mortification she had felt on discovering that Colin, an aspiring actor, had been rehearsing more than his lines with at least one female thespian.

'I won't say I told you so,' Rob said, 'but you know I never liked the guy. He wasn't right for you – not nearly bright enough, for starters.'

'Well, clearly *he* didn't think I was enough for *him*,' said Stephanie, and immediately regretted volunteering the information.

'What?' Rob's antennae were up. 'Did he mess you around, Steph? I don't believe it, the little waster! Why—'

'Please, Dad,' Stephanie hissed, 'it doesn't matter now. It's over.' She hurriedly forked some risotto into her mouth.

'Well, you did the right thing, sweetheart.' Rob stabbed his asparagus, eyes darkening at the idea of anyone hurting one of his beloved daughters. 'If he was messing you about, he's more of a fool than even *I* thought he was. You could do a lot better for yourself. You're a gorgeous, bright, beautiful girl and any man would be incredibly lucky to have you. And don't you ever forget that.'

'What are you two muttering about?' Carrie asked from across the table.

'Oh, nothing.' Stephanie tried frantically to think of a different subject. She was fed up with being the one who got things wrong in this family.

'I was just telling Stephanie,' Rob began, 'how glad I am that she's got rid of that excuse of a boyfriend – whatever his name was.'

'Dad, please, I don't want to talk about it. We're through, it's over, no hard feelings on either side. Colin and I had some good times. Things just reached their natural conclusion.'

'Any guy who's stupid enough to mess you around and even *contemplate* hurting you isn't worth defending, Steph. He deserves the boot and nothing else,' Rob told her.

'I wasn't defending him,' Stephanie demurred, 'I just don't want to talk about it, okay?'

'Your father's quite right for once, Stephanie,' said Carrie lightly, although Stephanie immediately picked up on the slight edge to her voice and simultaneously clocked the look of exasperation that flitted across Rob's face.

Oh God, Stephanie thought, what now? What eggshell had been stepped on this time? The evening had been going so well. Please don't let them start, she begged silently as tension seeped across the table.

Just then a discernible hush descended on the restaurant, followed by a ripple of excited murmurs, and Stephanie realised her sister had arrived.

Escorted down the six steps into the room by the delighted proprietor and followed by the handsome Stuart trotting a respectful two steps in her wake, Ali was making an entrance worthy of an Oscar winner. She looked stunning, although Stuart, Stephanie saw, had put on quite a bit of weight since she'd last seen him.

'Oh my God!' squealed Carrie as her gorgeous daughter glided across the room. 'Ali! Darling!' Suddenly everyone was on their feet.

Ali looked amazing, thought Stephanie. She was wearing a little black slip of a dress that wound round her like a bandage and probably cost as much as at least one surgical procedure.

When she hadn't seen her for a while, Stephanie forgot just how gorgeous her sister was. And tonight she was sparkling, almost as if she was lit up from the inside, although Stephanie knew from experience how much hard work went into the so-naturally-glowing-I-hardly-ever-wear-any-make-up-look that all models had to perfect.

The dinner had been a great idea, Stephanie decided. Her mother's face had been a sight to behold as it had dawned on her that Ali had flown in specially for the occasion. Ali jetted around so much, she hadn't been home recently. It had been clever of Dad to arrange it all and now her mother was having a ball.

Dad, too, was in excellent form, relishing the fun and being his charming, incorrigible self. Now he was chatting easily with Stuart, of whom he seemed to approve. And why wouldn't he?

When it came to prospective partners for one of Rob's precious daughters, Stuart Mitchell ticked all of the boxes. For starters, he was Irish. Stephanie knew this was a huge relief to both her parents, given the sometimes dubiously exotic people with whom Ali mixed in the mercurial world of high fashion. Although they had grown up in the same suburb, Ali and Stuart had met in New York, where Stuart had been posted with his firm. He worked for Frank Farrelly, her father's close friend and business associate, and, as a first-class-honours business graduate, not to mention ex-international rugby player, his career path was well and truly on the ascendant. Frank had made it no secret that he was grooming Stuart to be his right-hand man.

Ali and he certainly made a handsome couple, Stephanie admitted, observing them across the table, where they held hands discreetly despite talking to Rob and Carrie on either side of them. Stuart, with his dark, brooding features, heavy-lidded eyes and athletic, stocky build, was the perfect foil to Ali's slender beauty, sculpted cheekbones, slanting green eyes and tawny blonde and bronze streaked hair, caught back tonight from her animated face in a dishevelled chignon. Stephanie thought Ali was more beautiful than ever. Thinner, too, if that was possible, although weight had never been a problem for her. As a friend had once remarked enviously, 'The greyhound gene clearly runs in your family.'

Stephanie hadn't taken offence, even though it had bypassed her, and she worked her curvier, feminine shape into a look that was definitely her own.

Speaking of which, Stephanie had forgotten about Toby, all alone on his first night in a strange environment. She hoped he hadn't done any major damage. He was on probation already, poor thing, if not borrowed time. With a bit of luck they'd be leaving soon – the coffees had arrived. She was feeling tired now, pleasantly muzzy, and ready to go home. Now Ali caught her eye and mouthed something Stephanie couldn't decipher.

'Shall we make a move?' Rob sat back in his chair and stifled a yawn, relieved that the evening had been such a success. 'I'll call for the car and—'

'Just a minute Dad,' Ali interrupted. 'The evening's not quite over yet.' Her lips curved in a playful smile. 'Mum,' she glanced meaningfully at Carrie, 'I know it's *your* evening,' the green eyes slanted mischievously at Stuart, 'and it's absolutely wonderful to be here for your birthday and have all of us together as a family . . .' She trailed off, squeezing Stuart's hand. 'That's why . . .' she paused for a second to make sure she had everyone's attention, 'that's why, I – that is, well, Stuart and I . . .' She took a deep breath. 'We're getting married!'

There was a dazed silence, and then the table erupted in

a flurry of hugs and congratulations. 'How fabulous!' Carrie was dabbing her eyes. 'We're just *thrilled*, aren't we, Rob?'

'Fantastic news. Well done, Stuart.' Rob hugged Ali, then shook Stuart's hand heartily.

'Brilliant! That's so cool,' said Stephanie. 'I always wanted a brother. The question is, are you ready for me as a sister-in-law?' She grinned.

The mâitre d', ever conscious of his celebrity guest and a clientele of fond onlookers, had more champagne on the table at a click of his well-timed fingers.

Forty-five minutes and a lot of gushing later, Stephanie looked at her watch. The gesture wasn't lost on Rob, who, tired also, and slightly peeved, was ready to head home too.

Of course he was pleased for Ali and, indeed, relieved – Stuart was a solid sort of guy, not like some of those weird people he read about that, God forbid, Ali might have got mixed up with. But he would have liked Stuart to ask him for her hand in marriage before they announced their engagement. Not that he considered himself old-fashioned about that sort of thing – marriage was often fleeting these days – but he would have liked a man to man thing.

He stifled another yawn. Still – he looked on the bright side – a wedding, and in four months. It was welcome news. A totally unforeseen reprieve. If Carrie had a wedding to worry about – and what a wedding it was bound to be – she would have to shelve her divorce plans at least for the time being. And four months was a generous amount of time. Anything could happen in four months – anything at all.

Rob heaved a long, shuddering sigh of relief as a weight seemed to drop from his shoulders. For the first time since he could remember, he felt as if someone had handed him a lifeline and he was going to hold onto it for all he was worth.

He gestured discreetly for the bill. 'How about we go home

to celebrate properly, eh?' He looked round the table at the happy faces. 'Shall I call for the car now, Carrie?' he looked questioningly at his wife.

'You go ahead Rob,' she replied, not quite meeting his eyes, 'I'll go with Ali and Stuart.'

'Fine.' Rob's face betrayed nothing as he signed and returned the bill.

'Great,' Ali said. 'Let's make tracks.'

'Steph,' he turned to his younger daughter, 'will you hitch a ride with your old man?'

'Sure thing, Dad.' Stephanie was itching to leave. 'Let's go.'

'Ready when you are,' said Rob, getting to his feet, and one by one, they left the table and the restaurant, followed by curious, envious and openly admiring glances from the diners they left behind.

The Spanish sun was sinking slowly behind the Andalucian hills after another glorious day.

In her house, Hope leaned back in her chair and stretched her arms above her head, then she did a quick word-count on her text. The writing was coming along nicely, and this latest piece she had been working on, describing the aesthetic, other-worldly atmosphere of the twelfth-century Franciscan monastery, had completely absorbed her. She had sat down at two, and it was already eight o'clock. No wonder she was as stiff as a board.

Outside, the murmur of voices and the click-clacking of feet on cobblestones meant people were heading to Antonio's. The little bar-cum-restaurant at the bottom of the steeply curving street was a carefully guarded secret of the residents and chosen few who knew of the delightful development of La Virginia.

Nestled in the hills above the old town of Marbella, La Virginia was as far a cry from the bright lights of the sprawling seafront and heaving bars and clubs of Puerto Banus as it was possible to imagine. Built some fifteen years ago, the little development of just one street was designed in the old Spanish style, a carefully constructed hotchpotch sprawl of little pastel houses, each one unique in its own charming way. Beginning at the top of a climbing mountain road, the little street indented sharply, weaving steeply down to where the quaintest houses, smothered with bougainvillaea and wisteria, sat next to each other. Halfway, the narrow street opened out into a tiny square, where a minute white stuccoed church stood as if it had been there for centuries. It was rarely used but Hope thought it would be the most romantic church ever for a wedding. There was room, at most, for about fifteen to twenty people. Past the little square, the houses continued precariously to Antonio's where La Virginia's colourful collection of artists, writers and craftspeople – the 'beautiful misfits', as her dear friend Oscar referred to them – discussed and dissected the goings-on of life as they knew it. Hope had lived there for the past eighteen months and couldn't imagine leaving. La Virginia was not so much a neighbourhood as a way of life, a charming, easygoing community that had become, in its own way, a family for its devoted and fiercely protective inhabitants.

Hope wasn't sure why she liked the atmosphere so much, but she had fallen as completely under its welcoming spell as if she had lived there all her life.

She had stumbled upon it by accident. On her way inland to meet an editor staying at a *finca* high in the mountains, her small rented Jeep had coughed, spluttered and died. She had pulled in off the road and called the car hire company, who assured her help would be on the way. With nothing to do but wait, she had strolled along the road, camera slung over her shoulder, and come upon the unobtrusive gateway that led to what appeared to be a communal car parking area.

Wandering in, she had been intrigued to find the six steps leading down to a steeply dipping cobbled road, and following them carefully, she found herself on the sweetest little street she had ever seen in her life. One of the houses had a To Rent sign outside it. She had scribbled down the number of the estate agent, who had set up a viewing for her.

If Hope hadn't believed in *déjà vu* before she walked into the terracotta-tiled living room of the little house, she became an instant convert. Every nook and cranny of the house seemed to beckon to her, saying look at this, don't you remember? The charming rooms seemed as familiar to her as an old and much-loved friend.

She met the next-door neighbour, a charming gay designer, who held the keys – and showed her round. The little house, called *Casa Esperanza*, literally had her name on it – *Esperanza* being Spanish for 'hope' – and it was love at first sight. Two bedrooms and a bathroom upstairs, a small kitchen and the living room downstairs, and outside, a beautiful old-world terrace, complete with a table and chairs overlooking the Andalucian hills.

Hope strolled out there now, breathing in the fragrant evening air. Leaning on the intricately worked wrought-iron railings, she gazed out at the view that she had come to think of as home. The house, she often mused, had found her and become the refuge she had so desperately needed at just the right time.

Two years ago she had been living in New York. Two years ago she had had a loving, exclusive relationship with Michael, her handsome, intellectual, architect boyfriend – or so she had thought. It was true: ignorance was bliss. And she *had* been blissfully happy. She had spent her days attending the New York Institute of Photography and during her time off she had wandered around discovering and recording the ever-changing the city. Sometimes she walked for miles without realising, her constant companion, the trusty second-hand Leica, slung over her shoulder. Evenings were spent cosily in Michael's loft apartment, where he worked, sometimes late, and she would listen to him explain his drawings. She was fascinated by his incredible vision and creativity. Weekends meant precious long hours in bed, lazily making love, and in the afternoons they scoured the flea markets and antiques stores for hidden treasures, ending up at their favourite Italian restaurant unless they were meeting the hip crowd whom Michael increasingly hung with.

'You've been sleeping with Suky!' Hope had said, numbed with the pain of double betrayal – the fact that Suky was a friend of her sister, Ali, had hit hard. Not that she could cry on Ali's shoulder because Ali wasn't that sort of sister: she was increasingly self-absorbed and had little or no interest in her sister's love life. She had proclaimed Michael to be selfish and narcissistic. Hope had smiled inwardly and bitten back the retort that the pot was calling the kettle black.

Hope hadn't grown up with a great picture of marriage. She'd seen what it had done to her parents and had vowed not to repeat their mistakes. But when she'd met Michael, suddenly romance had seemed full of possibilities. She was captivated by his creative genius, his lazy, confident charm, his classically Waspish good looks, and she fell hard. Michael, she was sure, was The One – and for Hope that meant forever.

Now she never wanted to see him again and she hid her pain behind a carefully cool exterior.

She had moved out of their loft apartment, put her things into storage and taken off for six months to 'do' South America, fulfilling a long-held dream. But she'd hoped to fulfil it with Michael, and it wasn't the same with a broken heart. With a degree in Spanish and Archaeology already under her belt, the language wasn't a problem, and the journal she had kept of the fascinating people and places she had encountered on her travels along with the accompanying photographs had resulted in the publication of a well-received book on Argentina. Inspired by its success, her publishers had encouraged her to deliver more and, taking the chance to explore the deeper nature of a culture she had come to love, Hope had begun her current work: an exposition of the real Spain, a country of post-civil war and post-Franco contrasts.

How ironic it was that the hurt Michael had inflicted had motivated her to create a new life and career for herself. And that was what she had thrown herself into. Men, as far as she was concerned, were off the agenda. It wasn't as if they didn't try: Hope was too much of an artist not to know that she was attractive. She had long, lean limbs, olive skin and dark hair. More than one person had commented on her resemblance to Yasmin Le Bon, but it meant nothing to her. Hope knew that what really mattered was how you felt inside, and despite her enviable exterior, her fragile confidence had taken a hell of a battering.

A tap on the front door reminded her that she had agreed to meet Oscar for a bite to eat.

'Just checking you hadn't forgotten.' He stood on the doorstep, his wide, handsome face belying his sixty-five years.

'Of course not,' Hope lied cheerfully, 'I'm just running a bit late. Let me jump in the shower and I'll see you there in ten, okay?'

'Take your time,' Oscar beamed, 'it's always a pleasure to wait for a beautiful woman. I'll be at my usual table upon which there will be a carafe with your name on it.' He sauntered off.

Hope showered quickly, then pulled on a sheer white cotton shift, heavily embroidered at the neck and hem with a blaze of pink and purple, then slipped her feet into her favourite faded pink espadrilles.

Minutes later she was walking into Antonio's, where Oscar, true to his word, sat at his table with a carafe of chilled rosé and two glasses.

'What a delightful picture you made walking in, my dear.' He stood up to greet her. 'I always think you could pass for a Spaniard until that wonderful Irish smile lights your face!'

'You're such a silver-tongued old fox, Oscar.' Hope sat down opposite him, smiling as she watched him pour the wine.

'Not a lot else left for me to be, dear girl,' Oscar said lightly. He sat back, lit a cigarette and inhaled deeply.

Hope chewed her lip. 'Now, now, Oscar,' she chided, 'you know that's not true.' She took a sip of her wine.

'Of course it's not.' He sighed. 'It's just that, I – miss him, you know.'

'I know you do.' Hope reached out and patted the ageing but immaculately manicured hand. 'We all do, and you're being so brave, really brave. You just have to go on being brave.'

Oscar had lost Bilbo, his beloved partner of thirty years, to cancer just three months previously. He had broken down only once in public, when the curtain had been drawn at the crematorium. Now he wore his loss with the elegant restraint of his artfully knotted pashmina. But his close friends knew that he suppressed his grief and worried about him, as Hope did now.

'Of course I will, dear heart.' He grinned suddenly, ever the performer. 'Now, tell me what you've been up to – I took the liberty of ordering the prawns,' he added as two sizzling plates of prawns drenched in garlic were placed in front of them with a basket of fresh bread.

'Just as well I don't have a hot date later on tonight then,' said Hope, wrinkling her nose as the garlic hit her.

'I assumed as much,' Oscar speared a prawn, 'although you should have.' He wagged an admonitory finger at her.

'My love affair may be over, but yours, dear girl, is out there waiting for you. It's about time you got off the shelf and went out there to meet it.'

'Gimme a break, Oscar, I'm only thirty!'

'That's the whole point – God, no wonder they say youth is wasted on the young. At your age I'd been married, divorced and was about to sow a lot of very wild oats before I met the love of my life. It goes so quickly, you shouldn't waste a minute of it.'

'I'm working, not wasting it.'

Oscar was probably the only person who got away with telling Hope she should be looking for a man, but even he was walking a thin line . . .

'That's another thing, this wretched work ethic thing! What's the matter with you young people? In my day we had fun! Good Lord, we talked to people, interacted – you just text, email and sit in front of computer screens for jollies. And they said we were deviant in the sixties.'

'You know perfectly well I have a book to finish and a deadline to meet, Oscar. After that, well, who knows? Anyway, it's horrible out there until they all go home.' Hope waved a hand to indicate the masses that descended on Marbella in the summer.

'Speaking of home,' Oscar raised an eyebrow, 'aren't you due a visit? It's been what, months now, surely?'

'I know.' Hope sighed. 'I just can't work myself up to it. It's Mum's birthday today, too.'

'You did remember?'

'Of course. I spoke to her earlier, sent a card and a present. I know I should be there, but I just can't be around them at the moment. I can't stand all the pretence, the undercurrents. I just can't stomach it.'

'Ah, me,' Oscar sighed. 'Relationships. Why do we bother, eh?'

'You got me there.'

'Do you think they'll divorce?'

'I don't know,' Hope was thoughtful. 'They probably *should* – they seem to get to the brink often enough, but then they chicken out. Doesn't make for a relaxing home life, that's for sure.' She thought now, with a familiar pang, of her childhood, and how she had felt, even then, that something was wrong. If at all possible, Hope tried not to dwell on the ongoing soap opera that was her family. If she was honest, it got to her a lot more than she let on. Despite countless reassurances to the contrary, Hope knew, with blinding clarity, that her parents would not have married without her imminent arrival. Since the moment she had discovered she had been conceived accidentally – her aunt, Carrie's sister, had made many veiled references to Hope's *premature* birth – she had struggled with the conflicting emotions. Always a rather earnest child, she had had a good relationship with both parents, but that revelation had changed her dramatically, albeit subtly. She withdrew, first into her school work and later to university. In the family, Hope was the reliable one, the pleaser, the high achiever. Results were obtained, seemingly effortlessly – only Hope knew how hard she worked for them. In reality, she felt like an outsider, as if she wasn't really a *genuine* member of the family. Her sisters, unlike her, had arrived in a well-planned and orderly fashion, so she'd felt she had to earn her place in the family. It wasn't enough to be good, Hope had to be better than that.

'The last five Christmases have loomed as an exercise in mounting tension from September onwards,' she continued. 'You know, will-they, won't-they, will-we, won't-we. It's exhausting. Don't get me wrong, they're great people, my parents, just not great together.'

'They must have been great together once. They produced

you, didn't they?' Oscar said fondly. 'Not to mention your gorgeous sisters.' Oscar had met both Ali and Stephanie on separate occasions when they had been visiting Hope.

'Yeah, well, that's debatable,' Hope said darkly. She was thinking of Ali and the way her job, with all its illusions, was so clearly changing her. Even though her parents were wealthy, they, and her Mum in particular, had instilled in their daughters the importance of real values. Ali, with her increasingly unreal life, seemed to be living on another planet these days.

She changed the subject. 'Enough about me, what have you been up to?'

Hope listened attentively as Oscar chatted about the latest gossip in the Old Town where, from his shop, he made and sold the delicate and beautifully handcrafted jewellery that was more in demand than ever. She tried to stop her mind wandering to the birthday dinner in Dublin – almost, but not quite, wishing she was there.

'Hands like spades,' Oscar said, shaking his head. 'Speaking of models, how is the exquisite Ali?'

Hope started and realised she'd drifted again. Oscar was telling her about a model with impossibly large hands the agency had sent him who was *not* what he was looking for to display his latest collection of rings and bangles in a glossy magazine.

'Oh, same as ever. Driving everyone mad, actually. She was trying to fly into Dublin as a surprise for Mum's birthday dinner,' Hope said. 'All going well, they should be tucking in as we speak,' she smiled at him.

'They'll miss you, you know,' Oscar ventured, looking at her astutely.

'Nonsense. Ali and Stephanie make quite a double act. I'd only be keeping the peace, and frankly, I'd rather not. I'll call home tomorrow to see how it all went.'

After a leisurely and typically entertaining supper, Oscar

called for the bill. Hope tried and was thwarted in paying
her way. 'I wouldn't hear of it, dear girl,' he glowered across
the table at her.

'But I *want* to contribute, Oscar.' She was exasperated.

'You already have, Hope.' He patted her hand. 'Dear me,
I dread to think of the young men you must be mixing with,'
he tutted. 'Imagine allowing a beautiful young woman to pay
for dinner! Good God, what's happened to chivalry, never
mind romance?'

Before Hope could reply, her phone bleeped on the table
beside her.

'Don't tell me,' Oscar said dryly, 'a verbally challenged
male suggesting an assignation?'

'No,' said Hope, her eyes widening as she read the text. 'It
would appear, according to Stephanie, that Ali's just got
engaged.'

'That's more like it,' Oscar said approvingly. 'A wedding
in the family. How lovely.' He grinned wickedly. 'Just think
what a beautiful bridesmaid you'll make.'

5

In her mews house, Olwen Slater sat at her computer with her headphones on. Courtesy of Skype, the new software she had downloaded, she was speaking for free to her best friend Claire, currently living in Australia.

''Bye darling girl, love you too.' Reluctantly, Olwen hung up, then went to the kitchen where she poured herself a glass of wine. Wandering back listlessly to the sitting room, she sat down on the sofa, curling her long legs under her. She reached for the remote control and turned on the music system, flooding the room with her favourite Sade track.

What a bloody day, she thought wearily. If she hadn't had Claire to talk to, she'd be an even worse wreck than she was. How on earth did people cope without girlfriends?

It was amazing what the human body was capable of, even when the mind and heart were in complete and utter turmoil. The hectic world of a current affairs television show had no respect for emotion or heartache: no matter what, the show went on. Today had been no different.

She had risen at five thirty a.m. – not a problem these days, as she wasn't sleeping. A half-hearted attempt at some yoga, followed by a light breakfast, and she was in her car and at the studios by seven-thirty on the dot. Over coffee and the newspapers, she chatted to her producer Pete about the show, which was to feature, among other things, a hard-hitting interview with the Minister for Health.

'You're looking tired, Ol,' he had mumbled mid-croissant. 'Hope you're not overdoing it.'

It amused her that her appearance was so important for her job: you had to look good to be on TV, but if you did, men in particular often assumed you must be more interested in flirting than debating.

'Nothing that a good night's sleep won't fix,' she said. 'I'm one of the lucky ones. At least I get to go home in one piece and sleep in my own bed, not stuck on a bloody trolley for thirty odd hours – although, yes, I am tired,' she stifled a yawn.

She loved her work, but sometimes the sheer pace got to her. The last couple of weeks had been relentless – and presenting the show was just the tip of the iceberg. Along with the regular slot, she had stipulated in her contract that every month she would produce a story with her own angle, sometimes political, sometimes more general to highlight issues that affected the state of the country.

For the last two weeks she had been doing the rounds of all the city's major A and E departments, determined to see the deteriorating situation at first hand and talk to patients. Olwen never relied on statistics: she believed in doing her own research, which had led to some interesting perspectives and made her the ace interviewer she was. Politicians and public figures had learned that a razor-sharp intellect lay behind the charm, and woe betide the unprepared interviewee who thought a pleasant chat would be the order of the day. When she was pressing for the answer to an awkward question, Olwen Slater was like a dog with a bone – there was no letting go.

'Ready for the drill?' Pete was referring to the Friday morning production meeting, at which ratings, research and upcoming material were discussed.

'Sure, let's go.'

They sat around the table in his office with two researchers, Pete's production assistant, Verity, and Petra, Olwen's PA, and he began by telling them that the ratings were at an all-time high.

'Terrif,' grinned Hugh, one of the researchers, who rarely uttered a complete word.

'Ugh!' said Olwen. 'Who killed the coffee machine? This tastes like dishwater,' she grimaced as she pushed the offending liquid away.

'I know,' Verity made a face. 'It's a new brand. Housekeeping's strategy – if it ain't broke, change it anyway.'

'Yuck.' Petra wrinkled her pert nose in disapproval.

Just then the door opened and Sam, the director of programming, came in, sporting his uniform of jeans and a stripy shirt, which today was a migraine-inducing purple-and-yellow combination.

'Hey, guys.' He lounged against the wall. 'Great news about the ratings. Just thought I'd pop by to congratulate you and all that.' He leered at Olwen. 'New haircut, if I'm not mistaken. Very nice.'

'Thank you, Sam,' Olwen said, smiling pleasantly, although the way he looked at her made her flesh crawl. She tried not to catch Petra's eye across the table, who was curling her lip derisively.

Sleazy Sam, as every girl in the studios referred to him, had a massive crush on her and went out of his way to bump into her. It was an open joke in the department, and one that was wearing thin with Olwen.

'Ahem.' Pete cleared his throat. 'Next week, as you know, we're focusing on the health crisis. Olwen will be inter-viewing the minister and—'

'Ah,' Sam interjected smoothly. 'Glad you brought that up, Pete. I just wanted to mention, not that it's of any *real* importance, but the minister is a relative of mine. Not close, but you know . . . family and all that.' He fixed Olwen with a smarmy grin. 'Don't give him *too* hard a time Ol, eh? It's not all his fault – very complex situation the government has on its hands, and to be fair, he's done a brilliant job with the mess the last lot left.'

'I'll be perfectly fair with him, Sam.' Olwen's voice was carefully modulated. 'He'll be treated just the same as any other of our interviewees.' *Unlike some of the poor buggers at the mercy of his scandalous cover-ups,* she thought.

'Right. Well, I'll leave you to it, guys. Doing anything interesting for the weekend?' The question was posed generally but was patently intended for Olwen, who ignored it, studying the notes in front of her. 'Well, good job on the ratings. See you Monday.'

Olwen breathed a sigh of relief as he left the room. She found his attentions to her repulsive and intensely disliked his habit of being rude to underlings, particularly the production assistants whom he treated with disdain. She had complained about it more than once. They were indispensable to the team and found Sam overbearing and arrogant.

Back in her office, with the relentlessly organised Petra patrolling outside, Olwen continued her research on the minister and tried to focus. She sure as hell wouldn't tell Sam she was going to put the minister on the spot about his aged mother jumping the queue of three hundred-odd people to have her knees done. She was looking forward to that, even more so now she knew he was a relative of Sleazy Sam.

'Coming for a drink?' Petra popped her head round the door. Olwen looked at her watch. It was past six o'clock.

'No, I think I'll pass, Petra. I'm going to try to catch up on some shut-eye. Have a good weekend. See you Monday.'

'No offence, but you look like you could use it.'

Olwen grinned at Petra's bluntness. It was one of the

things she liked most about her PA. She valued her direct-
ness and was equally direct with her. In TV Land, this saved
many expensive, time-wasting and often futile discussions.
She only wished everyone in the department had Petra's
incisive manner. Both she and Olwen understood each other
and had a great working relationship. Early on in her career,
Olwen had vowed never to become one of those professional front-of-camera women who treated underlings badly.
She treated her staff with respect and empathy and never
demanded more of anyone than she was prepared to give
herself. The upshot was that her department loved her. They
could confide in and trust her. The downside was that they
could tell her she looked wrecked, and she would know it
was the unvarnished truth.

Gathering her bag and briefcase, Olwen slipped out of
the office, grateful not to run into any other cheery souls
heading for a Friday evening drink after work. She drove
home, let herself in and only then felt she could relax. She
took a long, hot soak, pulled on her favourite sweatpants
and comfort fleece, and went downstairs. After a microwave
dinner, she picked up the phone to her closest friend.

Talking to Claire had been a help, of course. She only wished
she wasn't so far away. They had been close friends for
more than twenty years and had survived flat-sharing,
marriages, divorce in Olwen's case, and now this . . . but
these days Claire was living in Australia.

Catching a glimpse of herself in the mirror across the
room, Olwen winced. She looked like shit. Her face was
haggard and she had lost weight. She looked pale, tired and
. . . what? Heartbroken? Was there such a thing as the heartbroken look? If there was, she must have been wearing it
for the last two seasons. Oh, the studio make-up and lighting
made sure she was always at her glamorous, gorgeous best

on screen, but those close to her had noticed the change. Pete had been particularly concerned. 'What is it?' he had asked over coffee one morning. 'Guy trouble?'

She had shaken her head, then turned away, terrified of the tears that constantly threatened.

'Well, if you want to talk about it, I'm here. You know that, don't you?' he had said gently.

Touched by his kindness, she had wanted to tell him everything, but good a friend though he was, she made it a strict rule never to divulge any aspect of her personal life at work. In her experience, it backfired on you big time.

Anyway, what could she say without looking like a complete and utter idiot? That she, Olwen Slater, talented and respected journalist, darling of the media, had fallen for the oldest trick in the book and become involved with a married man? No, not 'involved with', she corrected herself. That didn't begin to describe the passion, the intensity, the tenderness, the need their relationship had awoken in her. And it had all happened so unintentionally.

Of course he had pursued her, there was no denying that. And she had allowed him to. She had found him amusing and engaging, his persistence flattering. She had never thought that she would agree to meet him for lunch, and the moment she had sat down at that table, she had known it was a mistake. Even then, she wondered sometimes, if she had left it at that, could she have escaped? No, was the resoundingly definite answer.

Because it was already too late. Olwen sighed, trying unsuccessfully to make sense of the incredible mess that was her life.

The chemistry between her and Rob had been too powerful, too compelling, too all-consuming. Although she had refused to admit it to herself at the time, she knew from that moment on she had been lost.

How had it happened? How could she have lost herself like that? She, who had always considered herself a woman's woman, how had she become what women everywhere feared and despised? How had she become *the other woman*? How had she wandered so far off course?

For two and a half years she and Rob wrestled with the agony and ecstasy of their affair. What had begun as fun had deepened into feelings of such tenderness, devotion and love, it still took her breath away.

Being single, Olwen had the freedom to negotiate at least some of the pressures that surrounded them, but for Rob the scenario was very different. He claimed his marriage had been unhappy for years, that he and his wife Carrie had little or nothing in common except the children, who were now grown up. Grown up but not gone, Olwen later learned. Along with a lot of other things she hadn't bargained on.

'It's not that I don't respect her, or like her,' he had confided early on. 'She's a warm, lovely person and the mother of my children, but there's nothing between us any more.'

'I really don't think it's fair to discuss Carrie with me, Rob,' Olwen had said, and a moment of awkwardness had ensued. How could she explain that she loved him beyond reason but hated herself for it? How could she say that no matter how often he told her about his unhappiness in his marriage, she was still consumed with guilt and anxiety? There was a part of Olwen, a vociferous part, that told her she wanted to respect his wife, and although she had pretty much silenced it, she balked at hearing Rob criticise the woman he had lived with for so long. She knew he was trying to make her feel better about the situation, but any reference to his marriage struck her like a physical blow.

That's how much she tried to repress the fact that he was

married at all. After all, when he was with her, it was just them, just their little world. The other, the real one, didn't need to intrude at all. Initially, that was.

'Your marriage is none of my business, and I'd prefer to keep it that way.'

'Of course, of course,' Rob had said hurriedly. 'You're right. It's just that . . . well, it's hard to explain.' His eyes had met hers pleadingly.

'You don't have to explain anything to me, Rob. We lead separate, independent lives and what we have together is incredibly special. Let's keep it that way, hmm?'

And they had, as far as they could. Eventually it became impossible – especially as their relationship deepened and they became closer – not to discuss their respective lives and the people in them. After all, it was the only way they could get to know one another properly. A shared social life wasn't an option, so instead they talked about events and happenings so that, over time, Olwen began to feel she knew Rob's family and friends as well as he did. But she never discussed his marriage with him. Until he talked about leaving Carrie. That was when her demons awoke.

Of course she wanted him to leave. She dreamed of it. But that was as far as she got. The reality terrified her, so she avoided the conversation at all costs. If Rob left Carrie, it had to be of his own volition. There would be no encouragement or pleading on her part. This was a decision he had to make on his own. She couldn't bear it if he regretted it later and, God forbid, blamed her. Although, increasingly, she was aware that life without him wasn't an option. Should she fight for him? Was that what he wanted? However she looked at it, Olwen knew that she was powerless, other than to walk away – and that was the one thing she couldn't do. Whenever she parted from Rob she felt as if her soul was being ripped out and shredded.

They didn't often manage to get away together: their schedules were too demanding. But on the rare occasions that they had, parting afterwards had been even more difficult.

The small house they had rented on the cliffs above the Atlantic in south-west Ireland one bitter January would be for ever etched on her memory. There, away from the world, no TV, no distractions, they had spent three blissful nights and days, filled with walks on the beach, crackling log fires and long, lazy love-making.

'Where do you think you're going?' Rob stretched out an arm and playfully tugged at her hair, then pulled her back to bed.

'I thought you were asleep.' She snuggled back into the warmth of his embrace. 'If you don't let me up, we don't eat, and I'm damned if I lugged all that food down here just to throw it away.'

'My God, she can cook too! You're *such* a show-off!' He nuzzled her neck.

'I'd hardly call throwing a couple of steaks on a grill culinary art, but yes, I do like to cook – and I don't know about you, but I'm ravenous.'

'Mmm, me too. I thought I'd made that perfectly clear.' He bit her neck lightly, sending shivers down her spine. 'But hurry, or I'll distract you for sure.'

After that first time away together, there was a subtle yet seismic shift in their relationship that had frightened and elated her. They had driven home in relative silence, hands touching, neither voicing what they both knew: that nothing would ever be the same for either of them again. They could no longer deny that this was more than just a passing affair. They knew how happy and contented they felt in the circle of their love.

Dropping her off at her house, Rob had declined her half-hearted invitation to come in for a while. It was hard enough to leave her as it was. 'I'll call you tomorrow.' He held her close. 'Gotta go.'

Olwen remembered noticing then how he never said he was going 'home'. But wherever it was, it was always she who was left.

There were times, she knew, when he was genuinely at his wit's end. He would come to her, or phone her, sometimes in the early hours of the morning, saying he couldn't stand it any more, that Carrie set his teeth on edge the moment she walked into a room, that he couldn't take the pretence, the charade that was their marriage, and, above all, that he wanted – no, *craved* – to be with Olwen. And she would listen, soothe him until he had calmed down and the situation which had seemed so unendurable had become manageable again.

It was after about a year that she had tried to end it. For Olwen, things had become unbearable. She loved him – he was part of her and she couldn't imagine life without him – but the implications were too ominous. She knew she couldn't live with herself if she was thought the cause, however unfairly, of his marriage break-up. 'But you won't be,' Rob had insisted. 'Carrie and I have had problems for years. All our close friends know that.'

'That may be,' Olwen had replied, 'but every break-up needs a scapegoat, and that scapegoat would be me. And what about you, Rob? Do you really think you could cope with the fallout? Your children taking sides? Not to mention your friends. And what about the hassle of separation – divorce? Think what it would do to your business interests. You'd have at least two years, maybe more, of complete and utter hell. There would be no escaping it, you know that, don't you? It would destroy us, I know it would. Even if you did leave, you'd last about six months and then you'd be running back, feeling guilty, desperately trying to negotiate a truce. And there's no pleasing everybody – certainly not in these situations.' She had looked at him sadly. 'I simply don't think you could cope with it, Rob.'

She had been right, even though he protested to the contrary. If there was one thing Olwen knew, it was human nature, and Rob was one of life's charmers, which was a major part of the problem. He had to be the good guy in everybody's books. Oh, it was all right, he and his male friends thought, to be a naughty boy occasionally. If you got the odd slap on the wrist for bold behaviour it was no more than you deserved. But walking out on a long-standing marriage and a devoted, supportive wife, well, that was different. That wasn't playing the game. And that was when things would get nasty. And Rob Armstrong did not have the strength of character to deal with the tough stuff. And all of this, not to mention *her* career, the publicity – the press would have a field day.

If only, Olwen sometimes wished, Rob and she were 'normal' people, leading humdrum, run-of-the-mill lives away from the constant glare of publicity. Not that the pain involved for everyone concerned would be any less, but at least they could deal with it privately.

So she had ended it – or tried to – at least twice. Each time she and Rob had been gutted.

'Please, Rob,' she had begged him as he looked at her with disbelief, 'you need to sort things out. This is awful. The deceit – it's not fair to anyone, least of all ourselves. I feel like I'm turning into a cliché.'

'But you know what my situation is. I can't just pull out now, not with this takeover at full throttle,' he reasoned. 'You know I want to be with you, darling – I want nothing more. Please, give me a little more time. I love you more than I've ever loved anyone.'

And she had been strong. She had insisted they have a break, but had never estimated the price she would pay.

The pain, the loss, the yearning had been too much. He would call her, text her, plead with her, and despite her best intentions, she would relent, and when they met again, for those first bliss-filled moments, they would wonder how they could ever have entertained the idea of not being with each other, however infrequently or furtively it had to be.

'Please,' he had begged, 'just for two days. Just jump on the plane – the ticket's waiting for you at the desk. Please, Olwen, I need to see you desperately.'

And she had needed him. So she had got on the plane to New York, grateful for the chance to spend time with him away from home and the gnawing reminders of reality.

He had seemed as ridiculously happy as she was, meeting her at the airport with an armful of red roses and a bunch of balloons tied to his sleeve.

'You are one crazy fool,' she had laughed and wept as she clung to him. He had abandoned the roses the minute he saw her, and a small crowd had cheered and whistled as he swung her off her feet, thinking, she supposed, that this was a happy-ever-after, long-awaited reunion.

And it had been. For another two magical days. New York in the autumn. A horse-drawn carriage in Central Park, shopping in Manhattan, cocktails at the Carlisle and a visit to Ground Zero, where they stood and remembered how life could change so irrevocably in a moment.

'I can't live without you,' Rob said suddenly. 'You know that, don't you?' He took her in his arms and held her tightly.

'Don't.' Olwen squeezed her eyes shut. 'Don't even think it.'

'You light up my life,' he whispered.

Then they had left, sober and silent, mindful of those who had been torn apart for ever.

She travelled home alone, awash with happiness but lonely

for him already, longing for a time when they could travel together whenever they liked; do all the normal things that other couples take so much for granted.

Back home, they had grasped every opportunity to be together.

Except this time. Olwen let out a long, shuddering sigh. This time it was finished for good. It had to be. Things had gone too far.

She thought back to the evening when she had heard her doorbell ring. It had been nine o'clock or thereabouts, and Olwen was just out of a lovely, long soak in a hot oil-scented bath. She had padded downstairs in her towelling robe, barefoot, hair scrunched up in a ponytail, and sat at her computer to research a public figure she would soon be interviewing.

When the doorbell sounded, she absentmindedly wandered out to answer it. She wasn't expecting anyone at that hour – Rob was away on business and most of her friends called to check that she was in – but she answered the door.

'Hello.' The expensively dressed woman on her doorstep smiled. 'I'm Carrie Armstrong, Rob's wife.' She paused. 'May I come in, please?'

To say that Olwen froze with shock would not be quite accurate. It was more that time appeared to slow down and stop as, with increasing horror, she understood the implications of the woman's visit.

'Of course,' she said, in a voice that sounded strangely calm, and then, inanely, 'I'm sorry.' She gestured at her state of undress. 'I wasn't expecting anyone at this hour . . .'

'Don't apologise,' Carrie said evenly. 'I realise this must come as a, well, an unexpected visit, but I thought it best not to contact you in advance, for both our sakes.'

Olwen desperately summoned all the journalistic training that kept her cool, calm and collected in every circumstance. Now, in her hour of need, it deserted her.

'Yes, of course, come in,' she said lamely, as if entertaining her lover's wife was an everyday occurrence.

Carrie followed her into the sitting room. 'Please,' Olwen waved to the sofa, 'sit down. Can I – er, can I offer you anything? A drink perhaps?'

'No.' Carrie was polite, but her voice was shaky. 'Thank you. I'll say what I have to and then I'll be on my way.'

Sitting across from her, Olwen cursed her stupidity in answering the door. Never had she felt so vulnerable, so open to attack, so – she looked down at her bare feet – so inappropriately dressed, and not a screed of make-up on her face, from which she could feel the blood draining completely.

Carrie, on the other hand, was the picture of cool, collected calm. The only giveaway was the slight edge to her voice. Olwen was acutely aware from her many interviews, how much of a giveaway a voice could be. Only her voice, and the way she kept her immaculately manicured hands clasped tightly in her lap, betrayed that Carrie wasn't completely in control.

Despite the incongruity of the situation, Olwen found herself taking inventory of the woman sitting across the room from her as she would anyone else she was talking to. Carrie Armstrong was not beautiful, but she took care of herself and had the money to do so. Her features (or was it her expression?) had a severity that was not softened by her hairstyle – the chestnut hair with copper lights was pulled back from her face in a tortoiseshell clasp. Her skin was well-maintained and spoke of regular facials. She was thin, through dieting rather than fitness, and there was an overall tautness in her demeanour that belied the smile she forced now. The black linen trouser suit she wore was an expensive designer number, but it did not flatter her colouring.

'I know,' Carrie began, 'that you've been having an affair with my husband for some time.' She looked Olwen directly in the eye as she spoke and Olwen felt a ripple of admiration for her. 'And,' she paused, 'whatever he may have told you, Rob and I have a good, enduring marriage.'

Silence.

'Oh I know,' she smiled wryly, 'we've had our ups and downs, as happens in most marriages. You were married once yourself, if I'm not mistaken?'

Did she imagine it, or was there a put-down in that comment? The implication that Olwen, unlike Carrie, had not managed to maintain her marriage.

'Yes,' Olwen replied, 'for a short time. I left – it was a bad situation.'

'Quite,' Carrie continued. 'Then you'll understand when I say that all marriages are an exercise in constant negotiation.'

'We – I – we don't discuss your, er, marriage.' Olwen cursed herself for sounding so pathetic.

'That's kind of you.' Carrie waved a hand. 'As I say, Rob and I have had our ups and downs, like everyone else. He has, how shall I put it, an inability to commit for any length of time, but like many insecure men, in the end, he needs the security of belonging, to be part of something stable . . . his family.'

This time the implication was clear.

Carrie continued, 'There's no other way to say this, Olwen – may I call you Olwen?' she asked, politely.

'Of course,' said Olwen weakly, feeling her face flame.

'You're not Rob's first affair, and I doubt very much that you'll be his last. I say that not to be cruel but because I believe it to be true. However well you may feel you know Rob Armstrong, believe me, I know him better.'

Olwen studied the floor intently.

'I have not come here to hurl insults at you, to threaten you or to scream abuse.'

Olwen wished the floor would open and swallow her.

'Why have you come, then?' Her voice, thank God, seemed to have regained its clarity.

'I asked myself the same question many times on my way here,' Carrie said. 'Believe me, it gives me no pleasure.' She looked away before returning her gaze to Olwen. 'I suppose . . . to let you know that I know. I've known about all Rob's . . . *flirtations*. Nothing will come of it.'

Olwen flinched.

'You see, Rob *needs* us, his family. Without us, he'd go to pieces.' She drew breath. 'It would be . . . difficult, to say the least, and he isn't good with difficult situations. He likes things to be easy, uncomplicated, manageable.'

'I love him.' The words escaped Olwen softly.

Carrie smiled sympathetically. 'Of course you do. Rob's a very lovable character, when he wants to be.' The first hint of bitterness had entered Carrie's voice. 'But love's not enough. God knows, I've discovered that much over the years. It would end in tears for both of you – and what would it all have been for? The damage, the hurt?'

There was an awkward silence.

'I don't know what to say,' Olwen managed eventually.

'Think about it. Think about what you're doing *to us* – and *to yourself*. Let him come back to his home and family.' Olwen noted she had omitted to say 'to his wife'. 'He needs us, we need him. We belong together. That's why we've lasted for twenty-nine years now.' She looked at Olwen. 'You're still young, single, you have a life ahead of you. Find someone free to share it with you.' She paused. 'At least think about what I've said, will you?'

'Of course.'

'Good.' Carrie stood up. 'I won't disturb you any longer.'
She made for the door, with Olwen following lamely in her
wake.

'No need to see me out.' She offered a hand to Olwen,
who took it numbly.

'Look, I know this is awkward, painful even, for you, for
us both – but what can I say? You seem like a decent person.'
Her eyes flicked over Olwen. 'I'm sure if we'd met under
different circumstances we'd have liked each other. You do
understand, I hope?'

'Yes.' Olwen stood at the door for the second time that
evening in her robe.

'Goodbye, then.' Carrie smiled. 'I *would* appreciate it
if you could keep this meeting between ourselves. Women
understand these things so much better than men, don't
you think? The children, thankfully, are unaware of this
latest, er, situation. That hasn't always been the case,
which has been distressing for them. Although they're
older now, they, well, they *worry* about their father and
me.'

With that, she disappeared into the night as Olwen closed
and double-locked the door, still feeling as if she was in a
dream, or, more appropriately, a nightmare.

There it was! The gauntlet had been thrown down. *The
children. Their father. Our family.*

It was only then that she began to shake. Despite the
warmth of the house, she felt chilled to the bone.

Unknown to Olwen, outside her house, Carrie had only
just made it back to her car. Her hands were shaking so
much she was barely able to put the key into the igni-
tion. She gripped the wheel until her knuckles turned
white.

She never knew how she drove home, but she did, her

breath coming in gasps, tears streaming down her face. Thankfully the traffic was light and she had only to contend with one red light, where she rummaged for a tissue and blew her nose, hoping that no one she knew would catch a glimpse of her in this state.

Why had she done it? Why had she been so stupid, so pathetic? What, in the name of God, had made her think that confronting the woman would make her feel better? It had made her feel a thousand times worse. It had been madness.

She understood now. Of course Rob was in love with Olwen Slater – how could he not be? She was drop-dead gorgeous. Carrie had seen her on TV and in the news-papers, but in the flesh she was a million times lovelier. Sitting in her house in her towelling robe with no make-up, she had been stunning, golden skin gleaming and line-free, blonde hair shiny and healthy, tied up in a youthful ponytail. No wonder Rob couldn't help himself – what man could? And the worst of it was that Carrie had known immediately, instinctively, that Olwen was a nice person. She hadn't been cold or bitchy. She had allowed Carrie into her house, which she had been under no obligation to do. She had been polite, had had the grace to look as mortified and horrified as Carrie had felt.

Also, she was clearly in love with Rob. Carrie winced. A woman, particularly a wife, could tell. Olwen wasn't after money or a good time – she didn't need Rob for either – she was simply in love with Carrie's husband. She was clearly miserable and uncomfortable with the arrangement too. But none of this made Carrie feel any better. On the contrary, she felt utterly defeated. She could never compete with Olwen. Carrie wasn't going to delude herself on that particular point.

Shaken and distraught after Carrie's departure, Olwen had

poured herself a glass of wine, still hardly able to take in what had just happened. She had picked up the phone and dialled Rob's number, which went straight to voicemail. She left a message, telling him she was ending it, that it was for the best, although she would always love him, that he would always be in her heart. She asked him, please, not to contact her.

She had done what Carrie had asked of her, if not in so many words, and what she knew was the only honourable thing to do. In a way, she had been lucky, she reflected. Somewhere at the back of her mind she had known that this day would come. They couldn't have escaped it for ever, and at least this way it had been discreet, civilised, not exaggerated in a blaze of headlines or sullied by vindictive, malicious gossip.

But, oh, *the pain.*

It was relentless. It gnawed at her day and night. She had never known anything like it. And it was clever: like a virus, it would mutate to suit a particular situation or environment. During the day, at work, to which she abandoned herself even more than usual, it was a dull ache, which meant she could interact with some degree of normality, although the effort it took was enormous.

But when she was alone, at home, during the evenings or at weekends, there was no escape from the hollow, mocking emptiness.

The nights were the worst. She would lie awake, tossing and turning until dawn, when she had to get up.

After two months of this, she had gone to her doctor, who had listened sympathetically and prescribed anti-depressants.

'Come on, Olwen,' he had said kindly in the face of her protest. 'You're no more invincible than the rest of us. Sometimes we all need a bit of help. These will take the edge off, make it easier to function.'

It was then that she had broken down.

'There, there, take your time,' he said. 'Have a good old cry. It's a nasty old business, this thing called love.'

She had taken the tablets for three months, then weaned herself off them. They didn't solve the problem, just made it fuzzier. She didn't want to be on medication long-term, and realised that, as yet, there was no cure for a broken heart. And that was what she was suffering from. She didn't need any doctor to tell her that.

She missed Rob. Not the excitement of the affair. Not the sex – although it had been magical. She missed watching him sleep, missed taking his hand in hers and pressing it to her face, kissing his fingers one by one. Above all she missed hearing his voice. She glanced, now, at her mobile phone, lying beside her. She had been so strong in not returning any of his texts or messages, although he had pleaded with her to reconsider. Eventually he had left her alone. How alone he would never in a million years begin to know.

She wondered what he was doing now, right this minute. Was he hurting too? Or had it come as a relief, to stop the deception? She knew he must love Carrie however much he protested to the contrary, or the marriage wouldn't have lasted so long. But he loved Olwen too, she knew he did.

It was more than the hundreds of times he had told her in text messages, emails, phone calls. The real love she knew he felt for her was unspoken, as hers was for him. The kind of silences and omissions that need never be voiced, in a look, a touch, a smile – those precious exchanges.

That was what got her through the really gut wrenching times, the times she felt so alone, so isolated in her grief. After all, who was to know what she was going through? It had all been secretive, furtive, clandestine, and so, it followed, would her pain.

Olwen pulled her fleecy round her tightly. It was getting

late. She would go to bed. Standing up from the sofa she jumped as her phone bleeped. She was almost afraid to pick it up.

It was a text from Rob. 'Nothing has changed,' it read. 'I love and miss you more than ever if that's possible and am going through hell. Hope you're okay. X'

Olwen sat down again, reading and rereading it, tears of relief coursing down her face, and felt, for the first time in months, as if someone had switched the light back on in her life.

6

'What the *hell* is that?' Rob stared at the large dog that was sprawled on the kitchen floor. Stephanie rushed to Toby's defence. 'I meant to say something on the way home,' she fixed her blue eyes on her father, 'but what with the surprise announcement and everything . . .' She trailed off, seeing Rob's face. 'Anyway, this is Toby,' she said defiantly. 'He's a greyhound-cross lurcher and he's Mum's birthday present. She's really thrilled with him.' She knew she was winging it heavily on this one. 'Please Dad, he's rescued and he'll be a wonderful pet. Just give him a chance. Anyway,' she continued, 'Mum's spending far too much time on her own these days. A dog to walk will get her out of the house and it's a well-known fact that it's a great way of meeting people.' She sat beside Toby who, satiated with the warmth of the Aga and the ongoing TV soaps, gazed at her adoringly, ignoring Rob completely.

'Is that a fact?' Rob had picked up the accusation underpinning her words. 'Well, present or no present, he's not staying. You want a dog, Steph, you keep it at your place. There's no way I'm living with that creature.' He regarded Toby with intense dislike.

Before Stephanie could retort, the front door opened and a cacophony of excited voices heralded the arrival of Carrie, Ali and Stuart.

★   ★   ★

'In here, everyone,' Stephanie called loudly as Rob pulled the cork from yet another bottle of champagne.

'Good idea,' said Carrie, coming in and putting down her handbag. 'Let's get the glasses.' She jumped as Toby nudged her playfully. 'Oops! Hello Toby.' She stroked his head and bent down to have a better look at him. 'You really are a very handsome chap, aren't you?' She fondled his silky ears. 'I think he's a great idea, Steph, now that I've got over the surprise.' Stephanie beamed as Toby arched his long neck, looking very aristocratic as he enjoyed the caresses.

'Well, I don't,' said Rob, pouring the champagne. 'He's not staying, and that's that.'

'Who's not staying?' Ali breezed into the kitchen, followed by Stuart.

'This creature.' Rob jerked a thumb at Toby. 'He's not staying.'

'Oh, and you are?' The acerbic retort was out before Carrie could stop herself. Leaning against the counter, she looked him squarely in the eye, daring him to contradict her.

She felt rather than saw him flinch, and was pleased. Fuck him anyway! Who the hell did he think he was to upset her life for twenty-odd years, then think he could call the shots? Well he could whistle, Carrie thought, suddenly feeling powerful. It was *her* birthday, *her* family around her, and it was *her* house, just as much as Rob's, so she had a right to say what would or would not go on in it.

'Toby is a very thoughtful and considerate birthday present given to me by Stephanie,' she began. 'I'll admit, he was a bit of a surprise, but you're right, Steph. I *have* been spending too much time on my own, and the house *is* awfully empty without you all.' Rob was chewing his lip and studying the floor. 'I think it's only right to give Toby a chance. We'll see how he settles in and take it from there.' Carrie smiled at the bemused faces around her, feeling a lot more uncertain than she sounded.

'Greyhounds are considered cool these days.' Ali's voice cut across the tension. 'They're the ultimate fashion accessory, if you're going to have a dog.' She smiled in Toby's direction. 'And I must say, his colouring is gorgeous.' His black coat, blonde legs, cute blonde eyebrows and two-tone face were stunning.

'He's much more beautiful than a greyhound,' Stephanie protested. 'And you're not a fashion accessory, are you, darling?' She stroked Toby's glossy coat, thinking for once in her life Ali was making sense.

'Well, he looks like a greyhound to me,' Ali said. 'Anyway, let's go into the den and have our champers in there. Then Stuart and I really must go.'

'The library it is.' Rob insisted on referring to the room where they always congregated as the library. It contained an antique desk and wall-to-wall shelving of old, leather-bound books, none of which he had ever read, that over the years he had bought in bulk when a dealer had tipped him off to a good house-contents auction. Intended as his study, the room was decorated as such, lined with dark green brushed silk. Two comfortable sofas, covered with white calico, and leather wing armchairs completed the elegant ambience. Of course, Rob had never worked there as he had intended and over the years the family had claimed it as a TV den and general gathering place, although Rob still called it the library.

Rob headed there now, grateful to escape the creature in the kitchen who was gaining admirers by the minute. And Carrie, who had seemed to be in a conciliatory mood earlier, now appeared to be spoiling for a fight. Typical, now that she had a captive audience. Rob placed the bottle on the drinks cabinet and, taking his glass, sat down wearily in an armchair. He was feeling it now, the deep-seated tiredness from the back-breaking effort of constantly playing a part. Absentmindedly he reached for his phone, hoping against hope that Olwen had replied to his message. Before he could check though, Carrie and the kids had trooped in, followed by the dog, who had assumed a certain air of ownership. 'Not in here,' Rob frowned at the sight of Toby. 'I won't have that creature in here, he can stay in the kitchen.'

'He's been in the kitchen all the time we were out,' said Stephanie. 'Anyway, he needs to get used to the house.'

Not if I have anything to do with it, Rob thought. Keep calm, he said to himself. It's been a long day and we've had a lot to drink. With a bit of luck everything will be back to normal in the morning.

Toby stood in the middle of the room, looked around, sniffed the air, then wandered over to Carrie, who was sitting on one of the sofas. He folded himself at her feet and rested his head on her knee. 'Oh, give it a rest, Rob,' she said, stroking Toby's head. 'It's his first day in a strange place and so far, he's been no trouble at all.'

Rob sat back, folded his arms and tilted his head to one side. 'Since when have you encouraged pets in the house? As I recall, Hope's hamster brought you out in a rash.'

'Perhaps,' Carrie said with a dangerous edge to her voice, 'since I'm enjoying some unexpected affection for a change.'

As Rob threw his eyes up to heaven, Ali cut in smoothly, 'Mum, Dad, about the wedding.'

'Yes, darling?' Carrie asked.

'Well, the most important thing, of course, is the location.'

'Surely you'll be having it here, at home,' Rob said. 'We'll put up a marquee.'

'That's sweet of you, Dad,' Ali went on quickly, 'but think of the invasion of your privacy. After all, I'm quite a celebrity now, by any standards, and you'd have paparazzi crawling all over the place. It was my first thought, too, to get married from home, but it would be too accessible. We'd be asking for trouble.'

'So where were you thinking of?' Carrie enquired. 'Not a hotel, I hope?'

Ali smiled, enjoying the expectant, captive audience. 'Good Lord, no.' She laughed prettily at the idea. 'We thought and thought, and suddenly I came up with the perfect place – private, secluded and wonderfully romantic.' She looked at Stuart, who returned her gaze adoringly.

'Where?' at least three voices asked in unison.

'The *Excalibur*!'

'What – the yacht?' Stephanie looked surprised.

'No, Steph, the spaceship,' Ali said a little tartly. 'It's the perfect, perfect location.' She clasped her hands theatrically. 'We'll have the church ceremony in the Orange Square in Marbella, and the reception afterwards on *Excalibur*.'

'Out of the question,' Rob spoke firmly. 'For starters, it would cost a bloody fortune.' He looked at Carrie for support, but her face bore a wistful expression.

'It's not as if you can't afford it, Daddy,' Ali told him coldly. 'Anyhow, if necessary, I can pay for the whole thing myself.'

'That's not the issue,' Rob snapped. 'Of course money's no object, darling, but it would be too much of a spectacle. It would draw too much attention to us as a family – and think of the security implications. What's wrong with a simple, elegant, reasonably quiet wedding here in Ireland? Anywhere you like.'

'Daddy, this isn't Posh and Becks's wedding, it's mine, and you seem to forget I have a profile to maintain. I have it on authority that I'm in line for a major cosmetics house contract, and this wedding is the perfect opportunity to create the suitable backdrop for my image. The *Excalibur* is the only venue that fits the bill. And since Frank Farrelly is your friend and business partner, he probably won't charge you for it at all, or he'll certainly give you huge discount.'

'She has a point Rob,' Carrie said, thinking of the romantic wedding she had been denied. 'It would be incredibly romantic, and the Orange Square in Marbella is so quaint, and we've spent so many happy holidays there. I'll talk to Jay about it tomorrow and we can see what she says.'

'I think it's a great idea,' Stephanie put in, 'and we'll get to see loads of Hope for once.'

'Yes,' Ali smiled, 'of course. That's partly why I wanted to get married in Marbella. She might even show up for it.'

'Oh, Ali,' Carrie was dismayed, 'that's not fair.'

'Of course it is, Mum. In fact, if Hope wasn't so stubborn, I'd ask her to do the photographs for me. After all, she is a professional, or so she keeps telling us. You've seen her stuff and some of the portraits she keeps hidden are brilliant. If she was focused enough, excuse the pun, she could be the next Annie Leibovitz, instead of doing all that boring landscape stuff.'

'Hope's a photo-journalist, Ali, not a fashion photographer, for God's sake,' Stephanie said crossly.

'But she could be, that's just my point. I offered to introduce her to all the right people – I could have set her up. She'd be making a fortune and having a life. But would she listen?'

'Let's not get sidetracked,' said Rob, thinking suddenly of all the incredibly beautiful girls Ali would be inviting, captive on a yacht. Perhaps it wasn't such a bad idea after all.

'What about you, Stuart?' he asked the groom in waiting. 'Did you have any say in this?'

'Whatever Ali wants is what I want,' he replied without missing a beat.

Rob felt himself rapidly going off Stuart.

'Well, that's that, then,' Carrie said brightly, her mood clearly improving. '*Excalibur* it is. I'll get straight on to Jay tomorrow, and once we have an idea of numbers, we can go from there. Rob, you can talk to Frank.'

'I knew you'd see it was the only possible place,' Ali beamed. 'Thank you, Daddy.' She got up and crossed the room to hug Rob. 'You'll see – it'll be fabulous.'

'With you as the star of the show, how could it be anything less?' Rob smiled indulgently at his beautiful daughter. Well, it looked like he was outnumbered on this one, but what the hell? It would be one heck of a wedding.

'Now, we really must go.' Ali glanced at Stuart, who immediately got up. 'Bye, Mum and Dad. See you tomorrow, guys. Oh, Steph, if you have a minute, could I pop upstairs with you? I need to find that top I lent you last time I was home.' She winked at her sister. 'I'll see you in the car in a mo, Stuart.'

'What's up?' Stephanie panted as she followed Ali upstairs and into her old bedroom.

'What's up?' Ali looked incredulously at her. 'Are you kidding? You could have cut the tension with a knife this evening.' She began to pace the floor.

'Oh, that.' Stephanie looked nonplussed. 'I thought they behaved quite well. At least they managed to sit at the same table without rowing. Why the sudden concern?' Stephanie was wary.

'Oh, come off it, Steph, you know perfectly well what I'm on about – and it's not going to upset my wedding, that's for sure.'

'No, I don't – really.'

'It's Dad and whatever other woman he's seeing.'

'I don't know what you're talking about, Ali.' Stephanie seemed truly bewildered.

'Well it's about time you did. Dad's having an affair.'

'An affair? What do you mean?'

'Stephanie, are you stupid or what? An affair. He's seeing someone else – having a relationship with another woman, you know?' Ali spoke as if her sister was a particularly obtuse three-year-old. Surely even Stephanie was up to speed with adultery. It was part and parcel of life, displayed in all its glorious abandon on every soap going.

'How do you know?'

'I've seen the disgusting phone messages.'

'What phone messages?' Stephanie was beginning to sound like a broken record.

'Dad's always leaving his phone lying around,' Ali said witheringly. 'I had my suspicions about him last time I was home, so I decided to flick through a few of his messages, and bingo, there it all was. Pathetic.' She raised her eyes to heaven. 'Declarations of undying love to and from both of them, whoever *she* is.'

'That's appalling.' Stephanie had paled.

'Exactly.' Ali's eyes were blazing.

'No, Ali,' Stephanie said slowly. 'What's appalling is that you went into Dad's phone messages. How could you?'

'Oh, for God's sake,' Ali said pityingly. 'Somebody in this family has to keep tabs on what's going on. Are you in denial or what?'

'Mum and Dad have been married for ever. Whatever's going on, or not going on, and you can't know for sure, Ali, it's absolutely none of your business.'

'Typical,' snorted Ali. 'You just can't face the truth. Well, they needn't think they're going to wreck my wedding. Whatever's going on, they can just bloody behave for another four months. It won't kill them. I simply *cannot* have any whiff of scandal surfacing about my family. It could totally jeopardise my chances of getting this contract. Stay Tru Cosmetics may be one of the hippest brands in the States, but its president comes from serious Bible Belt country and he won't consider even the merest suggestion of anything unsavoury,' she paused theatrically. 'They're totally into family values and everything has to be whiter than white. The reason I'm in with such a good chance is they think I'm a modern day Grace Kelly with a family to match. Divorce or adultery just isn't an option. Not until I've signed on the dotted line, anyway.'

'Who said anything about divorce?' A note of panic had crept into Stephanie's voice. 'It's not as if they're splitting up – are they?'

'You're too damn right,' Ali shot back. 'Not if I have anything to do with it. They've had the last God knows how long to sort out their marriage, and neither of them has done a single thing to confront the issue. Whatever's going on, it isn't going to spoil my wedding day.' She drew a deep breath. 'Besides, Stuart's parents would be horrified. They're very straight, dignified people.'

'Does Hope know about this?' Suddenly Stephanie wished her eldest sister was there now. Hope always knew what to do, and Ali's dramatics were frightening her.

'Oh, don't be ridiculous. Hope doesn't give a damn. It's all her fault anyway – if it wasn't for her, Mum and Dad wouldn't have got married in the first place.'

'Ali, for God's sake, stop it!' Stephanie looked at her incredulously. 'That's an awful thing to say! Really, really awful.'

'Yeah, well, you know what they say about the truth – it hurts. You might as well get used to it.'

Stephanie looked as if she was about to cry.

Ali relented slightly. 'I'm sorry, Steph, I didn't mean to

upset *you*. It's just all this tension gets to me – and the wedding's going to be so stressful.'

'No, it won't,' Stephanie said, more confidently than she felt. 'It'll be fine, everything will be just fine.'

'I hope you're right, really I do. In the meantime, keep an eye on them and let me know if anything looks like it's going to blow.'

'Okay,' said Stephanie miserably. 'Now we'd better go downstairs, or they'll think something's up.'

'You go ahead. I'll follow you in a few moments.'

After Stephanie had gone downstairs, Ali lit a cigarette, inhaling deeply. This was proving harder than she'd thought. Her career was precarious enough at the best of times, but now it was make-or-break time, and the competition was tougher than tough. Ali wasn't stupid. She'd heard the rumours, felt the knowing glances of younger girls coming up. *She's so over. Ali was great, but she's, like, really yesterday.* Everything was riding on this contract. Every model had her day. They all knew it. And the best way to leave the business was to win a prestigious cosmetics contract for a couple of years, then retire to marriage and baby-making before you reinvented yourself, if you were so inclined.

Ali was prepared to bow out. She couldn't complain, the industry had treated her well, but she was going to do it on *her* terms. She would bow out in style. And she was damned if her family were going to blow it for her – she'd sooner kill them.

'Well, that was quite a turn-up for the books, wasn't it?' Rob said to Carrie after they had seen everyone off except Stephanie, who had elected to stay the night in her old room.

'Yes.' Carrie stood at the door of the oak-panelled library. 'It certainly was.'

'Fancy a nightcap to round off the celebrations?' He eyed the near-empty champagne bottle.

'No thanks.' Carrie ran a hand through her hair and yawned. 'I'm going to bed.' Then added, 'Rob?'

'What?' Rob said warily.

'I want this wedding to be perfect for Ali. Do you understand what I'm saying? Absolutely perfect.'

'Of course. So do I. Why wouldn't it be?'

'Oh, please,' Carrie threw him a withering glance, 'it doesn't change anything, you know. I'll still be speaking to my solicitor about what I said this morning. But, well, there's no point in doing anything until after the wedding, is there?' A note of uncertainty had crept into her voice.

'No,' Rob agreed heartily. 'I certainly wouldn't have thought that would achieve anything constructive.'

'I suppose another few months won't kill us.'

'No, no, of course not. Carrie, I—'

'I meant what I said, Rob, but I'm emphatic, as I expect you to be, that between now and then, nothing, and I mean *nothing*, is to spoil Ali's big day.' The unspoken implication hung in the air. 'Do I have your word on that?'

'I've already said as much,' Rob scowled.

'Fine. Just so long as we understand one another. Thanks for dinner,' she added, 'I'm going to bed.'

When Carrie had gone, Rob drained the last of the champagne into his glass. It wasn't as if he wanted it, but he needed a few minutes to let things settle in his head. What a day! First Carrie asking for a divorce, then Ali springing this wedding business on him. Of course he was happy about Ali's news. Stuart was solid and clearly adored her – and why wouldn't he? Rob reflected wryly. He knew his parents vaguely too, decent sorts, if a bit on the dull side. And Stuart had good prospects too – Frank Farrelly spoke of him in glowing terms. He'd call Frank tomorrow and make enquiries about *Excalibur*. He couldn't help feeling excited at the prospect, despite his protests. *Excalibur* would indeed be a fabulous setting for the reception, and – he brightened considerably at the thought – if Carrie had a wedding to organise in Marbella, she'd be spending a lot of time there between now and then.

God, what he wouldn't give for some peace. Everyone seemed to be on his case these days. Carrie and her divorce, and Ali was going to be a nightmare if everything about this wedding wasn't just so. Looking around the sumptuous room, Rob found himself longing for the cool, uncluttered calm of Olwen's home. There he could really relax, be himself. It was his refuge from the prison that had become his life. Here, well, he was just paying the bills, and he got little or no thanks for that. Standing up wearily, he pulled his phone out of his pocket and listlessly checked his messages. There it was, the number he'd been longing to see. Olwen had replied. Quickly he clicked on the message icon, hardly daring to read the contents. 'It's been hell for me too, I love and miss you as ever x'

Feeling a great sadness lift from the pit of his stomach, Rob offered up a silent prayer of thanks to a deity who had finally seen fit to throw a drowning man a lifeline. He had not lost her. Tomorrow he would ring her. They would work something out. They always did. Life without her was unthinkable.

Heading upstairs to his room, Rob climbed into bed and the minute his head hit the pillow, slept the sleep if not of the just then of the mightily relieved.

Further along the corridor Stephanie tossed and turned, sleep evading her. Ali's outburst was doing escalating rounds in her head. Dad having an affair? Maybe Ali had got it wrong. Everyone knew how unreliable text messages were. You could read the wrong thing into something totally innocent, and Ali was a drama queen at the best of times – Hope was always saying so. Thinking of Hope, Stephanie checked her phone for a message, but there was nothing. She had texted her earlier about the surprise engagement, but maybe she hadn't got it yet. Mind you, she hadn't known then that the wedding venue they were thinking of was Marbella. Wait 'til Hope heard that! Stephanie sent her another text to update her.

It all seemed unreal. Not that Stephanie had been unaware of her parents' problems over the years, but somehow things had always returned to an even keel. Now, though . . . and then there was Ali's wedding. It was strange, Stephanie thought, that although they had all left home and were all grown up, it still mattered so much. It felt, well, *weird*. Poor Mum. She must have been going through a horrible time. No wonder she seemed so sad these days, and that she hadn't been thrilled with Toby. Poor dog. Stephanie's last thought was of him before sleep finally overtook her. He wasn't even one night with his new family and already it looked like he'd be the victim of a broken home.

Downstairs, on his bed beside the Aga, Toby stretched sleepily, blissfully unaware of the precarious nature of his new surroundings.

It was strange, this new place, and he missed the other dogs he had left behind in the rescue centre. But he was warm and comfortable, and he liked the female who had brought him here very much. The older one was nice too, although he could sense she was stressed. He wasn't sure about the alpha-male though. Canine intuition told him that an undercurrent of unhappiness ran through the house. Toby sighed. He could only do what generations of his kind had done and would go on doing. He would give his unqualified and unconditional love to whoever required it. Drifting off to sleep, front paws twitching, he dreamed happily of chasing something small and furry into the distant horizon.

7

Jay paced the drawing-room floor and glanced yet again at her mobile phone. Nothing. Fuck Frank anyway. He was supposed to be here tonight. That was the deal. Tonight they were expected at exactly eight o'clock at the National Museum of Fine Arts annual dinner. It was now four and she hadn't so much as heard from him in three days. Nothing unusual in that, but even by his standards he was cutting it fine. He had been entertaining clients on the yacht, and Jay knew *exactly* what that entailed, she thought grimly as she brushed aside the disturbing images that floated as near to the surface of her consciousness as she would allow them. If he even *dared* to let her down in public . . . She sat down abruptly at the horrifying thought, then pulled herself together. No, he wouldn't. Not tonight. Frank cared very much what people thought of him, despite his protestations to the contrary, and Jay had honed the art of playing on this useful aspect of his character to a fine art.

From her vantage-point on the large, silk-covered sofa, Jay gazed distractedly about her. Beneath the vast Adam mantelpiece, a gas fire blazed at full power, its orange and blue flames flickering with a vigour that matched the myriad thoughts whirling in her mind.

An onlooker would have observed a small, meticulously groomed woman sitting in a room that screamed of money. The polished parquet floor gleamed beneath a carpet worth several years' salary to an average couple. The warmly painted walls were hung with magnificent mirrors that reflected the paintings and sculpture that had been arranged elegantly in groups by the adviser Frank had hired to acquire the collection. Crystal bowls and silver candelabra stood in military precision on occasional tables strategically placed under windows swamped with opulent drapes. As Jay chewed a thumb-nail absentmindedly, her eyes rested on the one object that, in her opinion, ruined an otherwise perfect room. The portrait, displayed in pride of place in the centre of the wall, directly opposite the door, of Frank's late mother. It never ceased to arouse Jay's intense irritation, but it was the one thing about which Frank had put his foot down. Looking at it now, Jay's mouth curled in a derisive twist. As if the ould bat had ever looked like that! Frank had had the portrait commissioned from an old photograph, when he had made his first million and she had been dead for ten years. Jay snorted. To look at it you'd think the woman had been a feckin' duchess! The shabby clothes and hatchet face had been replaced with an elegant lace blouse and soft features. And the wistful serene expression hinted at a decorum that was as far beyond her as the dictionary she would have had to look up to spell the word.

Shit! The resounding crunch meant she had unwittingly chewed through one of her immaculately constructed gel nails. In a moment of rare clarity, she wondered what in the world she had come to if she was chewing through her false nails with her false teeth? Not that veneers were *false*, exactly, but as far as Jay was concerned, no body part was safe from constant alteration. She was very firmly of the Sharon Osbourne school of thought when it came to self-improvement. *If you can't see it on the outside, what the hell point was there working on the inside?* Anyway, it was hard enough being small in stature, and Jay liked to add length wherever possible. Longer nails and bigger, better teeth were simply part of the package. She viewed her mangled nail now with disgust. Damn! No chance of a patch-up before tonight. She would just have to do the best she could to make it inconspicuous. She got up wearily and paused to pick up a photo of her youngest son, Gerry. At twenty, he was away with his pals on his gap year, somewhere unpronounceable in the Far East, last she heard.

'Hiya, Mum, how's it going?' The line had been bad and he had sounded very far away.

'Gerry, how are you, sweetheart? Where are you?'

There had been a torrent of information and then the line had gone dead.

It was quiet without the elder three boys at home. Although their constant rambunctious behaviour had driven her mad over the years, she missed them. There was the Sunday lunch ritual, which included various transient girl-friends and other pals, but these days someone was always missing. Frank Junior was living in New York, pursuing his real estate dream. Terry was in Miami, studying marine biology and Mikey was playing soccer morning, noon and night.

That was life, Jay reminded herself sternly. No point getting maudlin. Crikey, if she wasn't careful, she'd be going down Carrie's route to morbidity.

Come to think of it, Carrie seemed to have gone AWOL too. It had been weeks since she'd heard from her. Jay hoped she had seen sense and taken her advice and abandoned the ridiculous divorce business she'd been so hell bent on. She had *warned* her not to go ahead with the insane plan. If she did, she'd live to regret it. Jay shuddered at the thought. The lawyers would be champing at the bit, and the gossips would have a field day. All of Rob's business empire would be gone through with a fine-tooth comb, houses would have to be sold, settlements made, and what, in the end, would she have achieved? Jay stubbed out the cigarette she had absentmindedly lit. Nothing more than *dowager* status. The ex-Mrs Rob Armstrong. A pity-provoking figure for women everywhere to gloat over. Oh, yes, they would *pretend* to support her, admire her courage, her integrity, her *independence*, but secretly they would be pitying her. That kind of carry on got you on the fast track to nowhere. Much better to do things the sensible way. Like Jay did. When that amount of money was involved, you had to play the game. It was the only way to survive. Frank might reckon he called the shots in their marriage, but that was only because Jay allowed him to think so. It was an arrangement that worked very well. Frank got to do pretty much as he liked so long as he showed up on occasions specified by Jay. In return, Jay got to remain Mrs Frank Farrelly and enjoy the respect, money and prestige that went with it. As long as you showed up as a couple at the important public and indeed family occasions, and lived in the same house, or houses in their case – Jay allowed herself a smile as she thought of her houses in Dublin, London, Marbella and Miami. It sometimes felt as if you were a swan, looking serene and untroubled as you glided along on the surface, while paddling furiously below to keep up. Well, wasn't that what most women were doing to some degree or other? Might as well be doing it in style. The important thing was not to rock the boat.

So why did she suddenly feel she was on such shaky ground? Jay wrestled with the unfamiliar feeling. It was silly. Of course Frank would show tonight – he couldn't afford not to. She would go upstairs and have a little rest. She had been overdoing it lately – too many parties, functions, charity events. Really, it was no wonder her nerves were frayed.

She headed upstairs to her bedroom, taking her phone with her. There, she went over to the Louis Quinze armoire and opened its secret drawer. Just a quick line as a pick me up. She hadn't been sleeping well lately, and the pills her doctor had given her were useless. She needed to think, to feel alert. Then everything would seem clearer. No harm in that.

Just as she had reclined against the pillows, her phone rang. She was about to launch into a well-rehearsed rant at Frank when she heard Carrie's voice.

'Carrie!' she exclaimed. 'How weird, I was just thinking of you. How are you?'

'I'm fine, Jay, thanks. I'm sorry I haven't been in touch, but, well, things have kind of overtaken me.'

Jay took a sharp breath. 'You haven't . . . have you?'

'No, no, I'm not calling about that, although I haven't changed my mind. Actually, it's good news. Ali and Stuart are engaged. That's what I wanted to talk to you about.'

'Carrie!' Jay squealed. 'How wonderful! That's fantastic news! How, when, where?' She rattled off the usual questions as her mind ran through a few quick calculations. If a wedding was on the cards, then surely Carrie couldn't possibly proceed with her divorce nonsense. As if on cue, Carrie came to the point.

'Well, she has her heart set on having the reception on *Excalibur*. I must say, Rob and I were rather surprised, but thinking about it, it would be a heavenly location, if, of course, it was all right with you and Frank.'

'Oh Carrie, you don't have to ask!' Jay said. 'Frank and I would be thrilled. I only wish I had a daughter myself who could look forward to a wedding there. Boys just aren't the same.' Jay thought of her four sons, who showed no signs of having a relationship lasting more than three months, never mind settling down. Quickly she scribbled down the dates Carrie gave her to run past Frank. 'I'll tell him this evening and I know he'll be as thrilled as I am for you. Then I'll get back to you.'

'Oh, Jay, that's so kind of you. You don't know how much it will mean to Ali,' Carrie said.

'Nonsense, you and Rob are our dearest friends, and Ali is like a daughter to us,' Jay gushed, thinking of the fun she, too, would have, organising the wedding with Carrie. She wished one of her own big louts of sons had been smart enough to land the most beautiful and talked-about girl in the country. 'Oh, Carrie . . .'

'Yes?'

'You know you'll have to spend quite a bit of time *in situ* to make the arrangements properly. I can help you with the right caterers, florists, that sort of thing, and you're welcome to stay at the villa for as long as you need to.' Jay smiled, thinking of the fun they would have.

'Thank you, but I wouldn't dream of imposing on you. You've been kind enough already. Hope is based down there now, so I thought I might rent a villa of our own. That way we can come and go as we please without disturbing anyone.'

'Well,' Jay was crestfallen, 'if you're sure. It seems silly, seeing as we have so much space in Villa Esmerelda, but at least you'll be nearby.' She brightened. 'I'll get on to the estate agent tomorrow and make sure you get a nice one. They're not all up to scratch, you know, and when Rob comes down—'

'Yes,' Carrie cut in quickly, 'that would be great. I'd appreciate it. In fact, I'd like to go down on my own as soon as possible, just to have a look round. I thought the week after next.'

'Perfect, I'll get on the case right away.'

Carrie smiled at the other end of the phone. 'Call me back as soon as you know – and make sure Frank's really okay with all of this, won't you?'

'Carrie, if I say it's fine, it's fine. Frank will be thrilled, believe me,' Jay said with more conviction than she felt, but she thought it was a *brilliant* idea. A wedding on the yacht! A celebrity wedding at that! And she would have an excuse to check things out in Marbella and sort out the little problem of Frank and his Polish companion – or was she Latvian? Jay couldn't remember. She made a mental note to see her private detective, or enquiry agent as they called themselves these days, so that she was fully briefed going into battle.

As Jay put the phone down, she felt an overwhelming sense of relief. She didn't like leaving the house in Marbella for too long, even if it was in the capable hands of their full-time staff. More to the point, though, she needed space and time to plan her next strategy for keeping her increasingly unpredictable marriage on track. Since Frank's yacht was moored in Puerto Banus, just ten minutes from their villa, she could monitor proceedings from there far more easily than she could from Dublin. *Excalibur* was off-limits to her, just as the villa was off-limits to Frank, without prior mutual consent. As long as he kept his exploits offshore, as agreed, everything would be fine. Jay exhaled. Oh, yes, it was high time she took matters in hand. As usual, Frank had let things go way too far. But it was still possible to stall the inevitable. It always was if you kept your head. Checking her watch, Jay noticed it was now a quarter to seven. She smiled as she heard Frank let himself into the house and begin his ascent up the stairs. She took a deep breath and fixed a welcoming smile on her face. No need for a scene after all. Not tonight. Tonight, the show that was their marriage would go on. And tomorrow, and the day after.

'Frank?'

'Rob! I hear congratulations are in order. That Stuart's a

lucky bastard,' Frank chuckled. 'How do you feel about losing your baby girl?'

'Some baby,' Rob said wryly. 'Of course we're all thrilled with the news. Stuart's a great guy and Ali seems besotted with him.'

'Well, I can vouch for him too.' Frank leaned back in his chair. 'As you know, he's been with me for four years now, bright guy, personable, good prospects and all that. At least now he might concentrate for a bit. I was worried there for a while that all this romance business was affecting his work. You know how caught up in it all they get at that age.'

'Tell me about it,' Rob said, thinking age had absolutely nothing to do with it. 'I suppose you've heard they want to hold the wedding on *Excalibur*?'

'Great idea!' Frank beamed, thinking of all the model friends Ali would undoubtedly be inviting. 'Jay was telling me all about it last night. Of course you can have the boat. You'd have total seclusion – the Spanish are first rate at security arrangements and I have my own people, of course, so there won't be any problem in that direction.'

'It's bloody decent of you, Frank,' Rob continued. 'You're sure it won't cause you any problems? I'd hate to interfere with anything . . .' All Frank's friends were well aware of how extensive Frank's entertaining on the yacht could be.

'Nonsense,' Frank said. 'It's only a day, or maybe two, eh? Although it'll be an expensive one! But what a party!'

'That's what I wanted to talk to you about. I insist on whatever the going charter rate is.'

'Don't be ridiculous, mate, I wouldn't hear of it.' Frank was adamant. '*Excalibur* is yours for the couple of days. Think of it as a wedding present for the young pair. As long as you take care of the other stuff, caterers and so forth, I can't think of a more appropriate event to hold on board.

After all, that's what she's for, and knowing you and Carrie, it should be quite a party.' Frank licked his lips. '*Excalibur* has hosted quite a few in her day, but she hasn't had a wedding in forty years, not since the Greek nuptials.' He was referreing to the famous billionaire who had first owned *Excalibur* and had been secretly married on the yacht in the sixties.

'Well, hopefully this wedding won't attract *quite* so much notoriety.' During the famous après-wedding celebrations, more than one famous actress of the time had been thrown overboard naked. The waiting press, in fishing boats a discreet distance away, had had a field day.

'We'll live in hope,' Frank quipped. 'Anyway, as I said, it'll be a pleasure. Just keep me abreast of details, and I'll give you my skipper's email address and phone numbers. He's the real boss of *Excalibur*. I just pay the running costs. You'll like him, he's a great guy. Rudi Weiss is his name and he's South African. Tell Carrie and Ali to liaise with him. Then it'll all be plain sailing.' Frank grinned at his own wit.

'Great, I'll be in touch. Oh, and Frank, thanks again, we really do appreciate it.'

'Don't mention it, old man. Let's get together soon. We missed you at the Fine Arts do the other night. I'd thought you and Carrie would be there.'

'Yeah . . .' Rob didn't try to hide the weariness in his voice. 'Well, things are kind of strained at the moment.'

'Hang in there, mate. It'll all settle down again. Just keep your head together. Anyway, there's nothing like a wedding to concentrate the girlies' minds, eh?'

'I'm counting on it.'

'Take it easy, mate.'

'Cheers, Frank.'

Frank shook his head. So, Rob was on the rack again – as

far as his marriage was concerned anyway. Well, it was par
for the course. Sure, wasn't he a victim in the marital stakes
himself? Most of his friends were in the same boat. How
could you find someone you'd been married to for nearly
thirty years a *turn-on*? It simply wasn't possible. Not with
the amount of mega-totty on offer these days. And if you'd
worked hard, back-breakingly hard, to build up a business,
made serious money, well, you deserved a few perks. That
was all there was to it.

Look at him and Jay. Childhood sweethearts from the heart
of the country, and look where they'd ended up! Top of the
rich list, and *that* was no small feat, Frank thought with a
glow of satisfaction.

He glanced at the photo of their wedding on the corner
of his vast desk and smiled. Had they come a long way or
what? Inspecting it now, he scratched his head. Jay was
hardly recognisable – her friendly Harley Street surgeon
had seen to that. The only similarity between the girl in
the wedding dress and a more current shot of her in a
family group was that if anything Jay looked even younger
than she had in 1975. As for himself, well, back then he'd
looked a right yobbo! And now, well, he was no oil painting,
Frank was the first to acknowledge that, but there was no
doubt that he'd acquired the appearance of *prosperity*. Yes
that was it. Jay was right . . . what was she always saying?
Clothes maketh the man. It was amazing what good grooming
and a well-tailored suit could do – covered a multitude and
in his case – Frank patted his stomach affectionately – a
fairly substantial paunch. And no amount of sit-ups or
workouts would ever change his short, stocky build,
although the wickedly expensive hand-made shirts added
inches to his shorter-than-average arms. And shoes, of
course. Jay had a *thing* about shoes and socks. Until a few
years ago he'd thought she was mad, but now, with everyone

from taxi drivers to politicians having 'makeovers', Frank acknowledged she had been right, as usual. Especially since he was always being complimented by various women on his collection of Tod's, Frank stretched out his short legs and craned his neck to check them under his desk. Who'd have thought a few rubber knobbles on the heel of a slip-on shoe would make such a fashion statement? There was no doubt about it: when it came to clothes, Jay knew what she was talking about, or if she didn't, she paid someone handsomely who did.

He drew the line at having his back and chest waxed, though. Jaysus! God only knew how much pain that would involve – any women he'd sounded out said it far eclipsed childbirth, and that had been enough for him. It was one of life's great ironies, he reflected, that hair grew freely where it wasn't wanted and never where it was needed. These days, he only visited his barber for a nose-and-ear job. The rest had required a more radical solution.

If only his dear old mother could see him now, he thought wistfully. She'd understand; she was the only woman who'd ever understood him. Jay had been a good wife, of course, and a great mother to their four sons, but she was a tough taskmaster and, *God,* could she spend money! Not that he begrudged it – sure wasn't that what it was for? And, to be fair, she kept herself in great shape, was always being mentioned in the best-dressed lists and gossip columns. Frank rather liked that. It was important for a successful man to have a high-profile wife who featured on the charity circuit. And if there were other women on the side? Well, Jay was a tough nut, but as long as he kept his side of the deal, she was prepared to turn a blind eye. It worked very well really, all things considered.

Or it had until recently. Frank sighed as he loosened his tie with fat fingers. There was no denying that something would have to be done – but what? Frank pondered his current predicament. Poor wee Ivanka, she'd been in a terrible state, bless her.

Of course, he'd known the minute he'd been introduced to her in Marbella more than a year ago that she was different from the others. His eyes had almost popped out of his head when he saw the stunningly beautiful blonde from Latvia waiting on his table.

'I am vorking as vaitress to pay for university. I study history of art,' she'd said in charming, halting English.

'Sure aren't you a work of art yourself,' Frank had told her admiringly.

She had been terribly flattered when he had asked her to meet him for dinner (Frank wasn't used to women feeling flattered in his presence, not until they knew how much he was worth at any rate), and Frank had put on a special show. When he had arrived in his chauffeur-driven Bentley to pick her up at the modest apartment she shared with two other Latvian girls, she had almost fainted.

But that had been nothing to the expression on her sweet little face when he'd taken her down to the port and one of his crew had ferried them in the sleek power-boat out to *Excalibur*. There they had enjoyed a candlelit dinner, with full crew in attendance, while the string quartet had played discreetly romantic melodies. Frank smiled mistily at the memory.

'Oh Frank,' Ivanka had breathed, 'even in the movies I have never seen such a beautiful yacht, and never in my dreams did I imagine I would ever be on one with such an interesting and clever man.' Her golden shoulders gleamed in the moonlight as she gave a barely perceptible shiver.

'Here, pet, you'll catch your death in that little slip of a dress.' Frank clicked his fingers and a crew member appeared as if from nowhere with a cashmere wrap, which Frank put solicitously round a beaming Ivanka.

'You are *so* kind, *so* thoughtful.' She gazed at him adoringly, her blue eyes darkening as the pupils dilated. 'Are all Irish men like you?' she asked playfully. 'If so, I must go there, yes? It is a wonderful, romantic country. I have Polish girlfriend who tells me this.' She nodded expectantly.

'Ah, well, now.' Frank basked in the unfamiliar glow of compliments, edging his chair a little closer to hers. 'I wouldn't know about *other* men, but I do know that this one appreciates a beautiful woman like yourself,' he winked broadly, 'and Frank Farrelly knows how to treat a woman. Yes, sirree, he does.'

'I'm sure you do,' Ivanka purred. Then, tilting her head to one side as the quartet played 'Strangers in the Night', she took his hand. 'May we dance, Frank? I would so love to dance to this beautiful music.'

'I can think of nothing I'd enjoy more, pet,' said Frank and stubbed out his cigar with fat, fumbling fingers. As he took her in his arms and felt the thrill of her cool, fragrant flesh, he hoped desperately she didn't find hairy backs a turn-off.

He had soon set her up in a fabulous new apartment and persuaded her to put off her return to university for the time being. After all, he could afford to send her to any centre of learning in the world, she would have her pick, but for the moment it was best if she stayed in Marbella.

And he made sure it was worth her while to do so. He still couldn't believe his luck that someone as sweet and trusting, not to mention beautiful, could be in love with him. Frank breathed deeply at the thought. But it was true! Sure wasn't she telling him so morning, noon and night, bless her heart?

And, of course, he had fallen in love with her. Who wouldn't have? The trouble was, things were happening a bit too quickly – but Fate had a way of intervening in these matters. Wasn't that what Ivanka had said? And she was right. It was destiny. Frank sighed. Of course he'd got a shock when she'd told him she was pregnant, but if he was worried, it was nothing to the state *she* had got herself into.

Calling to her apartment, he had found her pale and wrapped only in a short towelling robe, pacing up and down the room as if she was unable to keep still for a moment.

She wouldn't even talk to him, just kept shaking her head and bursting into tears.

'You don't understand,' she had gulped finally. 'This is the end for me. This is disaster!' she had sobbed.

Frank had been *really* worried then. He had honestly been afraid she'd do something stupid, like harm herself or the baby, God forbid. He shook his head, remembering the night vividly, only a few weeks ago, that he had called to see her and, to his consternation, had found her in a state of near-hysteria.

Finally, after a stiff brandy (and that was just for himself) and a lot of cajoling, he had wrung the truth from her. She had been inconsolable, far more upset than he was. Her parents would disown her, she sobbed. She would be put out on the street to fend for herself. Her dreams of university would be over. When he had stupidly suggested 'having the situation taken care of', the hysteria not only returned but escalated. She would burn in hell for ever. She would be excommunicated, her soul condemned to trawl the very bowels of the underworld for all eternity.

Frank remembered being strangely impressed by her sudden command of the English language at the time, although he had quickly redeemed himself to focus on the problem at hand. When he assured her that he was actually chuffed at the news (this, in part, was true), she began to calm down.

Of course he'd take care of her and the baby. Sure it was his own flesh and blood, what else would he do? They would have the best of everything, and Ivanka could study whatever she wanted to – he could afford any number of nannies to care for the child. It was such a relief to see her smile again and regain her equilibrium. He had assured her that everything would be fine and stroked her beautiful hair. She looked up at him adoringly, eyes still brimming with tears, and told him he was a saint, a truly good man, that God would reward him for his kindness, and how she loved him more than anything in the world. And he said he loved her too. And it was true, he *did* love her. Ivanka *needed* him, and Frank had forgotten how good a feeling that was, for someone to really and truly need him. It made him smile and melt somewhere deep inside in a part of him that had become hidden beneath the quest for accumulation of material things that still left him feeling somehow *lacking*.

Minutes later, they were in bed and Frank would never have believed such mind-blowing sex could exist outside the pages of a steamy novel. Pregnancy obviously agreed with her, Frank thought as he stood shakily under the shower, his knees threatening to give way. He certainly couldn't ever remember Jay responding in a like manner. When he emerged to see Ivanka sitting naked on the bed, her long hair trailing over her small, perfect breasts, as she stroked her flat, golden stomach tenderly, he would have dived on her all over again if he'd been fifteen years younger. Instead, he smiled at her. 'Didn't Frankie tell you everything would be all right, pet?'

'Oh Frankie,' she breathed, getting up to wind her arms round his neck, nestling her head against his shoulder, 'I am so happy.

I never could have believed it. I am truly blessed to have met a man such as you.' She looked adoringly up at him, then sadness flickered across her beautiful features.

'What, pet?' Frank put his hand under her chin, tilting her face up to his. 'What is it?'

'It is Jay I feel sadness for.' She chewed her lip. 'Will she be very upset to be divorced?'

Before Frank could recover his breath to muster a reply, she continued, 'But it is our baby we have to think of now, yes? He or she must have a proper father and mother. We must be a little family together, you, me and our baby, and I will make you so happy, Frankie.' She kissed him lingeringly. 'So very, very, happy,' she murmured. 'That's all that matters, no?'

Entwined in another erotic embrace, he had attributed the sudden chill he felt to the fact that the towel he had slung round his hips had dropped to the floor.

Frank shook himself out of his reverie and back to the present as the intercom buzzed on his desk. 'Your appointment with Mr Cartwright is confirmed for this afternoon at three, Mr Farrelly.' His secretary's tones were clear and crisp.

'Thank you, Penny,' Frank replied, getting up to stretch his legs. He had a business lunch in town, and he would go from there to his appointment with Ireland's foremost family law solicitors. Not that he was *really* serious about this whole divorce business, but it didn't do any harm to be forearmed. And when Jay got wind of the impending baby, as she was bound to, he could do with all the armour he could muster. He shivered involuntarily.

Although, thinking about it, maybe it would be for the best. After all, Jay was a tough old bird, not trusting and innocent like his sweet Ivanka. And as for love! Well, Frank was aware that Jay tolerated him, but love? Nah! They were a good team, though, and they'd had some good times, but the boys were grown up, they would understand. In fact, they were hardly models of restraint themselves, he chuckled, chips off the old block. Jay didn't *need* him. As long as he looked after her financially and saw that she was well taken care of in that respect, she'd be fine.

It would probably come as a relief to her. They were fond of each other, of course they were, but things had changed, and he had found a woman who loved him for what he was. A beautiful, sweet, innocent girl who hung on his every word and trusted him implicitly. He couldn't let her down. Oh, yes, it would be expensive, and the shit would hit the fan big time, but it was nothing he couldn't handle. He had a whole new life just waiting for him.

Catching sight of himself in the wall mirror, he straightened up. He wasn't looking half-bad these days he acknowledged. The new toupèe took years off him. He had thought about a transplant, but at the last minute had been too squeamish to go through with it. Anyway, the people in London had known what they were doing when they'd kitted him out with his three new crowning glories. 'Had a Cut', 'Need a Cut' and 'Just Right', the manager had explained while he showed Frank how to rotate the three toupèes, imitating the normal growth of real hair. That way, it was totally authentic, no chance of anyone suspecting it wasn't his own, that, God forbid, he was wearing a 'rug'. Sheer artistry. Nobody had a clue. Ivanka thought he looked even better without them, but Frank wasn't that confident, not yet anyway. Of course Jay thought he was off his rocker. She'd laughed herself silly when he'd come home sporting one – but that was her problem.

He was holding up pretty well for his fifty-three years. *Distinguished.* That was what Ivanka told him he was. Frank reached for his jacket and gave himself a final once-over. Not bad, not bad at all, although, he reflected momentarily, if the baby was a little girl, he hoped for her sake she favoured her mother in the looks department.

Who'd have thought it? Frank Farrelly, expectant father – at his age! With a spring in his step, Frank left his office, and calling ahead to the restaurant on his mobile, ordered a bottle of vintage Krug to be waiting for him on arrival.

8

Despite the impressive forty-two-inch row of indents snaking round the left side of his deeply tanned back and torso, Rudi Weiss wore his real scars on the inside. All the same, having escaped the jaws of a Great White shark made a good conversation piece, and the girls loved to listen to his adventures. The lucky ones got to trace the length of his death-defying scar with gentle fingers, eyes widening ever so slightly as they risked running a tentative tongue along its delicious ridges – just as Lola, the Russian lap-dancer, was doing now with not a little skill.

Rudi gripped her long blonde ponytail and pulled her head back playfully. 'No can do, sweetheart,' he said, extricating himself expertly from her clutches. 'I've got to meet a guy in the port in half an hour – business.'

Lola looked petulant. 'You never have time for me any more,' she said in her charmingly cultivated accent. Winding a long coil of hair through her fingers, she watched him pensively as he pulled on his jeans and well-worn deck shoes. 'You are becoming bored with me, no?'

'With you, Lola?' Rudi laughed. 'Never.'

But they both knew he was lying. He couldn't help it. Despite having his pick of the most beautiful and sexually adroit girls on the planet, Rudi had never been hooked by any of them. Over the years, it had led to several awkward encounters. Whenever possible, he tried to let a girl down gently and just drift away – given his job, that was the easy part.

But not for the girls. It didn't matter if they were older or younger, heiresses or career girls, married or single – women fell for Rudi hook, line and sinker. That he took his immense sex appeal for granted just made him all the more lethally attractive.

None of this, however, was on his mind as he helped Lola off the yacht and onto the waiting power-boat, where, arriving in the port minutes later, they caused a considerable flurry of attention with their combined film star looks.

A few minutes later, disentangling himself from Lola's reproachful farewell embrace, Rudi went on his way with a vague assurance to hook up with her after she had finished her late-night shift at Olivio's. With her endless legs and amazingly flexible body, she was, without contest, the star attraction in the exclusive club.

Twenty minutes later, Rudi stood at the bar in Carlo's, where the hard-core sailors drank, and ordered a San Miguel. At three in the afternoon it was quiet, and only a few of the regular crew who frequented the place were there, finishing their beer and tapas, swapping stories of antics on their boats and outdoing each other with tales of dreadful owners.

'Rudi! How ya doin', mate?' A well-built, ruddy-faced Australian got up and slapped him on the back. 'Thought I might run into you down here. Come and join us. How's the floating brothel?' he referred, snidely, to *Excalibur*.

'Still afloat, Brad.' Rudi grinned good-naturedly, although in truth it irritated him intensely that his boat was considered game for such jibes. He was a serious sailor and it annoyed him that along with the obvious aspects of the job as skipper, he had to deal with and deflect the many rumours and stories that abounded regarding *Excalibur*. 'It's good to see you, I'd really like to, but I've got to meet someone right now. Catch you later?'

'Sure thing. We're in for the week, then taking the boat down to Gib. Hope you've left a few senoritas for us poor Aussies?' He winked at his companions. 'Rudi here's quite a ladies' man. Mind you,' he continued, 'I wouldn't have thought this was the kind of joint you'd bring a sheila to.' He laughed loudly.

'Even I know better than that, Brad,' Rudi retorted. 'This is strictly business. In fact, here he is now – you'll have to excuse me.'

Right on cue, Enrique B'stardo swept into the little bar with all the posturing arrogance of the acclaimed bullfighter he had been. 'Rudi.' He air kissed him assiduously on both cheeks, then sat gingerly on a bar stool. 'I have news for you,' he said, patting the carefully arranged bouffant hairdo that added a vital two inches to his meticulously maintained physique.

Rudi scowled as he heard the titters of the butch Aussies. He hated Enrique's over-the-top mannerisms. If he hadn't known better, he'd have sworn he was gay.

'San Miguel?' Rudi nodded at the barman, knowing the drill.

Enrique was as tight as his obscenely fitted trousers, and if Rudi wasn't forthcoming with the drinks, whatever news Enrique had would be withheld.

'Thank you, my friend. Actually, I'll have a brandy and a *café negro*. I've had a very stressful day.' Enrique gesticulated. 'Crazy legalities, how you say? Red letters?'

'Red tape,' Rudi offered.

'Yes, yes, that's it. Red tape. Everything is always tied up in red tape these days.'

'Tell me something I don't know.' Rudi gestured for another brandy as Enrique downed the first in a single gulp.

'I had a call from our friend Frank this morning.'

'Oh yes?' Frank Farrelly was the Irish multimillionaire

owner of *Excalibur*, the most notorious yacht in the Med. As such, he was Rudi's boss.

'Oh, yes.' Enrique grinned. 'He's coming tomorrow with a few friends. I thought you might like the advance warning.'

Rudi frowned. 'How many of them?'

'No idea. He just said that he and a few friends would be down for a week or so. He wants to get started with the new development.' Enrique snorted. 'That's if he has a better hope than I have of cutting through this "red tape", and *I*,' he said significantly, 'am a Spaniard. What hope has he, a mere Irishman?' Enrique sniggered.

'Shit,' Rudi sighed. 'That means the girlfriend'll be in tow.'

'That's a problem?'

'Mrs Farrelly is also in town,' Rudi said pointedly.

'Ah,' Enrique nodded knowingly. 'Women. They are all the same.' He raised his eyes to heaven. 'Spanish, Irish, Italian, whatever, always jealous, jealous, jealous.'

'Believe me, jealousy isn't Jay's problem,' Rudi said, 'or if it is, she's learned to hide it well. Frank and she seem to have an amicable enough arrangement, as long as things don't get too out of hand.'

'Out of hand?'

'As long as Frank doesn't push it – you know, overstep the mark.'

'He does not strike me as the discreet type.'

'You're right. He's about as discreet in his womanising activities as King Kong. Now apparently the girlfriend's pregnant, or so I'm told. It's not going to help things.'

'Ah, no. That is not an ideal situation. Does Mrs Farrelly know this?'

'Not that I'm aware, but not much seems to escape her attention. If she doesn't know already, it's only a matter of time.'

'You think they will divorce?' In this worrying new light, Enrique immediately resolved to bring extra pressure to bear on moving the development forward. Divorce was not good news. In his experience, properties were dispensed with, assets frozen, and the only people who ended up getting paid were the lawyers.

'I doubt it. I don't think either of them would be keen on that idea,' Rudi said thoughtfully. 'The deal is, Frank keeps his activities to the boat, but when Jay's in Marbella, that can be a bit tricky. The trouble is, I get to be the go-between. It's not a part of the job I relish.'

'In Spain a strong woman is admired.' Enrique smiled approvingly.

'I gotta go, mate.' Rudi downed the last of his beer. 'Thanks for telling me about Frank.'

'Not so fast.' Enrique bared his over-perfectly crowned teeth. 'That is not *all* the news.' He gestured to the waiter for another refill.

'There's more?' Rudi didn't like the sound of this.

'Oh, yes, indeed.' Enrique was enjoying himself. 'You will be happy to hear you are to host a wedding on *Excalibur*, a very glamorous affair, by all accounts.'

'Get outta here!' Rudi roared with laughter. 'Give the guy a chance, mate. Frank's not even divorced yet – and even if he was, I can't see him getting hitched again. Even by your standards, Enrique, that's stretching the odds.'

'But no, I am deadly serious, my friend, and it is not Frank. The wedding in question is that of the daughter of his close friend.' He raised his eyebrows. 'A supermodel no less, and I know this to be true, because it is I who will be acting as wedding planner. A dear friend of mine has already offered my services in this respect, and relayed my reputation to your Mrs Farrelly. I am to meet with her next week.'

'You? Organise a wedding!' Rudi hollered. 'Mate, now you're really taking the piss!'

'I will have you know, Rudi, that here in Spain I am famous for my elegant and exotic functions. Anyone who is anyone hires Enrique B'stardo to oversee the details.'

'And what about your property interests?' Rudi asked archly.

'As you know, I dabble – that is how you put it, yes? It is, as you say, a sideline of mine.'

Rudi shook his head. 'I don't like the sound of this, not one little bit, mate. Not on my boat.'

'It is true.' Enrique patted his hair. 'If you do not believe me, ask Frank. So we will be working even *more* closely together for the next couple of months, you and I.'

'Whatever,' Rudi said darkly, recognising the ominous ring of truth. 'I'll get hold of Frank, find out what it's all about.' He shrugged. 'But a wedding . . . it's not a good idea.' Visions of hysterical women and shrieking guests were already looming in his mind. 'Anyway, I gotta go, mate.'

'By the way,' Enrique called to Rudi's retreating back, 'I am very close to getting that information you are after. Another day or two at the most.'

'Good.' Rudi turned. 'Let me know right away.'

'Of course.' Enrique inclined his head. 'You can depend on it. *Hasta mañana*, my friend.'

As he made his way along the port en route to *Excalibur*, Rudi ignored the admiring glances from scantily clad women sunbathing on neighbouring yachts. All his life it had been the same. Even back in his dirt-poor days in South Africa, where he had joined the Merchant Navy at fifteen to escape his alcoholic mother and the series of vicious, abusive men in her life. Nobody had missed him. The only kindness he could remember had died with his stepfather when Rudi was just nine. His two younger brothers, both fathered by different men, were shiftless and jealous of Rudi, as were his mother's successive boyfriends.

Standing a lanky and self-conscious six foot three, even at fifteen, Rudi's stunning good looks and sex appeal had sent out a potent signal to every woman within a mile radius.

The navy had been tough but, along with gruelling hard work, had brought him the freedom he had craved. From then on, his passion for the sea and boats had dominated his life. When he left the navy at twenty-one, he went back to Cape Town, where he bought a boat, then another. Within five years he had built up the most efficient line-fishing fleet on the Cape. It was bone-shattering work, in dangerous and unpredictable conditions, but the money was good. And every month, without fail, he sent a generous cheque to his mother, for which she never once thanked him. Life was tough, and the men he worked with tougher, but it was a living, and a good one at that – although it had very nearly cost him his life.

That day was indelibly printed on his memory. They had been winding up the catch in the treacherous stretch of water known as Shark Alley where, in spring and early summer, the tourists would take 'adventure cruises' to see Great White Sharks in search of prey off the waters of Seal Island.

The weather was rough, a storm was blowing in, and the boats were pitching and lurching appallingly. A sudden wave engulfed them, and panicked shouts ensued as one of the men had been swept overboard, banging his head on the stern as he went over. He was attached to the boat by a rope but had lost consciousness. In a flash, Rudi dived in after him, grabbed hold of him, and three of the crew hauled them back to the boat.

The injured man went up first, then Rudi, hanging onto the rope for dear life, gasping for air. Nobody saw the shark rise out of the water and Rudi's howls of pain were lost in the wind, but the water turned red beneath him as the shark slid back beneath the churning water with a chunk of Rudi's flesh in his jaws.

The air-rescue service had flown both men to hospital, where they recovered, miraculously in Rudi's case. After several painful operations and skin grafts, he decided it was time to call it a day. He sold his fleet for a considerable sum and resolved to see the world in a more luxurious fashion, now that he could afford it. Unwilling to give up the sea, he turned to racing yachts, where his undeniable talent and fearlessness earned him one America's Cup victory and a reputation as the most talented skipper any crew could hope for. If Rudi Weiss was on your team, you were halfway to winning already.

Racing was an education in more ways than one, and Rudi was a quick study. Mixing with some of the wealthiest people in the world, he developed a taste for expensive toys and even more expensive women. The yacht owners were only too happy to encourage him in both pursuits – anything to keep Rudi on board – but after a while, he always became restless, leaving miserable men and even more miserable women in his wake.

He'd done Australia, America and the Caribbean in style. Now it was time for Europe. The Mediterranean was waiting, and he had a more pressing reason to get himself there than merely sampling the delights the continent could offer.

The fortuitous introduction to Frank Farrelly, the gregarious Irish multi-millionaire who had, in a blaze of publicity, bought the infamous *Excalibur*, formerly owned by a Greek tycoon, couldn't have come at a more opportune moment.

Frank was looking for a skipper to manage it and its crew of fifty, and he was willing to pay big bucks for the best. The yacht would be moored in Puerto Banus, a ten-minute drive from Marbella, playground of the rich and the dubiously richer.

More importantly for Rudi, it was the summer home of his father – the man who had refused to acknowledge his existence and had abandoned his mother. This mind-boggling fact had been revealed to him on his last visit home, when Jake, his mother's ageing boyfriend, had been wheedling Rudi to bankroll him in his latest hare-brained business venture. When Rudi had refused, Jake had flown into a drunken rage, hurling abuse and accusing him of thinking himself 'better than all of us because of your bloody aristocrat Spic of a father'.

There was silence, punctuated only by his mother's drunken giggle. Rudi turned a deathly pale. 'Just what the hell are you implying?' he had said through gritted teeth.

'Ask your bloody whore of a mother,' had been Jake's final word on the subject.

'Is this true?' Rudi turned to her. 'Why didn't you tell me?'

She had looked at him wearily as she drained her drink. 'It wouldn't have made any difference, sweetheart. He never wanted you, never wanted me,' she had slurred. 'We were better off without him. The bugger of it all is,' she had laughed bitterly, 'you're the goddamn spitting image of the handsome bastard.'

A week later, she had died, falling down the stairs in her small house, where Jake had found her body at dawn, returning from one of his many nights on the tiles.

Going through the small box of personal effects Jake had left for him, Rudi had found the photograph. It was his mother looking young, beautiful and, for once, happy. Behind her, his arms encircling her waist, was a man, tall, dark and disturbingly handsome. Turning the snapshot over, Rudi read his mother's faded handwriting: 'Me and Emilio – Marques de Alba, Cordoba y Rincón! Marbella, Summer 1973.'

Rudi looked again at the face that stared out at him from the photo. The date was about right, Rudi thought, and there was no mistaking the resemblance. If this was true, and this *marques* was still alive, he would track him down. He would make him pay for every miserable year he had put Rudi and his mother through. And he didn't much care how he went about it.

Eighty degrees of skin-searing Marbella sun streamed down on Jay as she hurried to her car, face shielded by over-sized shades that closely resembled the facial protection worn by riot police. Her appointment with her dermatologist at the Molding Clinic had run late. She'd have to step on it to make it home in time for the private detective. Not even that thought could diminish her high spirits as she slipped behind the wheel, lowered the roof and revved the powerful engine. She loved it here: she thrived in the heat, the fun, the non-stop partying, the full-on *glamour*.

She edged the sleek car onto the road, accelerated hard and sang along with Beyoncé, savouring the rush of warm wind that carried the heady aroma of sand, sea and a cocktail of sun lotions.

Approaching the turn-off to the Golden Mile, as the row of fabulous seafront mansions was affectionately known, her expression softened. Ahead lay Villa Esmerelda, the magnificent home she and Frank had built, finished only two years ago, in happier times. The sight of it restored her equilibrium instantly. For the moment, she would put the worrying matter of Frank and his scheming bitch of a girlfriend out of her head. Perhaps she had overreacted. In all likelihood, it was just another stupid fling, another gold-digging bimbo on the make. Well, she had seen off plenty of those before and no doubt would again. Frank would never leave her. They had been through too much together. Even he acknowledged he would never have got to where he was without her.

She drove through the vast wrought-iron gates and pulled up outside the front door as Maria, one of the staff, was polishing the already gleaming marble steps. '*Hola*, Señora Jay,' the robust woman greeted her, goggle-eyed at the number of bags Jay carried, which all bore elegant designer logos. 'You need help?'

'No, thank you, Maria.' Jay's gimlet eyes scoured every available surface for dust as she swept inside.

'A gentleman.' Maria gestured towards the sitting room. 'He is waiting for you.'

'Thank you, Maria. Tell him I'll be with him in a moment, will you? Oh, and ask Juan to bring in the rest of my bags.'

Jay ran upstairs to the bathroom, checked her reflection, washed her hands, freshened her lipstick and returned down-stairs. She paused briefly outside the sitting room door and took a deep breath, fixed a smile on her face and girded her loins.

'Mrs Farrelly.' The slim, unremarkable man in light summer casuals rose to his feet and held out his hand.

'Mr Smith.' Jay shook it and gestured for him to sit down again. 'Can I offer you some tea or coffee?'

'Thank you, no. Your, er, housekeeper kindly brought me some.'

'Good,' said Jay briskly. 'Now, let's get down to business shall we?'

'I must warn you, Mrs Farrelly, that one of the more unpleasant aspects of my job is relaying information that is not always well received.' He looked her directly in the eye.

'What exactly are you saying?' Jay fixed him with an equally determined gaze.

'You're not going to like what you hear.'

'I rarely do, Mr Smith.' She smiled grimly. 'Please, go ahead.'

Half an hour later, Jay settled her account with Mr Smith and showed him out, saying she would be in touch if she needed further assistance.

When he had gone, she went into the kitchen, opened the fridge and poured herself a glass of chilled white wine. From there, she made her way out onto the back veranda.

Beside the smaller of the swimming pools – the larger infinity pool was on a lower level – a table was laid out immaculately, as always, for an elaborate lunch in case Jay, on a whim, had invited a few friends round. Thankfully, today, she hadn't. For once the place was quiet. Maria had retreated to the staff villa, where she and her husband Juan resided, for her daily siesta. Although it was only April, Jay felt her skin turning puce from heat despite the rigorously applied sunblock. She pushed the button to lower the yellow and white striped awning so that the table was shaded and sat down. She needed to think.

Sipping her wine slowly, she went over the events relayed to her by Mr Smith.

He had been right. She hadn't wanted to hear any of it. But she had sat straight backed, her face carefully expressionless, as she had listened, leafing through the incriminating shots, to every unsavoury morsel.

She sat now, trying to gather her racing thoughts, noticing, with mild amusement, the tremor in her hand as she brought the glass to her lips.

Frank's bit on the side was pregnant – check.

She was Latvian – check.

No. Posing as Latvian. She was, in reality, Russian – check.

Why, Jay wondered, would someone pretend to be Latvian? Probably she thought it more glamorous – or maybe it solved immigration problems. She had been working as a waitress until Frank had set her up in considerably more style down in the port, where she was, by all accounts, serving up other, more exotic menus.

Most worrying of all, Frank had consulted with Ireland's foremost divorce lawyers.

Jay paled at the thought. This was as bad as it got. Divorce itself was bad enough at any time – *but for a husband to instigate it!* She put down her glass abruptly. It was unthinkable. She had to act quickly – but how? She threw back what was left of the wine and began to pace. Two rounds of the pool did nothing to clear her racing mind. If anything, the sound of the gently lapping water served to agitate it more.

She retreated inside and in the kitchen, she poured more wine. Then she prowled about the house, checking every room.

Maria and her younger sister Manuela, just two of the fleets of staff that frequented the villa on a daily basis, had done a meticulous job. Not even Jay could find fault with anything. The guest suites, like the rest of the villa, or mansion, as it was known locally, were an oasis of style and tranquillity that most people had only ever seen in the glossiest of travel and interiors magazines. In the master suite, she put her glass down on the dressing table and kicked off her shoes. Without her trademark five-inch heels, she suddenly felt very small.

She sat down on the bed, stretched out her feet and wiggled her toes, whose nails were painted a fashionable frosted burgundy. 'Why?' she asked out loud to the empty room.

Why was *nothing* ever enough for some men? The answer was not forthcoming. Sitting on her bed feeling very afraid and very alone, Jay Farrelly put her head in her hands and wept.

9

Not far away, in the sleepy Old Town of Marbella, the Marques de Alba, Cordoba y Rincón was also wrestling with a pressing predicament. Strolling along the narrow streets with his copy of *El País* tucked under his arm, he was reflecting on the precarious circumstances in which he now found himself.

At fifty-seven, he still cut a handsome figure – tall, erect and, as befitted his noble ancestry, eminently aristocratic – from the tips of his manicured fingernails to the soles of his handmade leather loafers. Crossing the Orange Square, he sat down at his usual table, put on his tortoiseshell Persol sunglasses, stretched out his long legs and unfolded the newspaper.

'*Buenas tardes, Marques.*' Miguel placed the espresso and small brandy, or *cortado*, reverently in front of him.

'*Gracias, Miguel.*' He nodded without looking up from his paper.

The square was still relatively empty, apart from the few locals opening shops or restaurants in preparation for business after the siesta. A few tables away, two matronly American women whispered covertly, nodding in his direction. The *marques* sighed. He knew what would happen next.

As surely as if he had written the script himself, one of the women approached him. 'Excuse me,' she began, 'but my friend and I were wondering . . . are you – you just *have* to be Sean Connery?' Without waiting for an answer, she thrust a menu at him. 'Could we have your autograph, please, Mr Connery? We're so, like, your number-one fans.'

The *marques* removed his shades and fixed her with a direct gaze. 'Madam,' he replied in the flawless English accent he had acquired at considerable expense to his late parents at Ampleforth College, the famous Benedictine public school, and later Oxford, 'you pay me a great compliment, but I regret I must fall short of your expectations.' He smiled briefly, revealing a row of startlingly white teeth. 'I am not, by any stretch of the imagination, Mr Sean Connery, and now,' he gestured to his newspaper, 'if you'll excuse me . . .'

'Oh, I—'

His demeanour did not invite further discourse on the subject, and the woman beat a hasty retreat. Thus dismissed, she made her way uncertainly back to her eagerly awaiting companion. 'It *is* him. It *has* to be,' the other woman argued. 'He has a house here, everyone knows that.'

'Well if it is him, he's downright unfriendly,' the autograph hunter grumbled, 'although I'll admit, close up, he's even more handsome. Usually film stars are disappointing in the flesh.'

'Not that one.'

The *marques* studiously avoided eye contact with the women as they gave him a final, furtive once-over on leaving the square. It had been the same for as long as he could remember. He was always being mistaken for the actor. In the beginning it had been amusing, but over the years had become tedious.

Taking a sip of his coffee, he contemplated the evening ahead. He would take a brisk walk along the seafront, meet up with Santo and Felipe for tapas and perhaps a game of cards, then retire.

At the thought of his shabby room above Santo's restaurant in the Old Town, the familiar feeling of despair crept
over him. That it should have come to this, that he, the
holder of one of Spain's most distinguished titles, was
reduced to a state of near penury. He smiled ruefully. Of
course nobody knew – nobody who mattered, at any rate.
At least in Spain, nobility were still revered, regardless of
their financial circumstances.

Every year, without fail, he still rented his private villa in
the Marbella Club – at a specially discounted rate – for the
summer season, and he was due to move in next week. But
this year would be the last he could afford. His linen suits and
handmade shoes had withstood the test of time and style. He
had long ago become proficient in performing a manicure on
himself. His expensive Persol shades had been his only recent
concession to fashion. He flinched inwardly at the memory of
their exorbitant price – but details were important.

For a moment he was transported back to the heady
days of the sixties, when he and his inseparable friend
Albert von Hohenlohe had cut a swathe through swinging
London and Europe. Prince Alfonso von Hohenlohe had
set up the Marbella Club in 1954, on the then unembell-
ished Costa del Sol, and ever since the club had become
the haunt of the burgeoning new jet set.

Their adventures and conquests had been the stuff of
dreams. And the women – my God – each more beautiful
and entrancing than the next. In the end, surprising no
one more than himself, he had married for love. His family
had never forgiven him for not honouring his obligation
to line the family coffers with a financially advantageous
union. At the time it had been something of a national
scandal: one of the most eligible playboys of the Western
world had married a mere air hostess. But it had been
worth everything. Maria and he had been blissfully happy

for five years. They had one adored son and then cancer had struck. She had died in his arms, a mere whisper of her former beautiful self, and part of him had died with her.

After that, nothing had seemed to matter very much. He did the best he could for his grieving son, but he had been an absent, uncommunicative father. He was too immersed in his own grief and loss to be anything to anyone. Carlos, brought up for the most part by his guilt-stricken aristocratic grandparents, had grown up to favour his mother in looks and his father in character. Happily embracing a career as a handsome, blond womaniser, it wasn't long before he was heavily into the drugs that never satisfied his search for fulfilment. He had left a trail of debt and broken hearts in the wake of his untimely death in a powerboat race. He had been one day away from his twenty-first birthday.

That had been in 1986 – it seemed many lifetimes ago. So much had changed since then, the *marques* reflected. So many of his old friends were dead. And somewhere along the way, the world had gone mad. Even in Spain, everyone appeared to be rushing, stressed and perpetually grovelling to the masses of new wealth emerging in Europe.

Of course there had been other women along the way – many – but no one had stolen his heart the way Maria had.

He shook himself back to the present. No use thinking about all that now. He had more pressing problems to deal with. The brusquely written letter from the bank had made that abundantly clear.

The solution eluded him. He had discussed and pondered it at length with Santo and Felipe, who were of the same opinion: there was only one thing to do. Emilio needed to find himself a wealthy wife. He smiled despite himself. He knew they meant well, his dear old friends, but apart from finding the idea of a convenient marriage distasteful, Emilio had only ever settled for the real thing. Love. He was one of the lucky ones. He had found it once and didn't expect to find it again.

Rudi powered the engine of the Riva and set off from the port towards 'his' boat, *Excalibur*. One of the biggest yachts in the Med, it was moored further out to sea than most, so he and the rest of the crew used either the extremely smart Italian-made power-boat he was cruising in now or one of the three RIBs – ridged inflatable boats – to go back and forth.

Ahead, *Excalibur*, all two hundred and fifty feet of her, lay gleaming in the afternoon sun. Rudi had to smile every time he saw her. In the world of big boats, Rudi knew *Excalibur* would be considered a bit of a joke to purists. A converted maritime 'survey' vessel, built by the CIA in the 1950s to keep watch on Russian submarines, she was, in modern terms, pretty much an 'old lady'. She was also slow, rather ugly and rolled like a pig.

Not having been built as a pleasure boat, she wasn't in the same league as a Saudi prince's yacht or, for instance, the *Ultima*, which belonged to the Revson family, who owned the Revlon cosmetics firm, or a host of newer, sleeker Bonettis.

But what the *Excalibur* lacked in sailing credibility, she made up for in fantasy. Thanks to the late Greek tycoon who had had her converted, *Excalibur* had hosted some of the most talked-about parties, business trysts, love affairs and honeymoons that, even today, were still the stuff of legends. Presidents, film stars and divas had all frolicked on board in her heyday.

Like all skippers, Rudi was fiercely defensive of his boat. *Excalibur* was home to a crew of fifty people at any one time, and it was his job to manage the day-to-day running of things, much like a managing director would manage a small company. Twenty deckhands, six stokers/engineers, five officers and a purser reported to Rudi, plus the twenty or so cooks, stewards, cleaners, bed-makers and cocktail waiters, who worked for guests and crew.

Rudi pulled up alongside the gleaming vessel and climbed aboard. She was pristine, having been painted last week. Steel rusts quickly in salt water, so painting was pretty much a year-round activity on board.

Thinking of Frank and his guest's imminent arrival and the careless damage they would inflict, Rudi scowled. His crew were the best and worked hard. It was difficult to sit back and smile when some stupid prick scarred the woodwork with a carelessly discarded glass or stubbed-out cigarette and empty-headed women left stiletto marks in their teetering wake.

'Yo, Skipper! Why the long face?' Rory, the first mate, looked up from his hand-held computer.

'Frank's coming tomorrow with guests. Don't know how many. I'll give him a call now.'

'No need, he's been on already. We have strict instructions to be ready to welcome him and fifteen others. Usual drill. Accommodation's already been allocated.' Rory waved a sheet of fax paper.

'Nice of him to consult me.' Rudi glowered. 'I only run the bloody show.'

'Don't get your knickers in a twist, mate. You know what he's like. That's why you're the best-paid skipper in the Med.' Rory laughed. 'Now, come on down and have a drink with me. There's at least three matters of high priority that need your attention. Not least of which is where we're going to spend our last night of freedom in port.'

'Speaking of last nights of freedom,' Rudi said, 'have you

heard anything about some bloody wedding party we're going to be having on board?'

'Don't tell me you've capitulated, mate.' Rory slapped him on the back, laughing. 'Lola and you'll make a *very* exotic couple.'

'Don't be ridiculous.' Rudi grinned. 'Marriage isn't for me. I've seen what it does to other people. Anyway, so many women, so little time.' He ducked his tall frame as he followed Rory below. 'Joking apart, that little weasel Enrique B'stardo told me in the port he has it on good authority that some bloody supermodel's chartered the boat for her wedding.'

'Really?' Rory perked up. 'That'll be fun.'

'Not with him prancing about as wedding planner and a slew of bird-brained models squawking round the place. It'll be a bloody nightmare.'

'Enrique! A wedding planner? You gotta be kidding!'

'I wish I was.'

Enrique B'stardo pulled up outside his small villa on the outskirts of Estepona. It had been a busy day and there was still a lot of work to do. Inside, he was greeted by the delicious smell of paella and his grandmother, who sat silently, swathed from head to toe in black as always, in the corner of the hall under one of the several bulls' heads that hung throughout the villa. As usual, she was engrossed in her crochet. She nodded at him briefly, then returned her attention to her handiwork. Since a series of slight strokes in recent years, she claimed to be deaf and hardly ever spoke, but Enrique had decided that this was a convenient ruse for her to indulge her favourite pastime of spying on him. The sight of her irritated him beyond belief.

'*Enrique, mi amor*! Is that you?' his mother, Fatima, called loudly from the kitchen.

'*Hola, Mama.*' He kissed her, then sat down at the kitchen table.

'I have made your favourite supper. Now let me pour you a glass of *fino*. You and I will have dinner together after I have fed your grandmother.' Fatima bustled about the kitchen, fussing over her adored only son, who had not only brought honour to the family with his glorious bullfighting days but had had the good sense not to be taken in by any of the mostly unsuitable girls who had thrown themselves at him over the years.

A well-preserved seventy-year-old with tanned, leathery skin, Fatima was a large woman, and proud of it. She dyed her plentiful hair a rather alarming shade of red, and favoured inappropriately high heels to show off her ample, if shapely calves. Widowed at thirty-one, she had devoted her life to bringing up her young son, and, forty years on, she still maintained her happily possessive hold on him.

For the most part, the situation suited Enrique. In fact, if it wasn't for the old crone of a grandmother, he would have been perfectly happy. He had his own suite of rooms, and if his mother knew about the women he brought back who occasionally stayed the night, she, quite rightly, made no mention of it. Of course, that only happened on rare occasions when he wanted to impress one with the formidable memorabilia of his glorious bullfighting days when he had been the toast of Spain. Ordinarily, Enrique pursued wealthy foreign women, who were only too happy to take him back to their tackily ornate villas.

His grandmother was another kettle of fish. She sat watching him with those beady little black eyes of hers and muttering her endless rosaries to herself. If it wasn't for his mother, Enrique would have had her in a retirement home like a shot, but this was Spain. The elderly were still entitled to end their days in the bosom of their families.

After dinner Enrique retired to his study, where he finished some work on the latest projections of the development Frank Farrelly had hired him to manage. He still couldn't believe his luck at being introduced to the obscenely rich Irishman. Truth be told, living on the past glory of his bullfighting days was cold comfort financially, and with his mother and grandmother to support, it wasn't enough to sell the odd apartment to a smitten tourist or a retired couple.

In the last few years, the stakes had risen considerably, and *everybody* in Marbella seemed to be 'in property', from euro-trash to so-called aristocrats – and that wasn't counting the Russians. Enrique shuddered – truly, things had changed for the worse in southern Spain.

His forthcoming business venture, though, would make him a lot of money if things were handled correctly, and Frank Farrelly wouldn't have the slightest idea of what was going on. Wasn't that why he had hired Enrique? A 'local' could deal with Spanish bureaucracy at its most frustrating. And if a little something extra fell into his pockets for his trouble, well, that was only as it should be.

Patting his carefully oiled jet black hair, Enrique smiled. Yes, it had a been a good day when he had met Rudi Weiss. Amazing how one thing led to another. And all because Rudi was on a mission to track down the Marques de Alba, Cordoba y Rincón . . . and he had paid good money for the information. It had been a doddle for Enrique to find out the details Rudi was after. Tomorrow, he would meet with him and discuss the situation, although Rudi had been tight-lipped about his interest in the *marques*: 'Just find out where this guy lives, and anything else about him, and let me know as soon as you can,' had been his instructions. Enrique had to admit he was intrigued. But it was enough for now that he had come up with the relevant information.

The rest of the story would unfold in due course, as they inevitably did.

It had been a long day and he was ready for bed, but just to unwind, he would surf a few porn sites on the web before retiring.

10

There was a God and he was definitely a man. Why had he ever doubted it? Rob Armstrong was whistling a happy tune as he sauntered into the kitchen to grab a quick cup of coffee before setting out on what would undoubtedly be one of the better days he had had of late. Although it was early, the house was reassuringly quiet. Carrie, who had been civil if remote lately, was out walking the dog – wretched creature. And Babs, their long-time housekeeper, wouldn't be in for a while yet.

He had a meeting in Kildare about a venture he was developing in conjunction with some UK bloodstock agents. He'd be finished there by lunchtime, hopefully, and then – Rob took a deep breath – he'd come back into town to see Olwen. The thought of it made his heart beat faster. They had arranged to meet that afternoon at her place, and Rob was unbelievably excited. No, he thought, smiling, that didn't even begin to describe the cocktail of tantalising sensations that flooded him when he anticipated their long-awaited reunion. They had spoken at length on the phone, and his relief at hearing her voice had overwhelmed him. She had been feeling as wretched as he had and, of course, when he'd asked if she would consider seeing him, she had agreed readily.

And now the day was here. He had backed out of a game of golf he had been looking forward to and, after the meeting in Kildare, was effectively free for the day. He sat down at the table, lost in fantasies of what lay ahead, and jumped as he heard Carrie come in through the front door on return from her walk.

'Hi,' he said chirpily, trying not to scowl at the dog that trotted elegantly behind her. She opened the sliding glass doors to the garden and let it out, hardly acknowledging Rob's presence. 'What are you up to today? Anything interesting?'

'I have a hair appointment, and then I'm going into town to meet the girls for lunch.' She poured a coffee. 'Ali's doing an interview with a journalist in the Merrion, and Steph and I are joining her afterwards.' She walked past him to open the fridge.

'That sounds like fun.' Rob was careful to sound casual. 'I've a meeting in Kildare, and then I've got the charity golf thing. I thought I'd let the worst of the traffic die down before I set off.'

Carrie seemed uninterested. 'I'll tell the girls you said hi.' She walked out, taking her coffee upstairs.

Minutes later, Rob heard the front door slam and the gravel crunch as Carrie drove off.

He let out a deep sigh. Great! No questions, no suspicious glances thrown in his direction. And why would there be? How could Carrie possibly guess what he himself hardly dared acknowledge? That only hours from now he would be holding the woman he loved and craved tightly in his arms. Pouring himself another coffee, Rob flicked through the paper, relishing the peace and quiet before Babs bustled in, talking ten to the dozen.

A plaintive howl accompanied by scratching on the door intruded on the calm.

Bloody dog! Rob scowled. Try as he might, there was no getting rid of it. Everyone had fallen in love with it. It followed Carrie around the house like a shadow and there wasn't a damn thing he could do about it. Suddenly a thought came to him. Serendipity! That's what it was!

His own car, which would have made the idea impossible, was being serviced. In its place, the garage had given him a Range Rover Sport to try. He had been toying with buying one – not that he was going to part with his Aston Martin – but the slick 4x4 would be fun to carry the golf clubs around in – and anyway, the Aston was a bit too visible sometimes. Rob leaped to his feet and grabbed the dog lead, which lay invitingly on the counter where Carrie had left it. He opened the sliding doors. The animal rushed in and dived onto its bed beside the Aga, from where he regarded Rob dubiously.

'Come on, boy,' Rob said gleefully, fastening the lead onto the dog's collar. What the hell was its name? Tommy? Tony? 'Toby!' That was it. 'Come on, Toby. We're going for a little spin, you and me.'

Ten minutes later, Babs cycled along the road as she had for the last twenty-three years, heading for Fairways, where she kept house and, indeed, sanity, she often thought, for the Armstrongs. Puffing slightly as she turned the corner at the village crossroads, she waved cheerily to Rob, who, eyes fixed steadfastly on the road ahead, failed to see her as he pulled out of the driveway and turned in the opposite direction. Hadn't she been right as usual? She'd been worried about the Armstrongs for a good while now. Carrie didn't confide in her as much as she used to, but she could read her as if she were her own daughter. Sure, she had been with them since little Stephanie had been a baby. They were like her own family, as she was to them. Babs sighed as she propped her bike against the wall and freed her trousers from their clips. She'd seen some comings and goings in those twenty-three years, that was for sure. And it just went to prove one thing. Money didn't buy happiness. A friend of hers had said recently, 'I've worked in some of the most

expensive houses in the country, Babs, and in my experience, the grander the home, the more troubles there are behind
the front door.'

But she loved the Armstrongs and adored the children,
although they were all grown up now and away from home.
Babs often wondered how long she had left with them now
that only Rob and Carrie were rattling around in that big old
house on their own. She had always pictured them retiring
somewhere nice, maybe to Spain or Portugal, one of those
sunny places where the Irish seemed to have taken over,
where they all played golf and had dinner parties with their
friends, and so forth. But of course that was the whole point
of it: if you weren't friends with each other, what did it matter
where you were? Nowhere was any good. Still, maybe there
was hope. It was great news, little Ali was getting married, a
wedding was always a lovely thing. Maybe that would bring
Rob and Carrie together again, make them value each other
and all their blessings, although somehow Babs doubted it.
It was a shame, she thought, a crying shame. They were such
lovely people individually, but together, they just didn't seem
to work. That Rob was a character, no mistake! Babs didn't
like to listen to gossip, but it was obvious to anyone with eyes
in their head that he was a ladies' man.

But sometimes, Babs thought, Carrie missed the point.
That sort of thing was always about insecurity, particularly
where men were involved. Babs blamed their mothers. If a
boy didn't get the right kind of mothering, he was hopeless
with women for life. And that was that. Unless, of course, he
met the right one, and even then it was a minefield. They
were always looking to be loved in all the wrong places, and
there were plenty of wrong women out there to help them,
she reflected grimly.

Letting herself in at the front door she called out a hello
which echoed, as she knew it would, through the empty house.

She would miss the silly dog today, she thought, smiling to herself. He was a lovely creature, and it had been a lovely thought of Stephanie's to get him as a present for her mother. He was great company for her, Babs, too, and she didn't mind him a bit. He was no trouble, no trouble at all. Of course, Carrie had told her that Rob wasn't a bit happy about it, not one bit, but she was overreacting, as usual. Sure, the poor woman was driving herself demented trying to antici-pate his every thought and move – that was half the trouble, thought Babs, but it wasn't her place to comment. And there now, hadn't she seen it with her own eyes? Rob was driving off with the dog looking out of the window in the back of that lovely new car. Off somewhere lovely, no doubt, for a nice outing, so it just went to show – you should never say never.

Animals had a way of getting round people that mere humans didn't understand. She had read somewhere recently that it was no accident 'dog' was 'God' spelled backwards. Yes, that was it. It was all to do with unconditional love. We could take a leaf out of their book, thought Babs. She made her way into the immaculate kitchen to start her rounds. She must remember to tell Carrie about Rob and the dog. She had known it would only be a matter of time before he took to him. Sure, who couldn't? The lovely, affectionate, silly creature.

She turned the television on, put on her rubber gloves and looked forward to her favourite programme when she'd have her tea break. It should be compulsory viewing, she often said. That wonderful Dr Phil had a lot he could teach the men of Ireland – and indeed, she reflected sagely as she attacked the sink, the women.

Today was going from good to better, Rob thought as he put his foot down urging the car along the N11 heading for Kildare.

The Range Rover was proving as good as its reviews, responding to the slightest touch on the accelerator, propelling its bulk powerfully ahead as it clung to the road, conjuring up images in his mind of what he would be doing later with Olwen.

The traffic had been a breeze. Once he was through the worst bottleneck, it had opened up beautifully – full steam ahead. There hadn't been a peep out of the dog either. In fact, Rob thought, if he hadn't been so fixated on the job in hand, he would have forgotten that the wretched creature was in the car at all. Toby was lying quietly on the back seat and hadn't made a sound. It was as if he knew something was up. Rob almost felt a flicker of guilt.

About an hour out of town, approaching the flat green stretch of land known as the Curragh, famous for an internationally known race track and home to a lot of sheep, Rob slowed down and pulled off the motorway and into a slip-road. He scanned the fields and stopped beside an iron gate. It was the perfect spot.

'Come on, Toby.' He opened the back door and the dog jumped out, keeping close to him as other cars sped past. 'Time for a pit stop, pal.' He wrestled with the gate, whose rusty bolts eventually slid back, then walked the dog through. Toby looked up at him, then squatted, relieving himself. He looked enquiringly up at Rob, who took off his lead. 'This is it, boy! Off you go! Go on! Shoo! Get lost!'

The dog gazed at him with what Rob felt was an unnecessarily bewildered expression. There was no time to waste. He climbed back over the gate, jumped into the car, slammed the door and took off. He didn't look back. With a bit of luck the animal would chase a few sheep and get shot or maybe it'd be run over. Either way he didn't give a damn. He was rid of it.

With a feeling of immense satisfaction, Rob rejoined the

motorway and turned up the stereo. Only this meeting to get through, and then he'd be on the road to *real* satisfaction.

Looking blankly around him in the strange field, Toby shivered. He trotted a few steps in one direction, then another, pausing to sniff the unfamiliar air. He wasn't sure what to do. Where was the alpha-male? He was nowhere to be seen. Toby stood on his hind legs to peer over the gate and backed down quickly as car after noisy car sped past. He didn't like this place. He remembered, dimly, having been somewhere like it before, a long time ago, before he had been rescued by the nice farmer who had brought him to the dogs' home. But now there was no one. He was alone, abandoned. He whimpered once or twice, but no one came, and the only other creatures he could see were a few sheep that grazed quietly, taking no notice of his plight. He was beginning to panic. He considered jumping the gate to follow the noise of the traffic and the car that had sped away without him when he stopped in his tracks. He heard a more urgent message, as old as the very fields that surrounded him. Standing stock still, Toby sniffed the air again. There it was. If he kept very still, he could just about catch it – the faintest whiff of the place he had left behind.

Concentrating with every fibre of his being on the instructions that age-old canine intuition was relaying to him, Toby did what he had been born to do. He located his direction and began to run.

The lounge in the Merrion Hotel was busy but not unpleasantly overcrowded. Ali had completed her interview with a prominent Irish style magazine and was sitting with her mother and Stephanie having some lunch before she jetted off to Paris.

'God, I *hate* doing interviews,' she said, pausing to bite into a smoked-salmon sandwich which she then left untouched for the remainder of lunch.

'Ali, darling, I'm worried about you,' Carrie said. 'You can't possibly be eating enough.'

'I'm fine, Mum, relax,' Ali said. 'I had a huge breakfast this morning,' she lied, 'and I have a swimsuit shoot in two days' time. I have to be careful. Most of the time I eat like a horse.' She eyed Stephanie's fillet steak hungrily.

It was an absolute nightmare, she thought, trying to stay thin, but it came with the territory. Thank God for solid, reliable, adoring Stuart. He was her ticket out of the rat race and back to some sort of sanity. He might not be a ball-busting tycoon, but he was doing well and more importantly, he idolised her. Ali had seen too many girls end up with no career and a big fat addiction to coke or heroin.

'Where's the shoot?' Stephanie enquired.

'Harbour Island,' Ali replied nonchalantly. 'It's off Eleuthera, the best-kept secret in the Bahamas.'

'Bummer,' Steph mumbled, tucking into her steak.

'I know.' Ali smiled. 'I'm flying out of Paris tomorrow. That's why I wanted us to catch up, Mum. God knows when we'll get together next.'

'But there's so much to do, Ali!' A look of panic crossed Carrie's face. 'What about the dress . . . and all the wedding plans?'

'The dress is a cinch, Mum.' Ali nibbled a crudité. 'Stella's doing it for me. She's already working on the sketches – I can't wait to see them.'

'Stella?' Carrie looked puzzled.

'McCartney,' Stephanie guessed, correctly, shooting her mother a look.

'Oh,' Carrie sounded deflated. 'How nice. But . . .' She hesitated. 'Don't you, I mean, I thought we could, well, look around.'

'Look around?' Ali stared at her as if she was mad. 'Why

on earth would anyone do that when Stella McCartney's offered to design their dress?'

'Yes, yes, of course you're right, darling, I just thought, well, if you're sure . . .'

Carrie trailed off, fantasies of choosing her daughter's wedding dress with her unravelling before her eyes.

'And now that we know I have *Excalibur* for the reception, all that's left really is the caterers, florists and so forth. That'll be fun for you, Mum, won't it? Stephanie will help, won't you Steph?'

'Sure,' said Stephanie dryly. 'It'll be a blast.'

Ali ignored her, turning instead to Carrie. 'Mum,' she said softly, 'there's something I've been meaning to ask you.' She paused, while Stephanie, across the table, tensed visibly. 'I know you and Dad have been having problems, and I know it's not easy, but . . .'

'Ali,' Stephanie protested, glaring at her.

'No, Steph.' Carrie smiled at her. 'It's all right. Ali's right. We do need to discuss this.' She took a deep breath. 'I've been meaning to talk to you both. It's just, well, the time never seems right, but now that we're here together . . .'

'Mum,' Stephanie blurted, 'you don't have to say anything, really you don't.'

'Dad and I *have* discussed divorce.' She failed to hide the quaver in her voice. She'd never thought she'd be having this nightmare conversation with her darling girls. 'And, all things considered, it's probably the best solution to our, em, problems. But you have nothing to worry about, Ali darling, we wouldn't dream of doing anything before – before the wedding.' The quaver became a strangled sob.

'Mum.' Stephanie looked stricken, horrified at the pain etched in her mother's face.

'I'm sorry, girls.' Hurriedly, Carrie took out a tissue and dabbed her eyes. She couldn't break down and cry now. 'It's just, well, the timing's so bloody awful. It doesn't seem so long ago that your father and I – well, you know. I never thought . . .'

'How could you have known, Mum,' Ali patted her arm sympathetically. 'But you're doing the right thing – in the long term, that is.'

'For God's sake, Ali!' Stephanie snapped.

'I don't know,' Carrie continued, 'maybe I should have done something years ago, maybe I should have let go sooner, but I – we just did the best we could with what we had and, of course, we had you three, and that made everything worthwhile. It wasn't all bad, you know – we did have some terrific times. We just weren't made to go the distance.'

'But you did, Mum,' Stephanie said softly. 'You did go the distance, every step of it.'

Carrie smiled sadly. 'Yes, you're right, Steph, we did – and now we've come to the end of the road. But Ali, I – we *so* don't want any of this to spoil your big day. And when we do go ahead with our plans, you needn't worry, any of you. It'll be very amicable, no fuss, no warring factions. We're way past all of that – we've already hurt each other far too much . . .'

'Well, I think you're being very brave and sensible, Mum,' Ali said firmly, 'but don't be *too* laid back about the whole thing. You need to make sure you get properly looked after, and if I know men, you're going to need a Rottweiler of a lawyer. It's all very well thinking everything will be sweetness and light, but when there's money involved things always get nasty.'

'Jesus, Ali.' Stephanie bit her lip as Carrie jumped to her feet.

'I'm just going to the loo. No.' Carrie waved Stephanie back, 'there's no need to come with me. I'm fine, really. I'll be back in a minute. It's just all a bit much at the moment.' She turned and walked away, fighting the tears that blurred her vision.

'You stupid, selfish, insensitive bitch!' Stephanie rounded on her sister.

'Oh, get a grip, Steph,' Ali retorted scathingly. 'You knew perfectly well this was on the cards, we all did. It's a little late to be throwing a hissy fit and overreacting. You're *twenty-three*, not a bloody kid. Besides, Mum's confided in me before and I knew she wanted to talk about it. She just couldn't bring it up.'

'Maybe that's because she didn't want to. Did that ever cross your mind?'

'Of course she did. She'll feel better now we've got it out in the open. It could be weeks before I'm around again.'

'It always has to be about *you*, doesn't it Ali? You don't give a rat's arse about Mum and Dad, you just want to make sure everything happens on *your* terms.'

'Oh grow up, Steph. You're just jealous because Mum and I have always been close. You're afraid Dad will run off into the sunset with this latest bimbo who'll push out a few babies and we'll be history. That's the way it is for the first family – I just want to make sure Mum's well taken care of, financially speaking, and I intend to make sure she is. Dad can go to hell.'

The thought of a second family hadn't even crossed Stephanie's mind, but seeing the abject look on her sister's face, Ali knew she had hit home. 'Divorce is a fact of life, Steph. You may as well get used to the idea that most marriages end in it.'

'If that's what you believe, why are you getting married?'

'Stuart adores me.'

'Mum adored Dad.'

'Things were different back then for women. Mum didn't have a career, she wasn't independent. I don't intend to let anyone walk all over me – and neither should you. If you learn anything from all of this, learn that.' Ali pulled out a

packet of Marlboro Lights and was about to light one when
she remembered. 'Shit, I keep forgetting you can't smoke in
this stupid country any more.' She scowled. 'And Steph, for
God's sake, don't go getting Mum all sentimental just because
you don't want them to break up. That really would be selfish.
Mum and Dad will be much better off divorced – at least
then they might be civil to each other and stop the ridiculous charade they've been playing. Mum needs to believe in
herself and make a new life for herself, and she won't do that
if you start whingeing and whining to play happy families,
okay?'

'Okay,' Stephanie said glumly. She had been about to
protest, but maybe Ali was right. Maybe divorce *was* the best
solution for everyone concerned, but that didn't mean she
had to like it. Seeing her mother return to the table, she
fixed a bright smile on her face as Ali motioned to the waiter
for the bill.

'Ali, that was lovely,' Carrie said, gathering her things. 'What
time are you flying out?'

'Six,' replied Ali, making a face. 'I'd love to stay and have
a stroll down town with you, Mum, but I have to make tracks,
I'm afraid.'

'Never mind, darling. Have a wonderful time on your shoot,
and promise me you'll eat properly, won't you?' Carrie hugged
her tightly.

'Of course I will.' Ali pulled away and kissed Stephanie's
cheek. 'Bye, Steph. Take good care of Mum for me.' With a
flurry of blown kisses, she ran outside and down the steps
of the hotel to where her limo was waiting.

Feeling suddenly diminished in the wake of her sister's
departure, and noticing the flicker of sadness that crossed
her mother's face, Steph linked her arm in Carrie's. 'Are you
rushing, Mum?'

'No, Steph, not at all, why?'

'There's an exhibition in the Hillsboro Gallery, some really interesting sculpture I've been meaning to go and see. How about we take a look at it now? It's only down the road.'

'That's a great idea. Come on, let's go.' Making a valiant effort to be cheerful, Carrie chatted gaily to her youngest daughter, who, she very clearly recognised, was more affected than she let on about the reference to the impending divorce. *Damn Rob anyway*, she thought, a stab of bitterness biting hard. *Why did it have to come to this?*

11

Rob stood outside Olwen's front door, so excited he was sure the whole street must hear the thudding of his heart. Armed with a bottle of champagne and the bouquet of spring flowers he had ordered from the florist round the corner, he held his breath, hearing, after what seemed like an eternity, footsteps approaching. The door opened, and there she was, as beautiful as ever, with that smile lighting her face.

'Hello, stranger,' she said. 'Come in.' And he did, feeling as if he had never been away, as if the last three months of hell had been no more than a bad dream.

'Oh, Rob, you shouldn't have,' she said, taking the flowers from him and kissing his cheek. 'They're beautiful.' She gazed at him with a mixture of shyness and adoration. 'Come into the kitchen. Can I get you anything?' she asked as he followed her down the steps.

'How about some glasses?' Rob grinned. 'I think we should celebrate, don't you?'

Olwen reached up to a cupboard and took out two champagne flutes with, Rob noticed, a slight tremor in her hands.

'Here, let me,' he said, taking them from her and placing them on the granite counter. He felt shaky too. It was always like this between them when they had been apart for any length of time. The chemistry between them made them jumpy, shy and timid with each other. He pulled the cork and poured the fizzing wine into the glasses, handing one to her as he raised his own. 'To you, my darling. It's *so* good to see you again.'

'Oh Rob,' she said helplessly, ignoring the glass he held out. And then she was in his arms, where he held her as if he would never let her go, burying his head in her neck, breathing her in, relishing her closeness, hardly daring to believe that this was really happening.

Olwen pulled away first. 'Come on, let's sit down.' She brought the glasses over to the nearby table. 'It's so heavenly to see you. I want to hear about everything you've been doing.' She led him by the hand to the table, where they sat next to each other, holding hands as they sipped the cool champagne.

'Thinking about you, mostly.' Rob smiled. 'I can't get you out of my head, Olwen. It's no use trying. You're there all the time, no matter what I'm doing.' He raised her hand to his lips and kissed the palm. 'It's been hell.'

'I know.' A long sigh escaped. 'Unutterable hell.'

'You've lost weight,' he said, noticing suddenly how frail she was, 'and you certainly didn't need to,' he added sternly.

'So have you,' Olwen countered, stroking his hand.

'It's a great bloody diet, this affair business, isn't it?'

'Oh, don't Rob.' Olwen shook her head. 'Let's not talk about it. Nothing matters now that you're here again.'

And it was true. Nothing else did matter when they were together. Talking to her, listening to her, Rob found himself beginning to unwind for the first time in months.

Later, they went to bed. That was the one place where they could be totally honest with each other. There was no need for words. Their bodies didn't lie.

They made love with a tenderness and passion that, as always, left them marvelling that they could ever, even for one moment, have stayed apart. Olwen satisfied a need in Rob that he hadn't even known existed, the same that he happily also answered in her.

Looking down at her now, as he held her in his arms, he saw the naked love in her eyes that always rocked him to the core. 'I adore you, you know that, don't you?' He searched her face for reassurance.

'Yes,' she whispered, smiling as she traced the frown line between his eyes with a finger. 'Yes, I know.'

They lay there, entwined, and Rob felt a peace he had never experienced with any other woman. How, he wondered, how on earth had he been so lucky, so incredibly blessed to have found her? This incredible woman who never asked anything of him, who calmed him, renewed him, made his life worth living, whose only unspoken plea was to spend as much time with him as he wanted to spend with her.

But that was the trouble. *No* amount of time was ever enough. 'Why me?' he asked suddenly, raising himself on one elbow, stroking her soft, blonde hair back from her face. 'You could have anyone, Olwen. Why me?'

'I might ask you the same question,' she answered, 'but you know why.' And he did. It was just that he found it hard to believe. Olwen was beautiful, intelligent and sexy, but she was also single, which made him uncomfortable when he thought about it.

Sometimes, he felt guilty about depriving her of a proper relationship, a family of her own, even. Sometimes he was envious of her freedom, her complete independence. When he had asked her about it once, she had laughed and said freedom wasn't all it was cracked up to be, and what good was it being free when the person you wanted wasn't? But she would rarely be drawn on the subject.

Sometimes, even, in his darker moments, he resented her for it, which was ridiculous, he knew. Olwen never played games with him, never tried to make him jealous as she could have done, as many other women would have done – but then, he reflected for the umpteenth time since he had met her, Olwen was not most women.

Sometimes, when their affair was at its most passionate, when he felt himself utterly consumed by his love for her, he would pull back, even though he knew it hurt her. Nothing major – he wouldn't phone her for a few days, he'd send a text instead. Sometimes he physically needed to put space between them. He'd let her down, break a date by jumping on a plane to play golf with the boys for a few days, but always he came back to her, and she never reproached him. There were never any probing questions, never any recriminations. It was almost, he thought, as if she understood. Understood his insecurity, his fear of not being in control, that this love, this passion might be his undoing.

'Penny for them?' Olwen stroked his face tenderly.

'I was just wondering,' Rob said gravely, 'have I told you lately that I love you?' He began to hum the tune to the Van Morrison song.

They got to the second verse before laughing themselves silly. It was one of the things Rob loved most about Olwen, her ability to be silly, and singing in bed was as silly as it got. Rob had a good voice; Olwen couldn't sing for toffee. She could, however, remember any lyric ever written and hold a tune. And they had whiled away many a post coital hour guessing the names, artists and lyrics to various tunes or film soundtracks.

He often thought if anyone could have seen them – she the smoothly articulate and composed TV personality and he the boardroom barracuda, acting like two kids playing hooky from school – nobody would have believed it. After an hour or two in Olwen's company, Rob, quite apart from anything else, always felt ten years younger.

'Don't know about you,' Rob said, sitting up, 'but I'm ravenous. Let's order some food in.'

'Me too,' Olwen stretched. 'But why bother ordering in? I can easily rustle something up for us.'

'That's too much like hard work, baby.' Rob trailed a finger down her spine, grinning as she shivered in response. 'I really fancy an Indian. I'll phone that new place – they deliver.' He reached for his mobile. 'The usual, Ms Slater?'

'Fine by me,' Olwen looked at her watch. 'No wonder I'm starving. It's seven o'clock already.' She slipped into her robe and headed for the bathroom. 'I was so excited about seeing you I forgot to have lunch.'

As she disappeared, Rob put a call through to the Indian takeaway and ordered. He had just finished when his phone bleeped to let him know a message was waiting. He dialled his voicemail and listened to his brother-in-law's crisp tones. He cursed, exasperated. 'Shit,' he said. He'd completely forgotten he'd agreed to meet him for dinner that evening. He thought about cancelling, but it was out of the question. Mark, Carrie's older brother, was an eminent barrister and handled a lot of Rob's corporate business. He wouldn't take kindly to being stood up.

'Darling,' he said as Olwen emerged from the bathroom, concern immediately clouding her face.

'What is it?'

He held out his arms to her. 'I'm so sorry, I'm going to have to leave earlier than I thought. It's Stephanie. She's been wanting to talk to me and I promised I'd meet her for a bite to eat this evening. It completely slipped my mind.' He chewed his lip, feeling guilty about the lie, but it was always better to claim a parenting appointment than something that could have been averted. 'Can you forgive me?'

'Of course,' Olwen said brightly. 'Don't give it a second thought. I do wish you could stay a bit longer, but if you've agreed to meet Stephanie, you can't possibly let her down.'

'You know I'd cancel if I could, don't you?' Rob looked as crestfallen as he felt. 'I was so looking forward to spending a proper evening with you. I can't believe I've been so stupid.'

Rob stroked her face. 'If it was anyone else, but Steph's been trying to talk to me for a while now, and—'

'Sshh.' Olwen pressed a finger to his lips. 'It's all right, really it is, you don't have to explain, I understand.'

'You're an incredible woman, do you know that?' He headed for the bathroom.

'So you keep telling me.'

Fifteen minutes later, Rob was showered, dressed and ready, if reluctant, to go. He checked his reflection in the mirror and followed Olwen downstairs.

Standing in the hallway, he kissed her and held her tightly. 'It's so good to see you again, my darling,' he whispered in her ear.

'It's good to see you too.' Olwen pulled away, smiling. 'We mustn't leave it so long next time,' she added mischievously.

'Gotta go. I'm late already.'

As she followed him downstairs to see him out, the intercom buzzed.

'Yes?' she said into the speaker.

'Indian takeaway for two.'

She opened the door. A delivery boy stood on the step with two bags of delicious-smelling food.

'Darling,' Rob shook his head, 'I'm really sorry, this is awful.' He handed the boy some cash.

'Lucky for you I'm hungry enough for two,' Olwen said wryly, pushing him gently out of the door. 'Go on, I'll see you when I see you.'

'I adore you,' he said and he really meant it, cursing his stupidity at having forgotten this meeting with his brother in law. Poor Olwen, left on her own with a pile of Indian food for company. 'Call you tomorrow! Bye, darling.' He slipped into his car, revved the engine and drove through the electric wooden gate, which slid closed behind him.

Minutes later he pulled up outside the hotel where he had

arranged to meet Mark and handed his keys to the parking valet. He made his way to the discreetly lit bar and noticed his brother-in-law had obligingly ordered a pint for him.

'Cheers.' Rob took a sip of the cold beer and sat down beside him. 'Sorry I'm late, got held up at a meeting. You're looking well,' he added, taking in Mark's tan.

'Skiing,' Mark said. 'I managed to get away for a week in Courchevel.'

'Good for you. How's business?'

'Crazy as ever. Which reminds me, I need to go through those contracts with you for the Knightsbridge deal. It'll have to be next week, though, I'm tied up 'til then.'

After chatting for a while, they went into the dining room for dinner. The maître d' ushered them to a table overlooking the fountains after which the restaurant was named.

'So,' said Rob after they had ordered, 'what was it you wanted to talk to me about?'

Mark, usually so direct, seemed reticent. 'Look, Rob,' he cleared his throat, 'I know it's none of my business.' He looked Rob directly in the eye. 'But, well, your Ali seems to be under the impression you're having an affair.' He paused, watching Rob's carefully neutral expression. 'And that you and Carrie are about to unleash some sort of ghastly divorce proceedings just in time for her wedding. You know what kids are like,' he continued. 'Ali confided in my Lisa, who told her mother, who mentioned it to me. I thought it would be better – that is, I said I'd have a word with you.' He looked about as uncomfortable as Rob felt. At that moment, the waiter brought their steak and salad.

When he'd gone, Mark held up a hand before Rob could speak. 'I'm not after any details, but if there's a divorce on the cards, it's better for everyone if we're all singing from the same hymn sheet . . .' He trailed off, picking up his knife and fork.

'Well . . .' Rob began, as calmly as he could as a million thoughts raced through his mind. Just what, exactly, did Mark know?

Rob adored his children, but Ali could be a major busybody at the best of times, and of course the girls would sympathise with their mother. It was only natural. But how much, if anything, did Ali know? Was this idle gossip she had picked up, or something more concrete? Had Olwen been talking? He dismissed that one immediately: it certainly wasn't in her interest for their affair to become public – but all the same, women were women. They talked.

'That's absolute nonsense, Mark,' he bluffed.

'It's only fair to tell you, Rob, that I took the liberty of making a few discreet enquiries and I know the girl in question is Olwen Slater.' Again Mark raised a hand before Rob could retort. 'You need to be careful, Rob. We're in the middle of some heavy negotiations and while your, er, personal life is none of my business, even if Carrie *is* my sister, the banks don't like unnecessary distractions, not to mention publicity. If this gets out, and Olwen Slater is a high-profile personality, there would be considerable exposure – newspapers and so forth. *Undesirable* exposure.' Mark was studying his face.

Rob didn't need to consider his reply. 'Look, Mark, Olwen's a fantastic girl and all that, but there's no way I'd leave Carrie for her – that's nonsense. We're just pals, really.' He was thinking frantically. 'Carrie and I, well, I'm sure it hasn't escaped your notice that for several years we've been leading increasingly separate lives.' He searched Mark's impassive face for sympathy and found none.

'That's not quite accurate, Rob,' Mark replied. 'You've been leading a separate life. Carrie's just continued being Carrie, hasn't she?' A touch of the cutting lawyer was coming into play here, and despite himself, Rob couldn't help feeling respect for his brother-in-law, not just in his defence of his

Fiona O'Brien

sister, but for having the courage to confront what he, her husband, did not.

'Carrie is free to do whatever she wishes. It's entirely up to her.' Exasperation was taking over Rob. He hated – no, *detested* – having to face the issue, let alone try to explain it to a family member.

'It's very simple, Rob,' Mark's voice was cool. 'Are you and Carrie divorcing or not? That's all I need to know.'

Rob sighed. 'I don't know, and that's the honest truth. We've discussed it, yes, but we've decided not to rush into anything before the wedding. Of course, Carrie and I would never think of ruining Ali's big day. How Ali could even think such a thing? And as for the other, er, matter . . .'

'I don't want to know, Rob.' Mark took a sip of his Bordeaux. 'Whatever you're doing is between you and Carrie. There is just one thing I want to say, though.'

'What's that?'

'Don't humiliate her. It's unnecessary. Carrie's been through quite enough already. And . . .'

'Yes?'

'Don't take this the wrong way, but there comes a time when a chap playing around *continually* on the side becomes a bit of a joke.'

'I see.' Rob's face darkened at the implication, but there was precious little he could say. Mark was on his second marriage to an attractive, younger lawyer but, Rob had to acknowledge, he had done it all above board. He and his first wife had divorced in a civilised manner and Mark had subsequently met and married his current wife, with whom, it appeared, he was more than happy.

Whatever hopes Rob had of enjoying the remainder of his evening were resoundingly dashed as a heavy wave of guilt crashed over him. This hadn't gone according to plan. He had been hoping for a pleasant man-to-man chat with Mark, and if the spectre of other women had arisen, well, he'd thought Mark would understand, that he would empathise with him, know it hadn't been easy for Rob all these years. He had hoped to emerge, if not shrouded in glory, then at least as the party who had stayed valiantly when many others would have long gone, but it appeared that was out of the question.

He thought longingly now of Olwen, overlooking how, minutes earlier, he had so easily dismissed her to Mark. How he wished he had stayed with her, cancelled this stupid dinner, which had been nothing more than another opportunity for a 'well-meaning' family member to attack him. But then, Rob recalled with a stab of bitterness, Mark and Carrie had always been close.

As if he had read his mind, Mark said, 'Contrary to what you might think, I haven't discussed any of this with Carrie, and neither do I intend to, unless she approaches me. But frankly, Rob, I'm worried about her. She's not looking well. All this must take a tremendous toll. You really should clean up your act, sort things out one way or the other for both your sakes – and, of course, the girls.'

They finished their meal in relative silence, punctuated by the odd benign comment about current affairs or business. Finally, Mark called for the bill. 'This is on me,' he said, brooking no argument.

'Well, er, thanks very much. That's, eh, very decent of you.'

'My pleasure.'

After the bill had been paid, they left the table and strolled through the bar en route to the lobby. 'Fancy one for the road?' Rob asked.

'No, thanks. I've got work to go over. Maybe another time.' The comment hung in the air.

'Yes, of course.' Rob tried not to sound relieved. 'Well, thanks again, Mark. It was good to talk things over.'

'Sure. I'll see you next week.' And with a wave Mark headed off. As he called for his car, Rob thought about ringing Olwen. It was ten thirty but it wasn't too late to spend some time with her – he knew she wouldn't mind, she was always thrilled to see him – but even he acknowledged it wouldn't be fair. After all, she had gracefully sacrificed the evening for him to meet, as he had led her to believe, his daughter. He couldn't very well turn up again unannounced – it would be a bit like saying, 'I fancied some afters. What about you?'

Anyway, he was tired, bone tired, but despite Mark he was happy. He smiled as he got into the car. Olwen always had that effect on him. She made him feel life was worth living. He would send her a text to say goodnight, that he loved her and was thinking of her, and then he would go home. This business with Mark was just an irritation, nothing that wouldn't blow over in a few weeks. All the same, Rob acknow-ledged, he had to be careful. He certainly didn't need any adverse publicity – although how anything to do with Olwen could be considered adverse was beyond him. Every man he knew would be drooling with envy if they knew about his relationship with her. Perhaps that was the danger. It couldn't be discounted that over the years he had fought some pretty dangerous boardroom battles – and not always fairly. He was under no illusions about his enemies. Many people, men and women, would be more than happy to see Rob Armstrong fall flat on his face. But it wasn't going to happen if he had anything to do with it. Rob accelerated on the main road heading for home. He was lucky, it was as simple as that. And as his mother used to say, it was better to be born lucky than rich. Happily for Rob, he was now both.

Banishing any troublesome thoughts, he concentrated on covering his tracks when he got home, in case Carrie was around. It was so perilously easy to let something slip with an innocent remark.

If he showed up at home now, he'd get brownie points for good behaviour. It certainly couldn't do any harm.

He had just let himself in at the front door and was looking forward to a nice nightcap in the library, followed by a reasonably early night, when Carrie emerged with a glass of wine in her hand and a face like thunder. 'You devious bloody bastard!' she said.

Rob froze as a variety of unpleasant possibilities ran through his mind. Had Mark, despite his assurances, talked to Carrie and landed him in it? Rob fought to keep his cool. 'Well, that's a nice welcome to come home to at the end of the day.' He paused, key in hand, sizing up the situation.

'Don't be fatuous, Rob. What the hell have you done with the dog?'

'I *beg* your pardon?' Rob's face reddened with anger as relief flooded him. Christ! He'd all but forgotten the stupid dog – but that aside, who the hell did Carrie think she was, attacking him before he'd hardly set foot in his own house? The bloody cheek of it! Anyway, he thought rapidly, whatever conclusions she might have drawn, she wouldn't be able to prove anything. Attack, in this case, was the best form of defence.

'You heard me,' Carrie articulated slowly. 'What have you done with Toby, my dog?' Her eyes glittered as she leaned against the library door, waiting for a reply.

'Yes,' replied Rob, eyeing the glass in her hand, 'I did hear you and I don't like your tone.' He closed the front door and walked past her into the library. 'If you're going to drink,' he looked at her scornfully, 'spare me the histrionics and delusional accusations. I haven't the faintest idea what you're talking about.'

'Is that a fact?' Carrie was fighting to keep her cool, thinking the two glasses of wine she had downed before Rob came in to stop her screaming with rage were not nearly enough. 'So when, exactly, did you last see Toby? In case you've forgotten, that's his name.'

Rob raised his eyes to heaven and gave a long sigh. 'Carrie, if you're spoiling for a fight, I don't have the energy or the inclination. As for the wretched dog, I don't know. The last time I saw him was this morning, I suppose, when you came back from walking him. You put him outside, and I left shortly after that. Why, what's the problem?'

'The problem is that you're a liar and have been for the greater part of our married life.' She grimaced. 'Most of the time I don't let it get to me – I learned to live with it a long time ago – but on occasions such as this, when you blatantly disregard my feelings, Stephanie's feelings and Babs's feelings, or those of a poor dumb animal who found himself at the mercy of your underhanded selfishness and cruelty, I begin to wonder just *who* the dumb animal really is around here.'

'I don't have to listen to this crap.' Rob picked up a sheaf of papers and made for the door.

'Oh, but you do,' Carrie continued, 'if you want your daughters to remain on speaking terms with you. Personally *I* stopped caring long ago about your moral ambiguities, but I dare say you wouldn't like Stephanie, or indeed Ali, whose wedding is imminent, to hear about their father's latest escapade. A particularly nasty one at that, even by your standards.'

'I don't know what you're on about Carrie, but if you'll excuse me, I need to get some rest.'

'Babs saw you, Rob,' Carrie said, playing her trump card, and watching Rob carefully as his eyes darted evasively in that way she knew so well. 'She saw you drive out in the Range Rover with Toby in the back seat. I rang her, naturally, the minute I got back from lunch with the girls and found Toby was gone. I thought perhaps she'd let him get out accidentally. It was then she informed me of your little outing.

Bless her, she thought you were taking Toby somewhere nice, for a run or something, or are you going to tell me she was hallucinating?'

Rob thought frantically. 'Actually, she's right.' He sank wearily into a chair. 'I had a meeting in Kildare, as you know, this morning, and when I saw the lead on the counter after you'd gone, I thought it might be a good idea to take the dog for a proper run.' Rob risked a glance in Carrie's direction. Her face remained impassive. 'I had half an hour or so to kill so I pulled off the motorway to let him out and he must have seen some sheep in the distance, because that was that. He ran off and no amount of calling would bring him back. I waited for bloody ages – nearly missed my meeting because of it.' He looked reproachfully at Carrie. 'Then I had to go. That's the trouble with those bloody rescued dogs. They haven't been trained properly, no obedience skills. Anyway, that's what happened.' He threw her a sheepish glance. 'If you want to know, I was afraid to tell you – I know it was stupid of me.' He held up his hands. 'And I knew how upset you and Stephanie would be, so I just thought I'd wait and see if he turned up, or someone phoned to say they'd found him . . .' He trailed off. 'It was cowardly of me, Carrie, but with everything that's been happening lately, I didn't want to be the cause of any more friction. I'm sorry, but that's what happened.'

'So I assume you alerted the usual dog-rescue centres?' Carrie asked. 'Phoned the pounds and so forth?'

'Er, no, I didn't. I had the golf outing after that, and— For God's sake, Carrie, the dog has a collar, doesn't he? If someone finds him they'll ring us. Now, you can think what you like, but I'm going to bed.'

'Go where you like, Rob, but you'd better hope that dog turns up. I won't say anything for the moment to Stephanie – she's not herself at the moment and I'm very worried about her. Our problems are affecting the girls badly, I can see that now, the whole situation is most unhealthy for them to be a part of. The sooner the wedding's over, the better. I've told Ali and Stephanie that we've discussed divorce, amicably, of course. I think they were relieved. I'm going to talk to Hope tomorrow, but I'll be seeing her soon anyway. I've rented a villa in Marbella, and I'm going down next week to get settled in and start organising the wedding. Stephanie's coming with me.'

'Fine,' said Rob. 'Whatever.'

'I imagine you'll enjoy the peace and quiet. But I'm warning you, Rob, if you do anything – I repeat, anything – to upset Ali's big day, I won't be responsible for what I do to you.'

'I get it,' snapped Rob.

'I hope, for your sake, you do.'

12

Hope had been prepared for the phone call, but not for how she would feel after it.

Now, sitting at her desk, she was unsettled and unable to concentrate. Ali was getting married in Spain, here, on Hope's doorstep.

She had been kept up to date with events via a series of dramatic text messages from Stephanie, and while she had been pleased to hear of Ali's engagement to Stuart and had phoned Ali to wish them every happiness, the news that the wedding was to be held in Marbella had come as a shock.

Not as much of a shock, though, as hearing the reception would be held on board Frank Farrelly's *Excalibur*, the most notorious yacht in the Med, let alone Puerto Banus. The press would be hanging around relentlessly, hoping for a salacious slant. Even Hope remembered the shots of the larger-than-life media tycoon, several years ago, frolicking on board with a party of girls who, unfortunately, did not include his wife. It had led to one of the most bitterly contested and expensive divorces in history.

Damn Ali. Of all the places in the world she could have chosen to have her wedding, why here? It would attract exactly the kind of attention Hope had spent her adult life trying to avoid. It would ruin everything. Standing up abruptly, she pushed her chair away from the desk and walked out to the terrace, where she lit a cigarette and tried to calm herself. Her mother and Stephanie were arriving in a few days and, it seemed, staying indefinitely, having taken a villa on the Golden Mile. 'So we can come and go as we need to,' her mother had said brightly.

Of course Hope was looking forward to seeing them, in a manner of speaking, but this was different. This was no ordinary visit. She wouldn't be able to escape when she felt claustrophobic. Family members would be camped very firmly on her doorstep, descending at will. Why, oh why, could she not have come from a normal family, like everyone else?

Hope adored her parents, but in the last few years she had found it increasingly difficult to be around them. She was well aware their marriage was not happy and did her best not to think about it. After all, it was their life and not hers. She had flown the coop several years ago and had her own dilemmas to deal with now. But with her mother sounding so fragile, almost brittle in her attempt at cheerfulness, Hope felt the familiar despair creeping up on her again. She couldn't help it. She would always feel responsible for them. It was ridiculous, she knew. Even after a spell in therapy while she lived in New York, she still blamed herself for them getting married in the first place. No matter how stupid she knew she was being in her head, her heart and her emotions told her it was all her fault.

Part of her felt sorry for them, trapped in a terminally dysfunctional loop, but another, increasingly insistent part was angry. While she was capable of empathising with their situation, Hope was, by nature, a confrontational person, too much so, she often acknowledged. But all the same, anyone sticking their head in the sand simply drove her nuts.

Unlike Ali, who positively thrived on drama, Hope craved peace and anonymity, sometimes solitude. Which was why living in La Virginia, working quietly on her book and her photography, suited her so well. In La Virginia, privacy was respected, yet you never felt alone. The little community was as closely knit as any family, but a respectful family, and that was why Hope loved it.

She went back inside and made a half-hearted attempt to work, then gave up. There was no point. A flea would have a better attention span than she did at present. Although it was only four o'clock, she decided to jump into her car and drive to the Paseo, where she would go for a leisurely walk and take some photographs. The light was perfect at this time of day, and the Paseo, the long walkway that stretched all the way from the Old Town to Puerto Banus, would be full of people walking dogs, cycling and roller-blading, while a stone's throw away on the beaches, the sun-worshippers caught the last, least harmful rays of the long hot day. If nothing else, she reckoned, it would take her mind off things.

Slinging her camera over her shoulder, she grabbed her shades and pulled on her favourite cowboy-style sun hat. She slipped her bare feet into well-worn espadrilles, went out and set off up the steep climb to the car park.

'Ali, darling! Come back to us, will you?' Rolf, the über-hot German photographer, looked out from behind the camera and smiled at her as he stood up to his knees in gently rolling surf. 'I know you've got a wedding to plan, darling, but can we put it on hold for now?'

'What? Oh, God, sorry Rolf. Let's go again. My fault.' Ali shook her head and forced herself to focus. Immediately the makeup and hair team waded in to rearrange the tousled surfed-up hair, add just another smidgeon of burnished bronze to her shoulders and cleavage and, yes, an artfully directed spray of sand to cling to the body oil applied earlier.

'Okay Ali, let's go. C'mon – nobody does it like you, baby.' Rolf grinned wickedly at her.

Automatically, Ali went into action, running through the lukewarm waves, surfboard clutched to her side, then coming out of the water, bending, twisting, kneeling in the sand provocatively, head thrown back, damp hair dripping down her back, anything Rolf demanded to get the mouth-watering shots that made swimwear companies the world over clamour for his services. In this case, the shoot was for *Fitness Illustrated*, the renowned sports magazine that featured a much-coveted yearly swimwear shoot. Neither the swimwear nor the featured model were easily forgotten.

'Great! Fantastic! Take a break, guys.' Rolf and his assistants went to check the film and Ali retired gratefully with the rest of the team to the makeshift hut erected for the shoot in the shade of the brushwood bordering the three miles of Coral Beach, so named because the sand was the palest pink. They had arrived the previous day, flying into Miami, and from there had taken a small plane to Eleuthera, one of the smaller islands, and then from there had made the five-minute boat trip to Harbour Island. Ali had smiled when she saw the old wooden sign nailed to the tree by the jetty that read, 'Welcome to Harbour Island, home of happy people!'

Now she flopped down in the shade and accepted a Diet Coke, which she sipped as the stylists fussed over the next array of bikinis, sarongs and surf gear.

Closing her eyes, she tried not to dwell on the last few days and her visit home. It had gone well, of course, and everybody had been thrilled for her and Stuart, but her parents . . . Ali wasn't comfortable about things. At least, she thought, she'd got through to Stephanie, who was unpredictable at the best of times, and being the baby of the family, was the most likely of them to say or do the wrong thing. But Hope . . . well, Hope was another matter altogether. Ali frowned. It wasn't that she and Hope didn't get on, just that they saw the world from completely different angles and dealt with it accordingly. And although Hope was far away from home, she seemed to wield even more influence over her parents than Ali could. Not that Hope ever took advantage of it, which irritated Ali: Hope should be making her opinions felt about the divorce, never mind the affair their father was conducting so blatantly. Ali scowled. He'd listen to Hope. He always did. Whatever anyone said, Ali knew deep down that her father adored Hope. She was his favourite even though Ali was the achiever in the family.

'OK, guys, back at the water in five!'

Ali sighed. It was only seven a.m.. The sun was up, the day was glorious, the beach looked heavenly, she had a fabulous wedding to look forward to. Why couldn't she relax and enjoy it all?

Babs was finishing her morning's work with the usual thorough inspection. The laundry and ironing had been done and the pile of freshly washed summer clothes had been stacked neatly in the hot press ready for packing. The house was as clean as a new pin, furniture gleaming and carpets hoovered within an inch of their lives. It was half past twelve and she was ready to set off home. Making sure that the alarm was switched on and everything else switched off, she pulled on her coat, ever mindful of the twenty-second slot she had to dash out and close the front door before the sirens were activated and a noise that would wake the dead was set off. She opened the door and was stopped in her tracks by a black flash that streaked past her and straight into the hall.

'Jesus, Mary and Joseph! What in the name of God—' she cried, steadying herself as the mad creature galloped about the hall as if it was a racetrack. Faster and faster he went, barking frantically, foam flying from his mouth as if he were a thoroughbred.

'Oh, Mother of God, my clean floor!' Babs stood back

helplessly as Toby ran in ever-decreasing circles until he collapsed, panting, in the middle of the hall, from where he eyed her balefully.

God help him, the creature looked done in, but any feelings of sympathy Babs had for him were rudely interrupted by an automated voice informing her that there was an intruder on the premises at level one and the alarm began to sound its siren.

Terrified by the high-pitched sound, Toby leaped to his feet and howled, scratching dementedly at the kitchen door in the hopes of escaping to his cosy bed.

This further confused Babs, who was desperately trying to remember how the damned remote-control gismo worked to turn the alarm off. She was still trying to turn it off when, a minute later, a squad car screeched to a halt outside the Armstrongs' front door and the nice policeman who came into the house found two individuals gripped in equal measures of trauma.

'I'm so sorry,' gasped Babs. 'I'm afraid you've been called out on a fool's errand. As you can see, it's a false alarm. I was all ready to leave the house when the dog dashed past me and I didn't turn off the alarm in time. I'm so sorry.'

'Ah, sure, don't worry about it,' said the guard. 'As long as everyone's all right?' He deactivated the alarm.

'Oh, we're fine, no trouble at all – at least none that can't be cleaned up.'

'We'll be off so.'

'Thank you again. You were very prompt in getting here, I'll give you that.'

'It's our job. Mind yourself now.' The big six-footer grinned at her, then made for the door. 'Nice dog you've got there. Sure you don't need an alarm at all with a hound like that to protect you.'

Babs followed the direction of his glance and saw Toby cowering under the hall table.

'He's just found his way home. He was lost, you see. I expect he's a bit upset by it all.' Babs wondered why she felt the need to defend him.

'Good luck.' The policeman waved, got into the squad car, and the driver sped away, spraying gravel.

Babs closed the front door and took off her coat. 'Come here, you big eejit of a dog! Where in the world have you been?' Left to themselves, Toby regained his sense of composure, emerged from under the hall table, trotted over to her and jumped up to cover her with big, eager licks. 'Get down out of that! Would you look at the state of you, dirt everywhere and scratched to bits. Come on into the kitchen with me 'til I make you respectable.'

In the kitchen, Babs found a cloth, ran it under the tap, wiped away the flecks of foam from Toby's mouth and scrubbed off the mud that had caked his hair. He had one or two nasty scratches, but nothing serious. She poured him a large bowl of water, which he lapped noisily, then opened the broom cupboard, retrieved his bed and set it beside the Aga, just as it used to be. Toby collapsed onto it gratefully and stretched out.

'I suppose I'd better give your mistress the good news, if you could call it that,' she said and dialled Carrie's mobile number.

Toby put his head on his paws, sighed deeply and waved his long feathered tail in response.

A week had passed since Toby's disappearance, and his unexpected homecoming was greeted with varying degrees of enthusiasm. Stephanie was ecstatic. She had rushed home the minute Carrie had rung her with the news, leaving a disgruntled lunch date staring moodily into his cappuccino.

Carrie, who had been more surprised than anything, was warmed by Stephanie's delight and smiled at the pair as Stephanie fed Toby some cooked sausages. Lately, Stephanie had been subdued and withdrawn, which was most unlike her. Carrie hoped the trip to Marbella and seeing Hope would lift her from the doldrums. Now that she had arranged it, she was looking forward to it too.

For the moment, though, reunited with her four-legged friend, Stephanie seemed more like her old self. She had decided to move home for the few days before they left for Spain. Her flatmate was more than happy to have their apartment to herself for a while, particularly since her sister would take over Stephanie's room for the time she would be away.

Babs, too, was pleased at Toby's return. She had become fond of him and his antics, even when he followed her around the house unless she shut him in the kitchen. Since he was back, he didn't like being left alone, so he trailed whoever was in the house like a shadow.

Rob was the only member of the household who wasn't happy about the reunion, but he was careful not to let it show. When he arrived home on the evening of Toby's return, after a tough day of negotiation with the bank, he could hardly believe his eyes when he saw the dog. Trotting out to the hall to greet the latest homecomer, Toby stopped in his tracks, put his head down and made for the kitchen, where he leaned against Stephanie and peered warily at Rob, who had followed him into the kitchen.

'Well, well, well,' said Rob, raising his eyebrow. 'I see the wanderer has returned.'

'I know,' said Stephanie, stroking Toby fondly. 'Isn't it brilliant? And he found his way home all on his own. Babs said he was in a dreadful state. She just opened the door and he ran straight in. He must have been waiting on the doorstep for hours, weren't you, pet?'

'Is that right?' said Rob, guardedly, aware of Carrie's amused expression as she sat beside Stephanie at the kitchen table, sipping a glass of water.

'We took him to the vet, of course, to make sure he was all right. He had some nasty cuts and scratches, but Mr Lavelle said he wasn't any the worse for it. Nothing that a bit of TLC wouldn't fix anyway. And you've got a lovely microchip now, haven't you, Toby? You'll never get lost again.'

'Speaking of going missing,' Rob ventured, 'what's the latest on the Marbella expedition?' He helped himself to a plate of chicken casserole, still bubbling on the Aga's hot plate.

'We're leaving on Tuesday. The villa's waiting, the flights are booked, and I got confirmation yesterday from a . . .' Carrie fished in her handbag and produced a piece of paper '. . . a Señor B'stardo – Jay put me in touch with him – that the church in the Orange Square is available. Father Logan was most helpful in organising the necessary release papers and so forth from this end. Honestly, I had no idea there was so much paperwork involved in getting married. Now all we need is Ali's birth certificate. I'll have a root through the files tonight.'

'Hope it's a decent villa you've got lined up.' Rob tucked into the casserole hungrily. 'Three months is a long time to spend somewhere that isn't up to scratch.'

Carrie smiled. 'Oh, it's perfect, right on the seafront, by the Marbella Club, and completely refurbished by Spain's most illustrious decorator, or so the agency said. It's owned by a Russian industrialist, can't remember the name. The photographs look wonderful and Jay's checked it out. She says it's the business. Six bedrooms, all *en suite* and separate staff accommodation. We'll be perfectly comfortable, won't we, Steph?'

'What about you, Dad?' Stephanie asked casually. 'When will you be coming down?'

'I'll let you get settled in first. Hopefully I'll manage ten days or so when things settle down a bit, and maybe a few weekends. Anyway, you girls will be having such fun you won't want me cramping your style.'

'At least you'll have Toby to keep you company,' Carrie said mischievously.

'What?' The look on Rob's face gave 'distaste' a new meaning. 'Christ, I'd forgotten about him.' He looked at the dog with loathing. 'Absolutely no way. He'll have to go into kennels. I'm not having that creature under the same roof as me.'

'Why do you hate him so much, Dad?' Stephanie was clearly upset.

'Relax, Rob,' Carrie said. 'I was winding you up. You needn't worry, he's coming with us.'

'What?'

'You heard Mum.' Stephanie's voice was accusing. 'He's coming with us. He's had his shots, he's got a pet passport and he's coming with us to Marbella. They actually *like* dogs in Spain, you know.'

'That is the most ridiculous idea I've ever heard. I think—'

'We've made the decision, Rob. Toby's coming with us. It's clearly not healthy for you two to be alone together. Kennels was an option, but seeing as the poor creature's only just been rescued from a dog shelter, it hardly seems fair to dump him back in care, and for such a long time. It would be cruel, by any standards.' Carrie looked at him contemptuously.

'I think the pair of you are off your bloody rockers – but as long as he's out of my way I couldn't care less. Mind you, now that he'll be lord of the manor at the villa, I dare say you won't be seeing as much of me as I'd anticipated.' Rob was livid.

'So, it'll be just like home then,' Stephanie quipped.

'Whatever,' Carrie said lightly. 'As long as you turn up to

give the bride away, I'm sure, as you quite rightly pointed out a minute ago, we'll all be having too much fun to notice.'

'Well, that's *very* nice – very nice indeed. I might remind you that I'm paying for this bloody carry-on and I think I'm entitled to a little respect in my own home. And I don't like your tone Stephanie, I don't like it at all.' Rob glared at them.

'Let's not go down the reminding route, Rob. I don't think there's anything to be gained from that at the moment, do you?' Carrie asked coolly.

'What I think,' said Rob, getting up from the table, 'doesn't seem to enter into this conversation, so let's quit while we're ahead. I'll be in the library,' he said, 'some of us have work to do.'

'What's the matter with him?' Stephanie asked when he'd gone.

'Don't mind him,' said Carrie, grinning at her worried-looking daughter. 'He just can't stand having his cage rattled, and it's been rattled quite a bit lately. I did warn you that Toby would be a problem.'

'Why does he hate him so much?'

'Your father is terrified – no, make that *petrified* – of dogs. All dogs. Big ones. Small ones. Anything with four legs and a bark reduces him to jelly.'

'So that's why we were never allowed one when we were little.' Stephanie frowned. 'Why's he so scared of them? I can't say I'd ever noticed it.'

'That's because, if you think about it, you've never seen your father around a dog until now, have you?'

'Now that you mention it, no, I guess not.'

'There you are. Let's just say he usually goes out of his way to avoid them. He was bitten, in a rather unceremonious fashion I understand, when he was little more than a baby.'

'What happened?' Stephanie was intrigued.

'Well, you know what toddlers are like, into absolutely

everything. Anyway, Granny Armstrong, bless her, was feeding the dog they had at the time. She put the bowl of food on the ground, turned her back to see to something in the kitchen and the next thing she knew the dog had taken a chunk out of your father's bottom. Not a serious wound, obviously, but let's just say it made an impression.'

'I can't believe he's never told us that. How hilarious.'

'Stephanie,' Carrie said, 'Dad has never even told *me* that story. Granny Armstrong did, and she advised me never to let him know that I knew. And if you've any sense, neither will you, however tempting it may be. It's a sore point.' Carrie chuckled. 'But I know it's true. I've seen the scar, barely visible, but it's there – exactly where Granny said it would be.'

'Too much information, Mum.' Stephanie wrinkled her nose and held up her hand to stop Carrie divulging any more details. 'I think I'll take Toby out for a walk. See you later.'

'See you.' Carrie gathered up the last of the plates to put into the dishwasher.

Too much information. Yes, she supposed it was. That was the trouble. At the moment, her whole life seemed to be about too much information. She walked quickly out of the kitchen and paused briefly outside the library door. She almost turned the handle, then thought better of it and went upstairs to run a bath.

How had it come to this? The familiar sinking feeling overcame her again as she undressed. How could you know every shade and nuance of a person, live with them, love them, then find yourself unable to be alone in the same room with them?

For a moment, a wave of sadness threatened, then she pulled herself together. She wouldn't get sentimental – and that was all it was. Sentimentality. In a few days she would be in Marbella, with two of her beautiful daughters and a wedding to arrange for the other. How fantastic was that?

And there was no way she'd let Rob and his antics spoil it for her. Those days were over, she told herself firmly.

Feeling surprisingly better, Carrie lit her favourite aromatherapy candle and lowered herself into the foaming water.

Downstairs, on the other side of the library door, Rob was scowling. He couldn't believe the bloody dog had found its way back. Of all the bad luck! Still, at least Carrie was off to Marbella in a few days. That meant more blissful time to spend with Olwen – although he'd have to be careful. His heart lifted. He wished he had the energy to go out now, but he was too tired. He would send her a text anyway, he thought reaching for his phone. 'Thinking of you, my darling, and wishing I was with you x.'

13

The first thing that caught Carrie and Steph's attention when they reached the arrivals hall in Málaga airport was a sign that read Armstrong.

'Look,' said Stephanie, accompanied by a prancing Toby, who was clearly ecstatic to be reunited with his mistresses after the short and, thankfully, uneventful flight. Behind them, Carrie pushed a trolley piled high with their luggage.

'Look, Mum,' Stephanie said again and pointed at the sign. 'That must be for us. Get a load of your man!' she giggled.

Carrie followed her gaze. Lounging against the gate of the arrivals hall, she saw a dark man of slender build and average height, dressed from head to toe in white. A fitted shirt revealed an expanse of gleaming olive skin to well below mid-chest. It was tucked seamlessly into hip-hugging tailored trousers, beneath which peeped a pair of white leather boots with two-inch Cuban heels. His raven black hair was heavily oiled and slicked back in a glistening coiffure that culminated in what could only be described as a duck's tail. It flicked up and out at the nape of his neck, around which hung three heavy gold chains. From behind his dark glasses, he gazed impatiently into the crowd.

'I thought we were getting a taxi,' whispered Stephanie. 'What's with the South American soap star?'

'We were,' said Carrie, trying not to laugh. 'At least, that's what I told Hope when she said she had to fly to

Madrid for the day. She said she'd meet us later at the villa. I told her not to bother about a car, that we'd make our own way.' They were approaching the apparition in white, who was looking at Stephanie appreciatively and Toby dubiously.

Carrie began uncertainly, 'Er, hello, I'm Carrie Armstrong, and this is my daughter, Stephanie. We weren't expecting to be met. Are you here for us?'

The man discarded the sign, stood to attention, clicked his heels and gave a short bow, baring a set of crowned teeth as he introduced himself. 'Allow me to present myself, Señora, Señorita. Enrique B'stardo, at your service.' He removed his shades and smiled broadly. 'Señora Jay tell me you arrive today, and I insist myself on meeting you at airport and driving you to villa. We will be spending a lot of time together, no, discussing wedding arrangements? I say the sooner we meet the better, yes?'

'Of course.' Carrie recovered herself quickly. 'Señor B'stardo, the wedding planner.' She frowned at Stephanie, who was staring at him, fascinated. 'How very kind of you. We had planned to get a taxi and now this will save us the trouble.'

'He is with you?' Enrique's smile faltered a fraction as he inclined his head towards Toby, who was panting in the heat.

'I'm afraid so,' Carrie smiled apologetically. 'But if it's a problem, we can—'

'Ees no problem. I have big car, many peoples fit in it. But Señora Jay, she no say you have dog accompaniment.'

'Oh, I see,' said Carrie, in the absence of a more suitable reply. Stephanie tried and failed to stifle a snort of laughter, which she followed with a cough as her mother shot her a look.

'Please,' said Enrique, taking the trolley, 'follow me.'

Outside, Carrie, Stephanie and Toby blinked in the noonday light and Enrique led them to a people-carrier parked close to the terminal.

'He is clean, yes?' Enrique nodded hopefully at Toby as he went to stow the luggage in the back of the car.

'Oh, yes, and sober,' Stephanie giggled.

'Excuse me?' Enrique looked bewildered.

'Yes, he's very clean,' said Carrie, poking Stephanie reprovingly as they clambered aboard and slid the door shut.

Behind the wheel, Enrique kept up a steady stream of chatter, mostly about himself, interspersed with the odd colloquial expletive directed at the many drivers he clearly felt to be incompetent.

During the thirty-minute drive along the seafront, Carrie and Stephanie learned of his bullfighting fame, his property business, his renowned soirées and other social functions.

'Goodness, what a very busy man you are, Mr B'stardo,' Stephanie said in the innocent tone that Carrie recognised all too well. 'How do you manage to organise weddings on top of all your other business interests?'

He smiled at her in the rear-view mirror. 'I have a finger in – how you say? Many puddings?'

'Pies,' corrected Stephanie.

'Ah, yes, of course.' He sighed. 'My English is not as good as it was at one time. I studied in Oxford town, you know, as a young student.' This was not altogether true, but Enrique had supplemented his school classes with Oxford English language tapes, so he saw no harm in embellishing the truth a little.

'Of course, I visit Dublin too, where you are from, very beautiful city . . . I think.' This in part was true. As a young man, Enrique had spent a wild weekend in Dublin, of which he remembered not a lot, except a series of smoky basement 'niteclubs' and girls who had enjoyed his practised dance routine. Stolen from the choreographed scene performed by John Travolta in *Saturday Night Fever*, it had gone down a treat. And so had more than one of the girls, as he recalled.

He had developed a strong liking for the Irish and their newfound wealth. Especially since so many were spending it prolifically, and wisely in his opinion, purchasing property on the Costa.

'Oh, look,' said Carrie. 'There's the Marbella Club. We must be almost there.'

Sure enough, just past the club, Enrique pulled off the main road onto a lane that led towards the sea. He stopped in front of a set of imposing electric gates and punched a code into the security panel. Slowly the gates slid open. He drove through and parked in front of an exquisite villa built in a simple yet ultra-modern style.

'Wow,' breathed Stephanie. 'This is cool, Mum. The pictures on the net didn't do it justice at all.'

'No,' agreed Carrie, pleasantly surprised. 'They certainly didn't.'

'Come.' Enrique began to unload the car. 'I show you around.'

Half an hour later, Carrie and Stephanie breathed a sigh of relief as Enrique departed, having arranged to meet them later in the week to discuss the wedding.

The house was, quite simply, beautiful. The bedrooms were on the lower level, generously proportioned and decorated in cool neutrals. All had *en suite* bathrooms featuring wet rooms and stunning individually designed baths.

Upstairs, there was a cleverly designated open living area, surrounded with mostly glass walls that allowed for the wonderful sea views and landscaped gardens to blend with the interior. Four huge sofas were sunk into a sitting space, three steps down, in front of a vast marble fireplace, presumably for use in winter. In each room, including the kitchen, there was a flat-screen TV, even though there was also a separate TV room, which resembled a small cinema.

'That's neat,' said Stephanie, flicking quickly through a confusion of channels. 'Look, we even get RTÉ,' she grinned. 'Now I won't have to miss *Fair City*.'

Outside, a marble patio was strewn with designer sunloungers, tables, chairs and a built-in barbecue. Beyond, on a lower level, seemingly carved into the horizon, the pool shimmered in the sunlight, its multi-toned blue mosaic tiling turning the water a hundred shades of aquamarine as it stretched to infinity.

'How about a swim, Mum?' Stephanie suggested.

'Good idea.' She followed Stephanie outside. 'We can wash off the journey, then have some lunch outside. How's that for a plan?'

On Jay's instructions, their fridge had been thoughtfully stocked with every conceivable luxury, including champagne and local wines, while a magnificent arrangement of exotic blooms held centre-stage in the hall.

'And champagne,' Stephanie called as she went off to change into one of her many bikinis. 'We have to drink a toast to our holiday or the wedding plans, or whatever.'

'Coming up,' Carrie called back, suddenly feeling lighter, now they were finally here.

Later, after a glorious swim and a light lunch, Carrie reclined on a remarkably comfortable sunbed with a glass of champagne and a new novel by her current favourite author. She glanced at her daughter, who, lying on her tummy, was fast asleep, a floppy sunhat perched on the back of her head, and an adoring dog resting his head on the small of her back. Looking at Stephanie, one arm curled under her chin, the other draped over the cushioned sunbed, Carrie had a vivid recollection of how she had looked as a baby, sleeping in just that very same position. She felt a sudden rush of love, and something else . . . a profound gratitude for her three beautiful daughters, her finest and, without doubt, most worthwhile achievement. Settling down to her book, she felt more at peace than she had in months. She was going to enjoy this special time with her girls, and whatever Rob did or didn't do, she wouldn't let him spoil one precious minute of it. In fact, she wouldn't even think of him at all, if she could avoid it.

As if in agreement, Toby walked over to her and nudged her hand. He stretched luxuriously, then collapsed onto the cool floor beside her and fell asleep.

'Carrie, you will come over this evening, won't you?' Jay pleaded. 'I'm dying to see you. Bring the girls, of course.'

'Oh, Jay, we can't tonight. We're a bit done in, to be honest, and I promised Hope a quiet evening – she's been in Madrid, so she'll be tired when she gets back, and we haven't seen her for such a long time. You don't mind, do you? You've been so good, having everything ready for us, and those lovely flowers . . .'

'Oh, nonsense,' Jay said. 'I suppose as it's your first night I should leave you alone, I'm just dying to catch up, that's all.'

'Me too, Jay, really. It's just—'

'It's all right,' Jay grinned. 'You know I'm impossible to insult. No umbrage taken. Lunch on Friday, then, at the Marbella Club – and I won't take no for an answer.'

'That would be lovely.'

'You met B'stardo, I take it? He's quite something, isn't he?' Jay chuckled.

'Well, yes, he certainly has a style all of his own.'

'Don't let that put you off. His dress sense is ridiculous, but take it from me, when it comes to functions that man is out on his own. My interior designer from Seville recommended him, and he knows absolutely everybody. He's still quite famous here from his bullfighting days and he's been very helpful to Frank, with his property thingy – knew all the right local palms to oil. Frank said he couldn't have managed without him.'

'He sounds quite a character, but as long as he does a good job with the wedding, that's all I care about. Ali, I'm afraid, can be very demanding, and she moves in such glamorous circles these days. Actually, the whole thing's beginning to intimidate me, if I'm honest.'

'Not a bit of it!' Jay said briskly. 'It'll be fabulous. Enrique B'stardo could handle a dozen supermodels and their demands with his eyes closed.'

'I hope you're right, Jay,' Carrie said, laughing.

'Of course I'm right. Aren't I always? See you on Friday. We'll talk about it all then.'

The walk before dinner had been a good idea, thought Carrie, linking Hope's arm as they strolled along the Paseo, watching the sun go down. Stephanie was ahead, revelling in the admiring glances Toby was getting from passers-by. It was true: the Spanish really did like dogs. For his part, Toby seemed to be adapting to his new home well. He loved the heat and trotted happily alongside Stephanie, his eyes fixed on the distance.

Glancing at Hope, Carrie was reminded of how like her father she looked. It always took her by surprise. Probably, she acknowledged, because they were so unalike in every other way.

'So how are you, sweetheart, really?' Carrie took in the beginnings of fine lines round the beautiful dark eyes, and although Hope was tanned, she thought she was a little pale and drawn. 'I hope you're not working too hard on that book of yours. You do push yourself awfully hard.'

'Of course I'm not, but deadlines are a necessary evil. Stressful but effective. Without them, I don't think I'd ever finish a book.'

'I worry about you out here, working away on your own.' Carrie frowned. 'Doesn't it get lonely?'

'Sometimes,' Hope smiled, 'but in La Virginia you couldn't possibly be lonely for long.'

'I do wish you'd come home, Hope. Won't you even consider it after you've finished this book?' Carrie had sworn she wouldn't ask the dreaded question, but she couldn't help herself.

'To meet a nice Irish guy and settle down?'

'Something like that. It wouldn't be the worst thing that could happen, would it? I mean, you'd like to get married and have a family of your own sometime, wouldn't you, Hope?'

There was an awkward silence during which Carrie inwardly acknowledged that her own marriage hadn't turned out that well. Hope, of course, was too kind to say so, although she could read Carrie like an open book. It wasn't the first time Carrie had felt the wash of guilt that maybe she wasn't the only one who had been harmed by her clearly dysfunctional relationship.

'"Sometime" is the operative expression, Mum,' Hope said, grinning. 'At least you're offloading one of us – one bride at a time and all that. Wait up, for a moment, I want to take a shot of you.' She called Stephanie back to join them.

The evening light was perfect, and Hope clicked away, moving expertly round her subjects, taking shots from all angles. 'There, that should do it. I think I've got some nice ones.'

'Good. Let's go back,' said Stephanie, 'I'm starving now. Must be all that fresh air.'

'Excuse me?' Nobody noticed the tall figure approaching them. 'Forgive me intruding on your photographic session,' the man spoke in clipped, cultured tones, with the merest hint of an accent, 'but I couldn't help noticing your dog. May I have a closer look at him?'

'Of course,' Stephanie beamed, delighted that someone as elegant as this man had spotted Toby's beauty. 'His name's Toby.'

'He really is a beauty, quite young too, if I'm not mistaken.' He looked to Stephanie for confirmation.

'The vet thought eight to ten months.'

'He thought?' The man seemed surprised.

'Well, we only got him about a month ago. He was in a dogs' home until then. He's a greyhound cross,' she explained, 'or a lurcher, as we call them.'

'Well, young lady,' the stranger continued, 'your Toby here is no greyhound, crossed or otherwise.'

'He's not?'

'Most certainly not. He's the finest Saluki I've seen in quite some time.'

'Saluki?' Stephanie and Carrie echoed.

'Yes.' The man stroked Toby, who was enjoying the attention. 'Salukis are the original Arabian desert hounds. Years ago, I used to breed them myself. Of course, the smooth-haired ones such as Toby are more unusual, but the feathered tail's a giveaway. That, and the feathers between his toes – see?' He held up Toby's paw, who gave it willingly. 'His colouring, too, is pretty much perfect. As I say, you have a very fine dog there.' The stranger smiled again at their bemusement. 'Allow me to introduce myself.' He held out a hand to Carrie, who was caught suddenly in his piercing dark gaze. 'Emilio is my name, Emilio de Alba. I must apologise again for the intrusion.'

'Not at all,' said Carrie, 'I'm Carrie Armstrong, and these are my daughters, Hope and Stephanie.' Stephanie grinned, but Hope was engrossed in a shot of something out to sea.

'It's a pleasure,' he continued, 'to see a beautiful dog with a beautiful family. I hope we meet again. Goodbye.'

'Goodbye,' murmured Carrie to his retreating back.

'Well, what do you make of that?' Stephanie was as pleased as Punch. 'See? I knew you were special, Toby! I just *knew* it! Greyhound, indeed!' She laughed. 'I'm going to look up all about Salukis the minute we get back.'

'At least wait until after dinner, Steph. After all, you're cooking, aren't you? Or did you actually learn anything on that course in London?'

'I will not only have met but exceeded all your culinary expectations by the end of this holiday, Mum, I promise. But wasn't that amazing? If he's right, that is. And wasn't he such a nice man?'

'Yes, he was,' agreed Carrie. *Very* nice, she thought, and astonishingly handsome.

Enrique sat back in the Riva as it roared out of the harbour towards *Excalibur*. One of the crew was ferrying him out to the yacht at his request to check on a few things. Enrique loved riding in the Riva. The beautiful Italian power-boat drew envious, admiring glances from men and women alike and, of course, they presumed it belonged to him. Mind you, Rudi would have frowned at him hitching a lift so sneakily if he'd known about it. He was meticulous – bordering on obsessive in Enrique's opinion – about cost control. Honestly, you'd think he was footing the bills himself, not the obscenely rich Frank Farrelly, his boss.

Anyway, thought Enrique, no need for Rudi to know anything about it. He had checked earlier and learned from

Lola, Rudi's charming current companion, that she was
meeting him for coffee in the Old Town, which meant Enrique
could potter around *Excalibur* to his heart's content – for an
hour or so, at any rate – without Rudi dogging his every step
and glowering at him. A man like Rudi would never understand the minute details that were crucial to making a wedding
perfect. And perfection, no less, was what Enrique B'stardo
guaranteed. Mind you, he was being well paid for it, thanks
to Señora Jay. She was a tough woman to deal with, Enrique
smiled, but an appreciative one, at least. Enrique couldn't
understand why her husband bothered with a silly tart, but
rich men were all the same. Always greedy for flattery and
fake adoration. Give him a woman like Jay any day – a strong,
clever woman. He was glad he had been able to help her.
And why should a rich woman, who took care of herself so
well, be denied the pleasure of a lover? And if Señora Jay
preferred her men on the young side, that was her choice.
As he had said to her, impressing her with his use of the
English language, 'What's sauce for the goose is sauce for
the turkey, no?'

She had laughed and agreed wholeheartedly. Enrique had
known exactly the young man to send her way, and he, by
all accounts, was keeping Señora Jay very happy indeed.
Enrique was not so happy about the cocaine. Better not to
get involved with those people. He left that to a contact of
his. All he had had to do was put them in touch with each
other. And now Señora Jay was happy. Happy and grateful.
He had been richly rewarded.

Pulling up alongside *Excalibur*, Enrique patted his hair
before he climbed on board. He'd have a good look round,
take a few shots and choose which decks would be best for
which element of the reception. That, and carry out Señora
Jay's instructions, of course.

★   ★   ★

At one o'clock on Friday, anyone who was *anyone* on the Costa would be lunching at the Marbella Club. Not in the MC Grill, although that was acceptable in winter, but as soon as one could sit outside, the exclusive poolside buffet lunch held forth. Here, perched on their privileged vantage point overlooking the deep blue of the Mediterranean, sleek, oiled sun-worshippers draped themselves on loungers watching the action from behind designer shades, and diners sat at strategically placed circular tables shaded by large yellow and white parasols. It was very glamorous.

Looking every inch the part, Jay sat at a table sipping a champagne cocktail. A bottle of Veuve Clicquot – Jay didn't believe in the cheaper but just as lovely local Cava – stood chilling in a bucket beside her, ready for when the girls arrived. For now, as she was a little early, the cocktail was a nice pick-me-up. Today, the temperature was in the early seventies, pleasantly warm and not too hot. The weather was still unsettled – before Carrie had come down, they'd had ten days of heavy rain. Jay shuddered at the memory.

She looked about her, indulging in one of her favourite pastimes: people-watching. A couple sunbathing, holding hands across their loungers, the girl sporting a generous solitaire diamond and a wedding band she admired regularly, oblivious to the fact that she was turning a dangerous shade of pink. Honeymooners, Jay decided. Beyond them, a beautiful bronzed girl, long-limbed, wearing only a gold thong bikini bottom, was oiling her breasts while her considerably older companion looked up from the book he had been engrossed in and leaned in lasciviously to murmur in her ear. Model-mistress-hooker material, for sure, Jay deduced. She'd bet marriage wasn't the nature of *that* particular partnership.

A couple of businessmen, Spaniards, sat in crisp, short-sleeved shirts and spoke urgently to each other and into their phones. She recognised a few regulars, most of whom, like her, had second homes in the town, at their usual tables. Waiters moved about efficiently and discreetly as the diners took their seats.

As soon as Carrie and the girls walked in, she spotted them and waved. They walked down the long flight of steps past the gushing waterfall that flowed down the wall into the swimming pool and made for her table, smiling.

What a good-looking pair those girls are, Jay thought. Hope, whom she hadn't seen for at least two years, was taller than she remembered, and had a natural elegance that was already attracting interested glances. Her hair was tied back and the slouchy combat trousers she wore with a simple white cut-off vest showed off her toned arms and enviably flat stomach.

Stephanie, not as tall as either of her sisters or, arguably, as beautiful, had a sweet little heart-shaped face, a slightly turned-up nose and huge blue eyes that dominated her face and were always heavily mascarad. Her hair was a mass of wild copper curls. The red sundress she had on made her look about sixteen.

Carrie, looking relaxed and tanned, was clearly the better for her a week away. In loosely cut linen trousers and a white halter-neck top, she looked, Jay noticed with a start, very well indeed. Her face had lost the pinched and haunted look that Jay had despaired about the last time she had seen her in Dublin and no make-up or beauty treatment could have erased it. That had to come from within.

Jay beamed as they reached her. It had been a great idea to get Carrie to come to Marbella, spend some time away from Rob – or, more to the point, and even more destructive, as Jay knew all too well – away from a constantly *absent* Rob.

'Hi you three,' Jay got up to kiss them. 'Who's for champagne?'

'Not for me, thanks,' Hope said. 'I have to work later and I won't do a thing if I start on the bubbly.'

'Not even one?' Jay was slightly annoyed. She hated anyone to put a dampener on any of her gatherings and not to have one teeny glass was really very boring. She'd forgotten how uptight Hope could be. She should relax more, go with the flow. She'd never get a man with an attitude like that.

'No, thanks.' Hope smiled but she was firm. 'You forget, you guys are on holiday, and that's great, but for me it's business as usual. I never drink at lunchtime – at least not when I'm working.'

'Don't worry, Jay,' Stephanie interjected. 'I'll drink enough for both of us!'

'Good girl,' said Jay, and filled her glass, then Carrie's. 'Here's to what will be the most talked-about, fabulous, on-the-cover-of-every-magazine wedding of the decade.' She raised her glass.

'To the wedding,' said Carrie and Stephanie. Hope looked a bit strained, Jay thought. Perhaps she wasn't so happy that her younger sister was getting married before her – and with such a splash. It was understandable, really.

'Now, tell me all the news,' Jay said, gazing fondly at the girls. She would have loved to have daughters of her own – so much fun to gossip with. 'Ali can't possibly be the only one with a gorgeous man in her life?'

'Count me out.' Steph wrinkled her nose. 'I'm off men big time.'

'Oh, that won't last long, sweetie,' Jay laughed. 'Besides, you have tons of time to meet Mister Right. What about you, Hope? Anyone special in your life?'

'No,' Hope replied, 'not at the moment, but I'm too busy

right now even to think of a relationship.' How she hated that kind of question, and Jay was so forthright in asking them, not indirectly either. Hope knew she meant well and that she was probably being over-sensitive as usual, but any kind of scrutiny of her love life or lack of one always made her deeply uncomfortable. Even Oscar was on her case these days, she reflected wryly.

Lunch followed briskly on the champagne, and was excellent. To start, the girls ordered gazpacho while Jay and Carrie opted for prawns and afterwards everyone helped themselves from the groaning buffet tables.

'Now, I've been thinking, Carrie,' Jay said. 'We need to go out to *Excalibur*. How are you fixed early next week? What about Monday, if I can arrange it?'

'Great. Whenever suits you.' Carrie nodded eagerly.

'And Hope, maybe you could come too. Not many people have been allowed take photographs on *Excalibur*, but I'm sure I can wangle something. It might make an interesting setting for you, and we'll need to take some shots to consider decorating angles – if you're not too busy, of course.'

'Of course not. I'd love to see *Excalibur*.' Hope sounded more enthusiastic than she felt.

'Good—'

Jay was cut off by a splash and turned to see a man execute a powerful front crawl up and down the pool. He did ten or twelve laps, then pushed himself up on the end of the poolside and effortlessly hauled himself out, wrapping a towel round his waist, which drew attention to his broad shoulders and long, well muscled legs. He slicked back his plentiful, if slightly receding hair and walked back to his sun lounger.

'Do you know who that is?' she whispered excitedly.

'No?' Carrie could only see the man's back as he leaned down to fold the backgammon set on the table beside him.

'That,' said Jay, 'is the Marques de Alba, Cordoba y Rincón.

He's a real aristocrat. One of Spain's oldest titles.' She spoke in a hushed voice. 'Isn't he divine? He's fifty-seven, and still looks like a movie star. Every woman in Europe has been after him at some time or other. Apparently his wife died years ago and he's never remarried. He's meant to be worth a fortune but, of course, money doesn't matter to the aristocracy.' Jay failed to see the irony of her comment.

'Of course not.' Carrie stifled a smile.

'Bet it does if they don't have any,' quipped Stephanie.

'Oh, I don't mean like that,' Jay said quickly. 'Of course they all *have* it, family trusts and so forth, land and, well, *things*. They just think it's vulgar to talk about it.'

'It is,' Hope pointed out.

Seeing as the course of the conversation had initiated with her, Jay, she could hardly disagree with Hope, although she didn't like her tone. There was definitely something disrespectful about that girl.

By now, the *marques* had gathered up his backgammon set and was wearing his shades and a white towelling robe. As he passed by their table, he stopped suddenly and looked quizzically at Carrie, then the girls.

'It is . . .' he paused for a fraction, frowning, then smiled broadly. 'Carrie, is it not? I almost didn't recognise you without your dog.'

Jay, whose mouth had dropped open, took a quick gulp of champagne, before rearranging her features into an expression of polite interest.

'Oh, of course,' Carrie smiled with pleasure as she recognised the handsome stranger who had taken such an interest in Toby. She wracked her brains frantically to remember, and thankfully the name came to her. 'Emilio.' Carrie held out her hand. Emilio took it in his own and bent over it, not quite kissing it, in a most elegant gesture that made her feel rather shy and awkward. 'And you remember my daughters, Hope and Stephanie?' she said.

The girls smiled and said hello.

'How could I not, such a beautiful family will always make an impression.' At this point Jay gave Carrie's ankle a sharp kick under the table, which brought her back to reality and Jay's pointedly expectant expression. 'This is my friend, also from Ireland, Jay Farrelly.'

Jay held out her hand and smiled up at him as he shook it in what she felt unfairly to be a most ordinary and less intimate fashion than he had exhibited to Carrie. 'Emilio,' he said, 'delighted to meet you.'

'We met Emilio while we were walking Toby. Actually, it was the day we arrived, wasn't it?' Carrie explained.

'Yes, indeed. Several days ago, certainly,' Emilio confirmed. 'By the way, where is the beautiful creature?' The way his resonant voice rolled over the words made Jay's legs turn to jelly. God, the man was divine – and titled!

'He's safely at home. He loves the heat – he's probably sitting in the sun as we speak,' Stephanie laughed. 'Although I made sure to put sunblock on his nose. I've been studying Salukis on the Internet since you told me what he is. You were so right. He shows every character-istic to a T.'

'They are beautiful animals, with a fascinating history. As I mentioned, I used to breed them many years ago on my *estancia*. I have a friend who still keeps a few. Perhaps, if you are here for a while, we might take a day trip and see them. You could bring Toby too, of course.'

'Oh,' breathed Stephanie, her eyes widening. 'That would be lovely.'

'That's very kind of you, Emilio.' Carrie winced as another kick found her shin. She glared at Jay, who was mouthing 'dinner'.

Stephanie had picked up on it, though, and before her mother had a chance to speak, she said, 'Why don't you come and have dinner with us and we can arrange something? Then you can see Toby again.'

'What a good idea!' beamed Jay. 'What about next week? You're not doing anything, are you, Carrie? And neither am I,' she added, deftly including herself in the invitation.

'Well, no, but—'

'I couldn't possibly intrude upon your holiday in such a fashion,' Emilio said diplomatically.

'You wouldn't be,' Stephanie insisted, 'would he, Mum? And it's not a holiday as such. We're here for three months to organise a wedding.' She rolled her eyes.

'A wedding?' Emilio raised an eyebrow. 'Are congratulations in order?'

'The bride-to-be is not with us,' Carrie told him. 'She'll be joining us nearer the time. My middle daughter,' she explained. 'And Stephanie's right, you wouldn't be intruding. We'd love to have you. Er, where can we contact you?'

'Here, at my villa in the club. Ordinarily I would give you my card, but—' He smiled ruefully and gestured to his attire or, rather, lack of it. 'They will find me for you if you telephone the main reception.'

'Well, I'll give you a ring then.'

'I shall look forward to it.' Emilio bowed imperceptibly and continued on his way.

'Well, I don't believe it!' Jay shook her head and let out a low whistle. 'You sly old thing, Carrie Armstrong.' She was only half joking. 'Not here a wet week and already you've wangled an introduction to the most eligible bachelor in Spain. I wouldn't believe it if I hadn't seen it with my own eyes. And not a word of it, not a single *word*, to your best friend.'

'Wangled an introduction? Don't be ridiculous, Jay. I had no idea who he was – none of us had. The girls can vouch for me.' Carrie seemed hurt. 'Anyway, *you're* the one who issued the dinner invitation – or as good as. And what on earth are we going to cook for him?' She was beginning to panic.

'Oh, don't get your knickers in a twist.' Jay's feathers were still ruffled. 'And don't pretend you're not thrilled to have him coming to dinner. Anyway, I'll be there too, so I can help break the ice. It's not as if you'll be on your own.'

Not if you have anything to do with it, thought Hope. She had watched the exchange with interest.

'It's true, though,' Stephanie was clearly enjoying the drama. 'Mum didn't know who he was, this count or whatever.'

'*Marques*,' corrected Jay.

'Well, *marques*, then. He was admiring our dog. We were mistakenly told he was a lurcher but Emilio put us straight. He said Toby was a Saluki, a genuine Arabian desert hound, revered in the dog world.'

'I'm sure,' said Jay dryly.

'Anyway, Mum, you won't have to worry about what to cook,' Stephanie continued, 'cos I'll do the catering. It'll be my first real dinner party – in the professional sense anyway.'

'Well, I don't know.' Carrie didn't like to sound ungrateful, but to be honest she hadn't seen much evidence apart from a very impressive-looking certificate from the cookery course in London where Stephanie had spent the last three months.

'Are you mad?' Jay was horrified. 'That man holds an ancient title. He—'

'Exactly, Jay,' Carrie cut across her, seeing the hurt look on Stephanie's face. 'He's just a man, whatever his title is.' She smiled at her daughter. 'That would be great if you'd do the food, as long as you're sure . . .'

'I wouldn't offer, Mum, if I thought I might let you down. I just want a chance to show off, that's all. So you can concentrate on dolling yourself up!'

'Stephanie!'

'Don't sound so shocked. It's perfectly obvious he fancies you – and he is kind of handsome, I suppose, for a wrinkly.'

Carrie laughed. 'He's not that much older than your father, and I don't think he'd be pleased to hear you calling him a wrinkly.'

'Well, at least he's a dog lover.'

'What did you think of him, Hope?' Carrie turned to her enquiringly.

'I thought he was perfectly charming.' Hope smiled at her mother. 'And I think it's great he's coming to dinner.'

'Well, thank God for that,' said Jay and gestured for the bill. If Hope had said anything negative, she wouldn't have put it past Carrie to change her mind and bottle out of the whole dinner altogether. She took what her girls said far too much to heart, in Jay's opinion. Maybe having daughters wasn't as much fun as it was cracked up to be after all. They appeared to take far too much interest in their parents' social lives, as far as Jay could make out. Boys were much easier in that respect. Anyway, disaster had been averted. She had been introduced to the most sought-after bachelor on any socialite's guest list – even if it had been in a most unexpected fashion. Emilio, Marques de Alba, Cordoba y Rincón really was a most exceptionally handsome man. He'd make an impressive addition to one of her gatherings. It would give the gossip-mongers something to chew over in Marbella *and* at home. Indeed, it would give Frank something to think about. There was no need for anyone to know he was thirty-odd years too old for *her* taste. Which reminds me, she thought happily, signing the credit-card slip. She'd better get a move on. She had an appointment to rush back to, and she certainly didn't want to keep the person in question waiting. Young people were *so* impatient.

★   ★   ★

Babs listened to the relentless drumming of the rain that had continued for three days on the trot and hoped they were having better weather in Spain. Well, it couldn't be any worse, that was for sure. She had been soaked this morning on her journey to the Armstrongs' house.

Now, safe from the elements, she went about her duties as usual in the big empty house. It was ridiculous, she thought, coming in every day when the place was immaculate, but dust settled the second you turned your back, and a house needed to be kept aired. And there was Rob. Naturally she had assured Carrie she would keep everything shipshape in her absence, leave dinner for him when required, and launder his shirts the way he liked them. No problem about that. It was just that during the last week or two, since Carrie and Stephanie had left for Spain, Rob hadn't spent more than a night or two at home. She knew he wasn't away on business because he had picked up his shirts and dropped off his daily laundry. So he was in the country. Besides, he'd have let her know if he was away. He had even left the odd note for her and, once or twice, their paths had crossed of a morning when he had rushed in or out while she was there. But that had been during the day. Whatever he was doing, he certainly wasn't spending his nights at home. Babs pursed her lips. It was none of her business. Mr Armstrong was her employer, a very generous one at that, and Carrie hadn't asked her any awkward or leading questions on the phone when she'd rung to check on things, so Babs didn't have to lie or compromise herself in any way. Not that she would have. She was a straight talker, Babs, had been all her life. But she would have hated to upset or worry Carrie in any way. Whatever was going on, Babs reminded herself, it was absolutely none of her affair.

She fixed her mind on happier thoughts as she went into

Ali's old bedroom to give it a hoover. They wouldn't feel 'til the wedding was upon them. She was going, of course. She wouldn't miss it for the world. And Carrie had been pressing her to come down a week or two beforehand for a proper holiday with them. At first Babs had said no. She didn't want to be in the way, on top of them while all the social palaver was going on, and there was bound to be plenty of that. But on hearing the disappointment in Carrie's voice, she had changed her mind. Maybe it *would* be a good idea. Things were bound to be hectic in the week leading up to the wedding, and maybe it wouldn't do any harm if she was there to stop things getting out of hand. And she missed them – missed the girls. Especially Hope, who had been away for so long. The only fly in the ointment would be her own daughters, who would expect her to go on their annual holiday to America – but she could do that any time. Babs decided to check the flight options that afternoon when she got home. She'd been a dab hand on the Internet since she'd completed the course for 'mature beginners' at her local vocational college. Rob had put her up to it, she remembered, smiling.

'Wouldn't use a computer Babs?' he had said, mock-disbelief written all over his face as he tapped into his state-of-the-art laptop on the kitchen table.

At the time, Babs had never seen anything like it. 'Wouldn't touch one.'

'That's only because you don't know how to.' He grinned wickedly. 'I'll show you.'

'No, thank you, Mr Armstrong,' she had answered firmly. 'It has nothing to do with not knowing how to use one, I simply don't approve of them. Too much margin for error. Give me a pen and paper any day.'

Rob had roared with laughter. 'They're the way forward, Babs,' he had said. 'You wouldn't want to get left behind, would you? Besides, you could email your family for nothing instead of running up expensive phone bills. They could be chatting to you every day.'

'That's what I'm afraid of.'

'Really, Babs! I'm disappointed in you. I never took you for someone who'd be afraid of anything, least of all technology.'

That had done it, of course, just as he had known it would. Babs had a stubborn streak and hated more than anything to resist a challenge. That, and the disappointment she had heard in his voice. She'd show him, the upstart! And she had, coming top of her class at the six-week evening course.

The next day, just after she'd come in from work, the doorbell had rung. Not expecting anyone, she opened the door cautiously to a young man holding a large box. 'Mrs Annie Buckley?' he had asked.

'That's me.'

'I have a delivery for you of one desktop computer from . . .' he checked his list, 'a Mr Robert Armstrong.'

When she had got over the shock she had made the young man a cup of tea and waited while he put it all together. Then he showed her how it worked, set her up with an email account and said another chap would be out within a day or two to get her on something called broadband. Babs had been too surprised at that stage to enquire as to what broadband was, but he assured her it was very useful indeed. Oh, there was just one thing, he had said, indicating where she had to sign the form to confirm delivery.

'What's that?' asked Babs.

'There's a condition.'

'A condition?' Babs was alarmed.

'Yes, from Mr Armstrong.' He fumbled for a piece of paper.

'Oh, yes, here it is. He says if he doesn't receive an email in twenty-four hours to this address, the whole lot has to go back.' He grinned.

'The scoundrel!' Babs chuckled as she took the piece of paper.

'Well, I'll be on my way. Thanks for the tea – and ring our customer-care number if you've any problems.'

As Babs closed the door behind him she glanced at the piece of paper with Rob's email address. It didn't occur to her until many weeks later that it couldn't be his company address. But then, she reasoned, an influential man like him must have many different addresses for the many different aspects of his business. But that was Rob all over, she mused affectionately, a scoundrel, but a lovable one, and generous to a fault.

She would check out the flights today and book one before she changed her mind. It would be lovely to spend a week or so with the people she now thought of as her second family. After all, this would be her last year with them; she had made up her mind to retire. Mind you, she'd been trying to do that for the last five years, but somehow Carrie had always persuaded her to stay on. She couldn't imagine life without them now. But everything came to an end sooner or later, and there was no avoiding the fact that she was getting on. She was by any standards a sprightly and healthy seventy-five, but even though the work wasn't strenuous and she loved coming to the Armstrongs', she didn't have the energy she'd once taken for granted.

That, and despite their protestations, she also pointed out that they didn't need her any more, so things couldn't continue as they were. Sure, there was only Rob and Carrie now, rattling around in the big mansion of a place. Surely they could move somewhere smaller together, or – the thought occurred to her more and more regularly these days although it brought her profound sadness – move to smaller, *separate* residences. She had to admit, though it pained her, that things on the Rob-and-Carrie front didn't look too good. You didn't have to be a psychologist to work that one out.

14

The excitement – or was it tension? – in the air was almost palpable. Sandi had been right, thought Ali as she and her agent marched into the advertising agency and were escorted straight to the boardroom. The big guns had been wheeled out. Practically the full board of BBDW, including the American executive creative director, who had flown in especially, was sitting round the table. She recognised the English creative director, a handsome man with long white hair brushed back from his face. He was an intelligent and respected figure in the world of advertising, with many award-winning campaigns under his belt in his long, distinguished career.

The creative teams, too, were easy to spot, fidgeting nervously despite their practised cool. Stay Tru was the agency's biggest account by far, and more than just its creative reputation would be on the line if the client was not kept absolutely happy. If they lost the account, heads would roll. But that was advertising, the nature of the game.

The chief account handler made the necessary introductions and tea and coffee were poured while the presentation team made last-minute adjustments to the audio-visual equipment and ensured for the umpteenth time that everything was in order.

The account handler checked his watch. 'It's already five past,' he said. 'I've never heard of Gerald J. being anything but on time if not early, just to keep people on their toes.'

'Relax. I'm sure he'll be here any minute.' The head of TV busied himself with his notes.

'No,' said the American creative director, 'Don's right. Gerald J. is *never* late. If there was any kind of hold-up they would have called ahead.'

'Try Reception again, just to be sure,' ordered the MD, a stocky man with a stern face. He'd got up from his seat and begun to pace the room.

Ali was impressed. She had thought the tension before a big runway show was mind-numbing, but compared to this, it was a walk in the park.

'Sit down, Alec, for God's sake.' The English creative director rolled his eyes. 'You're acting like you've got ants in your pants.'

'Oh yeah? That's nothing to what you'll have in yours if this casting goes the wrong way. We can't afford to hit a wrong note – not one. Sorry,' he added to Ali. 'It's just that we're under a lot of pressure.'

'So I see,' she said, smiling. 'Look, either I'll be right for them, or I won't. Either way, I'm sure your campaign will go down wonderfully.'

'Thanks.' Alec sat down again. 'But we've put you forward, Ali, and if Gerald J. turns you down, he'll ditch the people who pitched you in the first place.'

'For Christ's sake, shut up, Alec, will you? There's not a lot Ali can do about it, is there?' snapped Don.

'Please, gentlemen, this is ridiculous, you're stressing Ali out,' Sandi said sternly.

'It's okay, Sandi,' Ali said and smiled sympathetically. 'Look, guys, I'll do my best, okay? That's all I can do.' She smiled beguilingly and the atmosphere lifted a little.

Just then the phone rang and everybody jumped. The account handler picked it up. 'It's him. They're showing him up now.'

From the boardroom, they heard the ping of the lift opening, followed by brisk footsteps and the breathless voice of Sally, the vice-president, as she paused in the doorway. 'On behalf of BBWD London, Mr Simmington, it's my very great honour to welcome you to the agency.'

Around the table, everyone rose to their feet, and there was a definite if inaudible intake of breath as Gerald J. Simmington moved forward smoothly to shake the eagerly outstretched hands.

'Hey, guys,' he said, smiling broadly, 'sorry I'm late, but the traffic was crazy.' His eyes flashed round the room, taking in every detail. 'As you can see, the old man couldn't make it, so you'll have to make do with me, I'm afraid.' He grinned disarmingly. 'Allow me to introduce myself, Gerald J. Simmington the Second.'

As introductions were made, Ali found herself gazing at a man who looked as if he had walked straight out of a Ralph Lauren ad. He was tall and blond with an athletic build. His chiselled face was movie-star handsome and his smile was white and perfect, but it never reached his steely blue eyes.

'You must be Miss Armstrong,' he said, his eyes roving appreciatively over her. 'It's a great pleasure to meet you.'

'Likewise,' replied Ali, smiling, although as his hand closed firmly round hers, a ripple of something that could only be called unease washed through her.

'Hi, *babyeee* . . .' Rob sounded pleased with himself, Olwen thought, as she held the phone awkwardly between her neck and shoulder, putting the final touches to some sushi she had gone to great trouble to make. The rack of lamb was roasting slowly and smelled wonderful. She'd hoped he would call earlier, as he'd said he would, about this evening's arrangements, but she'd gone ahead anyway, rushing home from work to have everything, including his favourite food, ready for the evening. She knew how busy he was, how unpredictable his life and business commitments were, but sometimes, just *sometimes*, she wished he'd let her know for definite if he was free so she could look forward to them spending some time together without the awful suspense that he would cancel at the last minute.

Lately, though, things had been wonderful. With Carrie in Spain, she had had him almost to herself for the last fortnight. She knew she should feel guilty, but the sheer pleasure of having him around, staying with her all night without having to rush off, enjoying some semblance of normality in their relationship, had made her incredibly happy.

She even found herself wondering what it would be like to have Rob coming home to her every day. When the bad stuff was over, they would have a civilised relationship with Carrie. Perhaps they could even have their own children. She barely ever allowed herself to even think about that. Much though she fantasised about having a child with Rob, Olwen didn't really believe she deserved such a thing. Blessings like that only happened to other people. But still, she could dream. And no dream could trump the one where she held their baby in her arms.

'Hi, darling,' Olwen felt a warm glow. 'Are you on your way?'

'Actually, no.'

'Oh,' Olwen held her breath, then forced herself to sound upbeat. 'What's up?'

'I've had a great idea.'

'What's that?'

'Why don't *you* come over *here*?' Rob couldn't think why he hadn't suggested it before.

'What, you mean to your place?'

'Yes, why not? I've got some champagne chilling, and we can order in.'

'Rob, I don't think that would be a very good idea.'

'Why not? I'm always coming to your place. It would make a nice change. Besides, you haven't seen where I live.' Olwen knew that Rob was keen to show her his fabulous mansion, and that with Carrie away, it would be the perfect opportunity. Also, she knew he was tired and had found it a strain to have to think ahead and bring a change of clothes with him. He'd been worried too about his housekeeper, Babs, noticing his absence. But . . . 'I'm not sure I want to.'

'Why not?'

'I wouldn't feel comfortable.'

'What do you mean? We'll have the place to ourselves for a five-star luxury weekend, just you and me.' She could hear that he was becoming impatient.

'I mean,' Olwen said quietly, 'that I wouldn't feel comfortable in another woman's home, Rob.'

'Oh, for God's sake, Olwen. It's my home too, you know. I pay for the damned place so I'm entitled to use it as and when I see fit.'

'Yes, you are, Rob.' Olwen's voice was strangely quiet. 'But I'm not. Frankly, I'm surprised you'd suggest such a thing. I have everything ready here. I assumed that as we arranged, you'd be round for dinner.'

'You mean you won't come here? Even though it would make things easier for *me*?'

'No, Rob, I'm afraid I won't.'

'Right, I see. Well, in that case, we won't be seeing each other this evening.'

'Fine, if that's what you want.'

'You know it's not, but you're being entirely unreasonable about this. Look—'

'I'm sorry, Rob,' Olwen said, 'but I meant what I said. Goodbye.' She hung up the phone.

★　★　★

What the hell was eating *her?* Rob shook his head in disbelief
as he stared at his phone. It was Friday evening and the whole
weekend stretched ahead of them. A blissful, hassle-free weekend that they could have spent in complete and utter luxury
and privacy. And Olwen had turned him down because of a
twinge of conscience about it being Carrie's house. Well, it
was his bloody house, actually. He'd worked for it, paid for
it, maintained it. He was perfectly within his rights to entertain whomever he wanted in it.

It hadn't bothered Olwen when they had snatched a night
or two in a hotel. Of course they went to her house ordinarily, but that's because it had been their only option while
Carrie had been in town. Rob really couldn't see what she
was making a fuss about. But he sure as hell didn't need it.
He got enough of that from his wife. Women! They were all
the bloody same. He was royally pissed off.

He got up and went into the kitchen, pulled the bottle of
champagne out of the fridge, then on second thoughts put
it back. Sod it! He wasn't going to sit around on his own. If
Olwen wanted to play silly buggers and waste a terrific
weekend, then that was her problem. He'd go into the Four
Seasons. There'd be plenty of action there on a Friday night
and he'd be bound to bump into a few mates. Come to think
of it, he'd been downright unsociable lately since he'd been
seeing so much of Olwen, and it wasn't good to neglect your
friends.

He threw on his jacket, grabbed his phone and thought
about ringing her back. No, let her whistle. He'd bent over
backwards for her these last few weeks and the least she could
do was accommodate him when he asked her to his place.
God knows, there were plenty of other women who'd be only
too happy to come. He slammed the door behind him and
scowled as he got into the Aston Martin. He'd leave the car
with the parking valet at the hotel because tonight he'd have

some fun, maybe even get smashed. He certainly wasn't going to be manipulated by any bloody woman – even if that woman *was* Olwen.

Olwen stared at the phone, willing it to ring. *Surely*, Rob couldn't be serious? Surely, inconsiderate though men often were, he could understand her reluctance to engage with him under the roof of his wife's house. It was unthinkable. Clearly it didn't bother Rob, but that he should be so insensitive to her feelings, so sure in his assumption that she would blithely drop everything she had so carefully planned and run over to his and Carrie's house, quite frankly flabbergasted her.

Another, more dangerous, realisation was crawling around in her mind. The realisation that he would want her, there, in the house he shared with Carrie and their children. His total lack of sensitivity for Carrie's feelings, or what they might be if she or, God forbid, one of his children, were ever to find out, didn't bear thinking about. With a sickening stab, Olwen found herself empathising with Carrie.

Abandoning the phone, she turned to the oven, took out the perfectly roasted rack of lamb, wrapped it in tinfoil and put it into the bin, along with the sushi. Then, realising they were having their first ever row – which was very different from a lovelorn parting for altruistic reasons – and, more importantly, wasting a precious evening that they could have been spending together, she ran upstairs and threw herself onto her bed, where she cried and wondered, not for the first time, why she seemed so ready to accept, if not engineer, all these occasions when she was left yet again on her own.

An hour later, the insistent ringing of the phone cut through her semi-comatose cry-in.

'H-hello,' she hiccuped, not bothering to look at the caller ID, hoping desperately it was Rob.

'Olwen?' She recognised the voice, clipped and familiar. 'Is that you?'

'Pete?' she answered. She tried hurriedly to compose herself. 'Yes, it's me.' She sniffed.

'Olwen,' there was a slight pause, 'are you all right? What's the matter?'

The concern in his tone did it – that he, her pal and producer, had picked up so quickly that something was out of kilter.

'Er, nothing's the matter – I just . . .'

'Olwen, what the hell is going on?'

And just as she was about to tell him everything was fine, she was just coming down with a cold and feeling a bit moby, she was sobbing incoherently, and hearing, from somewhere in the distance, the firm, incontestable statement that he was on his way over, whether she liked it or not.

Much later, when they were still talking in the kitchen, Olwen wondered distractedly why she had never noticed how attractive Pete was, even though most of the girls at the station had wild crushes on him to which he seemed oblivious. It was one of the many nice things about him.

She had told him everything, against her best instincts, and he had listened, nodded occasionally, and let her ramble on until the whole sorry story had emerged. He had sighed a couple of times but he had never said the awful words she had dreaded: *Olwen, how could you? How could you, of all people, be so stupid?* Perhaps, she guessed, because he knew somehow that they were the very questions with which she berated herself day and night.

Then, while they ate scrambled eggs – Pete had been keen to investigate the earlier discarded rack of lamb, but Olwen had remained firm – and drank a particularly nice New

Zealand Sauvignon Blanc that he had thoughtfully brought with him, he began to ask a series of deceptively innocent questions with the ease of the brilliant and talented producer he was.

The interview, for that was how Olwen came to think of it with affection later, had been constructed so cleverly that she, a talented interviewer herself, had failed to see the objective he had set out to achieve.

He had asked her, with genuine interest, to tell him again about the beginning. And Olwen, feeling better now, warmed by the wine and Pete's comforting presence, was all too ready to divulge it.

She told him of the heady, exciting days when Rob had pursued her relentlessly, stopping at nothing, refusing to take no for an answer. She told him, haltingly, tearful again, of the moment she had fallen in love with him.

'You can be that specific?' asked Pete curiously, leaning forward across the small kitchen table. 'When?'

'It was Mother's Day,' Olwen said with a rueful smile. 'Two years ago.'

'Go on.'

'Well, we'd been seeing each other since January, and this was March. We hadn't slept together. Anyway, it was Mother's Day, and I was feeling a bit low, I suppose, and I decided to go out, probably to the shops or something, and opened the door. There, sitting on the porch, was a beautiful bouquet of flowers. I knew they were from him because it was the florist he always used, although there was no message. I sent a text message to thank him but I never got a chance to ask him about it until the next time we saw each other, here, maybe a week later. We were on the sofa and I was lying in his arms. I said, "By the way, why did you send me flowers on Mother's Day?"'

'What did he say?' Pete was deliberately off-hand but was on red alert.

'He was quiet for a minute and then he said, "This is going to sound kind of silly." "Go on," I prompted him. "Well," he said slowly, "you don't have a mummy, and you're not a mummy and I thought you might be feeling a little low."'

There was a pause as Pete digested this. He swallowed, but not for the reason Olwen presumed. 'I know,' she sniffed, 'it got to me too. I just couldn't believe a man could be so unbelievably intuitive, so sensitive to my feelings. I mean he *got* it. He went right to the very heart of it. He *understood.*'

Pete nodded slowly, not trusting himself to speak.

'Imagine! He had his own family to look after – his own mother's still alive, and of course there's his wife – and he *still* thought of me, went out of his way to make sure I wasn't left out on a day that quite frankly I find pretty difficult.'

Pete knew that despite Olwen's career-girl front she adored children and would love one of her own. He also knew that her parents were dead, and she had gone through a difficult divorce. Despite her outward air of assurance, Olwen Slater, Pete knew, was very much on her own, and wonderfully attractive quarry for an unscrupulous predator such as the one with whom she most assuredly and unfortunately seemed to have fallen in love. And that was the problem. He knew he had to move with the utmost delicacy here. This man was no slouch in the seduction stakes, but Olwen was vulnerable. And if there was one thing Pete detested, it was a manipulative, greedy, selfish married man who preyed on vulnerable women.

'What about the next year?' he asked casually. 'Were there flowers on Mother's Day then? Or this year?'

Olwen thought for a moment. 'No, now that you mention it, there weren't. But he always sends flowers on my birthday and Valentine's Day. I guess he'd made his point. Actually,

I think he was quite embarrassed about it afterwards.' She laughed.

I bet he was, thought Pete grimly. He'd achieved his objective.

'And this year? Your birthday's in February, isn't it?'

'Sure is. You have a good memory.'

'Were there flowers, trips away, a nice surprise?' Pete was pretty sure that Olwen had been working round the clock at the time, and his instinct told him that this had nothing to do with advancing her career.

Olwen chewed her lip. 'Well, no, but we were on an "off" period,' she explained. 'I'd finished it with him about a month or so earlier . . . of course! How could I forget? It was before Christmas. I told him not to contact me, and he was respecting my wishes.'

'I see,' said Pete. 'So, how did you get back together?'

'Oh, it's hard to explain. We can get by for two, maybe three months without each other, and then we always cave in. I swear to myself I won't see him again, answer any of his texts or phone calls, and then, just when I'm feeling abysmally miserable without him, he'll phone or text and that's it. We're back together again . . .' She paused. 'It's like – he's like a drug to me. I guess we're both addicted.' She raised sad eyes to his. 'I'm hooked on him. It's as simple as that. I'm in love with him. Big time, you know, the I-can't-live-without-you-stuff. And,' she stifled a sob, 'the really scary part is that I don't think I can.'

He patted her hand. 'I'm sure it won't come to that, hon.' He willed her to believe – to *know* – she was so much more than the morass of a relationship she was embroiled in. 'And when you get back together, it's great, right?'

'Oh, God,' Olwen breathed, 'better than that. Neither of us knows how we managed without each other. It's like we can't live without each other although we keep trying to pretend we can, until one of us falls apart. We've had such great times together, and Rob's so, so understanding, so sensitive. Well, he just gets me. And I know, deep down, there's nothing he wouldn't do for me.'

Except leave his wife, of course. Pete's face remained carefully impassive as the thought filtered through his mind.

'Oh, I know what you're thinking,' Olwen smiled, and took a sip of her wine. 'You're thinking he's married and he won't do the one thing you need him to do above all else, which is leave his wife.'

Silence.

'But that's just it. I don't *want* him to.' She looked at him, willing him to understand. 'Leave his wife, that is . . .'

Oh, God. Pete fought not to put his head in his hands. It's worse than I thought. This is *way* beyond the loop of love. This is use me, humiliate me, let me suffer, but on no account let me put my needs above or, God forbid, *alongside* this fucker's. This time Pete had to work quite hard to keep his face and voice impassive.

'You really don't want him to leave?'

'No, well – oh, God, it's so hard to explain.'

'Try.'

'Neither of us was looking for this.' Olwen's face was working. 'It just – I don't know – it just happened.'

Sure, thought Pete. You're half right. *You* weren't looking for it. But you sure were prime fodder for it. He was beginning to see a very different side of Olwen, which he found fascinating. A side she kept hidden, perhaps, most of all, from herself.

'And now?'

'Now? Well, I don't know. I love him, Pete. I know him. I understand how tough all this is for him. And I don't think leaving his wife . . . I just don't think he could handle the fallout.'

'Are there kids?'

'Yes. Three girls.'

'Tell me they're younger than you are.' He was only half joking.

'Eldest is thirty, youngest twenty-three. Photo-journalist, model and student, respectively. Stephanie, the youngest, is still discovering herself, I guess.' Olwen smiled.

Almost as if she was talking about her own family. Pete shuddered.

They were old enough to be judgmental, young enough to pull the parental heartstrings, and always, always, the right age to be daddy's girls, he thought despairingly.

'And you?'

'As you well know, I am thirty-eight and a half.' Olwen grinned, but sadness flitted across her face.

'And what about kids, Olwen? Don't you want some? Would he do that for you?'

'Oh, I wouldn't even go there.' Olwen played with a strand of hair, twiddling it round a finger. 'Anyway, he had a vasectomy years ago, after his youngest was born.' She remembered him telling her.

'So you don't want to have a child with the man you love so much who loves you back. You wouldn't even want to discuss it?' He held his breath.

'You don't understand.' Olwen was becoming fractious. 'There are so many pressures, so many other things to take into account . . .'

'Of course,' Pete murmured. Everything, he thought, except yourself.

After Pete had gone, reassured that she was all right, or as all right as she could be under the circumstances, Olwen cleared up the kitchen things and headed for bed. It was eleven p.m. and so far, not a phone call from Rob.

She wondered miserably if he was sitting at home, feeling as wretched as she was. She climbed into bed, willing herself not to think, not to go over in minute detail, every nuance of their fight and, more importantly, not to dwell on the disturbing train of thought Pete had set in motion. She couldn't think. Wouldn't. She just wanted the oblivion of sleep. As if on cue, the familiar churning began in her stomach.

The Ice Bar was buzzing. God, it felt good to be out and about. Rob had met up with an old mate for a few pints, which had led to dinner, and then Paul had suggested the Ice Bar. Rob hadn't been there in a while, and now, at ten p.m., the place was humming. An unending stream of women came through the swing doors, prowling, hungry women on the make. Paul was enjoying it big time. 'Jaysus, Rob, how come you never told me this place was full of top totty?' He eyed a buxom blonde lasciviously. She licked her lips in response.

'Dunno,' Rob was feeling pleasantly woozy. 'Haven't been out much lately.'

'Too much work, mate. Wanna watch that – you know what they say.'

'Rob!' The female voice took him by surprise. 'I haven't seen you around for a long time. Where have you been hiding?' It was Tanya, an old girlfriend. They'd had a satisfying affair – gosh, it must be ten years ago now – until she had become too clingy and he'd ended it. Last he heard, she'd moved on, taking up with another married man, who had left his wife and with whom she had had three children in quick succession.

'Tanya! What a surprise! Wow, you're looking great.' He greeted her warmly. And she did look great. The years, or a friendly needle-wielder, had treated her well.

'Thank you, sweetie.' Tanya flicked back her long blonde hair. 'So are you. Oh, you won't have met my friend Suzi, will you?'

Suzi turned out to be American, with a killer body and a hawk-like face that just managed to stay on the right side of good-looking. She was incredibly sexy. 'Hey, guys, good to meet you.'

Paul, Rob's mate, looked as if he was about to faint.

Aware of the envious glances being thrown their way by men and women alike, Rob lost no time in ordering more champagne. Later he couldn't remember when someone suggested going to Renard's, Dublin's hottest and most exclusive nightclub, frequented by celebrities and the mega-wealthy, but at the time it seemed like a good idea, particularly since he was guaranteed not to run into one of his daughters.

It had been fun for a while, but now, at three a.m., Rob had had enough and made his getaway.

Outside, he tried without success to find a cab and had no intention of joining the long queue that was forming down the street. He remembered leaving his car at the Four Seasons and now it looked as though he might just have to walk back there. He could always get a room and drive home in the morning.

Damn Paul. He had sloped off earlier, pleading a golf competition the next day, and Tanya in particular had been none too pleased that an invitation to continue partying with Rob had not been forthcoming.

Never mind, Rob thought, shivering and pulling his coat closer as he walked up Dawson Street. He would ring Olwen. Just the thought of her gave him a warm glow. He would ring her, she would drive in and get him, and they would spend the rest of the night making up. He knew they'd had a stupid fight over something or other that she'd been unreasonable about, but he couldn't quite remember what.

Anyway, it didn't matter. Olwen adored him and she'd be thrilled to hear from him. She always was, at any time of day or night.

The ringing of her mobile didn't wake Olwen as she lay tossing and turning, unable to sleep. She picked it up, saw it was Rob's number and was overjoyed. He must be feeling as awful as she was. God, she hated fighting with him – it was so stupid. Nothing was worth the pain and anxiety of separation.

'Rob?' She began.

'Hi, babyeeee,' Rob sang down the phone. 'Are you pleased to hear me?'

'Rob?' Olwen couldn't believe her ears. 'Are you drunk?'

'Of course I am, baby,' he used his most cajoling tone. 'I wouldn't be ringing you if I wasn't.'

'What did you say?'

Rob swayed slightly on his feet and tried again – that last attempt hadn't sounded quite right. 'Baby, *please*, don't be nasty to me. I'm in town and I'd love to come and see you?' There, that was better.

'Do you know what time it is?'

'Oops. It's three o'clock.'

'Yes, Rob, it's three o'clock. Three o'clock in the morning.'

'You shouldn't be up so late,' he mock scolded her, 'go to bed immediately – and I'll come and join you, 'cept I can't find a taxi anywhere.'

Olwen was hit by the sinking realisation that Rob was completely pissed.

'Baby, it wasn't my fault,' Rob whined. 'It was the girls, Tanya and – and – whassername who wanted to go to Renard's.'

'You've been in Renard's?' Olwen tried not to scream. 'You've been *carousing* in Renard's with a couple of birds while I've been going out of my mind because of you and your stupid, selfish ego ruining our weekend.'

'S'not ruined, baby,' Rob wheedled. 'You can come and pick me up – I can't get a taxi *anywhere*, I'm outside the Shelbourne – and then we can go back to your place . . . please?' This usually worked. 'Please, baby – I'm dying to see you. I need you.'

'Do you really, Rob?'

'Of course I do. I always need you, baby.' This was becoming confusing. 'But I really, really need you to come and pick me up.'

'Rob?'

'Yes, baby?'

'Fuck off.'

'Well, that's not very nice. Why are you being so mean?'

'At this hour of the morning, when you're clearly drunk, I'm not going into that.'

'So you don't care that I'm stuck here in the middle of town and you won't come and pick me up? You don't want to see me?'

'No Rob, I won't and don't.' Olwen had never employed her strength of character so well, despite the fact that every fibre of her wanted to jump straight into her car and go and get him.

'How am I supposed to get home then?' Rob asked sulkily. 'Walk?'

'Yes. On your hands for all I care. And don't even think about ringing me again tonight – or should I say today?' Olwen hung up.

Just as luck would have it, a taxi came round the corner at that very minute and screeched to a halt as Rob practically threw himself in front of it.

'Where to, mate?' the driver asked as Rob hauled himself in.

For a moment, Rob nearly gave Olwen's address. He knew he could apologise, get round her, even in this state. She could never resist him in person. But fuck her! He was going home to peace and quiet. He gave the driver his address. He had seen another side of Olwen tonight. Boy, that woman could be a real bitch, he thought indignantly, before quietly passing out.

That did it. Whatever hope Olwen had had of getting some sleep had been knocked on the head. She knew she should be livid at the way Rob had treated her, but she felt wretched. To think that while she had been agonising about their row, going over and over everything in her mind, he had been blithely out on the town.

What hurt even more was that it hadn't even been the kind of drinking episode guys throw themselves into to cope with their inability to share or handle their feelings. As usual, Rob had simply had a good time. He appeared to have forgotten what had transpired earlier, as if it had been no more than a slight inconvenience. That was how much it had meant to him. How much her feelings meant to him.

Olwen got up and went downstairs to make a cup of tea. It was now three twenty. Not the time of day to contemplate things in a sane or rational manner, but there was no avoiding the thoughts that were whirling around in her increasingly miserable mind.

She sat down at the kitchen table, remembering Pete's kindness and concern earlier. How he had insisted on coming round and had stayed to listen to her, comfort her, and hadn't left until he was quite sure she was all right. Well, that was a joke, Olwen thought ruefully. She was far from all right. It was just that, increasingly, there seemed to be less and less she could do about it. She felt powerless in the grip of the love she felt for Rob and, until now, had assumed he felt for her. Now, all of a sudden, she wasn't so sure.

She thought of the flowers that arrived on her birthday and Valentine's Day, which seemed now to emphasise that on all of those days she never saw him, except for little more than half an hour.

She thought of the early days when he had talked to her, phoned her, on a daily basis and how recently those phone calls had become more infrequent and unpredictable.

'Love you, baby, must rush, talk later' had taken the place of languorous, loving conversations.

Lately, text messages, which she hated, had taken over unless Rob wanted something. Then he phoned.

Delving deeper, and remembering Pete's quietly probing questions, she admitted to herself that it hadn't been entirely out of altruistic reasons that she had ended the affair on the two previous occasions. It had been out of fear – not the fear that they would be found out, although she certainly didn't relish that, but the cold terror that closed round her heart when she felt Rob slipping away, perhaps without realising it, losing interest. It hadn't been a ploy on her part. She wasn't playing hard to get. She simply couldn't bear the thought of him ending it, so she would end it first.

But then, of course, he would want her back. He'd work hard to win her over, yet again, and she would go back to him, loving him, and there would be those first heady bliss-filled moments of reunion when she believed, sometimes with a fervour that surprised her, everything he so earnestly said and promised.

Like the time she'd met him in London.

'Thank you,' Olwen said to the porter who had shown her to their suite and insisted on carrying her small holdall as she tipped him.

When the door had closed behind him, she had unpacked,

laying out her expensive lingerie and the stockings Rob loved
her to wear. She ran a hot bath, filled with bubbles, and sank
into it, relishing the thought of the night ahead and the sheer
excitement of seeing him again. Afterwards she had smothered herself in her favourite body lotion, sprayed her perfume
liberally and dressed carefully, seeing a woman in the mirror
so clearly infused with happiness and desire.

They hadn't seen each other in about a month and Rob
had texted her relentlessly, until eventually she agreed to
spend a night or two with him in London to 'discuss' things.

She met him, before dinner, in the bar, and his face had lit
up at the sight of her. Of course, it was as if they had never
been apart. She was as hungry for him as an addict needing
her next fix. In the taxi on the way to the restaurant, he told
her how beautiful she looked, how he had missed her, how
wonderful it was to see her again. When they walked through
to their table, Olwen felt weak with delight, thrilled beyond
imagination just to be with him, to go out and do what normal
couples take for granted. Once they had ordered, Rob got
straight down to business.

'I've been thinking,' he said, gazing at her intently.

'About us?' Olwen held her breath, not sure what was
coming next.

'I think you should have a baby.' He took her hand.

Olwen had been taken totally by surprise. 'I've never even
mentioned kids.' And she hadn't. She was sure of it. A woman
in love would rather cut out her tongue than pressurise a man
by suggesting such a thing. 'Why would you say that, Rob?'

'Because I think it would be good for you,' he said simply.
'You'd be a wonderful mother, and I know you'd love a baby.'

'But you've had a vasectomy.' Olwen couldn't believe the
turn the conversation was taking. It was beyond her wildest
dreams.

'They can be reversed. A friend of mine had it done – he's

remarried and his second wife was keen to have a child of her own. I'll talk to him about who he went to. You could investigate too, hmm?'

'You'd do that . . . for me?' Olwen was astounded. 'Why?' She knew it was a stupid question but she really needed to hear the answer.

'Because I love you madly.'

Olwen had thought then and there that she would die of happiness. He really loves me, she thought. He's not just saying it. He really, *really* loves me.

He had uttered the words she had wanted to hear above all. Better, *much* better, than if he had said he was leaving Carrie. This way, she could savour the reality she had only contemplated in her wildest fantasies: the longed-for child with the love of her life. And this way, she thought, no one got hurt. Everyone could be kept happy. Rob wouldn't have to go through the hassle and disruption of leaving Carrie. Carrie would not have to go through the pain and humiliation of publicly losing her husband, even though she had lost, or perhaps never had, his love. This was not just what Olwen surmised. It was what Rob told her in no uncertain terms on every possible occasion.

The rest of their brief time together passed all too quickly. They took in a musical, Rob worked the following day and Olwen went shopping, they met for lunch and, again, that last evening, had a wonderful, romantic dinner, then made love back at the hotel. The next morning, first thing, Rob was on a plane to Atlanta, and Olwen, feeling beyond lonely, checked out later and got the lunchtime flight to Dublin.

That trip had taken him away, unexpectedly, for three weeks. Broken, fragmented weeks, when it had been impossible for him to talk to her for more than a minute, and even his text messages were less frequent than usual. He had asked her to find out the name of a specialist in vasectomy reversal and, on the one occasion she did get to talk to him for more than three seconds, she mentioned that she had in fact tracked one down whose credentials were excellent. Rob had sounded first distracted, then briskly disinterested, and suddenly had to go.

As swiftly as the line went dead, Olwen's fragile hopes crashed and burned with it. In that instant the lifting, soaring feeling that she had harboured, had foolishly allowed to grow in her heart, was cruelly dashed. Later she wondered why she hadn't pinned him down, asked him pointedly – had he not meant what he had so definitely said to her about having a baby that memorable evening in London? She knew the answer. Her pride told her she didn't want to demean herself by appearing desperate, needy. Her heart told her she was just too damned afraid of losing him – even the very little of him she had claim to. So she had hung on, as she was doing now. As Carrie must have been done for so many soul-destroying years.

Except that Carrie, Olwen reminded herself, had her children. Apart from her career and a painful divorce under her belt, Olwen had really very little indeed.

After the nightclub incident, Olwen didn't hear from Rob for two weeks, although she knew he was around. He was putting a big deal together in Dublin – she remembered him telling her that it would be a relief not to be jumping on and off planes for a while. He'd been looking forward to spending time with her.

One day, she passed him in traffic. He was heading in the opposite direction in his Aston Martin. If he saw her, he didn't acknowledge it.

With a sickening lurch in the pit of her stomach, Olwen realised he was punishing her. What surprised her most of all was not how petty or puerile his behaviour was, but how very much it hurt. The pain of being ignored was bad enough, but worse was the sudden shock and realisation that maybe Rob Armstrong wasn't quite the man she'd thought he was.

15

'Ooh, that must be it,' said Stephanie, pointing to the power-boat that sat sleekly in the water, moored, as they had been told, opposite the restaurant in Puerto Banus. 'Look, the red one, over there.' She pointed at the Riva as Carrie and Hope followed her.

One of *Excalibur*'s crew, whom Rudi had sent out to meet them, waved and jumped on to the gangplank to help them aboard.

'Señoras.' He smiled politely. 'Good morning. Let me help you down.'

Once they were comfortably seated, he untied the rope and put the boat into gear, manoeuvred her carefully past several yachts and out of the harbour. He pushed the throttle forward and they surged through the water towards the vessel that lay waiting ahead.

With the wind whipping her hair round her face, Carrie got caught up in the collective excitement. She could hardly believe they were about to set foot aboard the most talked-about yacht ever. And to think her own daughter would have her wedding reception on it. It was the stuff of fairy tales, except . . . Carrie pushed any negative thoughts from her mind. The sun was shining, the Mediterranean was a deep blue, and her two daughters were laughing and chatting in front of her. It was a good day, and she was determined to enjoy every minute of it.

Ten minutes later they pulled up alongside *Excalibur*, which towered over them. The crewmen helped them aboard. 'Oh, there you are, darlings!' Jay had appeared on deck from somewhere below, followed by Enrique B'stardo, whose hairdo seemed to precede the rest of him. 'Isn't this fun?' she said gaily. 'Enrique has been looking around so he can get a feel for the space.'

'Señoras.' Enrique shook hands with Carrie and Stephanie and was introduced to Hope, whom he had not yet met. 'A pleasure again.' He inclined his head.

'This is the bride?' he asked delightedly, gazing at the elegant Hope.

'No, no,' laughed Carrie as Hope scowled and Stephanie sniggered. 'I'm afraid the bride won't be with us for quite a few weeks yet, so far as we know. This is my eldest daughter, Hope. Ali, who is working at the moment, is the bride-to-be.

'Ah, I see.' Enrique was relieved. The more bride-free time he was allotted, the better, in his experience. 'But an understandable mistake, no? Now, we take a look round and I tell you my ideas, yes?'

'We'll follow you,' said Carrie.

'D'you mind if I wander around on my own for a bit to take a few shots?' Hope asked Jay.

'Good Lord, no. Of course not. Just try not to get lost, sweetie, or fall overboard,' Jay laughed. 'Let's all meet back here in half an hour, hmm?'

'Great,' said Hope, feeling relieved to escape, at least for a little while. 'See you in a bit.'

Carrie and Stephanie followed Enrique and Jay below as they began the guided tour. Until now, Jay had been reasonably unfamiliar with the boat. She had made the most of the last week when, thanks to the prospective wedding, Frank could no longer keep *Excalibur* and whatever secrets she might harbour to himself. Whenever possible, Jay, and Enrique in her absence, had gone over her with a fine-tooth comb looking for incriminating evidence about Frank and his extra-marital exploits. This, however, was not an easy task with the crew coming and going about their duties, especially Rudi. Although Jay had to admit he was the sexiest man she had ever seen, he had an irritating air of propriety about the boat. Almost, Jay thought, as if she belonged to him. Which, as skipper, in nautical terms, she did, particularly in Frank's absence. Rudi guarded *Excalibur* as jealously as an MD his first fledgling company, and that included, on Frank's instructions, keeping uninvited and unwanted wives off her.

What really irritated Jay about Rudi, though, had happened a little more than a year ago when she had been introduced to him by Frank on one of their rare visits together to Marbella.

At thirty-three, Rudi, wearing only a pair of cut-off denims and Ray-Bans, had sported an eye-wateringly perfect body with a perfect tan to match. His face, with the slightly hooked nose, full, sensual mouth and hooded eyes, had reduced Jay to near meltdown.

When Frank had gone back to Dublin, she had called Rudi to Villa Esmerelda on some invented business about Frank, whereupon, on arrival, she had very generously, with just the right degree of sophistication, propositioned him. Not only had he turned her down flat, but he did so in a most ungentlemanly manner, hardly bothering to conceal his impatience and anger.

Jay had been furious, but there was nothing she could do about it. Since then he had been detached, polite and distant, which she had done her utmost to return.

Now, however, he was not in evidence, much to Jay's relief, as she and Enrique showed Carrie and Stephanie round. The bar ran in a semi-circle of polished marble, and the surrounding stools were rumoured to have been covered in whales' foreskins by the tycoon who had once owned her. Of course, Frank had had a complete makeover done on her since he had bought her, but Jay wasn't sure about the bar stools. She wouldn't have put it past Frank to keep the wretched foreskins even though he swore the stools were newly covered. All the same, Jay – not that she often got the chance – was never comfortable sitting on them.

'Now,' Enrique said, 'cocktails will be served on deck, as the guests arrive. Then, I think, they can filter down through the bar area, yes?' He didn't wait for a reply, but continued to share his ideas, with very impressive sketches and story boards to illustrate the kind of backdrops he had in mind.

Outside, on the upper deck, Hope had found her way up a narrow stairway that led to an even higher deck. From there, if she positioned herself at an awkward angle and leaned over and down, she could get some incredible images of the lower decks, which looked, from where she stood, almost like the set of a Broadway musical, with the sun beating down on uniformed crew members scurrying about in seemingly choreographed precision.

She was on her fifth shot when a voice interrupted her.

'Just what do you think you're doing?'

Hope almost dropped her camera and had to grab the railing for support as she wheeled round.

'Shit!' She glared at a tall man glowering down at her. 'What the hell are you doing creeping up on me like that? You scared me to death!' She checked her camera to make sure it was still in one piece.

'Good.' He had a trace of an accent that Hope identified as South African. 'That was my intention. I suppose you must be the bride, but let me tell you now, this deck is out of bounds, and it's forbidden to carry out any photographic activity on board my boat without permission.' He looked at her impassively. 'Now, if it wouldn't be too much trouble, I'd appreciate it if you'd follow me back to the lower deck.'

'*Your* boat!' Hope almost laughed. 'For your information, I know perfectly well whose boat this is, and it's not yours, whoever you are.' She was bordering on rude, but she didn't care – fright had made her angry. If there was one thing she couldn't abide, it was overbearing, arrogant men, particularly good-looking ones who thought they were God's gift to the universe. This deckhand, or whatever he was, qualified on all counts. As for assuming she was the bride, well, that was an occupational hazard around here. She saw no reason what-soever to enlighten him.

'I may not have paid for it,' he replied coldly, 'but believe me, it *is* my boat in every respect that matters. And what I say goes.' He turned on his heel. 'That means *you* follow *me* below, right?'

Hope held her breath and counted to ten as she descended the steps behind him, deliberately not replying. What a premier-league fuckwit! At the bottom he strode ahead, then down another level, and finally Hope found herself back on the lower deck, where Jay, Enrique, Carrie and Stephanie had congregated to meet her as arranged.

'Oh, Hope, there you are,' said Jay. 'Did you get any inter-esting shots? You missed all the fun down here.'

Hope didn't trust herself to speak.

'Well, sweetie?' Carrie looked at her questioningly.

'Yes,' Hope forced herself to smile. 'I got some great ones, thanks.' She noticed with pleasure that the deckhand didn't look happy about that – but he had heard it from the horse's mouth. She had her permission so he could stuff his lecture where the sun didn't shine.

'We thought we'd have lunch on board before going back to port,' Jay continued, glancing at him. 'That shouldn't be a problem, hmm, Rudi?'

'Of course not, Mrs Farrelly. I'll have the small dining room ready in just a few minutes.' His expression betrayed nothing.

'Thank you, Rudi.' She gave a small, cold smile, 'I see you've already made Hope's acquaintance, and of course you know Enrique, but let me introduce my friend Mrs Armstrong and her daughter Stephanie.' Rudi shook their hands.

'Rudi Weiss,' Jay explained, 'is our captain.'

'Pleased to meet you, Mrs Armstrong.'

'Please, call me Carrie.' She took in the tall, handsome young man and smothered a smile as Stephanie tried not to drool. Hope, on the other hand, seemed pointedly disinterested.

'You'll be seeing Mrs Armstrong and her daughters quite a bit, Rudi, as the wedding arrangements are dealt with. But of course Frank's told you about this already. I know you'll help them at every possible opportunity.'

'Of course, Mrs Farrelly.' A muscle flexed in Rudi's jaw as his eyes flickered briefly over Hope. 'My congratulations and best wishes to the bride,' he replied.

Was it her imagination, Carrie wondered as she watched the exchange, or had that comment been directed at Hope?

Jay led the small gathering into the dining room where champagne was waiting for them in an ice bucket.

'Shall I play Mama?' said Enrique coquettishly, reaching for a bottle.

Rudi had anticipated that they would stay for lunch, so he had briefed the kitchen before Jay had arrived. It was superb. The conversation centred on the wedding and Enrique became particularly excited at the idea of so many guests being ferried out by helicopter. Although glamorous, it would be hugely distracting and noisy. They decided that the helicopter would only be used in cases of absolute necessity. Otherwise, two small boats, suitably decorated, of course, would ferry guests out to the yacht.

'Mmm,' said Carrie, taking a sip of champagne, 'these prawns are even better than the ones we had in the club last week, Jay.'

The mention of the lunch in the Marbella Club jogged Jay's memory about another important engagement. 'That reminds me, Carrie,' she smiled brightly, 'have you rung the *marques* yet to invite him to dinner?'

Carrie was caught in a collective gaze of interest from around the table. 'Er, no, I haven't.'

'Why on earth not?' Jay didn't wait for an answer. 'And what evening were you going to suggest?'

'What about Saturday, Mum?' Stephanie suggested. 'That would be good for you too, Hope, wouldn't it? You wouldn't have to worry about work. And I'll have all day to buy and prepare the food.'

'Saturday suits me,' Jay beamed. 'Why don't you ring him when you get back, Carrie, and we can all confirm it?'

Before Carrie could answer, Enrique said casually, 'I assume you are referring to Emilio, Marques de Alba, Cordoba y Rincón?'

'That's right,' Jay said, 'do you know him?'

'We have not been formally introduced, but of course everyone in Marbella would know of the *marques* – much as they would know of me but might not necessarily have made my acquaintance,' Enrique explained gravely and gave a little laugh. 'We are both, in our own ways, a little famous, yes? But I would very much like to meet him. The *marques*, I understand, is a most interesting man . . .'

'Well, then, you must come to dinner too, mustn't he, Carrie? It won't hurt to have another man at the table, at any rate.'

'Of course, Enrique.' Carrie tried to avoid Stephanie's eyes, which were rolling dramatically in horror. 'If you're free on Saturday?'

'I will make it my business to be free for you, Señora Carrie,' Enrique said obsequiously, and took a deep breath. 'I hope you will not think it presumptuous of me, Señora, but it might be a good idea, if you are having this little soirée, to invite Captain Rudi along too . . .'

'What?' Jay asked sharply. 'Why on earth would you invite him?' she asked.

For some reason, Hope was looking equally perplexed across the table.

'Well,' Enrique continued smoothly, 'there is a lot of work to be done regarding the wedding, and Rudi, as Señora Jay must already know,' he smiled across at Jay, whose face was a study in polite detachment, 'needs a lot of persuading about anything on *Excalibur*. He is fiercely protective of his yacht, no?'

'Well, he needn't concern himself with the wedding. Frank has given full permission for Carrie and her daughter, who are our dearest family friends, to have their every wish catered to. All Rudi has to do is carry out instructions.'

'I understand, Señora Jay,' Enrique's head inclined alarmingly, 'but surely, it would be wise,' he looked at Carrie, 'for us to at least include him in the arrangements, rather than issuing instructions.' He delivered his killer punch. 'After all, it would make my job so much easier. I do not want to have to fight a man such as Rudi on every point, especially near the time of the wedding. I will need everybody's full co-operation.'

'I don't see why not,' Carrie said. 'I think it's a good idea, and it will even up the numbers a bit.' Secretly, she was relieved at this sudden addition of menfolk to the arrangements. For some reason, having the *marques* with only her, Jay and the girls for company was a little unnerving. 'Will you be able to manage, Stephanie? I'll help, of course.'

'I'll be fine, Mum, really. I do know what I'm doing and it'll be fun.'

'Well that's settled,' Carrie said. 'Jay, will you let Rudi know he's invited?'

Before she had a chance to reply, Enrique closed the deal. 'I will relay the invitation myself, Señora Carrie, with your permission. I have to speak with Rudi later regarding some of the proposed wedding plans. It will be a pleasure for me to let him know he is invited.'

When Jay, Carrie and the girls had been ferried back to the port, Enrique remained on board, waiting to discuss what had transpired over lunch with Rudi, who, being his usual elusive self, was nowhere to be found.

As he sent out a crew member to search for him, he could barely contain his excitement. This would make Rudi sit up and take notice. Not only had he tracked Rudi's father down, as he had promised for the agreed fee, but now he had made the opportunity for him to become acquainted with the man over dinner. Enrique shivered with anticipation. That would be worth quite a considerable bonus. He sat down again in the dining room and helped himself to more champagne while he waited for Rudi. He tried to decide which excited him more: the thought of the exorbitant fee he would demand, or witnessing a father meet his unknown son for the first time.

They would resemble each other closely in one way for sure. They were both, by all accounts, arrogant bastards.

Later that evening, in his villa at the Marbella Club, Emilio replaced the telephone receiver and smiled. Holding the piece of notepaper up to the light for closer examination, he studied the address he had noted down.

Villa Tsarina, The Golden Mile, Marbella.

His brow furrowed in concentration. If memory served him, that must surely be the magnificent newly built villa owned by the Russian oligarch Pietrovich.

Whatever Irish background this Mrs Carrie Armstrong was from, she was obviously wealthy. And, on reflection, she was a very attractive woman. Not in the obvious sense, of course, but over the years Emilio had had his fill of obvious women. No, there was something . . . soft and reassuringly wholesome about Carrie Armstrong that appealed to him.

Mind you, he would have to double-check his wardrobe. It had been a long time since he'd been invited to a decent gathering. And anyone residing in Villa Tsarina for three months would put on a first-rate production.

Oh, of course Carrie had said it would be casual, a barbeque probably, very relaxed, but if he knew women, and Emilio prided himself on being something of an expert, that could mean a villa full of the most glamorous and wealthy people on the coast. He had better take care to be looking his best.

Then, glancing up, he was caught unawares by the sight of his reflection staring at him from across the room. He ran a hand through his plentiful dark hair, now liberally streaked with grey. He was in good shape, despite his years, which he attributed gratefully to his genetics rather than to any serious attempt at exercise. He was six foot three, his broad shoulders tapered to a pleasingly trim waist with only the merest hint of a paunch, and his long muscular legs still caused many a flutter among the female population of Marbella. Even now he turned heads when he wandered to the pool for his daily fifty lengths, then an hour of sunbathing, a game of backgammon and a light lunch. After this ritual, he retired to his villa, followed again by admiring glances.

He thought now of going to dine in the club, then ordered room service, preferring to be alone. Flicking on the sound system, his favourite aria – or rather, their favourite – from *La Bohème* flooded the room, 'Che Manina Fria', 'Your Tiny Hand Is Frozen'. For a moment, tears threatened and he blinked them away, surprised by the vehemence of feelings he fought hard to ignore. Of course, it was the music that did it – Maria had always said he was a sentimental old romantic at heart, and with her, he had been.

He listened now to the exquisite voice of the tenor, singing the tragic lyrics. Brushing away the tears, he allowed himself to remember his beautiful, frail Maria, her beauty, her bravery when he could no longer be strong in the face of her ever-increasing frailty. She had laid her hand on his and told him, her big brown eyes shining with love, that everything would be all right as long as they had each other. And how he had tried to believe her, though he could feel her life force ebbing, as he held and tried to warm her cold and fragile hand in his.

16

Frank Farrelly sat in his huge television room, sunk bliss-fully into one of the four sofas that flanked two walls. The TV was blaring, food was on the way, he was on his own and all was well with the world.

He was in a particularly good mood. In the last couple of weeks he had pulled off an indecently successful merger with an American company he had been chasing for years. It would propel him even higher up the rich list. It had been hard work, the last couple of months, those Yanks didn't give anything away easily, but after a few strategic boardroom onslaughts they had seen they were fighting a losing battle and had come to their senses and capitulated. Frank and his company now held a 51 per cent stake in one of the biggest insulation companies in the US. It was no small feat. But the travelling between the States and Ireland, the late nights, the sweet talking on and off golf courses, the trips to the élite lap-dancing clubs and general post-takeover celebrations had taken their toll. Frank was exhausted.

Now, in Dublin, he was relaxing at home. He had shed both his shoes and his toupèe and was eagerly awaiting a Chinese takeaway he had ordered – he wouldn't have dared to if Jay had been in residence. But she wasn't. Frank grinned. God, but there was nothing like a bit of real peace and quiet. He was going to take a few days off and concentrate on recovering. Get in a round or two of golf, nothing strenuous, maybe even have a massage.

He had to be in good nick for the following week, he reminded himself, when he'd be heading down to Marbella. The bankers who were funding the merger were coming for a three-day jolly to stay on *Excalibur*. It was all part of the corporate roundabout. They had pulled out the stops for him and now he had to show them a good time. Just the boys, some real heavy hitters, mind, but he'd put on the usual show – golf, dinners on *Excalibur*, a night or two in the port, maybe some polo in Soto Grande – and send them home tired and satisfied. No doubt about it, whoever said there was no such thing as a free lunch had got it right. He sighed. Still, he thought eagerly, he'd see Ivanka soon, and that would be worth the trip in itself. Then he frowned. He had almost forgotten Jay was down there too. Hmm. That might be a problem. Usually their arrangement worked quite well, but when other people from Dublin were around, Jay wasn't so easy to manipulate. She liked to Keep Up Appearances. She said it was important not just for their boys, but for his businesses that they presented a united front. And in fairness, she did a good job of it. But with these bankers having to be entertained on *Excalibur*, Jay and not Ivanka had to appear as hostess.

Bankers were a funny bunch at the best of times – Frank wouldn't trust them as far as he'd throw them. They could be stuffy buggers, too. Not all of them liked to let their hair down. Never mind, he thought as he heard the front-door intercom buzz. He'd find a way to see Ivanka. Unlike Jay, she wouldn't make an almighty fuss if he couldn't spend as much time with her as she'd have liked. There was always the next time.

He stood up and patted his stomach, which was rumbling loudly. He wasn't half looking forward to this. He shuffled out to the front door in his socks and opened it to take his order from the young Chinese boy. Frank put the bag on the hall table and counted out the cash, making sure to give the boy a generous tip. It couldn't be much fun, he thought, racing around delivering meals on a wet Friday night when everyone else was having a good time. The boy took the money and held something out to him. Frank thought he was handing him back the change.

'No, no, that's all right,' he said. 'That's for you.' He had already turned to close the door.

'No, mister,' the young man protested. Now Frank saw that he was proffering an envelope. 'This for you, too.' He thrust it at Frank and jumped back quickly into his car and shot off.

Frank looked puzzled. He couldn't think what it might be. It didn't look like one of those special-offer leaflets those places circulated. He picked up the bag, tucked the envelope under his arm and went to the kitchen, where he got out a tray and a plate, then opened a bottle of beer. He headed back into the TV room to eat in peace and catch up on the Heineken Cup rugby he had missed while he was away. The envelope sat on the tray. Something about it bothered him.

He could never eat happily while there was any sort of paperwork that needed to be checked – a habit that he had acquired as a young boy when he had inadvertently thrown away a not inconsiderable sum of money sent to his mother by a relative in America. He had picked it up with the old newspapers he had been told to throw out. When his mother discovered the money was gone, Frank had to not only leave the house but leave the county until he had earned the same amount to return to her. It had taken him three hard months on a building site and left him with a lifelong regard for even the most inconspicuous-looking piece of paper, which he would check and re-check before disposing of it. It drove Jay mental.

Reluctantly he put aside the tray and took up the envelope,

which on inspection bore two words only: 'OPEN PLEASE'. That struck Frank as strange, although there was no knowing what lengths marketing people would go to these days. Maybe it was a begging letter – he was used to those too. God knew how people got hold of his home address, but once you were a multimillionaire, nothing was sacred. He opened it and pulled out a folded piece of A4 paper.

At first, he couldn't make out the two squiggly lines of writing, but the image above it looked vaguely familiar. He reached for his reading-glasses and put them on and realised he was holding it upside down. He turned it round and recognised a photocopied picture of himself, one that had been used many times in newspapers for PR purposes.

It was a close-up, in black and white, of Frank looking businesslike and serious. In this instance the eyes in the shot had been cut out. The words above the photograph read, in slanted writing: 'Take a good look, Mr Frank. This is what it will be like to have your eyes gouged out.' That was it. Frank felt a bit peculiar. He didn't know whether to laugh or to take it seriously.

A vague feeling of unease crept over him. Fifteen minutes later, the food on the tray beside him had gone cold. That didn't bother him. His appetite had deserted him.

Frank wasn't the only one who was tired. Rubbing his eyes, Rob sat with five of his top tax people and accountants round a boardroom table going over, for the umpteenth time, the purported tax breaks involved in the bloodstock company he was just about to invest in. It was two a.m. and their deadline was nine o'clock. They couldn't afford to miss a trick.

'That's it,' Barry, the senior tax consultant, said. 'We've tied up the last loophole. I can't see any reason not to go ahead.'

Rob yawned. 'Great. Good job, guys. See you here at eight for breakfast. We'll call it a day after we've signed.'

Outside, he got into his car and made for home. God, he was tired. He'd been working round the clock, as usual, to take his mind off his increasingly unsatisfactory domestic situation.

It had been two weeks, maybe more, since he had spoken to Olwen, and that conversation had been strained, to say the least. Well, the bits he could remember. Now that he had calmed down, he couldn't say he blamed her for her reaction to his late-night call. But she needn't have been quite so sharp. After all, it wasn't the first time he'd phoned her in the wee hours, and it wouldn't have been the first time she'd driven into town to pick him up. She'd done it on several occasions when he had been on the tear. She'd been happy to have a chance to see him and spend time with him. But on those occasions they hadn't been having a row. His brow furrowed again as he thought about the lost weekend.

He missed her, he really did. Just thinking about her made him feel horny.

Rob pulled up outside his house and let himself in, flicking on the lights and finding the vast hallway suddenly eerie. He shivered. He hated coming home to an empty house – always had. Even on the few occasions over the years when he and Carrie had almost split up and he had moved out – he owned apartments galore he could stay in – he had lasted three days at most. Not because he missed Carrie, but because he missed the noise, the routine, the hustle and bustle of a home that revolved around *him*.

The last two weeks had been awful. Work had helped to take his mind off things, and he had spoken to Carrie and Stephanie, who seemed to be having a whale of a time in Marbella and were in no hurry to press him on when he might be coming down to join them – but he was lonely.

At least the whole wedding palaver was progressing without incident. Carrie had rattled on about some wedding-organiser chap, visits to the yacht and how everything was shaping up to be absolutely fabulous. Well, something was.

He went into the kitchen and found a note from Babs saying there was a casserole in the fridge that would heat up in twenty minutes if he fancied it. It occurred to Rob that he hadn't eaten since breakfast and was ravenously hungry – even if it was now three a.m. He got himself a beer, put the casserole in the Aga and sat down at the kitchen table. He turned on his phone, which had been off all day because of the meeting and checked his messages. Nothing, apart from a couple from his secretary. Rob stretched his legs with a sigh and a heavy heart. He'd call Olwen. He couldn't leave it like this. He needed her. That was all there was to it. Then, remembering it was three a.m., he decided to text her instead. That way she couldn't accuse him of phoning her in the middle of the night. If nothing else, she'd wake up tomorrow to a message telling her how sorry he was, and how very much he loved and missed her. Couldn't do any harm.

Beep! Olwen's phone vibrated on the bedside table beside her, rousing her from semi-sleep, where she tossed and turned in the grip of uneasy dreams. She reached automatically for the phone, hoping and praying it would be Rob. Rubbing her eyes, hands trembling, she read the message: 'I'm so sorry my darling, I have behaved like a wally, I miss you so much. We need to talk. I adore you. Please may I ring you? x'

Olwen sat up, turned on the light and read it again. She looked at the clock. It was almost five past three in the morning. Clearly Rob couldn't sleep either. How gut wrenchingly miserable she had been. How stupid they'd been to waste even a moment of precious time they could have spent together. And all because of a thoughtless remark.

Olwen had gone over the scene a thousand times. Yes, of course she'd been hurt, but why couldn't she have talked the whole thing through calmly and reasonably instead of reacting the way she did and hanging up on him that Friday evening?

Of course his suggestion had offended her, but he hadn't meant to, she was sure. He was just being thoughtless, and had been tired and had wanted to stay in his own home for a change. She could understand that. She should have been more tactful in her response. And then when he'd phoned her up from town, clearly pissed, well, she'd been annoyed of course, but again she had overreacted. She could have just laughed and told him to call her the next day when he'd sobered up.

Instead they had spent two miserable weeks of sleepless nights feeling wretched. Well, *she* had, and now, oh, God, it was *so* good to hear from him. She fumbled quickly to reply, ignoring the small voice that warned her it was absolutely the wrong thing to do.

'I'm so sorry too, darling, have been miserable, of course I'd love to hear your gorgeous voice x'

Olwen lay back on the pillows and sighed, still holding the phone in her hand. She hoped he'd call her straight back, but perhaps he'd just sent the text and gone to sleep or turned off his phone until morning. Either way, she didn't care. She was just happy to know he was thinking of her, that he needed her as much as she did him.

Well, that hadn't taken long. Rob's heart lifted at the sound of his message alert. He grinned as he grabbed the phone. He had wolfed down the casserole and was about to wash it down with the last of his beer. He read the message happily. Olwen was awake. Better still, she had responded, and instantly.

He'd thought he'd have to wait until tomorrow at the earliest. It was better than he could have hoped for. He'd ring her now. Strike while the iron – or in this case, the woman – was hot.

'Baby,' he said silkily, injecting just the right amount of regret into his tone. 'Are you talking to me? Will you forgive me?'

'Oh, Rob.' He heard the smile in her voice and imagined her in bed with the phone to her ear. 'It's so good to hear you,' she sighed.

'Not as good as it is to hear you.' He meant it. God, he'd almost forgotten what her voice did to him. He loved her voice, soft, modulated and so, so sexy.

'Of course I've forgiven you,' she murmured, 'and I'm sorry, so sorry about everything.'

'Don't be. It was my fault. I behaved like a prick,' he said, relieved and elated. 'And I'm going to make it up to you.'

'You don't have to, darling. Just promise me we'll never do this again – never fight like that. It's been – I've been so miserable, so wretchedly miserable . . .' Olwen's voice caught.

'Darling, don't cry, please. I love you so much.'

'I'm sorry,' Olwen sniffed. 'It's just been so hard trying to keep up a front at work and I missed you so much.' Her voice was almost a whisper.

'I know. I missed you too. It's bad, isn't it?'

'Awful . . . Rob?'

'Yes, baby?'

'What are we going to do?' For the first time there was uncertainty, fear even, in her voice.

'We need to talk. Don't worry about it now. I'll call you tomorrow, okay?'

'Okay . . .'

'All that matters is that I love you. Now go to sleep, or I'll make you have phone sex.'

That raised a small laugh, which he was glad to hear.

'Night. I love you,' she said softly.

'I love you too, more than I've ever loved anyone.' He meant it, he thought as he hung up. He did love her more than anyone – ever. It was just that . . . Christ, this was so difficult. He was relieved, that was for sure, that Olwen had been so ready to forgive him, to talk to him, but something else niggled him. Something he had heard in her voice. She had sounded kind of strung out. He was worried about her. He knew how much she loved him – how could he not? – as he did her. Now, for the first time, it began to worry him. No matter how delightfully it had started, an affair always became acutely stressful if love was involved. But . . . Rob couldn't think as coherently as he would have liked. He was so tired. But maybe, the thought hovered uncomfortably as he got into bed, this was becoming a problem. One, perhaps, that was too big even for him to handle.

The applause was deafening as row after row of fashionistas rose to their feet to reaffirm Claude Verdun as king of the Parisian autumn-winter collections. For the finale, the models had once again paraded down the runway, followed by the designer and then the pièce de résistance, Ali in the wedding dress, looking exquisite, the scene all the more poignant as everybody knew she was soon to be married. Under the explosion of flashbulbs, she continued to do what she did best, smiling, posing, showing off the gown to its best possible advantage, until Claude took her arm and escorted her backstage. The collection, it was unanimously agreed, had been a triumph.

Backstage, he kissed her hand. 'Ali, you were fantastic – as always.'

'Nonsense,' Ali laughed. 'It's your clothes that do it. How could any woman *not* feel fantastic in them?'

'You're still the best.' He beamed. 'None of the other girls come close!'

As he disappeared into the crowd of well-wishers, Ali smiled after him. Claude was sweet but, like actors, designers had huge, fragile egos, matched only by their huge insecurities. You could never flatter or reassure them enough. She understood this perfectly and it was that, along with her professional reliability, that had secured her a place at the top. There might be younger, prettier girls snapping at her heels, but Ali did more than make clothes or make-up look great: she made people feel good while she was doing it.

Struggling out of the dress, she handed it carefully to one of Claude's assistants, then pulled on her skinny jeans and a T-shirt. She slathered her face with cleanser and meticulously removed the layers of painstakingly applied make-up. Checking her mobile, she noticed a message from her agent, Sandi. 'Ring me!' it said.

'Ali!' Sandi's voice was brisk. 'Heard you were a sensation today. Well done, girl.'

'News travels fast.'

'Oh, Claude was on not five minutes ago in raptures, bless him. But that's not why I rang you.'

'Oh?'

'Stay Tru have finally been in touch. It's down to you and the Ukrainian girl, but Sarah, my mole, says the money's on you. Apparently they love you, and Gerald J. Junior was very impressed at the meeting. What he says goes – even with Big Daddy. In fact, he'll be in town next week.'

'Who? Gerald J. Senior?'

'No, Junior. He wants to have dinner with you, so if you have any plans, hon, cancel them.'

'Dinner!' Ali exclaimed. 'What for? Can't we just have a meeting or something – lunch, even?'

'Relax, Ali, for heaven's sake, it's a formality. He just wants to chat, go over a few things in a relaxed setting. Jeez, for twenty million smackeroonies I know plenty of models who'd be only too glad to have dinner with him. He's a nice guy, Ali, and jolly easy on the eye too!'

'He knows I'm engaged, doesn't he?' Ali chewed a nail absentmindedly.

'I don't think that rock on your finger has escaped anyone's notice, Ali! Of course he knows. It's part of why they like you so much – squeaky-clean image and all. Anyway,' Sandi cut to the chase, 'I took the liberty of accepting on your behalf.'

'Sandi!' Ali protested in vain.

'Seven thirty at the Ritz next Wednesday. Be there. Just think of the contract, Ali, think of the furore you'll cause in the industry. Think of all those millions!'

Right, thought Ali. That's all you're thinking about for sure. She scowled at her end of the phone.

'Okay, I'll do it.'

'Good girl. Ring me afterwards and let me know how it went. We're nearly there, Ali. By the end of next week you'll be the new face of Stay Tru.'

'How're you doing, Steph sweetheart?' Carrie wandered into the kitchen, from which a variety of delicious smells were emanating. From where she stood she could smell sautéing garlic, the tang of juicy Spanish tomatoes and the tantalising aroma of chorizo.

'Mum,' Stephanie sighed. 'For the last time, everything's fine.' Her face creased with exasperation. 'Why can't you just trust me?'

'Oh, darling, I'm sorry, but I'm so nervous. I can't sit still and they'll be arriving any minute.'

'All the more reason for you to sit down, have a drink and relax,' said Stephanie, firmly 'while I grab a quick shower and get dressed – if that's allowed, of course.'

'You haven't even changed, Stephanie, hurry!' Carrie lifted a lid and breathed in deeply. 'Mmm! It smells gorgeous.'

'Just don't touch or fiddle with anything.' Stephanie had turned into quite a little Tartar in the kitchen. 'I'll be gone for fifteen or twenty minutes max, okay?'

'Okay,' Carrie said doubtfully, desperately wanting to check and snoop on everything.

'I mean it, Mum. You'll ruin it if you start messing. Everything's perfect, and I'll be back in a mo. You look fab, by the way.' Stephanie gave her mother an appreciative once-over. 'Is that a new dress? I'm sure I haven't seen it before.' She eyed the white silky number that plunged in a Grecian neckline and clung in flattering swirls of fabric to below Carrie's knees. A wide bronze belt cinched her slim waist and matched her high-heeled shoes. Her legs were tanned and bare.

'I've had it a while,' Carrie lied. She didn't want her daughter to guess just how much trouble she had gone to with her appearance.

'What your mother means is that it's belonged to her for more than twenty-four hours and less than forty-eight.' Jay had come into the kitchen. 'I'd call that pretty new, Carrie, wouldn't you?' She grinned. 'Now, where's that champagne? I for one have an empty glass.'

'In the fridge,' said Stephanie. 'I'm outta here. See you in fifteen and don't touch *anything*.'

'Hope?' Carrie went back to the dining area. They had debated eating outside, but as it could turn cold suddenly after dark, they had decided to eat at the large glass and steel dining table inside, with the glass doors open onto the main patio. They retracted at the touch of a button, and the patio was artfully lit by carefully placed spotlights. The pool, also lit, was a liquid blue against the velvet darkness of the approaching night.

'Mmm?'

'Are you sure the table looks all right?' Carrie stood back and studied it critically. She had spent most of the afternoon arranging and rearranging it.

Hope got up from the sofa, where she had been flicking through a magazine, and walked over to her. 'Mum,' she said softly, putting her arms round her, 'it's *fabulous*. The food will be fabulous. *You* look fabulous. Now, sit down and chill, will you?'

Carrie laughed and had the grace to look a little shamefaced. 'I suppose I am getting a bit worked up about everything. It's just been such a long time since . . .'

'Since what?' asked Jay as she joined them, having topped up her glass. 'You entertain all the time at home, Carrie.'

'That's different,' Carrie protested.

'Why?'

'Well, I don't know – it just is.' How could she say it felt strange – no, *weird* even – to be entertaining on her own like this? Not to be waiting nervously for Rob to show up, hoping he wouldn't be late, and the relief she would feel when he'd breeze in. Her fear would evaporate as the whole room picked up on his mood and the gaiety began in earnest.

Now she was in a strange house in another country, with two of her daughters, granted, and her dear friend Jay, waiting for three men to arrive whom she had barely just met. Suddenly a wave of panic gripped her. She wanted in that exact moment to flee the house, the holiday, the wedding, *everything*, and run home to Dublin, to her home – to Rob. Except, she reflected miserably, Rob probably wouldn't be there. He never was.

She was saved by the bell, which rang loudly, making them jump.

'Well, don't just stand there!' Jay gave her a dig. 'Go and greet your guest, whoever it is.'

Jay took another gulp of her champagne. Despite her bravado and her enthusiasm for spending an evening with Emilio, Marques de Alba, Cordoba y Rincón, Jay was *not* looking forward to sharing the same space for any length of time with Rudi. In fact, the idea made her downright uncomfortable. Ever since the 'episode', she had almost felt his derision seeping from his every pore.

She couldn't believe her bad luck that day on *Excalibur* when Enrique had suggested including him in their gathering. It was really too bad . . .

'I do hope I'm not late.' Emilio was very handsome as he stood in the doorway proffering a bottle of vintage Krug. 'It is an occupational hazard with us Spaniards, but I made a special effort to be punctual.' He grinned, revealing his movie-star perfect teeth.

'Of course not, come in. You're perfectly on time – and thank you.' Carrie accepted the bottle of champagne. 'You shouldn't have.'

'My pleasure,' he said, following her to where Hope and Jay stood, sipping their drinks.

Minutes later, a glass of champagne in hand, Emilio had dispelled any potential awkwardness and was telling an amusing story that had his audience laughing. Just as he was about to get to the punchline, the doorbell rang again.

'It's okay Mum,' called Stephanie, fresh from the shower and wearing a pretty smocked tunic and huge wedge sandals that looked impossible to walk in. 'I'll get it.' She opened the door eagerly. 'Welcome to Casa Armstrong,' she said to the two figures silhouetted in the dusk.

'Señorita.' Enrique's muffled voice came from behind a vast arrangement of flowers he was holding. He drew himself up to his full height of almost five foot ten and half inches in heels, but he still had to peer round them. 'It is an honour,' he said and handed them to Stephanie.

'Hi,' said another, following Enrique inside. 'Rudi Weiss. We met on *Excalibur*.'

'Oh, I remember,' said Stephanie. The captain, who even to her critical eyes was hotter than – well, just plain hot. She reckoned he was in his early thirties or thereabouts, far too old for her, but still, fun to flirt with.

'Here, let me take those for you.' He lifted the flowers from her – she was staggering under their weight.

'Thanks,' she said. 'You can put them over there.' She pointed to a table by the wall. 'Come and get a drink – Mum?'

Carrie greeted Enrique and Rudi warmly as they joined the gathering and Stephanie headed back into the kitchen, enlisting Hope's help with dishing up.

Once introductions had been made and glasses refilled, the conversation turned to the spectacular house. As Enrique held forth about his tenuous links with the architect who had built it, Rudi asked Carrie if she'd mind if he took a look outside.

'No, of course not, be my guest.'

He went lazily out on to the patio and down the steps towards the pool. There he let out a long breath, then took in another. Man, that had been some act to pull off. He fingered the collar of his open-necked shirt distractedly. He had done it. He had shaken hands with and been introduced to the man in the world he loathed above all others. Emilio, Marques de Alba, Cordoba y Rincón, his very own, very absent, very negligent father. Rudi strolled around, pretending to notice the lush, fragrant plants, but aware only of his pounding heart. He had had no idea, not an iota, of how much this meeting would affect him. He was finding it difficult to breathe, let alone speak. To think that the son-of-a-bitch up

there, holding court, laughing, talking, had been the bastard
who had let him and his late mother live in poverty. Rudi
was shaking with suppressed rage. That he had taken the
man's hand, and not his bloody throat, as he had wanted to,
showed the measure of his resolve. His moment would come,
he was sure of it. Then he would have his revenge. In the
meantime, he took another deep breath. He might as well
find out as much about the guy as he could. He glanced up
at the house and saw Enrique gesticulating wildly at him
from the window. Time to go back inside. Time to fraternise
with the enemy.

Stephanie had outdone herself, no doubt about it. Carrie, a
good cook herself, was seriously impressed and proud of her
despite her earlier misgivings. The designer cookery course
Stephanie had completed in London certainly seemed to have
paid off, and everyone had exclaimed over the wonderful
food.

They had sat down to chilled mint and pea soup, followed
by a paella that, according to Emilio, rivalled the best he had
ever tasted. For dessert, Stephanie had made her own favourite
Banoffee pie, with lashings of whipped cream, and a mouth-
watering Cointreau sorbet. Now, with cheese and coffee about
to be served, she and Hope cleared the table discreetly as the
hum of conversation increased as appetites were sated and
tongues loosened by a succession of well-chosen wines.

In the kitchen, safely out of earshot, Stephanie babbled as
Hope loaded the dishwasher. 'Don't you think Rudi's
gorgeous?' Stephanie handed her a plate, flushed and happy
with her culinary triumph. Hope, she thought, was not in
good form, despite the success of the evening. All through
dinner she had been her usual polite self, but the only time
she had come to life was when she had been having an earnest
discussion with Emilio about a Franciscan monastery she had

been researching for her book. It had turned out that an uncle of his had been the last abbot. Hope had listened with rapt attention to his encyclopedic knowledge of the monastery and, indeed, history of the surrounding area.

'No, I don't,' Hope said shortly. 'I think he's rude and arrogant, actually. And his manners are appalling – he's barely said two words all evening.'

'Rudi by name and ruder by nature,' giggled Stephanie. 'When you're that sexy, it just adds to your appeal.'

'Don't be ridiculous, Stephanie. He's just a pain in the arse. I don't know why Mum invited him. He obviously feels he has better things to be doing than sitting here with us, that's for sure.'

'He probably has,' observed Stephanie. 'All the women within a twenty-mile radius I'd say would be a very viable option. But I, for one, am not complaining. Just look at him – those lovely long legs, and did you notice his hands? They're beautiful. I always think—'

'Oh, for God's sake, shut up, Steph.' For some reason, the eulogy was making Hope increasingly angry. 'He's just another sulky, self-obsessed, arrogant man, and he might as well have "serial womaniser" tattooed on his forehead. Believe me, I know the type well.' *And so should you*, she almost added, but snapped her mouth shut before the hurtful words could escape. It was true, though. Years of finding out about their father's various affairs, watching her mother try to hide her pain, listening to the rows she wasn't supposed to hear late at night as a little girl had left their imprint. Hope had listened to them, sometimes sitting on the top stair in her nightie, too afraid to go back to bed until the shouting stopped. It did, eventually, but was usually followed by the slam of a door, the sound of her father's car starting, and then, worst of all, silence. Hope would hurry back to bed when she heard her mother's footsteps, then stay still as a mouse when her mother opened the door to check on her and Ali, who would always be sound asleep.

After that, Hope would put a pillow over her ears to block out her mother's muffled sobbing, but no matter how she tried, the sound seemed to get right inside her head. She had wanted to cry too, to run in to her and get into her bed and tell her not to cry, that it would all be all right, cuddle up beside her and fall asleep. The way they used to when she was very little and her father would carry her back into her own bed when she was fast asleep. But somehow, she knew instinctively that this would not be the right thing to do. So she waited, as long as she could, before falling into a fretful, exhausted sleep.

In the morning, pale and subdued, she would come down to breakfast and was always astonished by the sight of her father at the kitchen table, having his coffee and maybe a slice of toast, then kissing them goodbye and rushing off to work. Her mother would be telling them to hurry up or they'd be late for school – and it was all as if nothing had happened. Hope would sometimes have a strange buzzy feeling in her head, as if she had imagined it all. As if the horrible fear that her daddy would not come back, that he had left them all in the middle of the night, as if the fear that had coiled in her stomach all night long had been nothing at all, just a silly dream.

Later on, when she was a teenager, she had felt a mixture of pride and peculiarity when her friends told her her dad was 'cool' on the rare occasions that he roared up in his latest sports car to collect her from school. Even stern-faced Sister Joseph, the headmistress, had gone a little pink and tittered when he had talked and joked with her. Her friends' mothers always asked hopefully was her daddy collecting her when she stayed at their houses, and had smiled fixedly when she had said no, her mummy would be coming.

It was later still, in her twenties, when well-meaning girl-friends would let slip they had seen her father in a restaurant or bar with someone other than her mother. Worst of all, a boy she knew at college, and seriously liked, said in clearly admiring tones one day it was well-known her dad was a 'player'. She had made her decision. She had studied hard, completed her finals, taken a gap year and never come back – except at Christmas or for the occasional flying visit, usually coinciding with her mother's birthday.

'Since when did you get to be a man-hater?'

Stephanie's question brought her back to the present.

'I'm not a man-hater,' Hope retorted. 'It's just that . . .'

'What?'

'Oh, I don't know, forget it.'

'Hope, you really need to wind down. You've been working way too hard. It's a nice evening. We're all having a good time. Just enjoy it, will you?' Stephanie shook her head in bewilderment.

'You're right,' Hope conceded, wiping her hands on a tea-towel. 'I'm sorry, Steph, it *is* a lovely evening and I didn't mean to rain on your parade. Dinner was fab and you did a great job. Everyone's saying so.'

'Good, and it's not over yet.' Stephanie grinned. 'He fancies you, you know, Rudi.'

Hope gave her a don't-go-there look. 'Don't be ridiculous.'

'He does, I can tell. The same way I can tell Emilio fancies Mum. Rudi's less obvious about it, but he keeps looking at you when you're not watching.'

'Now you really are imagining things.' Hope swatted her with the tea-towel. 'Come on, let's get back out there.'

'Typical.' Stephanie gave a long-suffering sigh. 'Ali's getting married, Mum's getting chatted up by a *marques*, no less, and you're getting lustful looks thrown your way. I'll be the only one without so much as a whiff of a holiday romance. It's not fair.'

'What's not fair?' Carrie asked, looking up from her conversation with Emilio and smiling at her two girls.

Emilio took the opportunity to ask permission, which was readily granted, to light a cigar. As with everything else, he executed the procedure with infinite elegance, sitting back in his chair and puffing thoughtfully.

'Nothing,' grinned Hope. 'Coffee's served.' She moved round the table to fill each cup.

Emilio took a sip of his coffee and surveyed the scene around him. He had expected something very different and had been pleasantly surprised. This was no flashy, over-the-top, let's-show-off-just-how-much-money-we-have party as he had assumed, with fleets of staff ferrying ridiculous canapés and awful designer cocktails about to suspiciously dressed people involved in equally suspicious business dealings. On the contrary, it was a delightful family supper with extremely convivial company and the whole evening reminded him of how much he missed such gatherings. The only fly in the ointment was the awful Enrique, with the gravity-defying hairdo and ridiculous mannerisms. But he was the wedding planner, so Emilio conceded that his inclusion was of necessity rather than desire. The Jay woman seemed dubious, too, and she was quite clearly taking something. Emilio had noticed her leave the table more than once in the last hour, and she had an aggressive set to her expression that he found off-putting. She was also throwing back the champagne liberally.

The family themselves, he thought, were perfectly charming. The young one, Stephanie, was clearly a terrific cook and a cheery little soul, while her sister Hope was very intelligent and well-read, if a little guarded. She had been hurt, he guessed, and needed careful handling, but the right man, well . . . Emilio smiled to himself. Whenever he came along, he would have found himself a wonderful girl.

★   ★   ★

A warm breeze blew in, carrying with it a heady mixture of bougainvillaea and the light tang of the sea below them.

Breathing deeply, Carrie looked around the table and tried to make sense of her conflicting feelings. The evening had been an undoubted success. Stephanie had catered beautifully, and Jay had been so impressed she had promised to get her to do a dinner party for her and assured her she would give her name to all her friends too.

Hope seemed happy, if a little withdrawn, but she always took a while to relax with new people. Carrie smiled inwardly. She had noticed, more than once, that Rudi's glance hovered with something more than polite interest in Hope's direction, although Hope seemed unaware of this. He was an incredibly attractive young man, she thought, but there was something about him she couldn't quite put her finger on. He had been perfectly polite all evening, but she had noticed something uneasy in his unguarded expression. Something raw that flared in his eyes. Something that, ridiculous as it might seem, had made her feel sorry for him. She couldn't for the life of her imagine what it was.

Part of her felt sad that they should be enjoying such an evening without Rob. Even though he was rarely around, it was different tonight, now that she knew it was only a matter of time before they separated formally. It was, she supposed, the beginning of the end.

Another part of her felt guilty exhilaration that she could relax and enjoy herself in the company of new people, who didn't know her simply as Rob's wife.

As if he had read her thoughts, Emilio touched her arm lightly. 'A penny for them?' he asked. 'Or should I say a euro?'

'Oh, they're not worth that much,' Carrie laughed, embarrassed to be caught deep in thought. 'I was just, um, thinking of home and family, how quickly the years pass . . .'

'Yes,' Emilio smiled, 'I know.' A definite shadow passed across his face. 'Your husband, he is joining you soon?'

'Probably.' Suddenly Carrie felt flustered under his direct gaze. 'Actually, I don't know, Rob travels according to his own schedule.' She hoped the smile she forced hid the uncertainty that underpinned her reply. 'He's very busy . . . you know how it is.'

'Yes,' Emilio said speculatively. 'Yes, I do know how it is.'

And somehow Carrie had the strangest feeling that he knew exactly what she was talking about. Suddenly she remembered, and cursed herself for her insensitivity. 'I'm so sorry,' she said. 'Forgive me, I forgot that your wife . . . that she, um . . .'

Mercifully he rescued her from the horror of being unable to find the right words.

'Thank you,' he said quietly. 'Yes, she died a long time ago now, but I miss her still. Not a day goes by . . .'

Carrie didn't trust herself to speak. Something about the way he had looked when he uttered those words, with such simple honesty, tore her heart in two. How dreadful for him, she thought, but how wonderful for his late wife. A woman who had known and inspired such love. It was something, Carrie suddenly realised with a wrench, that she herself would never experience. Or, at least, she hadn't so far. Her children loved her, of course, but—

'Forgive me, I have made you sad.' Again his hand was on her arm. His eyes, kind, wise, looked into hers.

'Oh, no,' she said, 'not sad. A little bit wistful maybe. She must have been a very special person.'

'She was. We had far too short a time together, but we were lucky. Some people never get to share the love that we did.'

Carrie swallowed. 'Do you have children?'

'We had a son. He was killed in a power-boat accident.

That was the only time I gave thanks that Maria was dead. At least she was spared that agony.'

'I can't imagine how awful that must be. How did you cope?'

'Badly, is the short answer. And I'm afraid I was not a good father. I was very angry, too angry. In a way, I often think that Carlos lost both his parents when Maria died. My parents took over his upbringing – it's not something I'm proud of. And, of course, I thought there would be time to make it up to him – but that was not to be.'

'What on earth are you two whispering about?' At the other end of the table, Jay was annoyed to be excluded from what was clearly a riveting conversation between Carrie and Emilio. She was finding the evening dull and even constant top-ups of coke and champagne weren't lifting her mood. Whatever they were discussing, they were getting far too cosy. Until now, she had been regaling Enrique with her theories of marble versus terrazzo as flooring material. He had been listening attentively to her, but she could feel that he was also trying to keep an eye on Rudi, who, sitting across from the *marques* and beside Hope, appeared sulky and uncommunicative. Every time Enrique tried to catch his eye, Rudi just scowled at him.

Emilio replied to her question without missing a beat. 'We were discussing life and how it can take you by surprise. I'm afraid I have been guilty of monopolising our hostess's attention, an understandable if selfish *faux pas*, I'm sure you'll agree.'

Jay didn't. Far from being mollified, the latter part of Emilio's remark served only to irritate her more. She decided to liven things up a bit, put a spark into the evening. She cast her mischievous eyes round the table, deliberately avoiding Carrie's questioning glance, until her gaze came to rest upon Rudi.

'Gosh, Rudi,' she began, 'you're being a bit of a damp

squib this evening. You haven't so much as opened your mouth, except to eat.' She giggled at her joke as the table became dangerously quiet. Before Rudi had a chance to reply, she leaned forward in a mock conspiratorial way that she guessed would show off her impressively arranged cleavage. 'Usually Rudi's the life and soul of the party, aren't you, Rudi?' She scanned her audience for reaction, but something in her tone had made everyone shift uneasily in their seats. 'Why, he's quite the ladies' man, you know.' She glanced around the table. 'A girl in every port – at least that's the conservative statistic – and as for *on* the boat, well, the mind boggles. You have quite a reputation, Rudi. As the best skipper in the Med, of course – and I should know. My husband has to pay him.'

An uncomfortable silence followed, which Enrique tried and failed to dissipate.

'Ah, Señora Jay,' he interjected, 'you have been listening to too much rumour – yes! I myself have suffered from such a reputation.' He patted his hair.

'Oh, I listen all right. "Listen and learn." That's what my dear old mother used to say, not that it got her anywhere. And I'll admit, Rudi, that you're almost obscenely attractive.' She looked him directly in the eye. He returned her gaze unflinchingly. 'But even *you* are not perfect. He has a scar, don't you, Rudi? A very impressive one, with a very impressive story to go with it.' She sat back, delighted at the distraction she had caused. 'Why don't you show it to us. Come on, be a sport and whip off your shirt. I'm sure the girls would love to see it!'

'Jay,' Carrie said, worry flooding her face, 'I really don't think this is the time or the place—'

'Oh, Carrie, don't be such a spoilsport. Rudi loves showing off his physique.' Jay looked around her belligerently. 'Well, what's the matter with all of you?'

'Jay, why don't you have some more coffee?' Hope was at her side, refilling her cup.

'Why, Miss Goody Two Shoes? Am I lowering the tone? What's the matter? Are you offended? Poor Hope's probably never seen a man naked, from the waist up or down. Never mind, hope springs eternal!' The cafetière froze in Hope's hands.

'That's enough.' The voice was quiet but steely. Six sets of eyes whipped towards the *marques*, whose affability had been replaced with authority. Only Rudi remained impassive.

'Perhaps a little fresh air would benefit Señora Jay?' Emilio looked pointedly at Enrique, who was torn between carrying out the unspoken request that he accompany her outside, and staying to enjoy the delicious tension that had gripped the table.

'There's no need.' Rudi's voice broke the spell. He stood up, smiling, but contempt flickered in his eyes. 'I was about to leave anyway.'

'Oh, Rudi, *please*,' Carrie protested. 'Do sit down, I'm sure Jay didn't mean to be, er . . .' Words failed her again.

'Uncouth? Coarse? Hurtful? No, I'm sure she didn't.' He looked at Jay with intense dislike. 'Thankfully I don't have to stick around to listen to her.'

'Are you insulting me?' Jay cried, attack being the best form of defence. 'Because if you are, my husband will have something to say about that, I can tell you.'

'I'm sure he will, after he's read my letter of resignation, which I intend to write tonight. He should have it first thing in the morning. And yes, I should imagine he will have something to say about that to you, although I don't think it'll be the conversation you envisaged.'

Jay paled visibly. Her mouth opened and closed but no words came out. He couldn't mean it, he was bluffing. Why, Frank was coming down next week to entertain a group of bankers on *Excalibur*! Rudi wouldn't dare quit. Frank would be incandescent with anger. Suddenly Jay was frightened. She looked desperately for her champagne glass but it had disappeared. Only coffee and water were within reach, neither of which would do the trick.

But Rudi hadn't finished. He'd planned to wait, to think this through, but he'd had enough shit – he'd taken it all his life, and he wasn't about to take any more, certainly not from his employer's drunken, offensive wife. He'd accomplished what he'd come down to Marbella to achieve anyway and now it was his turn to throw a spanner into the works. He was almost finished. Almost, but not quite.

'As for you,' he turned to Emilio, who had put down his cigar and was watching him with interest and admiration, 'don't think you can take the moral high ground, mate. You're no better than she is. At least with Jay, what you see is what you get, but you, you're nothing more than an impostor. Add that to your title and try it for size.'

A collective gasp went round the table. Emilio sat very still, the only discernible movement being a muscle flexing in his jaw. Carrie looked as if she was about to pass out and Enrique seemed transfixed with horror. 'Rudi,' he said imploringly, 'I beg of you, do not do this.'

'I don't understand.' Carrie looked lost.

'Apparently we have a very angry young man here,' Emilio said, smiling thinly. 'While I can empathise with the anger, I confess I find it a disproportionate response with which to address the offence from which it originated. You might remember we are all here at the invitation and most generous hospitality of our hostess and her daughters. That carries a degree of obliga-tion, does it not, in even the most basic societies.'

'Is that a fact?' Rudi stood stock still, but his outrage was palpable. 'You'd know all about obligations, of course, being an aristocrat.' He gave a mean little laugh.

'Young man—'

'Don't bloody "young man" me, you obsequious dick! You're nothing but a bloody fraud.'

For the briefest of moments, Emilio wondered how, as seemed to be the case, this Rudi person must have found out about his lack of financial status, which he was accusing him quite correctly of being fraudulent about, but more to the point why on earth he could possibly be so angry about it.

The evening had taken on an almost surreal atmosphere. Rudi's impassioned attack and apparent dislike of Emilio had to be nothing short of insanity. But then things took a definite turn for the worse.

'That man sitting there calling himself an aristocrat, posing as a sophisticated, elegant, discerning individual, is nothing but a cheap bastard whom I' – a bitter laugh escaped – 'it would appear, have the misfortune to call my father.'

The deadly silence was accompanied by a disturbing chill that seemed to envelop the little gathering. As astonishment gripped the already riveted audience, Emilio, Marques de Alba, Cordoba y Rincón, stood up slowly. 'How dare you?' His anger was palpable in the ominously quiet, modulated tone. 'How dare you, whoever you are, and whatever plot you may be harbouring in your clearly insane mind? My son died in nineteen eighty-six. How dare you,' he continued, 'disrupt an innocent evening to trade on such loss, such sorrow, for your own callous, cruel and delusional ambitions? I suggest you leave at once before I call the police.'

'Sweet Jesus!' muttered Jay, who had grabbed someone's half-full glass and swigged it.

Still Emilio and Rudi stood facing each other, the silence punctuated only by a strange keening sound from Enrique, who, head in hands, was rocking back and forth in his chair, saying 'Aye-aye-aye-aye-aye.'

'Is this true?' asked Carrie, looking helplessly from one angry face to the other.

'Don't be ridiculous,' Emilio said. 'It's a joke, and one in very poor taste.'

'If it's a joke, then I assure you the joke was on me,' Rudi said through clenched teeth. 'Here.' He slung across the table the photograph he kept with him day and night. It landed in front of Emilio. 'Take a look at that and what's written on the back. It might jog your memory. Clearly my late mother had a penchant for bastards – God knows, she took up with enough of them after you. But being left alone, finding yourself pregnant and penniless, can't have been a bundle of laughs, any more than fending for herself with a baby in tow.'

Emilio had picked up the photograph. The blood drained from his face and he sat down abruptly, staring at the faded picture. 'It can't be. It's impossible,' he whispered. 'I had no idea, no idea at all. I swear . . .'

'Sure you didn't. You were probably too busy screwing your way through Europe with your aristocratic chums, clocking up more notches on your belt.'

'I never—'

'Don't lie, Marques, it doesn't become you. I know she tried to contact you. I have the letters – returned, all of them. "Unknown address", I believe, very convenient. If you need further proof, I'll be happy to undergo DNA testing, although,' he looked contemptuously at Emilio, 'I'm not sure I want it confirmed that I'm related to you.' He turned to Carrie. 'I'm sorry for spoiling your evening like this – it truly wasn't my intention. I just couldn't listen to any more hypocrisy. Something snapped. Forgive me, please.' Before anyone could say anything, he left the table and strode to the front door.

Enrique was the first to react. 'I must apologise,' he said. 'I have no idea what has come over my friend Rudi – I have never seen him behave in such a manner. Please, Marques, accept my apologies on his behalf for his, er, extremely unorthodox behaviour.'

Emilio looked at him as if he were a particularly unpleasant insect, and turned to Carrie. 'My deepest apologies, Carrie, for this – this outburst. I really don't know what to say.' He suddenly looked defeated and put his head in his hands.

Carrie was overwhelmed with sympathy for him. Suddenly common sense returned and she took charge of the disintegrating evening. 'Stephanie, get some brandy for Emilio. Hope, order a taxi *now*. Enrique and Jay can share it. Enrique,' she looked sharply at him, 'you will see that Jay gets home safely, won't you? She's in no state to travel unaccompanied.'

Both Enrique and Jay opened their mouths to protest, neither having any intention of leaving a scene of such intrigue, and were silenced by a look from Carrie who had realised, with something close to amusement, that years of dealing with a wilful husband and contrary children had imbued her with more authority than she might have suspected.

'Here,' she said gently to Emilio after the taxi had departed with a reluctant Enrique and unsteady Jay. Hope and Stephanie had cleared the table and were discreetly tidying the kitchen. She handed him a generous balloon glass of brandy. 'Drink this. You've had quite a shock, to say the least.'

Emilio seemed to be miles away, his face ashen under the tan. He was still looking at the faded photograph, turning it over and over in his hands.

'Is there anything I can do?' Carrie asked, feeling genuinely worried about him.

'No, thank you. You have been put through quite enough

as it is. I still cannot believe what happened. It was such a
nice evening until . . .well . . .'

'It's none of my business, of course,' Carrie ventured, 'but
the photograph . . . is it . . . did you know the girl?'

'Oh, yes,' said Emilio. 'I knew her. I remember her well.'
Then, to Carrie's horror, tears rolled down his face.

'I'm so sorry.' Carrie hesitated, then put her hand on his.
'How insensitive of me. Of course you don't want to talk
about it.' Grief was etched across his face.

'You couldn't be more wrong.' He took out an immaculate handkerchief and blew his nose. 'If you don't mind
listening, I would like to talk about it very much. It's been a
long time since I felt I could talk openly to someone about
my life.'

'If it helps,' Carrie poured some brandy for herself, 'I think
I know exactly how you feel. Why don't you start at the
beginning?'

In the kitchen, Carrie's mobile rang. Hope, who was just
about to slip away, picked it up quickly. She checked the
caller ID and saw that it was Ali.

'Hi, Ali,' she said, moving outside, where she could speak
to her sister without disturbing Carrie and Emilio.

'Mum?'

'No, it's Hope.'

'Oh, hi, Hope. Put me on to Mum, would you? It's her
phone I'm ringing, isn't it? I need to ask her something.'

'Sorry, Ali, she's busy. I'll get her to ring you in the morning.'

'What do you mean, busy? It's midnight there. How could
she possibly be busy?'

'We're having a dinner party Ali, and she's still talking to
one of the guests. I'm not going to disturb her. Whatever it
is can wait 'til tomorrow.'

'A dinner party! Well, that's lovely! I don't suppose anyone remembers I've got a wedding to organise down there. Hope, put Mum on to me immediately. Of course she'll want to talk to me.'

'Goodnight Ali.' Hope grinned and turned the phone to silent. The she glanced at her mother and Emilio, deep in conversation. Carrie was clearly fascinated by whatever Emilio was telling her. Hope knew she had done absolutely the right thing.

17

The sun was streaming through Carrie's window, bathing her face in warmth. She had forgotten to draw the curtains last night and stretched lazily, nuzzling into her pillow as she hovered on the brink of wakefulness. Opening her eyes, she saw that it was already ten o'clock. Most unlike her to sleep so late – then she remembered. Last night, the dinner party, Rudi's extraordinary revelations and, most interesting of all, Emilio's story.

They had sat up until three, Carrie listening at first to his extraordinary life and then, gradually, sharing details of her own. Not that she had much to tell him. Either she was a very easy read, she thought, or Emilio was an exceptionally intuitive man. She was pretty sure it was the latter. It was funny, she mused, how she could feel so comfortable with someone she had only just met, someone whose life was a million miles apart from her own, yet to whom she had happily confided details she would never have shared with another living soul.

And then, of course, there had been Rudi. Emilio had been shaken, to say the least, by his outburst. But according to his account of events, it appeared that the whole thing might be true, and there was no doubting the resemblance between the two men. Carrie wondered why she had missed it before.

Getting up, she pulled on her robe and padded up to the kitchen, left immaculate by Hope and Stephanie, who were, presumably, asleep, Stephanie downstairs and Hope in her little house in the hills.

Carrie made some coffee, then took a mug and the cafetière outside with her and wandered down to a table that overlooked the pool. She'd have a swim later, but now she needed to think.

'She was the love of my life,' Emilio had told her of his late wife. 'In a way that I could never have imagined or anticipated. From the moment I set eyes on her, she enchanted me. It wasn't just the way she looked, although of course she was pretty, beautiful, even, but she had a quality that captivated me completely, you know?'

And Carrie replied truthfully that yes, she did know, but Emilio's version had sounded so much more romantic than her own – until, of course, his beloved Maria had died of cancer at the age of thirty-two, leaving a shattered husband and motherless little boy. It broke Carrie's heart to hear the pain in his voice as he relived it. She thought of all the years she had loved Rob, and wondered, in spite of herself, if it had been worth it. All the years taking refuge in her girls and the increasingly infrequent good times to avoid contemplating the cold truth that clutched now at her heart: the awful suspicion that he had never loved her and never would. That nothing she did would ever change that. Now, that realisation was beginning to set her free. Deep down, Carrie knew that Rob Armstrong was capable of loving only one individual above all others, and that was the one he saw every morning in the mirror.

For five years after his wife's death, Emilio said, he had thrown himself into his work, collecting, building and enhancing an already renowned art collection. His parents had never acknowledged either him or Maria since they had married – he had neglected his duty to form a suitable and financially advantageous alliance with a family of similar pedigree – but had stepped in to care for his young son, Carlos. They moulded and trained him assiduously in the ways of generations who had gone before him – but failed miserably to fill the yearning loss of a confused child for his beloved mother.

Emilio had known this, deep down, but couldn't bring himself to do anything about it. He travelled Europe, America, Russia, hopping from one plane to the next and rarely stopping anywhere for more than a few days. When he visited his home, he would bring gifts for his young son, and later, when he was a teenager, motorbikes, cars and boats. To his friends, Carlos had freedom they could only envy, and looks that made women drool. On the outside, he had it all, but inside, he remained an orphan.

For Emilio, eventually, there were other women, some of whom he grew fond of – but no one came close to Maria. 'It wasn't fair to them. I could see that. For me it was comfort, a passing thing. I always made it clear that I would not be getting involved in a relationship, but—' he smiled ruefully. 'You know, of course, as a woman, that is not enough.'

Carrie thought of, and empathised with, the many women who must have fallen in love with him.

'So it was better to end it. At least I was always honest. Do you think that was fair?'

'Well,' said Carrie, considering, 'it was truthful and nothing is fair in love, really. Someone always has to be the loser.'

'Not always, if you find the right person.' His eyes held hers.

'But look what happened to you,' Carrie couldn't help pointing out. 'You found her only to have her taken from you.'

'True, but I would do it all again a thousand times over. That's the difference.'

'Tell me about the girl in the photograph.' Carrie looked at the faded shot and smiled at the image of a young Emilio and his strikingly lovely companion.

'Mary Jane was her name. She was lovely. I met her when she was travelling with a group of her friends. She was very athletic, I remember, a fantastic swimmer. She used to run every morning, too, along the beach. Believe me, in those days, that was an unusual sight. We had a month or so together. I found her very interesting. She was from South Africa and, of course, her life was as different from mine as it was possible to be. She was very warm, very spontaneous. We had a lot of fun.'

'And then?'

'She was moving on with her friends through Europe, and I had my work to attend to. We exchanged addresses, of course, but she planned to travel for the rest of the year and we knew it was unlikely we would meet again. Believe me, Carrie, Mary Jane was a free spirit, she was not bound by convention. It was one of the things I most admired about her. We both knew what we had was a holiday romance, for want of a better expression. But I had no idea of what had transpired after- wards – if, indeed, it is the case that this young man Rudi is my son. I swear to you, Carrie, if I had any . . .'

'The letters Rudi spoke of?' Carrie prodded gently.

Emilio gave a bitter laugh. 'Of course I never received them. She would have written to me at my parents' address, at the *palacio*. I was travelling so much at the time, and I kept an apartment there, but if my parents got hold of them – well, you can imagine the rest. They would most certainly have been returned. They weren't bad people, my parents,' he added when he saw Carrie's face. 'This was Old Spain. They would have seen it as their duty to protect Carlos, the grandson they had just recovered. They were very different times, unfortunately.'

'What are you going to do?' Carrie asked, topping up his glass.

'What can I do?' He shook his head. 'It seems to me it is

very much up to Rudi what happens next. Of course I want
to meet him again, talk to him, but ... well, it would appear
that I am probably the last person now that he wants to have
anything to do with.' Emilio shook his head. 'If he is my son,
I have lost him before I could even try to be a father to him.
I seem to have a talent for that.'

'Don't imagine the worst, Emilio. I'm sure it won't come
to that. You've both had such a shock. There's bound to be
recriminations, misunderstandings. You're just going to have
to approach it one step at a time. But I do think you need
to talk to him.'

'I very much want to,' Emilio sighed. 'But somehow, after
what he said earlier, I doubt he'll want to talk to me.'

'Let's just wait and see, hmm?' Carrie patted his hand, and
he placed his over hers.

'You are a very special woman, Carrie. Your husband is a
lucky man.'

'I'm not sure he sees it quite that way.' The words escaped
before she could stop them.

Emilio's eyes searched her face. 'Then he's a fool.'

Carrie avoided his gaze.

'Thank you so much Carrie, for your kindness tonight, for
listening. It means a lot to me.'

Shortly afterwards, he had left and Carrie had gone to bed,
sleeping almost immediately, and soundly. So soundly she
didn't hear Toby, who, unwilling to be deprived of this unexpected late night activity and company, nudged open the
door of her bedroom, climbed very quietly onto the bed
beside her, sighing as he sank into the cool Egyptian cotton-
covered duvet, and rested his head on the gentle curve of
Carrie's hip.

Now the sun was hot and Carrie gathered up the empty
mug and cafetière, then made her way inside. In the kitchen,
as she was opening the dishwasher, the doorbell rang.

Thinking it was Felicia, the housekeeper, she opened the door.

'Señora Carrie Armstrong?' the small man enquired.

'Yes.'

'For you, Señora,' he smiled. He handed her a bouquet of two dozen white roses, then leaped back into his van.

Carrie fished for the card, which nestled at the base of the bouquet, and opened it:

'Thank you a thousand times for your hospitality, graciousness and, most of all, your kindness to me last night. I hope you will do me the honour of having dinner with me. Would you call me if that is acceptable to you? Emilio.'

Carrie took the roses into the kitchen, found a vase and filled it with water, then arranged them, breathing in their delicate fragrance. Standing back to admire her handiwork, she reread the card that accompanied them again and smiled. *I hope you will do me the honour of having dinner with me.* The old-fashioned courtliness made her smile, and she felt an unfamiliar warmth unfurl in the cold, lonely place she called her heart.

As she made her way downstairs to change for her morning swim, she glanced into a mirror and saw her face was flushed and happy. For the first time in as long as she could remember, Carrie understood what it felt like to be courted. She slipped into her bikini, applied sunblock and felt a shiver of excitement run through her. Outside, she moved the lounger to her preferred spot and lay down, soaking up the warmth of the sun and feeling strangely giddy. It was a feeling she resisted at first, with something approaching firmness, before happily succumbing to it, realising with a start she hadn't felt anything like this since she was sixteen years of age.

★   ★   ★

Jay was not having a good morning. Despite the dose of Solpadeine, vitamin B complex and the chilled gel eye mask, the throbbing in her temples refused to subside. This was accompanied by unrelenting nausea, which escalated rapidly whenever an offending flashback reared its ugly head. What, in the name of God, had possessed her? she wondered, sinking back into the pillows.

And it had all started so well.

But then everything had gone wrong. She had been so looking forward to meeting the *marques* and getting to know him, but he had been seated next to Carrie at dinner – *surprise, surprise* – and from then on she had had to listen to Enrique, who had seemed much more interested in Rudi. Probably gay, but if he was, he must surely know he was wasting his time with Rudi, she thought darkly. The champagne had done nothing to relieve the building tedium of the evening and so she'd indulged in a little coke. So what? It wasn't as if she hadn't done it a million times before. But maybe she had had too much sun yesterday. Anyway, she had only been trying to have a little fun, liven things up a little, and then Rudi – well, it had been all *his* fault, Jay thought with a vengeance. Actually, she felt a little better thinking about it. On reflection, any misdemeanours she had committed must have been totally overshadowed by Rudi's extraordinary outburst. Then she remembered the end of the evening, Carrie's polite but firm instructions, and finally the humiliation of being bundled into a taxi by Hope, accompanied by an equally reluctant Enrique, and the sullen journey home. Both of them equally resentful of their expulsion from what had turned into a riveting evening.

She wondered what had happened after they left. Rudi had already gone, which had left Carrie and Emilio on their own. *Hmm.* Carrie was a smooth operator, Jay thought to herself. Underneath that act of being devastated by Rob's infidelity, she was no slouch when it'd come to pouncing on the handsome and extremely eligible *marques*. Jay couldn't blame her, she supposed. Curiosity overcame any embarrassment and she resolved to ring Carrie immediately. But then another far more sinister memory inserted itself firmly at the front of her mind. Rudi! What was it he had said? That he would be sending Frank his letter of resignation first thing this morning. Shit! She had totally forgotten about that. He couldn't! She wouldn't let him. Frank would kill her. And exactly what would Rudi say in this letter? Jay's blood ran cold at the thought. She had to stop him – but how? God, what a mess. What an almighty bloody mess. Throwing off her eye mask, panic overtook nausea as Jay grabbed her phone and, with trembling fingers, punched in Carrie's number.

'Jay.' Carrie sounded cold at the other end of the phone.

'Carrie, you've got to help me,' Jay blurted. 'Rudi can't resign. It would be disastrous. I can't explain now, but I have to come round and talk to you.'

'I don't see what I can do about it, Jay. I can't say I blame him. Your behaviour really was—'

'Carrie, please. I know it was all my fault, but please, no lectures now. I've got to stop him. Can I come over?'

'No, wait,' Carrie said. 'I'll come over to you. Stay put, I'm on my way.'

'Oh, Carrie, thank you. I'm at my wit's end. You have no idea what disaster this could spell for me.'

'Like I said, I really don't see what I can do.'

'We'll figure something out, at least I won't be on my own. I'm going out of my mind here – I can't even think straight.'

'Well, let's hope he doesn't do anything hasty,' Carrie said. 'I'm sure he won't,' she added, hearing the panic in Jay's voice.

'I hope for my sake you're right,' said Jay, and hung up miserably. Still, at least Carrie was coming over. And she had

sounded calm and sensible – both of which felt quite beyond
Jay in her present state of mind.

Another glorious day had given way to a balmy evening on
the coast. The sun was low and warm and not a cloud hovered
in the sky. Stephanie decided to take Toby for an early evening
stroll to the port. She had been lazy today, basking in the
sun and the afterglow of her successful catering début. Her
mum was out somewhere so she and Toby had the house to
themselves, which had been nice, but was now a bit too quiet.

She showered and dressed quickly, pulling on a halter top
and a little handkerchief skirt she had found in a flea market
in Paris. She left her hair to dry naturally, falling in masses
of unruly curls past her shoulders. What a night it had been,
she thought as she put Toby's lead on and he jumped into
the car beside her. All that stuff about Rudi and the *marques*,
how weird, if it was true. Imagine meeting your father for
the first time at a dinner party. Stephanie tried to imagine
how that would feel and couldn't. Oh well, they would just
have to figure it all out between them. At least her family
didn't seem quite so dysfunctional now. Emilio had seemed
very upset about the whole thing, and why wouldn't he be?
She had been surprised to see him crying, though. She thought
for a moment and realised that she had never seen a man
cry before – certainly her father had never cried – not in
front of her at any rate. There was something rather nice
about it, she decided. And her mum had been so good with
him, but she was always fantastic whenever anyone was upset.

She and Hope had left them to it after they had tidied up,
and there had been something warm and comforting about
watching Emilio and her mother sitting there talking and
talking, and seeing her Mum look so . . . content.

She pulled up at the port, parked the car and walked towards
the harbour, Toby trotting happily beside her. At six o'clock,

the sun was still warm, and the crowds that would descend later were not in evidence. It was Stephanie's favourite time of day. She strolled along, pausing to admire a particularly splendid yacht and the rows of expensive cars that lined up alongside them. She decided to stop for a cup of coffee and slipped into one of the many open-air restaurants, settling herself so she could people-watch and enjoy the deliciously cool breeze. Toby sat gracefully at her feet, attracting admiring glances.

The waiter came over and she ordered a cappuccino. Then she saw him, sitting at the next café, deep in conversation with a very pretty blonde girl who had the longest legs Stephanie had ever seen. There was no mistaking Rudi. Squinting as she tried to get a better look, she took in the distinctive profile, the slightly hooked nose above the sensual mouth, and the dark hair, sun-bleached at the ends to a coppery gold. He ran a hand through it now, seeming distracted as he spoke. And Stephanie realised, suddenly, that the girl was crying. It was quite angry crying, Stephanie deduced, and Rudi looked increasingly uncomfortable as he tried to placate her. Eventually she got up from the table, said something to him, grabbed her bag and legged it, leaving Rudi alone. Stephanie thought he was genuinely upset, but he was probably used to it, she thought. She'd bet her bottom dollar that a lot of girls had tearful outbursts around Rudi. He was just one of those guys who threw your hormones into turmoil whether you liked it or not. Rudi tossed some change down on the table and got up to leave. Shrinking back in her chair and studying the menu intently, Stephanie hoped he wouldn't see her or, at the very least, she could pretend not to have seen him. He was almost past her when Toby gave a friendly bark and stood up, wagging his long tail in recognition. Stephanie waved awkwardly. 'Hi,' she said, pulling Toby back as Rudi walked over to them.

'Hi, Stephanie.' He sounded subdued. 'Mind if I sit down?'

'Sure, be my guest, I'm having a coffee, would you like one?' She couldn't for the life of her think what else to say.

'No, thanks. I just wanted to apologise for last night. I hadn't intended any of that to happen and I'm afraid I ruined a really nice evening for your mother and Hope.'

'Don't worry about it. Mum's cool and Hope doesn't get out enough. It will have done her good to see what goes on in the real world. I wasn't sure about it initially, you know, my sister having the wedding down here' – Stephanie knew she was babbling, but she always did when she felt awkward – 'but now I think about it, it's good for Hope to be around her family again. She's become way too reclusive.'

'What made her decide to have it here?' Rudi sounded curious. 'It's not exactly a reclusive spot for a wedding.'

'Oh, Ali's not the reclusive one – she adores being in the spotlight.'

'Ali?'

'My other sister, the model,' Stephanie explained, as if he was stupid. 'The one who's getting married.'

'Oh, so Hope, she – she's not the—'

'The bride?' Stephanie shrieked with laughter. 'You must be joking, although everyone's jumping to that conclusion. There's as much likelihood of Hope getting married as, well, as me.'

'What do you mean?'

'Let's just say once bitten and all that. Hope guards her personal space big time – and she's not very keen on men just now – no offence.'

'Can't say I blame her.'

'Well, that's refreshing to hear.'

Rudi grinned. 'We have our moments. Seriously, though, would you give me your mother's phone number? I'd like to apologise to her for last night.'

'Sure. Give me your phone. I'll key it in.'

'Thanks,' said Rudi, getting up. 'I'll call her later. I'd better go, got stuff to do. Good seeing you, Stephanie.'

'Take it easy.' God, he was gorgeous. She watched him lope away, his long legs tanned a deep mahogany. Pity he was so old . . .

She finished her coffee and set off back to the car, stopping occasionally to rifle through the racks of clothes that beckoned from the sidewalk. She was admiring a pretty white cotton top when she heard snarling. Before she knew it, Toby had dived off the pavement, taking her with him.

The first thing she noticed when she had regained her footing and pulled Toby up was a beautiful Boxer, with ears clipped in the fashion that was now forbidden in Britain and Ireland. The second thing she noticed was that most beautiful guy Stephanie had ever set eyes on was holding its lead.

'*Lo siento*,' said the god apologetically, having regained control of his dog.

'That's okay,' said Stephanie breathlessly, taking in the lean, dark-skinned frame, the razor-slash cheekbones, the soulful dark brown eyes and mop of jet black curls. In a pair of faded three-quarter-length cut-offs and beaten-up leather gladiator sandals, he looked like the king of the gypsies. When he smiled at her, a big lopsided grin, she felt her legs go weak and her head spin.

'*Perdón*,' he said and rattled off a string of Spanish.

'Sorry, I don't understand. *No comprendo*.' She cursed her limited linguistic skills.

'English?' he asked.

'No, Irish – *Irlanda*.'

'Ah, Irish.' The grin became wider. 'My English not so good, but I like Irish people very much. Your dog?' He reached out to stroke Toby's head.

'Yes. Toby.'

'Yours?' Stephanie didn't feel brave enough to touch the Boxer, whose lips were still curled back as it glared at Toby.

'Not my dog. I, ah – how you say? – walk him for exercise. Daytime job, yes? In the evenings, I work there.' He pointed to a large restaurant on the corner of the port that Stephanie knew well. 'Luis.' He held out his hand.

'Stephanie.' She shook it, trying not to look as though she had been hit by ten thousand volts.

'Maybe we walk together sometime, with dogs, yes?' His eyes twinkled hopefully.

'Good idea,' said Stephanie, then took a deep breath. 'How about tomorrow?' she heard herself say.

'Tomorrow.' He rolled the word over, making the Rs sound like treacle. 'Yes, tomorrow is good. Evening?'

Stephanie nodded eagerly.

'Five o'clock? I meet you at the top of the port. Then we can walk along Paseo, yes?'

'Great. See you tomorrow, then.'

'*Hasta mañana*, Stephanie.' He pronounced it Stephan*eee*, drawing out the last syllable deliciously. Then he walked away, throwing another grin over his shoulder.

Stephanie walked to the car on air and passed the journey home in a complete daze.

She let herself into the house and called her mother, but she was still out. Then she went to get Toby his dinner and bent down to hug him, looking earnestly into his eyes. 'You are the best, most wonderful dog in the world, you know that? You are *such* a clever boy to introduce me to Luis.' She savoured the name. It sounded incredibly romantic. 'We're going walkies with him tomorrow.' Her voice rose to a squeak, 'Tomorrow, Toby, what about that?'

Had he understood what his mistress was saying to him, Toby would not have approved of the prospective outing, but, as she was just about to hand him his dinner, topped with his favourite treat of chopped sausages, he did his best to look eager and even leapt about a little to show that he was entirely enthusiastic about whatever was making her so happy.

At eight o'clock in the evening, Carrie was still with Jay, and reluctant to leave her.

When she had arrived, at about eleven that morning, Jay had been in a terrible state. Although she was somewhat calmer now, she was still most unlike herself. Carrie was worried. The Jay she knew was cool, calm and resolutely collected, up until last night, at any rate. Carrie couldn't work out what had got into her.

'What's going on with you, Jay?' she had asked as soon as they had sat down with some coffee. Jay had raised her cup with a tremor in her hand. 'You really were out of line last night, you know. What was it all about?'

'Carrie, don't,' Jay begged. 'Don't give out to me. I know I was horrible, especially to Hope, but I was so, oh, I don't know.' As Carrie watched, tears began to run down her friend's face and she started to sob.

'What is it, Jay?'

'I was jealous, pure and simple.' She reached for a tissue and blew her nose.

'Jealous?' Carrie asked incredulously.

'Yes, jealous,' Jay said, finding a strange sort of relief in being honest. 'I was jealous because Emilio was paying you far too much attention, Rudi was ogling Hope, who must be the only girl on the planet who wouldn't notice it, and I was left with Enrique, who was fidgeting like he had ants in his pants and had no more interest in talking to me than, well, anyone else.' She paused for breath. 'I suppose I had too much to drink as well.'

'And the rest.'

'Oh, Carrie, everyone does coke these days. I've done it for years – it's brilliant for keeping the weight off.' She blew her nose again. 'Anyway, everyone seemed to be having such a good time except me – and that Rudi, well, he just gives me the hump.'

'Rudi? Why?'

Jay grinned. 'I once propositioned him and he turned me down.'

'I don't believe you! Rudi?'

'What? That I propositioned him? Or that he turned me down?'

'Well, both. When?'

'Oh, it was ages ago, some time last year. Don't look at me like that, Carrie. He's divine, and I like younger men. It's not a crime, you know. They're less judgmental, and so much fun, and they appreciate you and, of course, they go on for—'

'Jay, I get the picture – but Rudi? Wasn't that a bit – I mean, he's Frank's employee, for goodness sake, of course he'd turn you down. You put him in an impossible situation. What did you think he'd do?'

'Oh, God, Carrie, what if he tells Frank? He said he was going to let him have his letter of resignation first thing this morning. Frank will kill me – it'll be the end.' She was sobbing again. 'He'll divorce me for sure.'

Carrie put her arm round her friend. 'Jay, you're over-reacting. Frank would never divorce you.'

'You don't understand,' Jay sniffed. 'It's bad, Carrie, really bad, and if Rudi resigns, it'll be all he needs. Frank's having an affair – not just the usual messing around he gets up to, the girl's after him big time . . . and she's pregnant.' Jay was sobbing noisily. 'I'm sorry I was such a bitch last night, I really am, but I've been sick with worry for I don't know how long and last night I just snapped.'

'Oh, Jay.' Carrie was trying to take it all in. 'There was me regaling you with my problems and all the time *you* could have done with a shoulder to cry on.'

'No, I couldn't. I was too proud. That's my problem. I didn't want anyone, even my best friend, to know that I've messed up. Oh, what'll I do? What'll I do if he leaves me for this girl? I couldn't stand it – the humiliation.'

Carrie watched helplessly as Jay dissolved again. 'Does he know that you know?'

'No – at least, I don't think so.'

'And you're sure about her being pregnant?'

'I've had a private detective investigate the whole thing for me – I've even seen the shots. I'll get them if you like. I have them here somewhere.'

'No, Jay, wait. I don't want to see them.' Carrie's head was spinning and she fought to hold on to common sense. 'Jay, you've got to talk to him.'

'Who? The detective?' said Jay, clearly bewildered. 'But there's nothing more he can do.'

'No. I mean Frank. You've got to tell him you know about this, tell him how you feel.'

'Talk to Frank? Are you mad? What would I say?'

'Tell him what you've told me. *Talk* to him.'

'Talking didn't get you anywhere, did it?' The hurtful words escaped before she could stop them. 'Oh, Carrie, forgive me, I didn't mean it to sound like that. It's just that I don't think talking will do much good at this stage.'

'You have to, Jay. For your own sanity. Talking may not have changed anything between Rob and me over the years, but it helped me. At least I know I did everything I could, left no stone unturned. Besides,' Carrie hesitated, 'Frank loves you. I know he does. That's the difference. And I think you love him too. Oh, I know,' she raised a hand to stop Jay interrupting, 'you might have grown apart over the years, and I know how hard the money, the success, the whole scene out there makes things, but I still think if Frank truly knew how you felt, if you were honest with him and with yourself, you'd have a fighting chance, really I do, I wouldn't say so otherwise. Where is he, by the way?'

'In Dublin, but he's coming down the day after tomorrow to entertain some bankers on *Excalibur*.'

'So you'll be together?'

Jay looked evasive. 'Well, in a manner of speaking. I suppose he'll want me to play hostess for a gig or two, unless he's moved her in already.'

'Well, then,' Carrie continued, 'there's your chance. Make sure you have a really good time together and talk to him.'

'I can't. You don't understand. Frank and I *have* no marriage, not really. We have an arrangement. We show up at functions and things together, but down here he stays on *Excalibur* most of the time and does his thing, and I have the house to myself to do whatever I want. That's the way it works. Or doesn't work now, I suppose.'

'Oh Jay, I didn't realise. You must have been so lonely – God knows, I know what that's like.'

'What about you? Are you still going ahead with the divorce?'

'Yes. Obviously we can't do anything until Ali's wedding's over, but as soon as it is, I'm going to push ahead with it.'

'What if you regret it? What if it turns out to be a horrible mistake? How can you see all those years, all that work, go to waste and just hand him over to someone else?'

'You can kid everyone else, Jay, but you can't kid yourself. I just can't do it any more.'

'I'm pretty sure I could.' Jay said. 'I'm not like you, Carrie. I'm not strong, not really, and I couldn't cope with being divorced, being on my own.'

'Jay, I'm not strong. God, sometimes I feel as if I've been

the most spineless woman on the planet,' Carrie sighed, pulling at a thread on the hem of her shorts.

'You're so wrong. You've always been strong. Look at you now, being brave enough to leave Rob and start a new life. I could never do that.'

'I don't think you'll have to, Jay. But let's take this one step at a time.'

'I don't have much choice, do I,' said Jay, getting up and heading to the fridge, from which she took a bottle of champagne. 'I don't know about you, but I need a drink. If you can stay a while longer I'll tell you all about it.'

And Carrie had stayed and listened as Jay related her account of the Russian girl with whom Frank appeared to be besotted and who, allegedly, was having his baby. They went over and over everything Jay knew, and by the end of the evening, Carrie felt as wrung out as her friend. When her phone rang, they jumped.

'Hello?' said Carrie, not recognising the number that showed on the screen. 'Oh, hello, Rudi . . . No, it's perfectly all right. You're not disturbing me at all.' She got up and walked towards the kitchen as Jay followed her, gesticulating wildly.

'Shush, will you?' she said to Jay, putting her hand over the phone so Rudi wouldn't hear. He apologised profusely for his behaviour the night before while Jay paced the floor like a caged animal and signalled at Carrie to let her talk to him. Carrie shook her head vehemently.

'No, no, of course, I understand, Rudi. There is, er, just one thing, though. I'm with Jay and she's very upset herself. She's hoping that you'll reconsider handing in your resignation – at least for the moment.' Carrie held her breath as Rudi sighed at the other end of the phone. 'It means a lot to her, particularly with Frank coming down so soon . . . and, of course the wedding . . . I see . . . Yes, of course I'll tell her, and thank you, Rudi, for phoning. I know it can't have been easy . . . Yes, goodbye.'

'What?' Jay gasped. 'What did he say?' The blood had drained from her face and Carrie thought she was about to faint.

'He said he was going to work the rest of his contract, which is up shortly after the wedding.'

'Oh, thank God,' said Jay, sinking into a chair.

'He said he was doing it to honour his obligation to Frank, not for you. Those were his words.'

'Who gives a fuck why he's doing it? The point is I'm off the hook – thanks be to Jesus!' Jay put her hands together and looked heavenwards.

'Jay!' Carrie said reprovingly.

'Well, really! Of course he's not doing it for me – but I would have done anything.'

'I think you need to write him a letter, Jay. I would if I were you,' Carrie said firmly.

'What on earth for?'

'To apologise for your behaviour, which was reprehensible, and to thank him for being so magnanimous and not dropping you in it, basically.'

'Humph! Magnanimous, my arse.' Jay was sounding more like her old self. 'He's just suiting himself, like they all do. Don't think he's doing this for any altruistic reasons.'

'You're wrong, Jay. You underestimate Rudi. I think he's a really decent person. Deep down, I suspect he's been hurt a lot. His childhood can't have been easy, by the sound of it. Anyway, you need to write that letter – and one to Hope.'

'Oh, really, Carrie. Now you're being ridiculous. I'll talk to her – take her shopping, buy her something nice.'

'Hope doesn't like shopping, but she *would* appreciate a letter. Come on, I'll help you, we'll do them now.'

Jay was too tired and drained for further resistance. 'You've got a queer one there, Carrie, in your Hope. I mean, she's lovely looking and everything, but a girl who doesn't like shopping – or men, by the looks of it.' Jay shook her head.

'She just hasn't met the right one,' Carrie smiled.

'Do we ever?'

18

In her small but beautiful fin-de-siècle apartment on Rue Vaneau, Ali dressed carefully for her prospective dinner date – appointment, she mentally corrected herself. This was strictly business but discussed over dinner. All the same, she felt uncharacteristically apprehensive. She settled, finally, on a sleek black and gold lace dress that clung to her alluringly and stopped just above her knees, with full sleeves and a simple square neckline that revealed enough pearlescent skin to be interesting but not so much as a hint of cleavage. Gold and black strappy sandals and a matching clutch bag completed the outfit. Her legs were bare and tanned and her hair was drawn back in an elegant chignon. A spray of her favourite perfume on her neck and wrists, a final check in the full-length mirror, and she was on her way. Outside, she hailed a taxi that drew to a halt beside her with a screech of brakes.

'The Ritz, *s'il vous plâit*,' she said, hopping in.

'*Oui, Mademoiselle*,' the driver said, smiling at her, stealing furtive glances in the rear-view mirror at his beautiful passenger as they sped across town to the Place de la Concorde and stopped outside the hotel. Ali paid him, then a doorman immediately appeared to help her out of the cab.

She had taken no more than three steps across the sumptuous lobby, when she felt a hand on her elbow.

'Ali,' said a voice with a deep southern drawl. 'May I call you Ali?'

She looked up to see Gerald J. Junior at her side, as groomed and handsome as any male model.

'Of course you can, Gerald.' She took the hand he proffered.

'Thank you for agreeing to have dinner with me at such short notice. I appreciate it. I'm sure you don't get many time slots.' He smiled his perfect smile at her.

'Not at all,' demurred Ali.

'Shall we go straight in?' He indicated the dining room. 'The table should be waiting.'

'Absolutely.'

It was seven thirty on the dot, and the magnificent room was pretty much empty. Nonetheless, the staff were on full alert, and they were ushered to what was clearly one of the best tables in the room.

'An apéritif, Mademoiselle?' the waiter smiled respectfully at her.

'Oh, I think this calls for champagne,' said Gerald J. 'Don't you, Ali?'

'That would be lovely. Perhaps just a glass,' agreed Ali.

'And mineral water for me, Antoine, with gas.'

'Of course, Monsieur, right away.'

'You're not having any champagne?'

'I don't drink alcohol,' Gerald J. said, smiling, as their drinks arrived. 'Cheers!' he said, raising his glass of water.

'Cheers!' Ali clinked her flute to his glass and wondered again why she felt so uneasy – almost as if she was walking into a well-rehearsed trap.

Over dinner, lamb for Ali, lobster for Gerald J., Ali found her dinner partner charming. He chatted easily, regaling her with amusing stories of his upbringing with his larger-than-life father. Then he enquired about her and listened with intent as she told him about growing up in Dublin.

'Sounds like you were top of the line when they were

handing out charmed lives.' Gerald said, a cynical smile playing on his mouth.

'I guess I'm lucky with my family and, yes, I've had a privileged upbringing of sorts – but no more so than you had, I'm sure.'

'And then you met Mr Wonderful from back home and now you're getting married. That's a storybook ending if ever I heard one.'

'Well, yes,' Ali felt uncomfortable again. 'I suppose so.' She couldn't put her finger on it, but there was something unfriendly in Gerald J.'s expression, although he was trying expertly to hide it. But Ali could sense it. And always there was the perfect smile that never quite reached his eyes.

'And this contract with us, with Stay Tru, that would be the icing on the cake, right?'

'Well, yes, of course.' Ali regarded him directly. 'It would be a great honour to be the new face of Stay Tru – any model would jump at the chance.'

'But you're not just any model, right? You're Ali Armstrong, more super than the supers. That's why we want you. Stay Tru only deals with the *crème de la crème*, especially when it comes to image.'

'That's nice of you to say so.'

'So, Ali, what about an after-dinner drink, a liqueur, perhaps?'

'No, thank you. Dinner was lovely and I hope I've answered all your questions satisfactorily, but I really have to go – early start tomorrow, I'm afraid.' Ali made to rise from the table.

'Not so fast, beautiful.' He reached across and gripped her wrist.

Ali was so shocked that she sat down again.

'Dinner finishes when I say it does.' He was still smiling broadly so that any onlookers would misconstrue the scene as a lovers' tiff. 'We haven't sealed the deal yet.'

'Excuse me?'

'Don't play the innocent, Miss Armstrong, you know how these things work. I – how shall I put it? I need to see how fresh and lovely you look first thing in the morning. I need to see if you have the characteristics of a *real* Stay Tru girl – you know, eager, hard-working, obliging, enthusiastic.' He leaned back in his chair and regarded her. 'Let me put it bluntly, Ali. You can come with me upstairs – or you can kiss goodbye to the Stay Tru contract.'

For a moment, Ali was speechless. Then, cold fury possessed her. She rose to her feet. 'You ignorant, asshole son of a bitch!' she said in a low voice. 'How dare you think for one moment that I would sleep with you. If that's what this is about, you can take your contract and shove it where the sun don't shine.'

'Nice language, Miss Armstrong. I'm surprised at you, surprised and disappointed,' Gerald J. drawled. 'But don't worry, there are plenty more where you came from. Younger – and prettier, too. Word on the street is you've had your day, honey. I was just giving you an opportunity to go out in style.'

Ali turned on her heel and stalked out of the hotel. She was damned if she'd let anyone see her burst into tears and run as she felt like doing. Outside, thankfully there were no paparazzi in evidence and she jumped into the taxi that pulled up.

Back in the safety of her apartment, Ali tore off her dress and sandals, pulled on a robe and flung herself onto the bed, where she sobbed until she fell into a fretful sleep.

'Here, drink this.' Ivanka handed Lola a shot of vodka. '*Salud*,' she said firmly, then knocked one back herself and placed the bottle of Absolut on the table beside them.

Lola drank the shot and stared at her friend with narrowed eyes. 'I thought you were pregnant. Surely you shouldn't be drinking.'

'Of course I'm not pregnant, but for the moment it suits my purposes. Whatever it takes.'

'What happens when he finds out?'

'He won't. Not until it's too late anyway. I could be pregnant at any minute, and he's so in love with me it won't matter either way. All I have to do is get him to leave his stupid wife.'

They sat in Ivanka's luxurious penthouse apartment in the port, overlooking the beach, which lay beneath them under a slender, silvery moon. Ivanka was proud of her apartment. She had made sure Frank had put it in her name, of course, and that he had bought it, not rented it, as so many other girls had made the mistake of allowing. Ivanka didn't believe in leaving things to chance. When you came from a two-bedroom flat in post-communist Moscow with eight other family members and a shared bathroom down the corridor, luxury became a priority. The only passport she'd needed out of her humble beginnings had been her stunning blonde good looks, which she had immediately put to efficient use. Emotion was a waste of time. So much excess baggage. She couldn't understand women who 'fell in love'. Love got you nowhere. Why, look at the state Lola was in now.

'I told you Rudi was a waste of time,' she said coldly, flicking ash into an elegant Waterford crystal fruit bowl. 'A man like that will never settle. Never have anything to offer you.'

Fresh tears trickled down her friend's face. 'But I love him, Ivanka. And the sex – you have no idea! Never in my life have I had such sex, such passion. He made love to me like he wanted to kill me and—'

'Pah!' Ivanka refilled Lola's glass. 'And where has it got you? He has finished with you, and you don't have a car or an apartment, jewels, nothing, only pain.'

'There must be something I can do.' Lola's face was stricken as she looked imploringly at her friend.

'You should never have given him an ultimatum. Men like Rudi, they can never be tied down. Not that way.'

'What else could I do?'

'What I did.'

'Get pregnant?'

'Of course.'

'Don't be ridiculous. You can't tie a man down much more firmly than by presenting him with a baby he doesn't want.'

'Ah, but that's where you're wrong, Lola. Rudi has no parents, no family. From what you have told me, his childhood was horrible. A man like that will crave to do the very opposite for his own child. I bet he'd be the most adoring father in the world – and he'd always have a special relationship with the mother of that child. If it's not too late, that's what you should do.'

'He'd never fall for it. And anyway, I think it *is* too late.'

'Don't be so negative. He'll be feeling bad about finishing with you – if you weren't too angry and didn't insult him too much. Did you?' Ivanka gazed accusingly at her.

'I can't remember,' replied Lola sullenly, downing another shot. 'Anyway, Rudi's funny. He has a very conservative side. He wouldn't want the mother of his children working as a dancer in the most talked-about club in Marbella.'

'It didn't put him off sleeping with you, did it?'

'That's different, and you know it.'

'No. You become different when you're the mother of the child. That's what changes things. If you want him, Lola, this is your only way of getting him back. Believe me, I know what I'm talking about.'

'What about you?' Lola refilled her glass. 'How's Mr Rich?'

Ivanka smiled. 'Frank's fine, thank you. It's his wife that's the problem. But not for long. Actually, he's coming down in a few days. He's entertaining clients on *Excalibur*.'

'Will you see him if he's with businesspeople?' Lola was used to the demands of the ruthlessly rich and their entourages.

'Of course I will see him. Although,' Ivanka threw back another shot and allowed a touch of bitterness to enter her voice, 'his wife will be acting as hostess.' Lola nodded, understanding. 'But it's me he'll be coming to afterwards. You will come to the club with me, won't you, Lola? I'll make sure we have a good time. Then, maybe, you will have the chance to get back with Rudi.'

Lola's face lit up. 'Of course! You're right, as usual.' Her smile faded. 'What is it? You seem on edge tonight.'

Ivanka drew a cigarette from the packet beside her and lit it, inhaling deeply. She wondered if she could trust Lola with her latest news. She decided she could. 'Igor's in town.' She blew a cloud of smoke across the room. 'I heard three days ago.'

Lola's face went pale. 'But that's impossible. He's was jailed, for life . . .'

Ivanka gave a bitter laugh. 'The sentence can be shortened, apparently, if you have the right connections and the right information to offer. Igor has always had both.'

'Does he know where you are?' Lola asked breathlessly.

'Of course. Why else do you think he's here? But he doesn't know that *I know* he's here. But it's only a matter of time. It just means I have to work faster. I won't allow him to ruin my chance of a new life with Frank.'

Lola shivered. 'Oh, Ivanka, be careful. Remember what he did to you when—'

'That was then,' she said shortly. 'I was young and stupid. Now, he'll be dealing with a very different person. It is already ten years.'

'Yes, but—'

'Don't worry, Lola, I can take care of myself. But be alert. He'll know you're here too and he may come looking for you. Tell him nothing. Remember, Igor's nothing but a bully and, like all bullies, a coward inside.'

Whatever feelings Lola had been harbouring of heartbreak over Rudi had been overtaken by a chilling fear. Igor out of jail. Igor on the loose. This wasn't good. It wasn't good at all.

Lola flicked open her mobile and called for the club limo. She had to perform this evening, which would take her mind off things – for the moment at any rate.

'Take care of yourself, Ivanka,' she said earnestly, kissing her on both cheeks as she left. 'And call me. Anytime.'

'Don't worry about me, Lola. I can take care of myself.'

The small private aircraft came in to land at Málaga at three p.m. and taxied to a standstill on one of the smaller runways which catered to the ever-increasing flow of private jets. Frank had decided to hitch a lift with a pal who was flying on to check out some property in Marrakech. Now, he and the three bankers he was entertaining descended the steps – Frank somewhat shakily, after a hard night, and were picked up by the waiting driver, who would take them straight to Puerto Banus. The guys were tired, and Frank's plan was to get them settled on board *Excalibur*, in the excellent care of his crew, then slip away to see Ivanka for an hour or so before dinner.

She was dying to see him, bless her, and had been texting him all day. Mind you, so had Jay, which was unusual. Generally she just barked instructions down the phone at him, laced with liberal threats of what she would do should they not be carried out. Frank yawned. He was very tired. He had nearly got himself into trouble: he had been on the point of texting a reply to Jay that was intended for Ivanka. It had outlined, in very basic details, what he was hoping to do to her later on that night. Frank was no wordsmith, which was why he enjoyed texting: you had to get straight to the heart of the matter, so to speak. No pussyfooting about. And that was what he was good at. All the same, he dreaded to think what would have happened had Jay received the raunchy message.

For a moment he felt sad.

What had happened to them? How had things turned out like this? When had Jay stopped being the person who made him laugh most in all the world? Because she had. Come to think of it, he didn't laugh much at all, one way or the other, these days. Not the way he used to. Great, big, rip-roaring shouts of mirth that rumbled through him and caught everyone around him up in it. Usually, it had begun with one of Jay's funny observations. And, by God, she could laugh with the best of them. He'd always said she should have been a stand-up comedienne, she'd have been a riotous success. She could even make his old mother laugh and that was tantamount to raising the dead. Frank smiled at the memory. Ah, well, that was life, wasn't it? Sure, nothing stayed the same.

The car turned into the port and drove slowly down the harbour to pull up outside Francesco's. The Riva was sitting elegantly in the water opposite the restaurant. Rory, the first mate, was at the wheel to greet them as per instructions. Frank and his travelling companions got out, handed over their luggage, which Rory stowed, then stepped down into the sleek power-boat. 'Welcome back Mr Farrelly, good to see you, sir.' Rory shook Frank's hand, and then, with a roar of engines and churning water, turned the Riva, revved her and sped away. The wind whipped past them and the salty sea air brought colour into their tired, pasty faces. Frank's heart lifted. Absentmindedly he patted his head to make sure that his current crowning glory was still there, failing to notice the amused glances his bankers exchanged with each other, clocking the by now familiar habit of Frank's that was the running joke du jour in Dublin.

'Well, lads, there she is!' Frank felt the familiar glow of pride. His ostentatious boy-toy lay ahead, gleaming in the afternoon sun.

Despite themselves, the bankers were impressed. No matter how prepared you were, *Excalibur* exuded a special kind of magic that was all her own. It wasn't just her majestic size, her sheer bulk or the immaculately uniformed crew of fifty-two all lined up on deck to greet the latest guests. She had something no other yacht could lay claim to and that was history. The kind of history that only the very, *very* rich could afford.

'Howya, Rudi.' Frank grinned with pleasure at seeing his skipper and gave him a resounding clap on the back, although Rudi greeted him with strict formality.

'Welcome aboard, sir, good to have you with us again.' He shook hands with each of the three bankers. 'Anita,' a statu-esque Swedish crew member stepped forward, 'will see that you are shown to your cabins.'

As if choreographed, three more crew stepped forward at her imperceptible nod.

'Your own personal butler!' Frank couldn't resist crowing. 'One for everyone in the audience,' he quipped, using the old *Late Late Show* line. 'What time is dinner, Rudi?' Frank asked.

'Eight thirty, Mr Farrelly, as you instructed. Drinks from seven thirty in the bar. If you need any refreshment prior to that,' he said to the bankers, 'just let your crew member know.'

'Don't worry, lads,' Frank grinned at the faces that were already lighting up. 'There's a fully stocked bar in every cabin if you're thirsty.' As the bankers disappeared below, he whispered to Rudi, 'I'm just going to pop back to port for a couple of hours. Got a bit of business to attend to.' He winked at Rudi. 'I'll be back in plenty of time for drinks. What time are you expecting my wife out?'

Rudi waved at Rory to bring the Riva round again. 'She asked to be picked up at seven thirty.'

'Right.' Frank did some mental arithmetic. 'In that case, I'll take the RIB. Better make it seven o'clock so you can send the Riva for Jay. I'll be back in time to get scrubbed up and ready to play Mr and Mrs Ships in the Night, eh, Rudi?'

'Got it, sir.' Rudi betrayed not a flicker of conspiracy in return to Frank's knowing look.

'See ya later, alligator?' Frank waved at his captain, his cheery face wreathed in smiles as he descended again, this time into the inflatable power-boat.

'Sir.' Rudi, ever a stickler for protocol, stood to attention and saluted his employer as he disappeared from view.

As Frank roared off back to port, Rudi grinned broadly and shook his head. Really, sometimes it was very hard to keep a straight face around that man.

By six o'clock that evening, Jay was getting tetchy. She'd had her hair done in the local salon, and although she'd said she wanted to be picked up in the port at seven thirty, she decided to go out to *Excalibur* earlier than planned. After all, she was going to get changed in the master cabin, where she kept a ready rack of designer evening gowns and cruise wear. Hanging around at home was only making her nervous. She rang Frank, but his mobile went straight to voicemail. She didn't leave a message. Instead, she rang *Excalibur*. Rory picked up and assured her he'd meet her in the harbour in fifteen minutes. Before she set off, she almost phoned Carrie again to beg her to change her mind and join them for dinner, then decided not to bother. Carrie had been firm. Jay had to do this on her own. Of course, it had nothing to do with the fact that Carrie had let slip that she was meeting Emilio for dinner that evening at the Marbella Club. There was nothing for it but to go and face the music, and the sooner she got to the venue, the better.

Juan, her gardener-cum-driver, dropped her to the port where, exactly on time, Rory was waiting in the Riva.

'Hi, Rory.' Jay was fond of the first mate, second in command to Rudi. 'Now, don't tear off in a rush – I've just had my hair done.' She tied a headscarf round her to protect it from the wind.

'And very nice it looks too. We'll take it easy, Mrs Farrelly, don't you worry.' True to his word, they rumbled slowly out of port into open water, where *Excalibur* lay majestically ahead, her white flanks shining in the late evening sun.

'Mrs Farrelly.' Rudi greeted her with chilling deference. 'Your cabin is ready. Is there anything I can get you?'

'No, thank you, Rudi,' Jay said breezily. 'I'll greet our guests in the bar later. Is my husband on board?'

'He had to remain in port to attend to some last-minute details. He's returning, I believe, at seven o'clock.'

'I see,' Jay said coolly. 'Well, tell him I'll see him in the bar.'

'Of course,' Rudi replied. 'If you need anything in the meantime—'

'Yes, thank you, Rudi.' She tried to sound dismissive, although she couldn't quite meet his eyes. 'I'll let you know.'

Jay went down to the master cabin, dumped her handbag on the bed and rifled through her extensive wardrobe. She would have to choose carefully. Finally, discarding some more elaborate designs, she settled on a discreet but beautifully cut sleeveless black Balmain cocktail dress that fell flatteringly to just below her knees. Not too long to swamp her and short enough to be alluring. It was, she decided, doing a twirl in the mirror, a masterpiece of tailoring. Her arms were in good shape, thanks to regular workouts – or was it carrying her own body weight in shopping – and on a whim, she grabbed a black velvet hairband and set it on her head so that her slanting fringe curved round her face and the rest of the feathered bob sat prettily in place. Very Jackie O. Just the effect she was aiming for. Slipping into a pair of black cut-away high-heeled stilettos and spraying herself liberally with Chanel No. 5, she wondered briefly if being married to Aristotle Onassis, never mind Jack Kennedy, had been any easier than it was being married to her own mad excuse for a husband. Probably not. In their own ways, she decided, they were all trouble.

She was just about to make her way down to the bar when she noticed Frank's holdall and briefcase on the vast super king-size bed. Both lay invitingly unlocked. Hmm. He'd obviously had more pressing things to attend to, Jay thought, trying not to let herself get wound up. Visiting the Russian whore, no doubt. Well, at least he wasn't having the woman play hostess tonight. The possibility had crossed Jay's mind and her blood had run cold at the idea of it. Then she would have known she was in trouble. As it was, there was still time, still everything to play for. She had a quick mosey through. Never hurt to keep up with things. It was part of her job, she reminded herself.

Nothing much in the holdall, the usual change of clothes and, God help us – Jay shivered with revulsion when her hand touched it and she recoiled instinctively – one of those ghastly 'syrups' he'd taken to wearing. She took out the offending article and looked at it from all angles. She couldn't help remembering one of her favourite episodes from *Only Fools and Horses*, when Del Boy had an assignment of toupées which the boys all referred to, in Cockney rhyming slang, as 'syrups' – syrup of figs = wigs. Despite herself, she sniggered. Talk about a mid-life crisis. You'd think it would be enough to own the biggest yacht in the Med or to be at the top of the European rich list, but no, Frank Farrelly had to go and make an eejit of himself wearing bloody toupèes – and, God help him, he was under the even greater illusion that no one was any the wiser. Jay shook her head in wonderment. He had looked perfectly all right without them. But would he listen to her?

Replacing the wig, Jay proceeded to the briefcase. Nothing much there either, the usual papers, stock reports . . . and then she found it. A large brown envelope. Something told her it was trouble before she opened it. Maybe, she thought with a chill, it was instructions to a solicitor. Divorce proceedings. Whatever it was, she knew it was bad news. Wifely intuition, she supposed. With trembling fingers she took out the papers. At first she thought she was mistaken. They seemed to be pictures of Frank, not incriminating ones. And then, as she read the printed script, she understood. They were threats. Blatant threats. The first one or two were tawdry enough: a photocopied shot of Frank with his eyes cut out and a similar threat in the written message. Another of a man with a cover over his head, terrorist style, and a rope round his neck, and finally, from a smaller, heavier envelope, Jay pulled a single silver bullet.

She sat down suddenly on the bed, breath sucked from her, trying to keep her head. Someone, somewhere, was threatening Frank – *her* Frank. And, knowing Frank, he was sticking his big stupid toupèed head in the sand and doing nothing about it. Jay bristled. She was about to return the evidence to the briefcase when she paused. There was only one person she could approach about this until she could contact her private detective in the morning. Even then she'd need copies of what she'd found. Much though it pained her to ask for his help, she knew this was no time to be squeamish. She picked up the bedside phone and dialled.

'Rudi, you've got to come straight to the master cabin. I need your help. It involves Frank. You might have reason to doubt me after my recent behaviour, but I promise this is a matter of life and death.'

The evening was progressing beautifully. Cocktails had been served on deck and the three bankers had emerged from their cabins, showered, refreshed and dressed for dinner. Smart casual had been the dress code, and the bankers, being a conservative trio, were sporting almost identical navy blazers, stripy shirts and crisply pressed chinos.

Frank had returned from his trip to the port and been unnerved to find Jay onboard ahead of schedule, but she had pretended not to notice his unease, instead telling him to hurry up and get changed. While he was showering, she chose a smart blue linen suit with a paler blue linen shirt for him and laid them on the bed.

By the time he arrived on deck to join them for cocktails, the string quartet was playing a lively number and Jay was chatting ten to the dozen with the bankers, who were responding to her wit and humour with increasing vigour.

When it became a little too breezy, they retreated to the bar, where the infamous stools were the focus of conversation.

'Is it true?' Joe, the most talkative of them, asked.

'Can't you tell?' Jay looked impishly at him and he laughed, his face turning a slightly deeper shade of pink.

Dinner was an elaborate affair, served unobtrusively, but the conversation was louder and livelier by the minute. Lobster was followed by either the finest Irish beef or local fish, washed down with a selection of Frank's finest wines. At last, the bankers were relaxing and beginning to unwind. Even Derek, whose expression was normally severe, was laughing heartily at one's of Jay's bawdier jokes.

Frank sat back, pleased. What had promised to be a tedious affair was turning out to be very good fun, and Jay, he had to admit, was playing a blinder. Perhaps that was because she was the only woman, he thought, and was enjoying the all-male company. After dinner was finished and coffees and liqueurs had been served, she suggested they all go into the port for a bit of fun. Frank was surprised and even more so when the bankers agreed readily.

'We're going into the port,' he told Rory. 'We'll take the Riva.'

'Right away, sir.'

'See you on deck in five, lads,' he said to his guests.

Minutes later they were whizzing towards the harbour, where the glittering lights beckoned and crowds were thronging. Now Frank felt uneasy. What if he ran into Ivanka? This was her turf, and he hardly ever went there with Jay, but he told himself not to worry. Sure, they were all having a bit of fun and what harm could a few more drinks do?

Joy's Piano Bar, or Jurassic Park as it was snidely referred to by young people who wouldn't have been seen dead in it, was heaving. A man of indeterminate age and origin was belting out a medley of well-known hits from the eighties, accompanied by a duo on bass and keyboard, and the older crowd were loving it. After three Mimosas and a couple of energetic dances with the bankers, Jay was feeling dizzy. She sat down to catch her breath and noted that Frank was chatting to a few people they knew from home and ordering yet another round of drinks. This was her chance. She went up to him, said hello to the pals, then claimed a headache and told Frank she was calling it a night. She'd get a cab to the house rather than going back to *Excalibur*.

'Are you sure, pet?' He was surprised. Up until now, Jay had seemed to be having a great time, and the bankers had enjoyed her company tremendously.

'Don't say anything,' Jay whispered to him. 'You don't want to break up the evening. I'll just slip away quietly.'

'Well, if you're sure?' He seemed genuinely disappointed. 'Will I not call Rudi or Rory to take you back to the boat?'

'No, I'll see you tomorrow, Frank. Let me know if you – well, if you want me to help out with anything.'

'I'll ring you in the morning – and thanks, Jay, for tonight, you did a great job. I appreciate it.'

'No problem,' said Jay as he bent to kiss her cheek. He missed, getting her smack on the lips, and she inhaled the familiar aroma that was uniquely Frank's. For an awful moment, tears threatened, but she smiled brightly, turned on her heel and blinked them away.

Outside, Jay pushed her way through the hordes and stepped off the pavement. She darted in front of a bright yellow Lamborghini, one of the many flash sports cars snaking their way through the port, drivers and passengers watching and being watched, hunters evaluating quarry. Walking as quickly as her trademark five-inch stilettos would allow, she reached Olivio's where, despite her petite stature, the doorman allowed her immediate access, taking in at a glance her jewels, the designer dress and the determined tilt of her chin.

Inside, allowing her eyes to adjust to the dim lighting, Jay made her way to the private bar where she slipped the girl guarding the reserved area a handsome tip and whispered to her discreetly. Standing a good foot above Jay, with a hawk-like nose and carnivorous mouth, the girl pocketed the money and flicked her eyes to the back of the bar. Jay followed her glance, slipping into a recently vacated booth from which she could locate her prey unobserved.

It didn't take long to spot her. Jay had memorised every

millimetre of the photographs, but none did the girl justice. Ivanka sat at the bar, dressed in gold from head to toe. Peeking out at her competition from behind the mercifully high curving back of the velvet-lined booth, Jay quietly let out a long, low whistle. She was stunning. Her pale blonde hair was drawn back into a ponytail from an exquisitely chiselled face with slanting cheekbones. Her skin gleamed and was covered only by what appeared to be a slip of gold satin. Her long, slender legs were crossed elegantly, and high-heeled gold sandals were secured to her feet with ribbons round her ankles. Her neck, wrists and ears were adorned with twenty-four-carat Cartier and a large solitaire diamond glinted on her left hand. The only flaws in the otherwise perfect portrait were the hard mouth and the coldness in her eyes.

Jay wanted to kill her. But first she wanted to kill Frank. That stupid, ignorant, feckin' gobshite of a man! To think he could contemplate for the merest glimmer of a second that a girl like her would be interested in him for anything besides his money. She wanted to scream. Feeling a cramp in her hands, she looked down and saw she was .digging into the seat back so hard she would leave claw marks in it. She told herself to keep it together and took a few deep breaths. A waitress passed and Jay ordered a glass of Cristal. When it arrived she sipped the ice cold champagne and forced herself to think calmly.

First off, the girl was a hooker. No doubt about it. Clearly an ambitious one, and possibly clever, but no match for Jay. Second, and this was the best bit, she was drinking straight vodka, as far as Jay could tell – she had seen her glass being topped up – and she was smoking. The girl was no more pregnant than Jay was, she'd bet her bottom dollar. If this creature thought she could sashay in and waltz off into the sunset with Jay's husband, she was sadly mistaken.

As Jay watched, Ivanka was joined by another girl, also

beautiful, also blonde, also scantily dressed with the longest legs she had ever seen. The girl kissed Ivanka's cheek and slipped onto a stool beside her, flicking back her curtain of shoulder-length blonde hair.

Shit! She had missed her chance. Jay had been ready to go over and confront her, show her who she was dealing with, but now she had been joined by the other girl, it wouldn't be nearly so effective. Damn. She could have kicked herself for not acting sooner. Hiding back into the high curve of her seat, she decided to wait, hoping the other girl might move on, but it didn't look likely: the two were deep in conversation. This came to an abrupt stop, however, when a tall, heavily built man walked into the bar, his mouth curled in a derisive smile. His dark blond hair was slicked back from his face, which, although handsome in a swarthy way, wore a threatening expression. Dressed in a black shirt and a white suit, he walked up to Ivanka from behind. Ignoring the other girl, he grabbed Ivanka's wrist, pinned it to the bar and grinned at her.

Jay watched, mesmerised, as the other girl legged it and the man sat down on her vacated stool. Ivanka stared at him contemptuously and, quick as a flash, stubbed her burning cigarette on his wrist. He merely laughed at her. Then he let her go and whispered something in her ear. Ivanka retaliated with what appeared to be a volley of abuse that Jay, unfortunately, could not hear above the pumping music. Then Ivanka got up, knocked back her drink, slammed the glass on the bar, turned and walked away defiantly – but not before he had slapped her roundly on her pert and very toned behind. He was still laughing as she disappeared among the bodies that bumped and writhed to the pulsing music.

Before she knew it, Jay was on her feet, following in Ivanka's wake. As she stood a good six foot in her golden sandals, her ponytail swaying behind her, it wasn't hard to keep track of her. Outside the club, Ivanka turned right and headed back up the port, walking swiftly. As Jay struggled to keep up, ducking and dodging crowds that occasionally obstructed her view, she couldn't help thinking what a ridiculous sight Ivanka and Frank must make as a couple. Her, tall, sleek and golden, and Frank, short, stocky and ruddy. Like an Afghan hound out walking with a bulldog. The crowds thinned as they reached the top of the port, where the shops ended and the apartments began.

Ivanka walked purposefully along the boardwalk by the sand, taking the beach route to some of the more exclusive apartment buildings. Jay stopped and took off her shoes – she had to, or she would have had no hope of keeping up with the girl's athletic strides. Checking her watch, she saw it was already three fifteen, although she felt she could have run a marathon, so much adrenalin was pumping through her. The beach was empty now, the moon hidden by cloud. Along the boardwalk, tall lamps stood on eerie sentry duty, throwing dim light on the shadowy doors that lay ahead. Darting quickly behind a palm, Jay waited breathlessly as Ivanka stopped and fumbled, fag still hanging from her mouth, for her key, which presumably eluded her. She mumbled an expletive.

Jay wondered what to do. Would she confront her now, outside? But what if things turned nasty? What if she was a karate expert or something? Still, she had come this far. Or maybe she should go back, think it over for a bit. She knew where Ivanka lived from the details her detective had supplied. But, of course, she had wanted to see for herself. And, if she was honest, she was getting a rush she hadn't felt in years from the sheer irresponsibility of what she was doing. Imagine her, little five-foot Jay Farrelly, following her husband's Russian Valkyrie of a whore in the middle of the night, right up to the hussy's front door—

Suddenly, a hand went round her waist, another over her mouth, and she found herself caught in a vice-like grip. Unable to scream or even to bite the perpetrator, Jay listened to a deep, heavily accented voice. 'Who are you?' She could smell the alcohol on his breath. 'And just what do you think you are doing following my wife?'

19

Carrie finished her twentieth lap of front crawl, turned on her back and pushed herself down the pool, floating weightlessly in the cool water, arms stretched behind her. At eight o'clock in the morning the sun was already bright, and she felt it warm on her face, its delicious heat caressing her chest and shoulders, as she idly watched the drops of water sparkling on her unsubmerged skin. She stayed like that for a moment, head back, hair floating round her, feeling for all the world like a girl in a shampoo ad. She felt special, and it was a very nice feeling she decided, one she could definitely get used to. She wiggled her freshly painted toes, admiring the deep red polish that highlighted her tan. Then she stood up, slicked the water from her hair and waded up the steps, pausing to stretch naked in the sun before reluctantly pulling on her robe.

Inside, she showered, slipped into a swimsuit and shorts and had breakfast sitting at the table on the patio, Toby at her feet, hoping for a piece of the toast which sometimes came his way.

There was no sign of Stephanie, and Carrie didn't expect to see her for some time since she hadn't come in until seven this morning. She'd have got away with it too, Carrie thought wryly, if she hadn't sent the huge vase on the hall table crashing to the floor. Carrie supposed she should have been angry – Stephanie had given her a hell of a fright – but when she had raced to the hall and seen her daughter's contrite and guilty face, eyes wide, hand clamped over her mouth, through which a horrified giggle had escaped, she had understood immediately that Stephanie was drunk. Carrie had sighed, led her to her room and taken off her make-up, trying to keep Stephanie upright on the bed. Then Stephanie had snuggled down, mumbled a few incoherent sentences, and fallen fast asleep.

Carrie had shaken her head and grinned before leaning down to kiss her on the forehead. Oh, for the resilience of youth, she had thought, gazing at her daughter's fresh, peachy complexion, where tomorrow there would be no telltale signs of the night's excess. Thinking of excess, Carrie frowned. She knew Stephanie was seeing someone – Luis, his name was, if she remembered correctly. She had said something about dog-walking, that's how Toby had found a new friend and so had she. More than a friend, Carrie deduced. Over the last few weeks she had scarcely seen her, and Stephanie, as hard as she might try, which wasn't very hard at all, was failing miserably at hiding the fact she was head over heels in love. Carrie smiled. Nothing gave her more pleasure than seeing her girls happy and Stephanie was a cheery soul, although Carrie had been worried that lately she was feeling a little low. Coming to Marbella had been a good idea, though – Stephanie was blossoming now, clearly basking in the attention of her new 'friend'. Which was another reason why Carrie was concerned.

Stephanie was spontaneous, open and easy to read. Yet she hadn't brought this Luis home to meet her mother – or even to hang out at the pool. God knows, they would have had plenty of space and time to themselves because Carrie had been out – here she felt a little twinge of maternal guilt. But whenever she had suggested it, Stephanie had demurred in a rather evasive manner. Carrie hoped Luis wasn't an older man, maybe married. There were such unscrupulous people around and with all the flash cash, sports cars and yachts, it would be very easy to turn a young girl's head. But that didn't feel

right. Carrie was sure of it. Stephanie didn't go for older men
– why, she thought Rudi was ancient, and he was only thirty-
four!

No. Instinct told Carrie it was something else entirely but
she couldn't for the life of her work out what. She would get
on the case later, she told herself firmly.

Now, she had to get ready for a polo match.

She went to her bedroom and rifled through her wardrobe,
wondering what on earth to wear. It wasn't as if she hadn't
ever been to a polo match, she had, several times in Dublin
at the Phoenix Park, and in London, when she and Rob had
been guests at the Cartier Tournament, and even to the Guards
Club, where she had seen Prince Charles and his two sons
carry away the cup to a delighted round of restrained applause.

But this was different. Emilio had suggested it as a last-
minute thing after they had had dinner last night.

She had seen more and more of him since the fateful
dinner party, now almost three weeks ago, and he was a
most delightful companion. Kind, considerate, terrific fun,
a gentleman and, yes, just plain gorgeous. She still had to
pinch herself. *Nice behaviour for a married woman,* the nasty
little voice reminded her. And for a moment she was crushed
with guilt. But then she rallied. She was doing nothing wrong.
She was simply having lunch, dinner and spending time with
a man whose company she found delightful and he, amazingly, felt the same way about her. There had been nothing
else, nothing to feel ashamed or guilty about. And nothing
sexual. Well, unless you counted the electric thrill she felt
when she saw him, or the roller-coaster ride that started in
her solar plexus and headed south when he took her hand,
or guided her protectively with his arm round her back. He
treated her as if she was the most fragile piece of Dresden
china.

Except, of course, last night. After another memorable

dinner at the Marbella Club, when they had talked and talked
– she had confided in him long ago about her marriage and
its imminent demise – they had taken a moonlit stroll along
the Paseo. It was there, at exactly twenty minutes past one,
with nothing but the gently lapping Mediterranean in the
background, that he had stopped, taken her in his arms and
bent his handsome head to kiss her. It had felt like the most
natural thing in the world. She had been astonished. Not that
he had kissed her, although she had been worrying about
that – she had never kissed anyone except Rob, apart from
a few teenage boys way back, and that didn't count – but
because she had been terrified at the thought of kissing anyone
other than Rob, afraid she wouldn't know how. That she
would recoil or, worse, clam up mid-kiss. And she had thought
Rob was the best kisser in the world. Kissing was so important, so *intimate*. But he hadn't kissed her in a very long time
– not like that. No! What Carrie was astonished at, *thrilled*
by, was that when it came to kissing, Emilio, Marques de
Alba, Cordoba y Rincón, was in a league of his own. And
what was more, he indulged in it slowly, artfully, masterfully,
as if he had nothing more important to do for the rest of his
life. And she – nervous, self-conscious Carrie Armstrong –
had responded in a very like and eager manner.

   She settled for a white linen scoop-necked sleeveless dress,
elegant but simple, and a medium-heeled pair of tan snake-
skin pumps with matching handbag. Her hair was almost dry
and just needed a quick finishing off with the straighteners.
She kept her make-up simple, allowing the glow, which had
nothing to do with the sun, to show through her semi-nude
base. She brought her favourite white floppy sun-hat and
popped her latest pair of shades into her handbag. It was a
two-and-a-half-hour journey by car to Soto Grande, where
the polo would be played, and Emilio would pick her up at
any minute. She scribbled a note for Stephanie and stuck it

on the fridge door, trying not to feel guilty at the lurch her stomach gave when she heard the doorbell.

If ever the expression 'impossibly handsome' was warranted, it applied to Emilio now, she thought, inhaling sharply at the sight of him grinning broadly at her. It wasn't the immaculate double breasted navy blazer and white linen trousers he wore so well, or the movie-star smile that dazzled her, but the genuine warmth in his eyes when he saw her.

'Carrie,' he said, taking her hand and kissing it. 'You look absolutely beautiful.'

She got into the passenger seat of the silver Range Rover he had borrowed from a friend for the trip and put on her sunglasses. Emilio closed her door carefully. Climbing in beside her, he drove out through the electric gates as the Gypsy Kings belted out 'Volare'. 'We're going to have fun today, Carrie,' he said, 'you and I, but I warn you, I will be very jealous if you flirt with any of the polo players.'

Never in her life had anyone said they would be jealous if she flirted with someone else. It was an extraordinary feeling and although she knew Emilio was joking, she realised, for the first time, that for most of her adult life, jealousy and insecurity had been her own constant companions. Feeling a sudden sense of exhilaration as they surged along the highway, Carrie flung her arm along Emilio's shoulders and caressed the back of his neck where his thick hair curled just above his shirt collar.

'You'd better be careful,' he warned, looking wickedly at her, his eyes dropping to her bare, tanned legs. 'I'm a very easily distracted driver.'

For three days Ali refused to pick up her agent's frantic phone calls. She was still too furious to talk about it. On the fourth day she relented.

'Ali,' Sandi's voice was shrill. 'What in God's name

happened? I've been worried sick! What's going on? And what did you do to upset Gerald J.? I can't believe it! He says you were rude and uncooperative, and the contract's going to the Ukrainian girl. What happened, Ali?' Sandi was distraught. 'That contract had our – I mean your – name on it.' She paused to draw in a shuddering breath.

'Let's just say there was a clause in it that I hadn't foreseen.' Ali was cool.

'What are you talking about?'

'The contract was mine, Sandi, if I had been cooperative enough to accompany him to his suite – and we're not talking about a nightcap. He made it abundantly clear that if I didn't sleep with him, I wouldn't get the contract. You can see how things transpired.' Ali sighed.

'Are you sure, Ali?' Sandi sounded disbelieving. 'I can't believe that of Gerald J., really, with his upbringing and everything. Maybe you misinterpreted it?'

'I've been in the business long enough to know a casting couch when I see one, and I'm happy to say that in all my long career, this was the very first time I'd come across it – which makes it all the more extraordinary. Anyway, I chose to decline his offer. I found it hugely insulting, quite apart from the fact that he's fully aware that I'm engaged to be married – which made it even more sordid. I'm sure you understand.'

'Yes, well . . .' Sandi's voice trailed off doubtfully. 'It's just such a – a tragedy. Twenty million dollars – and that was just for the first year. All that work for nothing.'

'Way too high a price, Sandi.' Ali was becoming impatient.

'Yes, yes, of course. You did the right thing,' said Sandi. She sounded as though she meant the opposite, that spending the night with Gerald J. would hardly have been a sacrifice considering the amount of money – not to mention prestige – at stake. 'Just as well you've got the wedding to organise, Ali.

This is going to cause a lot of talk in the industry. There'll be speculation and it won't all be flattering.'

'I really don't care, Sandi,' Ali said, and she didn't. She was worn out and thoroughly disillusioned.

'Well, you say that now . . . look, why don't you pop down to Marbella? The wedding's about the only thing that will distract the press from the Stay Tru débacle. I'll issue a statement and try to deflect things, damage limitation, if you like, but it'll affect your career, Ali. This would have been the big one.' Her voice was heavy with regret.

'Like I said, it was too high a price.' Ali put down the phone and lit a cigarette with trembling fingers. Whatever she had pretended to Sandi, the whole thing had shaken her badly. Sandi was right. She needed to get away. She'd go down to Marbella to be with her family. She had a wedding to plan. There was no need to mention the Stay Tru business, and if she had to, she could always say she'd changed her mind. Suddenly brighter, she picked up the phone and dialled her mother's number.

Hope crossed the main street in Marbella and headed into the maze of narrow, twisting streets where she dropped off her disk at a local print shop. Her own printer had packed up just when she needed to review some material, and she hated reading her copy on screen. At four o'clock, the Old Town was quiet and sleepy, and she decided to drop in to Oscar's shop and see if he fancied a coffee in the Orange Square. Reaching the brightly painted wooden doors that led through a small courtyard to the discreet shop from which he sold his beautifully crafted jewellery she stepped into the cool interior, where he was dealing with a customer. He winked at her. 'Hope, dearest, give me a minute.'

At her name, the customer turned – and Hope saw, with a start, that it was Rudi.

'Hello, Hope,' he said. His expression was pleasant, but she immediately sensed the guardedness behind it.

'Rudi,' she said, 'hi.' She hadn't seen him since the night of the dinner party, and in light of what had happened, she felt suddenly awkward and tongue-tied. She wasn't sure if she felt awkward for herself, or for him. He looked tired, she thought, and rather drawn but, as Stephanie had never ceased to point out, undeniably gorgeous.

'You two know each other?' Oscar's eyebrows were raised in a manner that Hope recognised.

'Er, yes, sort of,' she stammered. 'We've met.'

'Well, well, well,' said Oscar, to nobody in particular, as he busied himself with the card payment. He gave a receipt to Rudi. 'It'll be ready for you on Tuesday, Rudi, how's that?' he said.

'Great, Oscar, thanks.'

'Now what can I do for you, Hope?'

'I was just wondering if you fancied a coffee.'

'I wish I could,' Oscar sighed dramatically. 'Unfortunately I'm appallingly busy, but Rudi, I'm sure, would be delighted to join you, wouldn't you, Rudi?'

Hope froze with embarrassment and glared at him.

'Sure,' said Rudi easily, slipping his credit card into his pocket. 'I was just going for one myself. I've got half an hour or so to kill before I go back to the boat.'

He ushered Hope ahead of him as they left the shop and Oscar waved them a cheery goodbye. 'See you later, poppets.'

'How do you know Oscar?' Hope asked, trying frantically to think of something to say as they walked the short distance to the Orange Square, where Rudi selected a table in the shade and pulled out a chair for her. He sat down across from her at the tiny table and stretched out his long legs.

'Everybody knows Oscar, don't they?' He grinned. 'What about you?'

'He's a neighbour.'

'You live in La Virginia?'

'Yes, I have done for the last eighteen months.' Hope ordered a cappuccino and Rudi an espresso from the waiter.

'I have a place there myself.'

'What?' Hope realised she must have sounded rude, but she couldn't hide her surprise. 'But I thought – I mean, don't you live on *Excalibur*?'

'Only when I need to, which, yes, is most of the time.' He knocked back his espresso and regarded her with amusement. 'But I need a bolthole, or I get cabin fever. When I moved down here a year ago I was intending to rent, but I saw this house for sale and couldn't resist it. I let it until a couple of weeks ago – my tenant was moving out anyway. It's number seven,' he added, answering her unasked question.

'Of course,' murmured Hope. 'I knew Marinella,' she referred to his erstwhile tenant, a talented, reclusive sculptor. 'Not well, but just to say hello to. She was a nice woman.'

'Good tenant too. But it suited me that she was leaving, particularly with the wedding coming up and B'stardo prancing around the place driving us crazy.' He grinned suddenly. 'I couldn't have hacked it without somewhere to escape to occasionally.'

'I know the feeling.'

'What are you escaping from?'

'Oh, family, mostly. But they seem to have caught up with me, at least until the wedding's over. Then, hopefully, things will get back to normal.'

'Well, not long to go now. Four weeks or thereabouts?'

'Yes, about that.'

'They seem nice, your family.' He was looking at her speculatively. 'Particularly your mum.'

'They are – she is. It's just that, well – oh, God, I'm sorry, I forgot.' She thought suddenly of the ghastly scene with the *marques*. 'Whatever happened after the dinner? Is any of it true?'

Rudi's face darkened. 'He's not trying to deny it, been calling me every day since.'

'And?'

'And nothing. I haven't taken the calls.'

'Don't you think it's worth at least talking to him? He seems like a genuinely nice man.'

'He wants us to take DNA tests. You know, the funny thing is, I've spent my whole life searching for my father, vowing I'd make him pay for everything my mother went through, and now it just doesn't seem worth the trouble.'

'But if he wants to meet you, don't you think – well, aren't you curious? I know he's really upset about it all,' Hope blurted out.

'How would you know that?' Rudi's voice was cold.

'He and my mother . . . well, they've become friendly. She said he's really gutted about the whole thing.'

'Yeah, well . . .' Rudi looked away. 'Bit late now, isn't it? Anyway, what good would it do? It's not like we have a lot in common or anything.'

'How do you know until you give him a chance – get to know him?'

He looked at her curiously. 'For someone who's avoiding her family, you certainly seem very keen for me to cosy up to mine – that is, if he does turn out to be my father.'

'I'm sorry, you're quite right.' Hope clammed up as quickly as if she had been slapped. 'It's absolutely none of my business.'

'That's not what I meant.'

For a moment his eyes locked with hers and Hope found it impossible to look away. She felt like a rabbit trapped in oncoming headlights, knowing danger was imminent, but transfixed, unable to flee.

'Rudi, darling!' The moment was broken. A blonde girl had appeared as if from nowhere. She bent down and slipped her arms round Rudi's neck. 'Rudi,' she exclaimed, ignoring Hope completely. 'I have been looking for you everywhere!'

'Actually,' said Hope, smiling politely as she deposited a ten-euro note on the table, 'I was just going.' She got up and grabbed her bag.

'Hope, wait,' said Rudi, but it was too late.

'Perfect timing.' The blonde girl slipped into her vacated seat.

As he watched Hope disappear round a corner, Rudi scowled. 'What the hell do you want now, Lola?'

Stephanie was in a bind. Well, a very delicious bind, she thought, watching Luis as he emerged from the dilapidated shower cubicle in his small, cramped, one-roomed *apartamento*, nestled in the heart of old Estepona. Although it was tiny by normal standards, Stephanie thought that it was the most beautiful place she had ever been in, painted in shades of deep red, pink and purple and festooned with artfully hung shawls and tapestries embroidered by his late gypsy grandmother. Now Stephanie lay in the small double bed that took up most of the room and was covered with what she thought of as a wildly romantic mosquito net, draped from a central pod, cocoon like, round the bed.

She stretched lazily, watching Luis as he pulled a comb through his unruly curls and tugged on his working clothes – black hip-hugging trousers, white shirt, black bow-tie – and reached for his white jacket, which she had pressed. It was the universal uniform of the waiter – but Luis didn't look anything like a waiter, Stephanie thought. He could have walked off the set of some amazing romantic, macho movie, like *Gladiator* or *Braveheart*, striding around in a sexy

armoured breastplate and very little else, except his gladiator sandals.

She looked at him now and grinned.

'What?' he asked, watching her from the mirror.

'I was just thinking how lovely you are.'

Luis scowled. 'Lovely? Men do not look lovely. That is for
girls. Men are handsome.' He was working hard at polishing
his English. He was ambitious and perfect English was a
necessity in Spain.

'But you,' he came over to the bed where she lay naked
except for a sheet round her waist, her curls tangled and
tumbling round her face, 'you, Stephanie' – he leaned down
to kiss her nose – 'are very, very lovely.'

'I wish we didn't have to go.'

'Hurry. Five minutes, or I will be late.' He tapped his watch.

Stephanie leaped out of bed and into the tiny shower, where
she reluctantly washed away the traces of their hungry love-
making. Luis did things to her body that Stephanie had only
believed existed between the pages of steamy novels. It made
her shiver just to think of it. Stephanie Armstrong was madly
in love. She was also, for the first time in her life, deeply in
lust. It was a heady combination. There was just one little
problem.

He had mentioned it casually on one of their walks along
the harbour, this time without the dogs. And Stephanie had
thrilled as he casually took her hand and held it as they walked
along. It was morning and the port was quiet, shops and
restaurants readying themselves for the day ahead. The sun
glinted on the water and the yachts gleamed white in the
early heat of the day. It was all so pretty.

'It's disgusting, don't you think?' A scowl clouded Luis's
face, making him look even more exotic.

'Sorry?' Stephanie didn't understand.

'This – this *crap*.' Luis mistook Stephanie's wide-eyed gaze for admiration. 'All this,' he gestured at the boats, the cars, 'just toys for stupid rich people destroying the planet. Globalisation. It's all round us. Everywhere you look now in Marbella, there is more horrible buildings, another ugly villa built for some fat cat.' He looked out at the harbour. 'When my grandfather was growing up, Marbella was a fishing village. Now look at it.'

'Oh,' said Stephanie.

'Where did you say you were staying?'

'Um, with a girlfriend at her apartment in the hills.' She tried frantically to think of the name of Hope's little street. 'La Virginia, that's it.' This was clearly not the time to mention that her family were staying in one of the swankiest villas on the coast.

Luis's brow wrinkled. 'I have heard of it, but I don't know it. It has a lot of artists, yes? Artists are good,' he said firmly. 'Your friend, what does she work at?'

'She's a writer.'

Luis nodded approvingly. 'I would like to write. And you, Stephanie, what do you want to do?'

I would very much like to have your babies and live in idyllic bliss in any fishing village of your choice in the world, thought Stephanie. The more remote the better. 'Um, well, I'm a pretty good cook,' she ventured, and he gave an approving grin. 'Maybe one day I'll have my own restaurant, or a catering company.'

'Restaurants very expensive,' Luis said knowledgably. 'A person would need a lot of money or wealthy people to invest.'

'Um, yes, yes, you're right,' said Stephanie. Failing to inform him that her father could set her up with a chain in the morning.

'Maybe we start our own restaurant one day, hey, Stephanie? I am learning very much in Olivio's.'

Stephanie beamed.

'I have idea,' he said. 'You are here for one more month, yes?'

Stephanie nodded.

'You get bored, yes? There is nothing to do here except be lazy in the sun. No one can do that for all the time.' He made a face. 'Maybe weekends, but otherwise, you go crazy.'

'Oh, yes,' agreed Stephanie eagerly, although she'd rather have been enjoying lazing about in the sun. But she did feel crazy – crazy and giddy and drunk with lust.

'Olivio's, where I work, they need restaurant-manager person. Don't need to know nothing except speak good English. Show peoples to tables, that kind of thing. Why don't you come for interview? They will love you. And you are good cook so you can learn more. Then we can work together. Good idea, no?' He looked as if he had just proposed that she join him for a week in a five-star hotel. And gazing into his dark brown eyes, she thought it was the most wonderful invitation she had ever received. 'I think it's a great idea, Luis,' she said.

'*Estupendo*! We go now, to see them.'

That had been last week, and she was due to start work tonight. She would ride to the port now with Luis on his little moped, arms wrapped tightly round him, and when he dropped her off, so he could start the early shift, she would grab a taxi back to the villa. Then she could get ready in peace and tell her mum she was going out – after all, she would be dressed nicely, she had to be, it was part of the job description, and her mother would have no reason to think she was doing anything other than going out on the town with her new friend. Here, she faltered a little. She knew it was only a matter of time before Carrie pressed her to introduce Luis – in fact, she had only avoided it so far because Carrie had been out and about so much with the *marques*.

Stephanie liked Emilio, she reflected, she liked him because he made her mother smile and laugh again. She liked watching her mother pretend not be excited when he called, or taking extra care with her clothes and her appearance, liked seeing her having fun. And, of course, that he was a dog-lover, just like Stephanie. She wondered briefly what her father would say about it all, then pushed the thought firmly from her mind. He was never around and he'd been horrid to Mum. In fact, Stephanie had thought that she – they – would miss him not being there, but so much was happening, they didn't have time even to think about him. Not even Mum.

It was nine o'clock when Rudi, exhausted after a particularly gruesome day on *Excalibur,* finally escaped to his house in La Virginia. Dealing with Enrique B'stardo and some of his more obscure suggestions for the wedding reception, not to mention his hysteria if such requests were not complied with, had taken its toll.

Now all he wanted to do was pour himself a large whiskey and watch a bit of soccer on Sky Sports before it started again tomorrow. He had made it to the small kitchen when he heard a discreet knock on the door.

'Who the hell . . .' he muttered, replacing the bottle of Jameson's he had just been about to open. Never had he felt less like a visitor. If one of his mates was wanting company, they were out of luck. He opened the door and his scowl deepened.

'Please may I come in? We have to talk.' The tall figure of the *marques* stood before him.

'I have nothing more to say to you.' Rudi made to close the door.

'Please,' Emilio protested. 'I promise I won't disturb you for long. At least spare me a few moments.'

Something in his expression made Rudi relent – or maybe he was just too goddamned tired to care. 'Please yourself.'

He stood back and allowed Emilio into the small front room, simply but tastefully furnished, with a spectacular view of the Andalucian hills.

Emilio sat on one of the sofas.

'Drink?' Rudi asked brusquely. 'I was about to pour one for myself.'

'Thank you. Whatever you're having.'

Rudi handed him a whiskey and sat down on the opposite sofa.

'I can understand how you must be feeling—' Emilio began.

'No, you bloody can't, mate, not in a million bloody years,' Rudi laughed derisively.

'Please,' Emilio held up a hand, 'I will say what I have to say once. After that, you never have to set eyes on me again. At least hear me out.'

'Fair enough.' Rudi's voice was hard.

'I have spent a lot of time thinking about and researching the situation that you, er, confronted me with that extraordinary night. That photo brought back a lot of memories – happy ones. Your mother, Mary Jane, and I had a great time together, but we both knew it was a holiday romance. She was travelling round the world with her friends and I had to return to my duties. We exchanged addresses, promised to stay in touch, and I never heard from her again. I didn't expect to.'

'C'mon, mate, those letters! She sent them to you – to the right address.' Rudi dared Emilio to contradict him.

'You must believe me, I knew nothing – nothing at all of her predicament, nothing of your existence. I swear on my life, and I can prove it, if you'll just listen.'

Rudi started at him.

'My father is long dead, but my mother is still alive, a reasonably sprightly and mentally alert eighty-seven-year-old.'

'So?'

'I paid her a visit last week in Madrid, at the *palacio* – the address to which you referred. I showed her the photo, explained the situation and asked her if she knew anything about the letters.'

Rudi held his breath.

Emilio sighed. 'It was difficult for her. We have been through a lot, with my first wife dying, then Carlos, my son.' He looked sadly at Rudi, who was now listening avidly to every word. 'And it was all so long ago. Finally she admitted that she had indeed received the letters your late mother sent. She opened the first and discovered presumably that you were on the way. She made the decision – a very wrong decision – to ignore the whole matter, return any other letters unopened and hope the matter would go away. Unfortunately, for both of us, it did. You must remember, Rudi, this was Old Spain. Times were so different. When my wife died, my parents stepped in to look after Carlos while I was working abroad – they thought they were protecting him. People were easily threatened in those days. A scandal, or what was thought of as a scandal, well, people did stupid things to avoid it. She is deeply sorry for what she did, your grandmother, and hopes one day that you will come to meet her at the *palacio* – your rightful family home – so she can tell you herself.' Emilio drew a deep breath.

'So you really didn't know anything about me?' Rudi shifted uncomfortably.

'I swear to you, Rudi, I knew nothing. That doesn't excuse the last thirty-four years, but please, can't we wipe the slate clean and begin again?'

A muscle flexed in Rudi's cheek as he fought to control his emotions.

'I implore you, Rudi,' Emilio's face was ravaged, 'I have already lost one son. Please, don't make me lose another.'

The silence that followed seemed to last for an eternity,

and then a smile spread across Rudi's face. 'I believe you. And you're right, it's time to leave the past where it belongs.'

Emilio seemed to lose ten years. 'Thank God!' he exclaimed. 'I was praying you'd give me a chance.'

'Another drink?' Rudi got up and retrieved the bottle.

'I'd love that.'

'I think it's a little soon for me to start calling you Dad, though. How about Emilio?'

'Call me whatever you like, Rudi.'

'And I guess we should have a DNA test, just to confirm everything.'

'Whatever you want. Although . . .' Emilio fished for something in his breast pocket, 'I think you might find this equally convincing.' He handed Rudi a photograph.

'Holy moly.' Rudi examined the shot of the young Emilio standing alone on a beach, grinning broadly. It could have been himself right down to the last detail. 'That's kind of spooky.'

'That's what I thought,' said his father, smiling proudly.

'Dad?'

Rob smiled at the sound of his middle daughter's voice. 'Ali, sweetheart! Great to hear you, how are you?'

'Actually, Dad, I'm very stressed, but it's a relief to talk to at least *one* member of my family,' she said petulantly.

'What do you mean, love?'

'Every time I call Mum or Stephanie they seem to be rushing out somewhere or they forget to ring me back. And Hope, of course, is no help at all. I've had to get that awful wedding planner to ring me. He says everything's fine and going perfectly to plan, but he *would* say that, wouldn't he? Anyway, I've finished my last big job so I thought it was time I went down myself. After all, there's only a month to go now 'til the big day and I'm terrified. I mean, all the invitations have gone out and everything – of course my people here are handling that – but I think I'll go down next week and get settled in, make sure everything's shipshape, excuse the pun.'

'That sounds like a great idea. I could use a change of scene myself, and I'd love to see my baby bride-to-be. How about we go down together, darling, and surprise everyone?'

'Oh, Dad,' Ali sighed, 'I couldn't think of anything nicer. I just know if you're around everything will be all right.'

'Not having second thoughts, darling, are you, I hope?'

'No, of course not, it's just wedding nerves. It's to be expected, I suppose – it's such a big production.'

'Nothing we can't handle. I have to be in London on the fifteenth. Let's meet there and we'll fly down together. I'll have the plane and it'll be just us.'

'Oh, Daddy, I knew I'd feel better once I'd talked to you. Call me with the times, and I'll see you in London. Can't wait.'

'Me neither, darling.'

Rob felt better the minute he hung up. The last few weeks *had* been stressful. The row with Olwen, the subsequent reunion and making up had exhausted him. Olwen, too, seemed wrung out, physically and emotionally.

She was also under a lot of pressure at work, and when they did get together, they were both tired. Something else had changed too, something he couldn't put his finger on. Olwen was different with him. Not as warm . . . the tenderness – yes, that was it – the tenderness she had felt for him seemed to have disappeared. She was cooler – remote, even. Perhaps she was still a bit cross with him. Or maybe it was PMT. Anyway, she'd come round, she always did. In the meantime, a bit of sun, a few rounds of golf and a change of scene would be just what he needed. And, of course, to catch up with his daughters. Carrie, too, would be pleased to see him. She'd sounded in good form the last couple of times he'd spoken to her. Of course, she'd be enjoying all the wedding business. It would have taken her mind off things. Things he hoped she would reconsider. Whatever else Rob needed, a divorce was not one of them.

Not now. Maybe over the next year or so, when things had settled down a bit, when he could think properly, get his head round everything. Right now he needed to relax. And Carrie would be pleased to see him, even if she pretended not to be. She always was. They'd have a few nice dinners together, maybe throw a party or two. There was bound to be a good crew from home there. Yes, Rob thought, it was a good thing Ali had rung when she did. It would be great to be together as a family again.

Whistling a happy tune, he called his secretary and told her to make the necessary arrangements.

20

Hope was fresh out of the shower when the doorbell buzzed. Her damp hair fell down her back and she was still dripping as she pulled a white bath sheet round her and padded downstairs. Only Oscar would call to her door at this time, and although he could sometimes be a nuisance, she was mindful that he needed company and friends more than ever now that he was adjusting to life without his partner.

She was tired, looking forward to some downtime, but forced a welcoming smile and opened the door. The smile froze.

'Hey, I'm sorry, I obviously got you at an, er, inopportune moment.' She could see the amusement in Rudi's eyes, and immediately felt herself blush crimson. 'I would have called, but I don't have your number and I thought it would be easier just to drop by. I wanted to apologise for the interruption when we were having coffee, and I was wondering if you'd have dinner with me tonight?'

'You don't owe me an explanation.' Hope felt ridiculously exposed.

'I wasn't thinking of explanations, just continuing where we left off. I was enjoying talking to you. Eight thirty suit?'

'Er, sure. Eight thirty would be fine.'

'Great, I'll swing by and pick you up.' He smiled suddenly, a heart-stopping, stomach-melting smile, then turned and loped away. Hope shut the door hurriedly and leaned against it, taking a deep breath. Why on earth had she said that?

Why hadn't she just said she was doing something else? After all, she could have been getting ready for anything. And then she remembered how long it had been since she'd been asked on a date. How long she had been celibate. Two years. Celibate was easy. Lonely wasn't. And Hope realised that she was lonely. Even if it had been of her own making. Apart from Oscar, who was heading for seventy, she had avoided and discouraged men since her break-up from Michael.

Now, she found she was excited by the thought of dinner with someone her own age. It was just a pity he was a lethally attractive womaniser – *so* not her type. Still, she reasoned, what harm could dinner do? And she was dying to hear more about what had transpired with the *marques*, Rudi's newly acquired father.

'I hope you don't mind a bit of a drive,' said Rudi, turning up on the dot of eight thirty in jeans and a casual white linen shirt.

Hope, who had agonised unusually about what to wear, was glad she had opted for a simple but pretty faded pink cheesecloth dress tied in a drawstring round her shoulders, gathered at the waist and falling in a series of gypsy layers to below her knees. 'Not at all,' she said. 'Where are we going?'

'You'll see,' he said, grinning. Then, 'You look pretty.' His eyes roamed over her appreciatively. 'Really, really pretty.'

'Thank you,' said Hope, smiling, then cursing the blush she could feel creeping over her cheeks. 'You look, um, very nice too.' And he did, she thought. More than nice, actually, pretty damn gorgeous, from his freshly washed hair to his well-worn loafers.

They strolled the short distance uphill to the car park where Rudi gestured towards an old silver Porsche 356 drop-top. He opened the door for Hope and she slid onto the red leather seat.

'Wow,' she said, 'this is fabulous.'

'I think so,' he said. 'I found her languishing in a collector's garage in Germany and couldn't leave her behind. A mate of mine helped me with the restoration work, which took about a year, and now, I can't imagine life without her.'

'How come I've never seen her in the car park?' wondered Hope.

'I keep her in a garage in town when I'm on the boat.' Rudi accelerated as the road opened up before them. 'Only take her out on special occasions.' Hope felt, rather than saw, his amused glance in her direction. She tried to think of a witty riposte and failed.

'So, how come you wound up in Marbella?' Rudi asked.

As the car turned off the main highway and wound up through the Andalucian hills while dusk settled round them like a mantel, Hope found herself telling him about her family, living in New York and leaving Michael for South America after discovering he had been unfaithful to her.

Rudi listened to it all, prompting her occasionally. 'After you've finished this book you're working on, what then? Will you stay?'

'Honestly?' Hope paused, 'I don't know. I can't see myself going back to Dublin, although I know my Mum would love me to. Right now, I guess, I'm taking it one day at a time.'

'It's about the best way I know to live,' said Rudi. 'Works for me anyway.'

Suddenly he turned off the winding road onto an even steeper one. Hope glanced at her watch and could hardly believe they'd been driving for almost an hour – it felt more like twenty minutes. Then on a bend overlooking a steep cliff, she saw a small hacienda-style house.

'Well, here we are,' said Rudi, turning off the engine. 'El Lupo – the best food and the best view in all of Andalucía. But don't go telling everyone – it's a well-kept secret.'

Inside, Rudi was greeted warmly by the proprietor, a fat man with a jovial manner who wove his way through the maze of tables with amazing ease for his size. 'I have reserved your usual table, Rudi.' He guided Hope to the window, which looked out onto the dark shapes of the mountain beneath them. Rudi hadn't been exaggerating, Hope thought. The view *was* breathtaking.

After they had ordered, she sipped her glass of rosé and, feeling surprisingly hungry after the long drive, nibbled at a breadstick. 'Your turn,' she said, fixing Rudi with a smile. 'Is it true, what Jay said, about the scar?' The moment she had asked the question she regretted it.

Rudi leaned back in his chair. 'Why do you want to know?'

Hope tried not to choke as a piece of breadstick lodged in her throat. She coughed, then gulped some water to wash it down.

'Are you all right?'

'Perfectly, thank you.'

'You haven't answered my question.'

'Neither have you – answered mine, I mean.'

'Yes.' His eyes were humorous, but something darker lay in their depths. 'It's true. It's quite impressive, even if I say so myself.'

'How did you get it?'

'Ah, now that *is* a good story.'

Over dinner, Hope listened as Rudi told her of his encounter with the shark, but she was even more fascinated by the story of his life, which he related simply and without rancour.

'It must have been difficult for you.'

'It wasn't easy.' Rudi shrugged and sipped his wine. 'Being poor and white in South Africa wasn't a lot of fun, but if I hadn't started out that way, I wouldn't have had the life I have now – and I wouldn't change that. Parts of it have been mind-blowing and recent events have been a revelation, to say the least.'

'The *marques*?' Hope raised an eyebrow.

'Yep. Dear old Dad. I took the DNA test and we're one hundred per cent related.'

'Wow! I mean, congratulations. I don't know what to say – how do you feel about it?'

'Honestly, I don't know. You're the first person I've told. There's a whole lot of stuff going on in my head, but none of it's what I expected. I thought I'd be angry and stay angry, but I guess I just feel sorry for both of us. I think he's more cut up about it than I am – and you were right. He is a decent guy. I believe his version of events, that he didn't know about me.'

'So what now?'

'That depends.'

After coffee, Rudi called for the bill and Hope was strangely disappointed when he paid it quickly, then suggested they make a move.

'Thank you' she said, outside, shivering in the chilly night air. 'That was really lovely.'

'My pleasure.' Rudi held open the passenger door for her.

The drive back was quiet. Rudi seemed lost in thought, staring ahead, and she was glad that the vibrant strains of the Buena Vista Social Club filled the car as they sped towards the highway, dispelling in part the tension that seemed to have enveloped them.

All too soon they arrived at the turn-off to La Virginia and Rudi pulled into the car park. They got out and walked the short distance to Hope's little house, Casa Esperanza.

'It really does have your name on it,' Rudi said. 'I only just noticed that now.'

'I thought it was a sign.'

'Do you always look for them?'

'That depends.'

'On what?'

'On what I'm searching for.'

'Hmm. That sounds intriguing . . . I wouldn't say no to a cup of coffee, if I wasn't imposing.'

'Er, no, of course not. Come in.'

Inside, Rudi's height seemed overpowering in the tiny house. As Hope went into the kitchen, she could hear him moving around, every fibre of her sensing his masculine presence.

She opened the cupboard, then remembered with a jolt. She walked back into the sitting room. 'You're not going to believe this,' she said, feeling incredibly foolish, 'but I don't have any coffee. I meant to get some today and it slipped my mind. I have plenty of tea.'

'How interesting. I'd say *that's* a sign.' He began to walk towards her.

'A sign?'

'Yes. A very definite sign.'

'Wh-what do you mean?'

'Coffee, tea . . . or me? Isn't that how it goes?'

'If you think for one moment that this was deliberate—'

'Hope, what exactly are you afraid of?' Rudi regarded her quizzically. 'I don't bite, you know. Well, not unless . . .' He trailed off, smiling infuriatingly.

'I'm not afraid of anything.'

'Really? You could have fooled me. How about this? Does this frighten you?' He trailed a finger along her jaw.

'Of course not, it's just that – I, that is . . .'

'Or how about this?' The finger was tracing her collarbone now, eliciting another set of sensations in regions Hope had all but forgotten about.

'Rudi, you don't understand.' Hope had rehearsed the speech to perfection. But for some reason he wasn't listening.

'Oh, I understand perfectly,' he said, his lips curving in a delicious smile. 'What I'm perfectly clear about is that you should stop gibbering and enjoy this.'

Then his arms were round her, one hand at the small of her back, the other hooked round her neck drawing her to him, and his lips were on hers, his tongue exploring as his embrace tightened, and Hope's body was suddenly talking a whole new game plan.

At home, in the luxury of Villa Esmerelda, Jay reflected on the events of the last few days.

Bizarre wasn't the word for it. If anyone had told her that she, Jay Farrelly, hailing from the depths of the Irish countryside, would be entering into negotiations with a Russian gangster built like a brick shithouse, and probably with a record as long as both arms, she would have said they were deranged.

As it was, she felt as if she was on another planet. No, she *wished* she was. Still, there was no other option. Desperate times called for desperate measures. And impending divorce was as desperate as it got. She knew it wasn't wise of her to let Igor come to the house, but what else could she do? At least, she thought, it would be safer than meeting him at some shady venue of *his* choice where God only knew what might happen to her. She had no illusions. She was way past her sell-by date for smuggling off into the white slave trade, but she still didn't relish being on her own with Igor on unfamiliar territory. Life was cheap to people like him. But Jay valued it more highly than ever at the moment – which was why she had been prepared to pay the enormous sum she had proposed.

Igor. She rolled the name around in her head. Actually,
after the initial fright he had given her outside Ivanka's apartment in Puerto Banus, he had turned out to be quite nice.
Nicer still when she'd told him she could make it worth his
while to help her out of a tricky situation. A mutually tricky
situation, as it transpired.

She had explained to him that she was not at all happy
about Ivanka's relationship with Frank, her husband.

And Igor turned out to be equally unhappy about it, not
unnaturally since he currently happened to be married to
Ivanka, legally and in the eyes of the Church. Jay wasn't well
up on Russian Orthodoxy, but Igor assured her they took
marriage extremely seriously, as indeed he did, a small point
that Ivanka, presuming he was still imprisoned, had overlooked.

Ever since his release six months ago, Igor had been
tracking her down, and in the process had learned of her
infidelity with the Irishman, whom he had also tracked down,
and to whom he had been sending threats of an escalating
nature.

Jay assured him she understood. Sure, the poor man was
out of his mind with jealousy, never mind betrayal. From
there it had been easy. Jay explained that Frank was a brilliant businessman, but very innocent and easily led in the
ways of the world. It was her duty, first and foremost, as his
wife to protect him from himself. Igor thought this was most
commendable.

After a suitable amount had been decided on – including
the apartment, which was already in Ivanka's name – that
would allow Igor and his unsuspecting wife to start a new
life, preferably far away from Marbella, they had come up
with the plan. All going well, it should be unfolding tonight,
while Jay was fast asleep, or pretending to be.

A text message from Igor would suffice as confirmation.

Half the money had been upfront, the rest on completion of a successful outcome. Jay hadn't told a soul. Not even the detective, who to date hadn't come up with the goods after she had had Rudi photocopy the evidence she had discovered in Frank's briefcase. She had to admit Rudi had been helpful at the time when it came down to it, despite everything that had happened.

The detective, on the other hand, had told her to stay well out of it and leave it to him, that it was dangerous stuff. Yeah, right! thought Jay. Tell me something I don't know. So she had dealt with the matter herself. When something mattered this much, it was the only way.

Getting into Ivanka's apartment had been easy. Breaking and entering were elementary when you had progressed to the heights Igor had reached in the world of crime. What he hadn't known already, he had picked up from a few interesting characters he had become friendly with during his incarceration.

He had timed it well. Ivanka strolled into the sitting room fresh from the shower, very inviting in a short white towelling robe, running a comb through her long, damp hair.

'What are you doing here?' she spat, freezing in her tracks as she saw Igor lounging on the sofa, drink in hand, a cigarette dangling from the corner of his mouth. 'And how did you get in?'

He got up. 'Not a very nice greeting for your husband, Ivanka.' He smiled dangerously. 'Although, of course, I don't blame you for being angry.' He was standing in front of her now as he trailed a finger along her jaw. 'It can't have been easy, these last three years. You must have missed me, baby.'

'Don't touch me!' She was backing away now, eyes blazing.

'Come now, we have some catching up to do, you and I.' He produced a packet of white powder from inside his jacket. 'Only the best, Iva, especially for our reunion. I have been thinking of little else.' He noticed her gaze flicker. He could always control her, always had and always would. He knew she wanted him. The chemistry they shared was unique. He had trained her since she had been barely more than a child. They were made of the same stuff, he and she. And the sex had always been fantastic. No one knew Ivanka like he did. No one could bring her to the brink again and again, reducing her to a state of quivering desire, desperate for release from the prison of lust that only he could build round her.

'For old times' sake, Iva, hmm?' He slipped the robe from her shoulders and cupped a breast, feeling her nipple harden as he stroked it with his thumb. 'After that I will go – if you want me to. I promise.'

He could feel her wavering, see the desire flaring in her eyes.

'Come, baby, we'll have a little party, you and me. Later we can talk . . .'

Frank had extricated himself from the dinner, given by a business associate from Dublin, as soon as he decently could – although, in fairness, it had been a good evening. He had tried to get out of it but Jay wasn't having that. As it turned out, it was pleasant to relax with friends from home, and the food and selection of wines had been excellent. Jay had been in good form too, keeping the table in stitches. When the party broke up and she headed back to Villa Esmerelda, he had almost suggested going with her.

The bankers had gone home the week before, and the thought of going back to *Excalibur* on his own had lost its appeal. But, of course, he didn't have to be on his own. He could drop in on Ivanka. She'd take care of him, although he was a bit the worse for wear with drink and wasn't sure if he was up to any amorous activity. Still, Ivanka was happy to cater to his every need. He would spend what remained of the night with her and go back to the yacht in the morning.

He let himself in quietly, using the key he kept with him at all times, and closed the door softly, feeling for the light switch in the hallway as his eyes struggled to adjust to the darkness. He walked down the short corridor to the sitting room, where a table lamp shone dimly.

Clearly Ivanka hadn't been expecting him. The room was in what Frank could only describe as disarray. Empty beer cans were strewn haphazardly round the room and a half full bottle of Stoli vodka stood open on a table, two glasses beside it. Then Frank shuddered. He noticed the Waterford crystal bowl he had given to Ivanka after he had won it in a golf tournament was filled with cigarette ash and butts. Frank had never seen the apartment anything but clean and tidy, and he was surprised at how distasteful he found the mess. Even after the most rowdy of late nights, Jay had always insisted on cleaning up every last bit of debris rather than come down to face it in the morning.

It was then that he heard the noise.

At first he froze, wondering if Ivanka was being attacked in her own home. A loud moan became a strangled scream, and unintelligible shouting ensued. Forcing himself to focus, Frank grabbed the nearest thing that came to hand – a bronze sculpture of a naked woman. He tiptoed towards the bedroom and tentatively pushed the already open door. There was a struggle going on, all right, and Frank's eyes bulged with outrage. Poor Ivanka was tied up, her wrists bound together above her head and some evil oaf was forcing himself on her. With a roar of rage, Frank rushed at the bed, about to swing the bronze at the offender, who on closer inspection seemed to be a good deal taller than him – taking up all and more of the six foot plus bed. For a split second, Frank hesitated, afraid of hurting Ivanka.

'Frank!' she gasped.

Before he knew it, the intruder had reached out and caught his hair. This caused further confusion as Frank's toupèe came away in his hand, and the man who, now that he was standing up, appeared to be about seven feet tall and built to match, let out a shout of shock.

Frank dropped the sculpture and clutched his head, feeling both exposed and terrified. Another howl ensued, this time of agony, as the sculpture landed on the giant's foot.

After that, it was all a bit of a blur.

The giant hurled aside Frank's crowning glory, then caught him by the throat holding him up as effortlessly as if he'd been holding a puppy. As Frank's head swam he peddled furiously, trying to gain footing on the floor, which seemed suddenly to be a good three feet below him. He was now eye to eye with the giant, who did not look happy.

'Vell, vell, vell,' the giant growled. 'I finally get to meet the little Irishman.'

Frank managed only a gurgled response.

'Leesten carefully, little man. If you ever come near my vife again, I will kill you. But only after I have ripped out your insides and fed them to my dogs. Understand?'

Frank did.

As he was thrown across the room, he heard Ivanka shout, 'You stupid prick, Igor! You have ruined everything! Frank!' she begged. 'Wait! I can explain.'

Frank picked himself up and, gasping for air, ran as fast as his legs would carry him out of the apartment and down to the boardwalk, where he threw himself into the first of a waiting queue of taxis. 'Marbella!' he stuttered to the nonplussed driver, who obligingly drove off in the direction Frank pointed.

Only when the highway hove into view and Frank had

assured himself that he was not being followed by a gun-toting crew of Russian Mafia did he let out a sigh of relief, although he was still shivering uncontrollably.

Jesus, Mary and Joseph! He could hardly take in what had happened. He'd been lucky to escape with his life! There was no telling what those kind of people would do to you. Frank didn't stop to consider whether or not it was wise of him to pitch up at Villa Esmerelda in the state he was in – he was too damn glad to be alive. He wanted to be somewhere normal, where the nightmare would stop, somewhere that vaguely resembled home. He couldn't have entertained the idea of going back to sleep on *Excalibur*. No, he needed to be at home – even if that meant risking Jay's wrath by waking her up at – what? – two thirty in the morning.

When he got out of the taxi, he fumbled anxiously with the intercom on the gate, still looking over his shoulder for anything ominous.

'Who's there?' Jay's crisp voice came across loud and clear. Frank found himself almost crying with relief. 'Jay, it's Frank,' he blurted. 'Quick! Quick! You've got to let me in.'

Immediately the gate slid open and Frank charged towards the imposing front door, which he banged on loudly.

'What in the name of God are you doing, Frank?' Jay asked, seeming remarkably fresh considering the time of night. She was wearing a white silk peignoir and a perplexed expression.

'Just let me in, will you, for God's sake? And Jay, don't give out to me.' Frank headed for the drinks cabinet in the huge front room. 'I've been attacked.' He poured a tumbler of brandy with shaking hands. 'I was lucky to escape with my life, I tell you.' Frank knew he was babbling, but he was beyond caring.

'Well, we must call the police immediately.' Jay made for the phone.

'No, no – no police.' Frank sat down heavily, wiped his brow, and swigged the brandy.

'But look at the state of you! What happened? What did they get – and where's your hair?'

'Jay,' Frank eyed her beseechingly, 'there's something I have to tell you. I've been a major arsehole, a first-rate gobshite – I can't even get my head round it myself.' He was shivering again.

'Haven't I been telling you that for years, you big eejit?' Jay sat down and put an arm round him. 'Look, whatever it is, you're in no state to do anything about it now. What you need is a hot bath and then straight to bed. We'll talk about it in the morning.' She was firm.

'But Jay, you don't understand. He's going to kill me.'

'Nobody's going to kill you, Frank – unless it's me. Now, get out of those clothes and I'll run you a nice hot bath, then get you a sleeping tablet. 'Now, Frank!' she commanded.

'Jay,' said Frank, overcome with extraordinary tiredness, 'have I ever told you you're an amazing woman?'

'No,' she said. 'Not that I can think of – but it's never too late to start.'

'Well, you are,' he said, his eyes brimming. And as he climbed the stairs wearily, he realised he'd meant every word.

While Frank sank happily into a hot bath with relaxing oils, Jay sat on her bed and punched in a reply to the text message she had received not half an hour earlier: 'Good work.'

Rob thought Ali was more beautiful than ever as she descended the steps of the private plane, paused to take a deep breath, and smiled at the two security guards who, Rob correctly suspected, had come to sneak a look at his famous daughter, rather than the aircraft to which they gave a cursory once-over.

Despite her protestations to the contrary, Ali showed no signs of the wedding stress she claimed was plaguing her.

Inside the waiting Mercedes, she patted Rob's hand. 'I'm so glad you're here, Daddy. I do miss you, you know.'

'I miss you too, sweetheart, and young Stuart better take very special care of you or he'll have me to answer to!' Rob gazed at her indulgently. 'I hope he realises how lucky he is.'

Ali smiled. 'Oh, he does, Daddy. You needn't worry about that. Stuart adores me.'

'Of course he does. What else could he do?'

Ali turned her face away and bit her lip. She reminded herself that she was going to ignore the upsetting events of the last few weeks. Ali wasn't used to rejection, especially not at this stage in her career, and although she knew she had done the right thing, she was still shattered at having lost the Stay Tru contract. The important thing, she thought, was that she had a fabulous wedding coming up. She was marrying a man who *did* adore her. There was nothing Stuart wouldn't do for her – and that was the only way to have it. One person in a relationship always loved more than the other – and far better for it to be the man. She had seen at close quarters where the other scenario got you, and it hadn't done her mother any favours, whatever she might say about good times in the early days. A man *had* to worship a woman, recognise her as the goddess she, Ali, undoubtedly was. It was the only way to have it.

'Well, well, well,' said Rob, gratified at the sight of the magnificent Villa Tsarina as they pulled up outside. 'Mum wasn't exaggerating when she said it was spectacular, was she?' He paid the driver, who deposited their suitcases on the doorstep. 'This should be fun.' He grinned at his daughter. 'Everybody's about to get a big surprise!'

He rang the doorbell and waited, tapping his foot expectantly.

For a long moment there was nothing.

Then the door was opened by a small plump Spanish woman wearing a maid's uniform – in her late thirties, Rob guessed.

'*Sí?*' she enquired, regarding them, Rob felt, with unnecessary suspicion.

Ali had enough Spanish to tell the woman who they were and progressed inside, followed by Rob. After a lot of shrugging and rapid-fire Spanish on the maid's part, it was established that no one was home. She showed Rob and Ali downstairs to the bedrooms and left them to it.

'Well, that's a nice welcome,' Rob said.

'Never mind, Daddy. No one knew we were coming. Let's just relax for a while. I'll fix us some lunch, I'm sure there'll be plenty of food in the fridge – and we'll surprise them when they get back. Mum's probably out doing the grocery shopping and Stephanie'll be at the beach or something.'

'Good idea,' agreed Rob, taking in his surroundings appreciatively. 'I'll just have a quick shower and see you back here for lunch.'

Later, after lunch and tired from the stress of the last few weeks, Rob had a quick swim and stretched out in the late afternoon sun, falling soundly asleep. Ali, jet lagged, had gone to bed for a siesta.

Rob awoke with a start, feeling chilled, and wondered where on earth he was. Looking at his watch he realised it was half past eight! He had slept for a straight three hours. He sat up, rubbing his neck, which felt stiff.

Inside, the house was in darkness. Ali must still be asleep and there was no sign of Carrie or Stephanie. Rob felt increasingly cross. Where the hell was everybody? He could ring Hope, he supposed. He had her number in his mobile, but he had promised Ali he would spend quality time with her. He decided to wake her. Then they'd go out for a nice dinner down in the port. Perhaps, when they got back, they'd finally catch up with the rest of the family. Rob wondered again where they were. He could ring Carrie, of course, but that would spoil the surprise. He enjoyed a little thrill of satisfaction that Carrie would feel guilty she hadn't been there to greet him. She was probably out with Jay. Well, she'd discover soon enough that he was here, thought Rob self-righteously. In the meantime, he was ravenous.

Unknown to Rob, he and Ali were not *entirely* alone in the house.

Toby had been enjoying a nice afternoon nap in the sun when he had woken at the sound of Rob's voice. He had shot downstairs into Stephanie's room, where he dived under the bed. He was hiding there now, as quiet and still as a mouse – despite the delicious smells of pâté and chorizo that had earlier wafted down to him. He sighed deeply. The alpha male person being around again was not a good sign. Not a good sign at all.

Refreshed after their siestas, Rob and Ali had a reviving glass of champagne, then set out for the port.

At nine thirty, Puerto Banus was humming. Beautiful people were strolling along past equally beautiful cars and yachts. But no one was as beautiful as Ali, Rob thought proudly, walking beside her, basking in the glow of the admiring glances that followed them. And he looked damned good for his fifty years. He had sex appeal and knew it. People would naturally assume that Ali and he were a couple. They would never guess they were father and daughter.

'What about here, Ali?' Rob stopped outside Olivio's, where a hovering waiter beckoned to passers-by. 'Looks as good as anywhere.'

'Sure Dad,' Ali paused theatrically, allowing just the right amount of time to elapse as she considered the restaurant so that the appropriate level of respect and gratitude would ensue on her entrance. 'As long as you're buying!' she quipped.

The restaurant was buzzing. Luis and his colleagues writhed in and out of the tables, performing gravity-defying balancing acts with their precariously constructed towers of plates, elaborate desserts, baskets of bread and stacks of menus to be thrust at newcomers.

He checked out table ten: a staggeringly beautiful girl had just slid into the banquette opposite her dining companion, a good-looking older man in his early fifties.

Pah! Typical. Rich older man, beautiful young woman. Luis saw it all the time. It sickened him. Not that he was jealous, far from it. He pitied men like that – and the women. Men whose biggest achievement in life was the construction of their ego. Men who could kid themselves that beautiful young women *were* in love with them and not with what they could provide. And the women were as bad. Give them a few years and they'd be chasing younger men, like him, for the sex and passion that were painfully absent from their lives.

He glanced round for Stephanie, but she was nowhere to be seen. She was probably in the kitchen, trying to pacify the stupid prick of a chef who had stepped in to replace Guillermo when he was taken to hospital. The last time Luis had looked, the kitchen had been in chaos. He checked out table ten again. There wasn't a 'best table' as far as this restaurant was concerned, but if there had been, that girl would probably have demanded it. She glanced about her now, checking her reflection discreetly in the mirrored wall opposite, tilting her chin as she listened to something her date was saying. Her companion looked round, somewhat impatiently, and Luis made the mistake of catching his eye. The man waved to attract attention and clicked his fingers. Luis swore silently.

Arrogant pig! Where was Stephanie? She should be dealing with people like him – that was her job. Reluctantly, he made his way over and dispensed menus, being careful not to look at the girl, who would expect an appreciative glance – well, she wouldn't get it from him!

'Just a minute!' the man said imperiously as Luis was about to slide off and collect yet more plates. 'I want to order some champagne.'

'Sorry,' Luis shrugged in international language. 'Ees not my job, I send wine waiter to you.'

'No.' The man's eyebrows knitted together in a way Luis recognised all too well. It was the expression of the eternally dissatisfied. 'I don't need to look at the wine list. I want a bottle of Krug fifty-nine. Have it brought to the table right away, please.'

The girl sat expressionless, but for a slight smile that curved her lovely mouth. But Luis was quick to spot the hardness in her eyes. 'Just a moment, please.' He slid away, careful to hide his disdain. However much he hated serving such obnoxious people, his job paid the bills, and he couldn't afford to lose it. Offend a customer, and you were history. Anyway, it was only one season. Everybody did what they had to do.

'A bottle of Krug fifty-nine for table ten, *de prisa*,' he muttered to Valerio, the wine waiter, passing him back to back as he made for the kitchen.

Five minutes later, Valerio was presenting the bottle for approval and pouring a taster glass for Rob, who sipped it and nodded. As Valerio began to fill Ali's glass, disaster struck.

Luis, slithering past to deposit coffee at the next table beside them, nudged his pouring arm so that the champagne gushed into Ali's lap, making her squeal in horror.

'*Por Dios!*' muttered Valerio, glaring at Luis, who was regarding the unfolding scene with horror.

'*Lo siento* – I'm sorry,' he gasped to his colleague, who was frantically gesticulating for help in the mopping-up department.

'You stupid, clumsy oaf!' muttered Rob.

'*Momentito, Señor,*' Valerio held up his hand. 'I bring another bottle for you.'

By now the entire restaurant was watching the drama as Ali, dripping champagne, stood up and attempted to mop herself with a napkin.

'Sweetheart, I'm so sorry!' Rob was on his feet too.

'Don't worry, Daddy,' she demurred. 'It's only champagne. It won't stain or anything.'

Just then another figure entered the scene. Flushed and hot from her negotiations in the kitchen, Stephanie took a few deep breaths and sallied forth, preparing to face the music at table ten.

'What seems to be the prob—' She stopped in her tracks.

'That ignorant oaf of a waiter you employ is the problem,' said Rob before he looked up. Then his breath caught in his throat and he spluttered.

'Ali!' gasped Stephanie.

'Stephanie!' Rob exclaimed.

'Dad!' she croaked.

'You know these peoples?' Luis was gazing at her in disbelief.

'Know us?' Rob snapped. 'I'm her bloody father! And what business is it of yours?' He stared at Luis as if he was an unpleasant insect.

'Shut up, Dad,' hissed Stephanie. 'Ali, sit *down*! You're making a scene. It might not mean anything to you guys, but I happen to *work* here.'

'I don't believe this!' Rob was looking at Stephanie as if she'd grown antlers. 'And how dare you tell your sister to sit down when this clumsy fool has ruined her outfit. If this is what they taught you on that outrageously expensive cookery course I paid for, then I've clearly wasted my money.'

'He's *not* clumsy.' Stephanie's eyes glinted dangerously. 'It was an accident, that's all. They happen.'

'Well, if that's how you treat your customers, never mind your family, this restaurant, never mind its staff, is clearly on a losing streak.' The nasty words tumbled from Rob's lips, anger and shock at his baby daughter's defence of another man hitting him forcefully.

'Really, Daddy,' Ali interjected smoothly, 'it doesn't matter. Steph is obviously finding work stressful. After all, she hasn't had any experience of it, has she? And I suspect her defence of this guy,' she waved in Luis's direction, 'has precious little to do with her job, if you know what I mean.'

'You're a nasty, evil-minded bitch!' Stephanie spat.

'Come on, Ali.' Rob gave Stephanie a look that would have reduced most people to a gibbering wreck, but strangely had no effect on her. She was quivering with rage. 'I'll deal with you later, young lady.'

Leaving the restaurant, Rob was livid to hear the sound of hand-clapping from amused onlookers. As Stephanie took a bow, it turned into resounding applause for the feisty little manageress who had told the difficult guests to get lost.

In any language, it had been a great performance.

It was a lovely end to another lovely day, thought Carrie as she sat at dinner in the Marbella Club with Emilio, Rudi and Hope, just the four of them, and Carrie was thrilled to see her eldest daughter relaxed, happy and glowing, at long last. Although she had denied there was anything serious between her and Rudi, Carrie suspected it was love and Rudi seemed to be equally smitten.

They had set out early that morning, Hope and she, with Emilio to visit his friend's country estate and had spent a wonderful day touring the estate and seen the Salukis he bred there. As Emilio had said, they were just like Toby. It was a pity Stephanie hadn't been able to join them, but she was working at a restaurant in the port and taking the whole business very seriously. Carrie was proud of her and had encouraged her wholeheartedly.

Now, though, she was tired. It had been a long drive, and although she had been delighted when Rudi had agreed to join them for dinner, it had meant delaying their reservation an hour.

'Have you heard from Ali lately, Mum?' Hope asked as Emilio and Rudi were deep in nautical discussion.

'Now you mention it, I haven't. Last time we spoke she said her gown was just about finished and they were working on the bridesmaids' dresses. I hope they're as beautiful as she says.' Carrie was worried, although both Stephanie and Hope had flown with her to Paris earlier to be fitted. Carrie's outfit had been designed in Dublin and was hanging in her wardrobe.

'It was hard to tell when we went to be fitted,' Hope grinned, 'but the sketches were lovely.'

'I'm so glad they sorted things out.' Carrie was gazing fondly at Emilio and Rudi, their dark heads close together as they talked. 'It means so very much to Emilio, you know.'

'He's a good man, Mum, Rudi knows that now – and he's good for you too. I'm glad you've found a friend in him.' Hope's voice was warm.

'I'm so pleased you think so, Hope. I was worried that – well . . .'

'Don't worry, Mum. You have a right to enjoy yourself, to have your own life – we *all* think so.'

'He's just a friend, you know.' Carrie added anxiously.

'Mum,' Hope said firmly, 'we all like him, he's a decent man, there's no need for any explanations.'

'You're right,' said Carrie, laughing. 'It's just that old habits die hard.'

'Then it's time you made some new ones.'

Coffee arrived with liqueurs. Raising his glass in a toast, Emilio said, smiling broadly, 'To family!'

'To family!' they chorused.

Ali and Rob arrived at the Marbella Club at just after ten, early still for dinner in Spain.

'We should have come here in the first place,' Rob muttered, still furious with Stephanie.

'Dad, Steph's going through a rebellious phase,' Ali said soothingly. 'She's still just a kid, really, even if she is twenty-three. The youngest always do remain babies, don't they? At her age I was financially independent.'

'Well,' said Rob, mollified, 'I hope you're right – but her behaviour was appalling, and as for that waiter—'

'Don't even think about it, Dad. He's probably some silly holiday romance. She won't even remember his name once she's home.'

'Table for two, please,' Rob said to the maître d' who hurried up to them.

'Are you residents?'

'No.'

'Have you made a reservation, sir?'

'No, I haven't.' Rob was becoming increasingly impatient. 'Look, have you a table or not?'

'One moment, please.' The man looked at him disapprovingly, but smiled unctuously at Ali, who beamed back. 'I will have a table set for you. Follow me, please.'

It was Ali who spotted them. 'Dad!' she exclaimed. 'Am I seeing things, or is that Mum and Hope over there?' She gestured to a table around which several waiters were hovering attentively. Her mother and Hope were sitting with two of the most handsome men Ali had seen in her life. The older one, she realised, was – unthinkably – holding her mother's hand while the younger one's arm was draped casually round Hope's shoulders. Hope, looking stunning, was smiling at him adoringly. Ali thought she was about to be sick.

'What the hell is going on?'

Rob followed her gaze and felt his face tighten. 'I have no idea,' he said lightly, 'but I'd very much like to find out.'

Since they had to pass the happy group to get to their own table, where the maître d' was waiting impatiently, there was no avoiding an encounter.

'Leave this to me, Dad,' Ali said thinly, and fixed a wide smile on her face.

'Mum! Hope!' she said brightly.

'Ali! What are *you* doing here?' Carrie exclaimed, delight overcoming her initial confusion. 'I thought you weren't due 'til next week.' And then she saw Rob. 'Hello, Rob,' she said coolly, regaining her composure quickly.

'Hello, Carrie,' Rob said, equally coolly.

Emilio had risen to his feet, as had Rudi.

After she had hugged Ali, Carrie said, 'Well, I must say, this *is* a surprise.'

'That's what we thought it would be,' Ali said lightly, 'but when no one was at home, and after we'd waited for you all afternoon, we got hungry, didn't we, Dad? We decided to go out for dinner.'

'Why didn't you phone any of us?' Hope asked.

'Well then it wouldn't have been a surprise, would it?' Ali said tartly.

'This, um, is a friend of mine, the Marques de Alba, Cordoba y Rincón. My daughter Ali, and my . . . husband, Rob.' Carrie made the introductions awkwardly.

'Delighted.' Emilio took in the situation in a flash. He shook Ali and Rob's hands firmly. 'Call me Emilio, please.'

'And this,' Carrie gestured towards Rudi, 'is Emilio's son, Rudi.'

'Pleased to meet you,' said Rudi, his face expressionless.

'Ali is our bride-to-be,' Carrie heard herself twittering, but she felt as if she was trapped in a bad dream.

'Won't you join us for a drink before you dine?' said Emilio. 'Then Rudi and I will happily leave you to your reunion.'

Ali was about to accept when Rob interjected and declined. 'Thank you, but our table's waiting. Nice to meet you. I might,' he couldn't resist adding, 'actually be lucky enough, one of these days, to catch up with my busy family.' He smiled, but failed to keep the sarcasm from his voice. 'Enjoy the rest of your evening. Goodnight.'

'See you later, Mum.' Ali smiled and shrugged regretfully at Carrie, then followed Rob to their table.

'Come, Carrie,' Emilio was at her side, ushering her from the table. 'Let me take you home.'

'You two go ahead. We'll follow in a few minutes.' Rudi squeezed Hope's hand under the table. 'I'll take care of this.' He gestured for the bill.

Moments later, he and Hope were leaving the restaurant. Hope glanced at her father and Ali to wave goodbye, but they were studiously avoiding looking in her direction.

'Well,' she heaved a sigh once they were outside, 'now the fun will begin. I knew it was only a matter of time. Having the wedding down here was *so* not a good idea.'

'I think it was a great idea.'

'You do?'

'Sure. How else would I have met you?'

He saw Hope into a taxi. 'I'd better follow Mum home, make sure she's okay,' she said.

'Good idea. I'll see you tomorrow.'

* * *

Back at Villa Tsarina, Emilio saw Carrie to the door and took her hand. 'Will you be all right?'

'Of course. It was a shock, that's all, but he was going to arrive some time, so it might as well be now.'

Carrie's voice was bright, but Emilio sensed her uncertainty.

'Remember, Carrie, you have done nothing wrong. Absolutely nothing. If you need me, I am just a phone call away.'

'Thank you, Emilio. It was such a lovely day until . . . this.'

'There will be other lovely days. Now, go inside, and don't let anything or anyone upset you. That's an order.' He brought her hand to his mouth and kissed it.

'I'll ring you tomorrow.'

'Only if you want to. Your family is here now – I don't wish to be an extra obligation.'

'Oh, Emilio, you are many things but never an obligation.'

'Goodnight, Carrie.' He climbed into the car and was gone.

Carrie went inside and headed straight for the fridge. She opened a bottle of champagne and poured herself a glass. She felt horribly guilty, no matter what anyone said, and the shock of seeing Ali and Rob, so unexpectedly and under such awkward circumstances, had left her nervous and on edge. She took a swig of her drink and jumped when she heard the door open.

'Oh, Hope, it's you,' she said thankfully. 'You gave me a fright.'

'Mum, come and sit down with me and we'll have a chat. I'll stay the night, if that's all right?' Hope poured a glass for herself too.

'Oh, would you, Hope? That would be wonderful. I – I don't know why this has had such a dreadful effect on me, but seeing your father and Ali like that, and not being there for them when they arrived, I – I—' Carrie burst into tears.

'Mum, don't.' Hope put her arms round her. 'It's been a terribly long day, although a lovely one, and Ali and Dad arriving like that was plain inconsiderate. Who needs surprises when we've a wedding in less than two weeks? It was silly of them. So what if they saw us out for dinner with Emilio and Rudi? It's none of their damn business.' Hope was surprised by the anger in her voice, but she was angry. A lovely evening had been spoiled and now her mother was upset – just when she had been doing so well.

'Come on, Mum. Bring your glass and we'll sit down over here. You're not to let this upset you. Really.'

Hope was not alone in her concern for Carrie. Driving the short distance back to the Marbella Club, Emilio was thoughtful. If he was honest, he was more than concerned – he was downright worried. At the moment, Carrie was fragile. She had been through a lot – more than a lot if you counted up the years she had stayed in a marriage where it appeared she had received little or no real love. That kind of thing wore away at a person's soul. And Carrie still loved her womanising husband. He could tell that from the look on her face when Rob had turned up, clearly irritated that Carrie wasn't jumping to attention as presumably she usually did. And Emilio had also registered the anger that had crossed Rob's face when he had seen him and Rudi with his wife and daughter.

He smiled wryly. He knew all about men like Rob. They were all the same, wanted their cake and to eat it too, and it didn't matter at whose expense. He hoped against hope that Carrie could be strong and would not succumb to another of Rob's manipulative schemes to ensure things turned out as he wanted them to, caring nothing for what it did to her.

Emilio winced at the thought of Carrie being hurt again.
More than anything he wanted to protect her, shield her from
pain and deceit, but all he could do was hope and wait. The
only person who could help Carrie now was herself.

Realising his total lack of control in the situation, Emilio
was consumed by frustration, followed quickly by despair –
and then it dawned on him. It had crept up on him unawares.
He was in love with Carrie, very much in love with her, and
it cut him to the quick that there was nothing he could do
but wait and see what happened – and give her his full understanding and support whatever the outcome.

An hour later, when Carrie and Hope were still talking, the
doorbell rang and Hope got up to answer it, throwing Carrie
a warning look over her shoulder. 'Leave this to me, Mum.'

'Thank you, Hope,' Ali said, breezing past her, followed
by Rob, who was quick to notice the open champagne bottle.

'Mind if I help myself to a drink?' He poured a glass and
handed another to Ali, who sat down opposite Carrie.

'What's the matter, Mum?' she asked innocently, seeing
Carrie's tearstained face.

'Shut up, Ali,' Hope snapped.

Ali glared at her, but before she could speak Rob said,
'What the hell is the matter with you girls? First Stephanie
insults Ali in that wretched restaurant of hers, and now you,
Hope, are snapping at her.'

'I thought it would be a lovely surprise,' Ali said reproachfully. 'It was Dad's idea, wasn't it, Dad? And, after all, it is
my wedding, and no one seems to give a damn about it.' She
began to cry quietly.

'Oh, Ali,' Carrie felt wretched, 'that couldn't be more
untrue.'

'Is it?' snapped Rob. 'I must say, I can't blame Ali. She told
me she couldn't get in touch with any of you and that the

wedding planner was the only person who'd return her calls. Now that I've seen what's been going on, everything's becoming a lot clearer,' he said, staring pointedly at Carrie.

'That's ridiculous, Dad, and you know it,' Hope retorted, glaring at him. They started as the door burst open and Stephanie stormed in. 'So, this is where you are!' She glared at them all. 'You've ruined everything!' she yelled, flinging down her handbag and pulling off her high-heeled wedges. She threw herself down on the sofa beside Carrie. 'Mum! Dad and Ali have ruined *everything* – everything I've been working so hard for.' Angry tears began to roll down her face as she remembered the stinging humiliation of having to admit to Luis that Rob was her father and Ali her sister and suffering his dignified but disdainful silence ever since.

'Oh, darling, whatever's the matter?' asked Carrie, momentarily distracted from her own feelings of guilt.

'*They*'re the matter.' She pointed at Rob and Ali. 'Why can't we be like a normal family? Why does everything have to be drama and – and making scenes?'

'How dare you?' yelled Ali. 'I did not make a scene! Just because you've got your knickers in a twist over some bloody waiter who's probably shagging you between courses! Honestly, Steph, listen to yourself!'

'Luis is *not* a waiter. That's just a summer job! He's a philosophy student, actually!'

'All this is getting out of hand,' said Hope. 'Ali, Dad, a surprise is all very well, but once you were both here you might have rung either me or Stephanie. We could still have made sure it was a surprise for Mum. It was silly of you and thoughtless.'

'Oh, that's right,' said Ali nastily. 'Protect Mum – of course you would, Hope, so she can cover up her cosy little liaison with some Spaniard calling himself a *marques*.' She laughed scornfully. 'Really, Mum, every continental over the age of consent claims they have a title. He probably clocked where you were staying, saw there was money and decided to ply you with well-practised lines and God knows what else since day one.'

Carrie flinched as if she had been dealt a physical blow. 'I *knew* there was going to be trouble between the pair of you before my wedding – I just knew it.' She flicked her eyes to Rob before returning her accusing gaze to Carrie. 'But I never in a million years would have thought it would be *you*, Mum, who would let me down.'

'Hear, hear,' added Rob, nodding his head in agreement.

'Mum's never let anyone down in her entire life!' yelled Stephanie, outraged. 'You stupid, selfish bitch! If you recall, it was *you* going through Dad's phone messages that started all this horrible business.' Stephanie began to cry now in earnest, all the pent-up fear and frustration pouring out. 'Ali said you're having an affair, Dad, that you've had loads of them. She read the messages. I told her it was a disgusting thing to do. But it's true, isn't it?'

There was a horrified silence that grew heavy with potential fallout.

'I wouldn't blame Mum for anything she did! Anything! You've been horrible to her – we've all seen it, how lonely she's been, how she always tries to keep cheerful for us even though inside she's probably hurting like hell!' Stephanie, feeling the pain of her own heartbreak, was discovering even more of an empathy with her mother.

'You went through my phone messages?' Rob stared at Ali incredulously, anger flaring in his eyes. 'Is this true?'

'So what if I did? Someone has to keep tabs on what's going on in this family. If Mum refused to face the facts about you and your stupid womanising, I certainly wasn't going to – not when it threatened to ruin my wedding and my career!'

Something inside Carrie finally snapped. 'Be quiet, Ali!'

she barked. Her voice was like ice. 'That's enough, even by your standards.'

Ali's mouth dropped open.

'Maybe I haven't handled things as best I could have,' Carrie began, 'but my priority before anything else was you girls and our family. And maybe that meant ignoring things I shouldn't have, but I can assure you none of it was done lightly or without deliberation. Over the last few years, my over-riding intention has been to keep this family together. Now I realise that meant sacrificing other, perhaps more important, things. It meant for one, Ali, that I chose to ignore, or maybe hide from myself, that you were turning into a first-class prima donna, a selfish, manipulative young woman, intent on always, but *always*, having your own way, even at your sisters' expense.'

Ali shrank back in the sofa, too shocked to resort even to more tears.

'It meant that I didn't pay enough attention to you, Hope, growing up. I let you handle far more responsibility than you should have because I was so grateful that you seemed able to cope with everything so calmly and gracefully, much as I always wished I could. But now, of course, I can see the toll that must have taken. For that, darling, I do apologise – from the bottom of my heart.' Carrie's voice wavered but she forced herself to go on.

The tears were sliding down Hope's face now.

'Stephanie,' she regarded her youngest daughter sternly, but with affection, 'I don't know what's going on between you and Luis, but we'll talk about it tomorrow. You should know, Rob, that Stephanie has catered several dinner parties down here, every *one* of which has been an unqualified success. Yes, she has taken a job, and yes, she *has* been working hard. Whatever ensued this evening I'm sure was *not* the result of anything instigated by Stephanie, whether it was an insult to her sister or indeed anyone else. Am I right?' she asked sharply.

No one said a word.

'I thought as much.'

'As for you,' she stared coldly at Rob, 'you have no right, no right whatsoever, to arrive here unannounced and on a selfish whim, implying insults and innuendo. Every one of us has been working hard to make sure this wedding is an unqualified success.'

She turned again to Ali. 'Do you think the services of Enrique B'stardo come free?'

Ali remained mute.

'He's a wedding planner, is he not? Isn't that what you wanted? Someone to plan your wedding to the last minute detail? Well, that's what he has done. That's *his* job, not ours. If anyone has been negligent, it has been you. Enrique has complained to me time and time again that you have not returned his calls – that *you* have failed to make important, relevant decisions when they were most expressly needed. Placing, as usual, more strain on everybody else.

'From the moment you announced your engagement to Stuart, you have had everything handed to you on a plate – even the location for the reception. That was thanks to Jay. Everyone has bent over backwards for you. The wedding of any girl's dreams has been choreographed for you, Ali – but all you can do is arrive down here feeling resentful and interfering in your parents' relationship, which is frankly none of your goddamned business.'

Ali gasped as if her face had been slapped. She looked now towards her father for support – but Rob, witnessing the surprising but not altogether detrimental turn of events as far as he was concerned, avoided her pleading gaze and kept his face impassive, waiting for what would unfold next in this extraordinary drama.

He didn't have long to wait.

'The door was open.' A familiar figure stood gazing down at the scene. 'I expect with all the excitement you forgot I was arriving today, but here I am!'

'Babs!' They uttered her name with a mixture of shock, relief and sheepishness.

Ali grabbed her chance to salvage her plight. She ran to Babs, flung her arms round her and began to sob. 'Oh, Babs, everyone's attacking me! They all hate me, even Mum. I'm not staying here to be treated like this. I'm calling the whole thing off. I'm cancelling the wedding!'

'Now, now,' said Babs calmly, patting her back. 'It sounds like it's time I put the kettle on. Don't know about you Armstrongs, but I could murder a cup of tea.'

'You're not listening, Babs! No one is! I'm calling it off! The wedding's off!' Ali's voice rose to a shriek.

'Do whatever you like, Ali,' Carrie said, far more calmly than she felt. 'That seems to have been the defining pattern of behaviour in most of your life so far – but understand this. If you call it off, you and nobody else will notify every guest. You will make every single, solitary, unpleasant phone call. Neither I nor your sisters will have anything to do with it – and neither, I imagine, will Enrique B'stardo when he learns that all his hard work will have been wasted on yet another of your whims. As for Frank and Jay Farrelly, I hardly like to think what they'll make of it.'

'I don't care!'

'Of course you don't,' continued Carrie, although she felt as if was walking through a nightmare. 'But, yet again, you are forgetting someone who does care. Someone who cares very much about all of this – and, God help him, about you. You might, just this once, pause to consider Stuart. It's his day too – and his life with which you are juggling so danger-ously and thoughtlessly. If you can throw all this away so lightly, then I would advise him – never mind you, Ali – to rethink *any* wedding plans.'

'I hate you!' Ali shouted. Then she turned on Rob. 'This is all *your* fault – you ruin everything in this family. *Everything*!' She fled downstairs and locked herself into her bedroom.

Carrie sat down and put her head in her hands. Suddenly she was all out of fight. She wondered, wildly, what on earth had come over her, what had come over them all – and what, more pressingly, would become of the wedding. For once, everyone was speechless.

She took a deep breath and sat up straight. 'Stephanie, go to bed. We'll talk tomorrow.'

'Okay, Mum.' Her voice was small. 'Sorry, Dad, I didn't mean to—'

'It's all right, Steph. Do as your mother says.'

She kissed them both and slipped away.

'Hope, would you show Babs to her room, please, and give me and Dad a few moments alone?'

'Sure, Mum, I'll see you in the morning.' Hope went to the kitchen.

'Look, Carrie, I—' Rob began.

'Don't. Don't even start. I'm not going there – not now. I know all about this one, just like I knew about the others, and I'm not going to listen to whatever lies you want to spin. Like I said before I came down here, I'm going to divorce you. It's over. It has been for a very long time.'

'Is that because of this *marques*?'

'Oh, Rob.' Carrie almost laughed. 'How typical of you to latch on to that of all things. Can even *you* kid yourself that Emilio would be the reason for me to leave you, to finally, agonisingly, break up this marriage, this family? How very selfish of you – or unaccountable, I should say. But then, self-examination was never your strong point.

No, Rob, it's not because of Emilio – not in the manner you're implying at any rate. But he has helped me make up my mind.'

'I knew he'd something to do with it. You've changed, Carrie.' It was an accusation.

'Yes, I have. I've changed because I've learned something very important, something I wish I'd learned years ago, something that you will never understand.'

'What?'

'I've learned that love doesn't have to be earned, worked for or deserved. It's given freely, without constraints. I've also learned that not everyone is capable of giving it. I've learned what real love is, Rob, from a man who knows it, has lived it and is willing to give it generously.'

'I don't know what you're talking about.' Rob seemed genuinely perplexed.

'Of course you don't,' said Carrie.

He sighed. 'I'm going to bed. No one's making any sense tonight.'

'Goodnight, Rob.'

She sat alone for a moment as despair fought with something else. She realised, with surprise, that it was relief. Enormous, overwhelming relief that she could finally say what she felt. Despite the pain, she was finally able to own up to what she had denied herself for as long as she could remember.

Her tears, when they came, were strangely comforting.

She didn't hear Babs come back, was only aware of her when she sat down and put an arm around her.

'Oh, Babs,' Carrie sobbed, 'what have I done? What have I said?'

'There, there, pet. You've done and said nothing at all, Carrie – nothing that hasn't been a very long time coming.'

She cried until there were no more tears. Then Babs made

her drink her tea. 'Babs, I can't believe none of us knew you were coming today.'

'Well, I did arrange it with Stephanie, and I texted her yesterday to remind her, but I suppose with all the excitement she forgot about it. Don't give it another thought. I'm here now.'

'I'm so glad,' sniffed Carrie, 'but what on earth are we going to do?'

'Listen to me, Carrie,' Babs said firmly. 'When I arrived the door was open. Whoever was in last forgot to close it.'

'Stephanie,' remembered Carrie. 'She was furious with Rob and Ali.'

'Anyway, I overheard most of what you said to them. I wasn't eavesdropping – it just wasn't a good idea to intrude in the middle – and just now I heard what you said to Rob. I know it's not my place to say so, but sometimes I think a body has to say what's right and proper.'

Carrie was suddenly afraid of what she might hear.

'Carrie, I've known you for twenty-three years. I think of you as my own daughter, and with every single word you uttered in the last twenty minutes, I was cheering you on. Every one of them needed to be said and every member of this family needed to hear them. You've been the backbone of this family and not one of them, not one single one, would be what they are without you. If you want my opinion, Carrie Armstrong, you've just had your finest hour. I didn't mean to upset you all over again,' she said as Carrie broke into fresh sobs, 'but you cry all you want to. Then get off to bed and everything will seem better in the morning. I promise. Come on. If you can show me through that maze of rooms downstairs, I'll see you to bed and bring you another nice cup of tea – or something stronger?'

Carrie, feeling almost too weak to walk, let herself be led

downstairs and put to bed. Then minutes later, Babs was back with fresh tea. 'If you need one, I've got a sleeping tablet?' she said from the door.

'No thanks, Babs, but thank you for – for everything.'

'For nothing!' smiled Babs. 'I'll see you in the morning, pet.'

21

It was nine o'clock when Carrie, after sleeping the sleep of the emotionally exhausted, woke up. Then she remembered everything, and was filled with dread.

She got out of bed slowly and drew the curtains, allowing the sunlight to flood in, wondering how everything could be so calm, so picture-postcard perfect, when the world as she knew it had shifted irrevocably on its axis.

She thought about going back to bed and pulling the covers over her head. Anything to avoid facing the ravages of the night before. Now, in the glaring light of day, last night's courage and certainty had deserted her. But there was no going back, no unsaying the words that had tumbled out so freely, so insistently. She would have to face everyone sooner or later.

She pulled on her robe, opened the door and was greeted by the unmistakable smell of bacon. Upstairs the kitchen seemed empty, and then she saw them, Stephanie, Hope and Babs, even Ali, sitting at the table on the patio tucking into a full Irish breakfast. For a moment, despite the normality of the scene, she felt as if she were suspended between two worlds, not knowing whether to go forward or back.

Hope saw her first. 'Mum, come and sit down. We've kept a plate warm for you, I'll get it now,' she said, jumping up. 'Isn't this a treat? Babs brought everything out with her.' And then they were all on their feet, except Babs, who sat and smiled expectantly.

Ali, pale and drawn, came over to her. 'Mum, I'm so sorry. What I said last night to you about, well, everything, it was unforgivable. I realise that now. I don't know what got into me. I'd do anything to take it back. You were right. I've been selfish and – and, well, I'm . . . you were right, everything you said. I've, um, already apologised to Hope and Stephanie.'

At this, Stephanie couldn't resist the flicker of a smirk.

'I just hope you can forgive me too?' Ali continued. 'Will you, Mum?'

'Me too, Mum,' Stephanie added. 'I'm really sorry, I was way out of line.'

'Of course I forgive you, girls,' Carrie said. 'Come and give me a hug.' And they did, all three of them.

Miraculously, the world shifted again for Carrie – back to the familiar and the beloved.

Better still, she knew now that she had been right to say what she had – to stand up to Rob and to rein Ali in – but she had been so frightened it would change everything. Her girls, at least, loved her still.

'Now,' said Babs firmly as they sat down, 'that's quite enough emotion for one holiday, wedding or no wedding, even by Dr Phil's standards. Let that be an end to it. I've only just got here and you have me worn out already.'

They decided to book massages, chill out and go for a leisurely lunch somewhere. 'I'll skip the massage, if you don't mind,' said Babs, 'but I'll join you for lunch.'

'Mum,' Ali said tentatively, 'if it's all right with you, I'd really like to meet your friend, er, Emilio – properly, I mean. He must have thought me rude last night – and, of course, you must invite him to the wedding – if you want to.'

Carrie smiled. 'I'd love you to meet him Ali, and he's just a friend but a dear one. And no, there's no need to invite him to the wedding. The guest list was decided months ago, and he certainly wouldn't expect to come, but thank you for thinking of him. I think, regarding the wedding,' Carrie said firmly, 'everything is fine just the way it is.'

'Oh . . . well . . . good.'

Carrie hid a smile as the bride-to-be tried not to look too relieved.

In the event, the venue for lunch was decided by Jay, who rang on Carrie's phone. 'I hear Bridezilla's in town.'

'How did you know?' Carrie laughed.

'News travels fast, and it's not as if Ali would go unnoticed. Anyway, Carrie, let's have lunch on *Excalibur*, and I won't take no for an answer this time.'

'Babs is here too, Jay. She arrived last night.'

'Even better. Meet me at the top of the port at two.'

While the girls cleared away the breakfast things, Babs finished her coffee with Carrie.

Ten minutes later, Rob appeared, in jeans and a polo shirt. 'Good morning,' he said warily. 'Any chance of a cup of coffee?'

'Good morning, Rob. Here,' said Babs, filling a cup for him. 'That's the last of it. I'll go and make a fresh pot.' She went inside, tactfully leaving Carrie and him alone.

'I did a lot of thinking last night, Carrie,' he began. 'And coming down here, announced or not, was a mistake.'

Carrie could feel her throat constricting as he spoke.

'I've got some business to sort out at home, so I'm catching the three o'clock flight to Dublin.' He rubbed his chin.

Still Carrie said nothing. She didn't trust herself to. She bit her lip.

'Of course I'll be back in time for the wedding, probably two or three days beforehand. I don't want to be the cause of any more . . . friction. And, well, I had thought that we – that is . . . well, what does it matter what I thought?' He sighed. 'Anyway, it's best all round if I go back now.' Rob stopped, apparently waiting for her to protest.

'If that's what you think,' Carrie said quietly, 'then that's what you should do.'

There was an awkward silence.

'Well, obviously *you* haven't any objections anyway,' he said, a note of disappointment creeping into his voice.

Since when did my objections matter to you? thought Carrie, but with every ounce of will she could muster, she determined not to ask or plead with him to stay.

'You'd better tell the girls, and reassure Ali especially,' Carrie heard herself say.

'Sure. Of course I will.' He got up, leaving his coffee untouched. 'I'd better make tracks. I'll call you when I'm, uh, coming back.'

'Fine.' Carrie couldn't meet his eyes. She was afraid she'd break down again. Instead she watched him walk inside, seeming suddenly older and, of all things, surprisingly vulnerable.

Carrie finished her coffee and went back into the kitchen just as Ali was coming out to find her. 'Are you all right, Mum?' she asked uncertainly.

'He told you?'

'Mmm,' Ali nodded. 'I think he's right and it's probably for the best. He'll be back this day next week. Then it's only four days . . .' She smiled brightly. 'We'll be all right, won't we, Mum?' She took Carrie's hand and squeezed it.

'Of course we will, darling. We'll have a wonderful time – I'm going to make sure of it.' Carrie fought to keep her voice steady.

'And now, you'd better get a move on. The massages are booked in Los Monteros in half an hour. Hope's gone home and she'll meet us there.'

Her mother had disappeared downstairs to get ready and Ali went to the sofa. She sat down, closed her eyes briefly and squeezed away the tears that threatened. It had been hard, putting on a brave face for her mum, but she had done it. Exactly as Babs had told her in no uncertain terms. Her instructions of last night still resounded in Ali's head.

Through her sobs, she had heard the gentle but insistent knock and had got up and opened the door. Babs had come in and sat on the bed, just like she had when Ali was little.

'Now, stop that crying, Ali, there's a good girl,' she had said, 'and listen to me.'

And Ali had.

'I know you're overwrought, pet, and you think no one understands you but, believe me, we do. Every girl has a right to get upset before her wedding. It's only natural. You see, exciting though the idea of beginning married life may be, there's also the unexpected realisation that another part of your life is coming to an end. That makes us all a bit unpredictable. Emotions can get out of hand, so to speak. But you're doing the right thing, Ali, and Stuart's a lovely man. I know you know that, but I'm telling you anyway. He loves you very much, and let me tell you, you're a girl that needs the love of a man like him. You love him, too, and you're going to have a wonderful wedding and you'll be the most beautiful bride anyone could ever imagine. You're the star of the show, pet, no one's disputing that, but you're not the only one participating in the production. Your sisters are doing their best, and it's a pretty darned good best, as far as I can make out.

'And then there's your mum. I've dealt with a lot of women in my time, Ali, and your mother is one of the finest human beings I've ever had the privilege to know. But she's had a rough time of it recently, and as usual she's been putting a good face on things. Things that would have made many a lesser person, well . . . bend under the pressure, let's say. I know you didn't mean those nasty, hurtful things you said to her, but she needs to hear that from you.

'Now here's what's going to happen. Tomorrow morning I'll have breakfast ready at half past eight. I want you to set your alarm now and be at that table with your sisters. The first thing you're going to do when your mother appears is tell her how sorry you are for your outburst tonight. Will you do that, Ali?'

Ali nodded. 'I didn't mean to be hurtful, Babs, it just sort of came out wrong.'

'All the more reason to put it right, then. An apology to your sisters and, indeed, your father wouldn't go amiss either. None of us is perfect, Ali, and marriages can throw a lot of unexpected curves at you – but one thing I do know is that your parents adore you. Now it's payback time.'

'I *am* sorry, Babs, really I am,' said Ali, tears starting afresh.

'I know you are, pet. But it's your mother most of all who needs to hear that. Eight thirty sharp, mind. Now, go to sleep and no more upsets. Promise?'

'Cross my heart.' Ali managed a weak smile.

'Good girl,' said Babs and closed the door softly behind her.

Now, Ali jumped as her phone rang. She looked at the caller ID and saw it was Stuart. She hurried outside to take the call without being overheard. Suddenly she wanted to hear his deep, reassuring voice, wanted to talk to him more than anyone else in the world. He was her rock, her number-one fan and she had taken him for granted. It wasn't that she had treated him badly, she just hadn't treated him very well. She could see that now. It was amazing how listening to Babs had given her a fresh perspective. From now on, Ali vowed, she would love and appreciate her future husband as much as he did her.

★   ★   ★

Rob was ready to leave, his suit-carrier slung over his shoulder. He had said his goodbyes, and now Babs was walking towards him from the kitchen.

'You're off then, so?' she said matter-of-factly.

'Yes,' he sighed.

'Well, have a safe flight then,' Babs smiled cheerily.

'Are you against me too, Babs?' he asked mournfully.

Babs folded and refolded the tea-towel she was holding. She looked him directly in the eye. 'No one's against you, Rob, except maybe yourself,' she said, surprising herself with the insight. 'You might want to think about that,' she added, 'when you're at home. See you next week.'

She stood at the door and waved as the taxi pulled away as once again, he slid away from Carrie and his family responsibilities at the first sign of trouble. It almost made her cry. She was so damn fond of that man, and he was so clever, had done so well and had made so much money, yet had thrown away by far his most valuable asset.

Rob Armstrong was a great guy, for sure, but he wasn't a patch on his wonderful wife.

Rob hadn't taken a commercial flight in a while, but now he was surrounded by the hustle and bustle and was grateful for the distraction. He was in business class, of course, so it wasn't as if it would be too much of a shock to the system, but he avoided searching out the airport lounge, preferring to immerse himself among the people cruising Duty Free and the other airport stores.

Thankfully, the flight left on time, and once they were airborne, Rob ordered a glass of champagne and sat back to await his meal. If nothing else, it would pass the time. He could hardly take in the events of the last two days. He was genuinely gobsmacked. Sure, he'd known things between him and Carrie hadn't been great recently, but for her to disregard him and carry on with this *marques* the minute his back was turned was quite disturbing. And then her attack on Ali – although Rob had agreed with most of it, particularly when he had learned that Ali had gone through his phone messages, God almighty! He shivered at the thought. Just what had she seen? Despite everything, though, he couldn't help feeling a bit proud of her. She was like him, on the ball. There was no way Ali would let anyone mess her around and – if he was honest – Rob was chuffed that she cared enough to keep tabs on him and what he was doing.

But Carrie had become a different person altogether. She didn't seem to care at all about him or about his feelings and their marriage was clearly about to be history.

He wondered if it was that menopause thing. He'd heard that could make women go completely doolally – mad as brushes – but then, she had looked all right. Well, more than all right. Carrie had looked great. Rob tried to eradicate the image that flashed intermittently through his mind of Carrie holding hands with the *marques* – Emilio.

Rob knew about the Emilios of this world. Smooth-talking continental bastards who had women drooling. Well, his wife wasn't going to be one of them. Rob wondered fleetingly if he was jealous, then dismissed the idea. Jealous of Carrie? Ridiculous. No, he felt more . . . proprietorial. She was *his* wife – and he didn't want her out there making a fool of him, never mind herself. He would have Emilio checked out the minute he got home. There was bound to be something undesirable about him, and if anyone could put a stop to this nonsense, it was Rob. His marriage wasn't going to be upset by some smooth-talking aristocrat. It would end on his terms – or not at all. Feeling better now that he had determined to take control of the disturbing turn of events in Marbella, Rob settled back to relax for the rest of the short flight. He was on his way home, away from all the madness, where he would sort things out and, of course, see Olwen. His heart lifted. She would be thrilled he was home early. He would see her as soon as possible and make sure they had a fabulous time. At least Olwen *really* loved him, Rob sighed contentedly. More importantly, she appreciated him. He would make it up to her. He hadn't been very nice to her of late, he reflected, but that was all about to change – big time.

Olwen was padding around in her oldest jeans, giving the Hoover a good workout. It was Saturday and she was having a clear-out and a bit of a spring clean. Apart from anything else, it was taking her mind off Rob in Marbella with his wife and family.

Olwen always found housework comforting – organisation out of chaos. Probably because she so rarely had to do it, she thought. Misha, her Filipina girl, came in twice a week but she had flu and Olwen was taking the opportunity to get reacquainted with every nook and cranny of her home. She had been doing a lot of thinking lately, too much maybe, some of it extremely painful. But as Pete had reminded her, nothing is going to happen, Olwen, unless you make it happen.

The phone rang, startling her.

'Rob! I thought you were in Marbella.'

'I was, baby, but not any more. Some urgent business cropped up and I jumped at the chance to come home – but that was just an excuse. Really, I needed to see you – badly. I don't want to be away from you a moment longer than I have to.'

'But Rob—'

'Whatever plans you have for tonight, Olwen, cancel them. I'm taking you out. I've booked a table at Guilbaud's and we're going to celebrate.'

Rob was on a roll, enjoying the surprise he had sprung on Olwen. He had thought it all out. If the girls had seen and condoned their mother out and about with that *marques* chap, then who could blame him if he wanted to enjoy a night out with Olwen? He was longing to be seen out with her anyway – he was fed up with all this hiding away stuff. So what if people talked? He didn't give a damn. He'd be the envy of every man in Dublin.

'What's brought this on?'

'It's long overdue, darling, but I'll explain everything when I see you. We need to talk.' His tone was heavy with meaning.

'Yes, we do, but not in public. You can come here, if you like – but I don't think it's a good idea to go out to dinner. You have a family wedding in less than two weeks.'

'Believe me, it hasn't escaped my notice.'

'Anyway, there's something I have to tell you, Rob, and I'd rather do it in private.'

Rob didn't push it. Maybe she was right. Maybe it was better to lie low for just a little while longer. After all, there'd be plenty of time for dinners in Guilbaud's, or anywhere else in Dublin for that matter, when he had sorted things out.

'Whatever you want, darling. I'm just looking forward to seeing you – I'll be there at eight, okay?'

'Fine. See you then.'

Poor Olwen, she sounded tired. Probably been overdoing it at work lately, she hadn't sounded as thrilled as she usually did when he suggested seeing her. She was probably just taken aback. Whistling a happy tune, Rob headed for the shower.

At eight o'clock, Rob was outside Olwen's house, a bottle of chilled Krug under his arm.

She opened the door and, once again, he was struck by how lovely she was – as always when he had been away from her. Tonight she looked exactly how he loved her best: jeans, a white shirt, bare feet and no make-up – well, none that he could see. She greeted him warmly, but there was restraint, a shadow of concern in her eyes as she turned away. He followed her down to the kitchen.

'Well, aren't you going to ask what we're drinking to, baby?' Rob filled two glasses.

'I'm not sure I want a drink.'

'Why ever not?'

'Rob, you were right. We do need to talk. There's something I want to discuss with you and I need you to listen.'

'I have something to tell you too, darling.' Rob looked earnestly into her eyes. 'I'm leaving Carrie. I am finally, once and for all, leaving her. I've made up my mind.'

'What?' Olwen seemed taken aback. 'Why? I mean, why now, just before Ali's wedding? I thought that was your and Carrie's priority. What's brought this on?'

He could see she was shocked. Well, of course she would be – shocked and thrilled.

He continued, 'It's no good. I can't do it any more. I can't go on like this. I knew the minute I got to Marbella that I could never share a house with Carrie again – under any circumstances. There's absolutely no future for us. It was harder than I thought, breaking it to her, but I decided I had to be honest.'

'How does Carrie feel?'

'What? Oh, she's upset, of course, but she knows we're at the end of the road, and she agrees with me that it's time for us to make separate lives. We had a long talk about it all and the girls seem quite calm about the situation too. There's Ali's wedding to get through, of course, but that will be over soon, and then, darling, you and I can begin the rest of our lives. What do you say about that?'

Something in Olwen's expression changed.

'I'm sorry, Rob. I don't know what to say.'

'Well, of course it's sad, but—'

'I'm sorry to hear it, Rob, because I've been doing a lot of thinking myself – and I've had a lot of time to do it.' Olwen looked sad. 'Things haven't been good between us, Rob, not really, not for quite a while now. Please,' she held up a hand to stop him interrupting her, 'I know they haven't because I'm the one on my own. You've left me alone, quite a lot recently, whether you realise it or not.'

'But all of that's in the past – that's what I'm trying to tell you.' He was becoming exasperated. Didn't she get it?

'I've been offered a job, Rob, a very good one as a co-anchor with NBC, the opportunity of a lifetime – but quite apart from that, I need space and time to get a semblance of normality back into my life. To regain some perspective.'

'NBC? But that's in—'

'New York,' Olwen finished. 'Yes,' she took a breath, 'New York, that's where I'll be based.'

'Are you mad?'

'No, I'm not. But I do know if I continue like this, with you, that I'll unravel. Being the other woman is sheer hell. There's no other word for it.'

'I don't believe I'm hearing this.' Rob was incredulous. 'I cannot believe you'd make a decision like this without consulting me – discussing it with me.'

'What do you think I'm doing now?'

'This isn't a discussion, you're presenting me with a *fait accompli*. You've already decided. I don't come into it at all, apparently.'

'You couldn't be more wrong, Rob. You'll never know how agonising it's been for me – but that's part of the problem, a very large part. Everything, but *everything*, has to be about you, doesn't it?'

'Now you're being ridiculous.'

'Am I? You know, I hadn't actually decided – not for definite. I still have to the end of the week to let them know. If, just for once, you'd listened to *me*, considered how it's been for *me*, if you'd encouraged me, supported me, asked me how I felt, what I needed, then I might have turned them down. But now,' she sighed, 'I'm going to say yes.'

Rob looked at her. This wasn't the Olwen he knew. This was – it wasn't unreasonable, it was *outrageous* behaviour.

'I'd like to wish you well, Olwen, but you're making a big mistake – the mistake of a lifetime.'

'If you really loved me, Rob, you'd let me have this time. Think of all the time I've given you over the last two and half years – all the times when things have been difficult for *you*.'

'There wasn't a lot I could do about it, was there?' Rob snapped. 'I do happen to be married, you know.'

Olwen held her tongue, biting back the very obvious reply and the torrent of rage that threatened to accompany it.

'Yes,' she said quietly, 'I do know.'

'I thought you loved me.'

'I do love you.'

'Then why *now*, when I need you more than ever?'

'I have to do something for *me*, Rob. I don't know who I am any more. Everything – *everything* – I've been doing for so long has been a reaction to you or to whatever's going on in your life. I have no control. Everything in our relationship is dictated by *your* circumstances. It always has been. Can't you understand that, at least?'

'I don't understand any of it. You're not making sense. None of this is.'

'Please, Rob, try to understand.'

'Do whatever you want. I've had enough. I came to tell you I've left Carrie, or as good as, thinking you'd be happy, for me, for us. Instead, well, it's been a very rude awakening.'

'How was I to know any of that?'

'It doesn't matter. I can see that now. I'll see myself out.'

Seconds later, Olwen heard the door slam and Rob's car driving away. She sat at the kitchen table, trembling, unable to believe she had said the words she had rehearsed so often. Her mind was reeling. So much had been left unsaid, but that was always the way. She had never told Rob about Carrie coming to see her, all those months ago. Now Carrie's words rang in her mind again. *You're not Rob's first affair, and I doubt very much that you'll be his last. Rob needs his family. Without us, he'd go to pieces. It would be . . . difficult and he isn't good with difficult situations . . . It would end in tears for both of you – and then what would it all have been for?*

That would have been bad enough, but there was one more nail in the coffin of their relationship.

It had been delivered to her at the studio, marked PRIVATE AND PERSONAL, and when she had opened it the CD was labelled clearly, 'Play this in private.'

Olwen was used to people sending her stuff. It came with the territory of being a celebrity – especially one who featured on TV. She was always being sent demo CDs of voiceovers. Usually she handed them to her PA, Petra, to dispose of, but for some reason she had shoved this one into her laptop and began to listen.

As the anonymous recording played, her heart had plummeted and her stomach churned. One voice, at least, had been instantly recognisable. The other belonged to someone called Mark, who, it transpired, was Carrie's brother.

She had played it so often now that she knew it by heart, and even though she had destroyed it, the hurtful conversation looped insistently in her head: *It's only fair to tell you, Rob, that I took the liberty of making a few discreet enquiries, and I know the girl in question is Olwen Slater. You need to be careful, Rob. We're in the middle of some heavy negotiations and while your, er, personal life is none of my business, even if Carrie is my sister, the banks don't like unnecessary distractions, not*

to mention publicity . . . There would be considerable exposure
– newspapers and so forth. Very undesirable exposure. And then
had come the bit that cut her to the quick, Rob's unmistakable tones, smooth and clear: _Look, Mark, Olwen's a_
fantastic girl and all that, but there's no way I'd leave Carrie
for her – that's nonsense. We're just pals, really. At that point,
the recording had ended. Just pals. Olwen had felt as if
someone had driven over her, then reversed for good
measure.

She hadn't told Rob about the CD. Of course he would
have had reason for outrage – his conversation being recorded
– but worse would have been his insistent denial and futile
reinterpretation of what he had so clearly said. How he hadn't
meant it – how he had had to say it because Mark was Carrie's
brother. But there were some things that couldn't be erased
– not from your heart, at any rate – and that recording was
one of them.

She had asked for and finally taken Pete's advice. She had
put out feelers for a career change and NBC had come up
trumps.

'Just for a while, Ol,' Pete had said. 'Just to give yourself
some space, some perspective. If Rob's serious about you,
he'll sort things out at his end. He'll wait. In the meantime,
you sure as hell don't need to be sitting around going out of
your mind. Look what it's doing to you already.'

Of course he was right.

She'd thought about it, agonised, taken a day off work,
claiming she had a bug – which she had never done in her
life – gone home and cried. Then she had made her decision: she needed to be as far away from Rob Armstrong as
she could be.

She was doing the right thing, the only thing. So why, if
she was doing the right thing, was she crying? The answer
was whispered clearly in her mind. She loved Rob with all

her heart. She just didn't trust him with it. Not any more, not now, not for a moment.

He'd break it, over and over, just as he had done Carrie's.

Olwen would not be enough for him. She realised that now. No woman would be because no woman could ever fill the deep, dark void of need and insecurity that Rob Armstrong had to fill for himself.

22

Rob sat in his favourite chair in the library trying and failing to concentrate on the *Financial Times*. Nothing, not television, not radio, not phone calls, broke the silence. His home was well and truly empty. Even Babs was missing.

He had passed the last few days at home in a daze.

As everyone presumed he was in Marbella, he saw no reason to alert them to the contrary and risk being sucked into another endless round of meetings and appointments. He let his secretary know he was back but unavailable, unless the matter was extremely urgent. Otherwise he put in his time on the golf course, determined not to think about or, rather, be overwhelmed by the incomprehensible behaviour of the women in his life. Life, however, was not being kind to him on or off the course, it transpired. His game was as appalling as his mood, leading more than one partner to remark on his uncharacteristic negativity – particularly with a family wedding to look forward to.

Yeah, right – like he was giving away *all* the women in his life, Rob thought bitterly.

He wrestled now with the unfamiliar sensation of deep pain, of loss. He was devastated at what had transpired between him and Olwen.

But that was ridiculous, he reminded himself sternly. Rob Armstrong had never lost anything in his life. Not when it mattered. But this was different. This time Olwen wouldn't be tucked away in her little house where he could picture her

– picture them both – and all the wonderful times they had spent together. This time she would be away from him. He couldn't – he *wouldn't* – think about it. Not now. He would work something out later. In the meantime, he would forget about her. He would ignore the little voice that told him he deserved it. That he had screwed her around once too often, had taken advantage of just how very much she had loved him. No, he would definitely not think about that.

There was, however, a chink of light at the end of the tunnel. He had hired a first-rate team of private investigators, used by the *crème de la crème* of corporate magnates, to check out Emilio, Marques de Alba, Cordoba y Rincón. If, indeed, that was his title. They were due to report back to him at the end of the week and had been paid more than handsomely to do so. Rob had every hope that they would unveil the unsavoury truth about the smooth-talking man who had turned Carrie's head so effectively. Well, Emilio had waded in out of his depth on this one, Rob thought. He would soon discover that Rob hadn't got to where he was today by standing aside and letting some gobshite Spaniard waltz in and upset *his* apple cart. Rob was known to be a fearsome opponent in a boardroom wrangle. And now, with his domestic situation in such threatened chaos, the gloves would be coming off. If Emilio was looking for a fight, he would get one. Rob had never been more up for it.

Only four days to go! Carrie could hardly believe how the time had flown. It had seemed like two days and not seven since Rob had gone back to Dublin, and now here he was, back again, being exceptionally pleasant – if subdued, she thought. Mind you, with the wedding campaign running at full tilt, anything not directly related to it faded into the background.

The dresses had arrived by courier and were the cause of much hysteria.

All of them fit like a dream, and even Stephanie could find no fault as she twirled and admired herself in the mirror.

Of course, Carrie had burst into tears when Ali had appeared in hers.

'Oh, Ali, darling, you look so lovely!' she exclaimed, watching her beautiful daughter emerge from the dressing room.

For once, even Ali seemed unsure of herself. 'Is it? Are you sure?' she said, staring at herself with the bemusement of every bride who had ever gone before her. Even super-models were not immune to it, not quite believing that the magical image reflected is really them. So much is invested in that image: hopes, dreams, *love*. And that was what Carrie felt just then. She was grateful that, whatever had gone before, she had this wonderful time with her daughters, something so special that nothing could ruin it.

The dress was deceptively simple, a slinky confection of draped satin and silk with delicate ribbon straps that wove through the dress, which flared gently from below the knee into a short satin train. The veil was silk tulle and encrusted with hundreds of tiny pearls.

Stephanie and Hope's dresses were simple ivory satin with shoe-string straps, cut on the bias and clinging in all the right places with a low flare to the ankle.

'Oh, girls,' said Carrie when she had pulled herself together, 'you all look so beautiful. It'll be perfect.'

Carrie focused on the day that was almost upon them. The first of her daughters was having the fairytale wedding that had been denied her all those years ago.

She offered up a little prayer now that they would all have happy, loving, fulfilling marriages or relationships and, more importantly perhaps, that if they were unhappy and hurting, they would have the courage to leave.

*   *   *

Babs had been having a great time. She had been out to *Excalibur*, which she declared she had never seen the like of, and had been spending a lot of time with Hope, whom she hadn't seen in such a long time. Babs didn't believe in favourites, but if she'd had one, it would have been Hope.

She had met and approved greatly of Rudi, although she was quick to spot Hope's reluctance to admit that she was in love. The pair of them were clearly head over heels.

'Well?' grinned Babs over morning coffee with Carrie and Hope in the Orange Square, after they had gone over the church details.

'Well, what?' asked Hope.

'Well, are you going to admit he's The One?'

Carrie hid a grin as Babs charged in where she herself had feared to tread.

'Oh, Babs, I don't know,' Hope laughed, embarrassed.

'What is it you're afraid of?'

'That's exactly what—' Hope stopped herself from blurting out that those were the exact words Rudi had said to her, that first night.

'Go on.'

'It's nothing . . . really.'

'Hope, I've known you since you were six and you were a hopeless liar then. I'm happy to say you're no better now. What is it? Why are you holding back?'

'He . . . well . . . he has a – a reputation, I suppose . . .'

'A reputation for what, exactly?'

'Well, being a ladies' man . . . a womaniser.' There. She had said it.

'Ah, I see. Do *you* think he's a womaniser?'

'I don't know – I don't think so. Well, I mean obviously he—'

'Hope, don't you think you might be *projecting* here a bit – as my good friend Dr Phil would say?'

Hope grinned. 'Maybe.'

'You listen to me. Sometimes it takes a bit of time to meet the right person. For what it's worth, I think Rudi *is* the right person for you – and he certainly thinks so too. Don't let other people's experiences or, indeed, old relationships distract you from that. And another thing,' Babs continued firmly.

'What?'

'As my dear late father used to say, it doesn't matter how many there've been before you as long as you're the last.'

'Oh, that's nice,' said Hope, smiling. 'I like that.'

'I thought you might.'

Carrie smiled, remembering the conversation. Babs, as usual, had been right, and had dispensed the advice that Carrie, given her own marital circumstances, felt unqualified to give out.

'Carrie?'

She jumped as Rob's voice interrupted her reverie. She shielded her eyes from the sun and popped herself up on her sun lounger.

'Sorry, I didn't mean to startle you.' He smiled, the corners of his eyes creasing in the way she knew so well.

'I was miles away,' she said. 'Well, three days away, to be precise. I can't believe it's come around so quickly.'

'Are you doing anything tonight?' The query took her aback.

'No – well, apart from going over the seating plan for the umpteenth time.'

'I was wondering – well, hoping, really – that you'd have dinner with me, just the two of us. We can still do that, Carrie, can't we?' A note of pleading had crept into his voice.

She hesitated, then: 'Yes, of course we can, as long as there's no discussions about . . .'

'Of course not. Promise. It's just that we may not get another chance, Carrie . . . not for some time.' The comment hung in the air.

'You're right. It would be nice. Where were you thinking of?'

'The Old Town? Frederico's? I thought I'd book for eight thirty.'

'Lovely.' Anxiety suddenly gripped her, but she dismissed it. Why shouldn't she and Rob have a civilised dinner together? And he was right, she thought, determined not to succumb to sentimentality, it *might* very well be their last dinner together for – well, goodness knew how long.

Carrie lay in the evening sun for another hour, then got up and went downstairs to get ready. She showered, dried her hair and slipped on the white linen shift she had worn to the polo match with Emilio. She thought of him now with affection. It was thanks to him she would be able to go out tonight and have a calm dinner with Rob. Because of Emilio, Carrie knew she had the confidence to do anything. The old Carrie would have been fretting, worrying and probably in tears by the end of the first course.

'Coming,' she called as she heard Rob say upstairs that the taxi had arrived.

She took one glance in the mirror and saw a glowing, confident woman looking back at her.

'Shall we?' he enquired, opening the door of the car for her.

In the Old Town they stopped for a glass of champagne in the Orange Square, still warm from the day's heat. Then they walked the few steps to the restaurant, which had been a favourite of theirs over the years.

Rob was on his best behaviour, although he seemed tired. Well, it had been a stressful time for all of them, not least herself. If Rob was feeling the pain, he had no one to blame but himself. They chatted easily through dinner, Rob keeping away from incendiary topics. Despite herself, Carrie felt her anxiety vanishing, and for a while it was like old times, when they could laugh and talk freely, away from the spectre of the other women that had been so much a part of their marriage. Now, though, they didn't matter any more because those days were behind her. Carrie was striking out on her own, living life on her own terms, discovering that it was an exciting and empowering journey.

'You look great, Carrie,' Rob said warmly as coffee arrived. 'Really great. I mean it.'

'Thank you.' She smiled, relaxed after the excellent Rioja they had shared.

'Much as I hate to admit it, and I do *really* hate to admit it,' Rob smiled wryly, 'that *marques* obviously agrees with you. If he makes you happy, Carrie, then . . .well . . . I'm all for it.'

Carrie swallowed, not sure how she felt at Rob's sudden generosity. 'Thank you, Rob. That's decent of you to say so.'

'It's not, Carrie, not good of me at all. If you must know, I'm jealous as hell.'

There was a pause. Rob continued, 'It's not a feeling I'm accustomed to, I'll admit, and I don't like it, not one little bit – but it makes me realise what a prick I've been to you all these years.'

'Rob, please . . .' She couldn't believe her ears – and wasn't sure she could handle any more of this extraordinary outpouring. Rob, jealous – of her? She would have laughed if it wasn't so tragic. Now, after all the heartbreak, he was uttering the words she had yearned her whole married life to hear.

'Please, Carrie, let me say this, it's important. I realise now what I'm losing and I can't – don't blame you in the slightest for walking away from me, but before you do, I want you to know if there was anything, *anything at all*, I could do to turn the clock back so none of this was happening, well, I'd do it. Anything. I mean that, Carrie. I love you, I always have. I just wasn't any good at showing it, and now I suppose it's too late. Is it, Carrie? Is it too late for us, really?'

Carrie tried to speak and couldn't. She looked at him helplessly, separated by a table width and thirty years of let-downs. She didn't trust herself to speak as she gazed into those treacle-coloured eyes that looked at her now with such warmth and listened to the voice she loved so dearly. She wanted him to go on and never stop. Tears threatened. Whatever she had expected tonight, it had never been this.

'So if Emilio makes you happy, well, I'm glad for you, but you need to be careful, Carrie.'

'What do you mean?'

'Well, there are a lot of unscrupulous people out there, men in particular.' The corner of Rob's mouth slid down as it always did when he was irritated. 'Because . . .well, because I love you, and want to protect you, Carrie, I had him checked out.'

'What do you mean?' Carrie was horrified.

'I mean exactly what I said. I had your *marques* checked out by the finest firm of private investigators in the UK – at great expense, I might add.'

'I don't believe this.'

'And they came up trumps. Your *marques* is broke, Carrie. Stony. On his uppers. On Skid Row. Owes the banks more than three hundred grand. Look, I know this must be upsetting for you, but you're still my wife, and you're a very wealthy woman, with or without me. You're bound to be a target for such men. They're on the make, pure and simple. Look, Carrie, I've taken care of you for nearly thirty years – I couldn't bear to see you throw yourself away on a cheap fortune-hunter.' Carrie shrank back in her chair. 'He also was an absent father until very recently, I believe?'

Carrie said nothing. Her expression was unreadable, although her eyes were boring into him.

'So you see, Carrie, I really do want the best for you – only the best. It's your interests I have at heart. I couldn't bear to see you get hurt, not again.'

Somehow, she never knew how, she found her voice. And somehow she managed not to scream or hurl every plate in the restaurant she could get her hands on at him. Somehow, she managed to keep calm – at least on the outside.

'This may come as a surprise to you, Rob, but I'm well aware of Emilio's financial situation. He told me about it. He was quite upfront.'

'Really?' said Rob. 'Then he's not as stupid as he looks. That's the clever way to play it, of course – getting the woman's sympathy. Really, Carrie, I'd have thought you'd know better.' His eyes were hard.

'You're absolutely right. I should know better – better than to have sat down for just one moment with you thinking I could have a pleasant evening without being lied to or – or manipulated by your *gross* behaviour.'

'Now, wait just a minute—'

'No, I won't. I won't listen for one more minute to your lies. I've had enough to last me a lifetime. How *dare* you have Emilio spied on by detectives?' Carrie practically spat the word. 'How *dare* you try to upset me and hurt me yet again with your selfish, underhanded motives? Emilio is the kindest and most honest man I've ever met – quite apart from being the handsomest.' Carrie couldn't resist the last bit, and it was worth it to see the anger that crossed Rob's face. 'And another thing,' she got up to leave, pushing back her chair angrily, 'he's certainly a much better kisser than you ever were.' With that she walked out of the restaurant and practically ran from the square to the main street. She threw herself into a taxi and started to sob. But it had been worth it all – nearly – to see the look on Rob's face when she had flung her last remark at him. His mouth had dropped open. And she had spoken only the truth, the whole truth and nothing but the truth.

'You look amazing, Mum.' Stephanie hugged her. 'Go on, hurry, or we'll all be late.'

Carrie wondered wildly if the striking woman wearing the red silk dress in the mirror was really her. The incredible matching picture hat had been designed for her by Philip Treacy and was a millinery masterpiece, curving round her face in a dramatic sweep with a large peacock feather. It made her feel like a million dollars, albeit a very shaky million dollars. Mother of the bride! She had always felt that expression sounded rather dowdy, almost matronly, but the glamorous woman gazing back at her was anything but.

'Come on, Mum, *hurry*! Go!'

'If you're sure.' Carrie was gripped by panic. She took a last look at the beautiful bride, who was uncharacteristically nervous and clearly glad to have her two sisters' down-to-earth moral support.

'Jeez, Ali.' Stephanie rolled her eyes. 'What's with you? It's not as if you haven't sashayed down every major runway in the world. This is just making another entrance. Relax, will you?'

'This is different. It feels *weird*.'

'That's 'cos you've never done it before. Wait 'til it's your third or fourth go – you'll wish you'd enjoyed this one more.'

'Stephanie!' said Carrie reprovingly.

'You should go, Mum! All the cars are here! Come on, we'll be right behind you.'

Then came the part Carrie was dreading. She walked slowly up the stairs, taking deep breaths that did nothing to stop the swirling in her solar plexus.

And there he was, standing with his back to her, glass of champagne in hand. She could tell how handsome he looked without him turning round. He seemed taller, his height accentuated by the beautifully cut tails. Hearing her, he turned with the familiar fluid elegance that it seemed to her he always moved with.

'Carrie,' he said softly, 'you look wonderful.'

For a moment she couldn't breathe as thirty years flashed before her eyes. There stood Rob, handsome and elegant, ready for the ceremony that she – that they – had been denied. There had been no romantic church wedding for Carrie, as she had dreamed of, simply a perfunctory registry office ceremony with her sister and Rob's brother Charlie as witnesses, and both sets of parents looking equally uncomfortable. Afterwards they had had a painfully awkward lunch then fled to the airport for their flight to Spain.

Now, a lifetime later, here they were. The stage was set, but the players had changed. Now it was their daughter they were accompanying to her wedding while she and Rob prepared to go their very separate ways.

Somehow she found her voice, which was surprisingly normal. 'You look terrific too, Rob,' and thankfully, the moment passed as Ali and the girls came upstairs and Carrie watched affectionately as astonishment and emotion passed over Rob's face as he regarded his beautiful daughters.

'One last glass of champagne?' Rob filled the glasses, glad, Carrie suspected, to have something to do to disguise his emotion.

'Not for me. You guys have one – but no more than five minutes.' Carrie made for the car.

Rob accompanied her to where the chauffeur stood, holding the door open for her. 'See you at the church, then,' he said, smiling with a hint of his old mischief. 'Save me a seat.'

'You can count on it.' The door closed, and she was off.

The car sped along the highway, then slowed and turned into the myriad narrow streets that made up the Old Town.

As they approached the square where the church stood, Carrie took a few deep breaths as the car drew to a halt. One last check in her compact mirror, and a smile as she breathed in the fragrance of the rose Emilio had sent her. She was keeping it in her handbag for luck.

Quite a crowd had gathered outside the church, made up of curious onlookers, both locals and tourists, and were being kept at a respectful distance by two Spanish police officers. As Carrie emerged from the car, a flurry of flashbulbs took her by surprise. The local paparazzi had made their presence felt. Then the chief usher was beside her, ready to escort her to her place at the front of the church.

'Mrs Armstrong,' Michael, a close friend of Stuart's, took her arm, 'you look amazing! And you're bang on time!'

'Thank you, Michael.' Carrie grinned up at him. 'Recovered from the stag party?'

'Just about. I take it the bride's on her way? Because there's a very nervous fellow waiting up front for her.'

Carrie assured him she was. 'They're about five minutes behind me.'

'Thank God for that! Now, if you'll allow me, it would be my honour to escort you inside. I must warn you, though, there's quite a crowd. Shall we?' Gallantly he offered his arm and Carrie slipped her hand round it.

'Let's go,' she said.

There was a ripple of excitement as Carrie entered the cool church, the guests knowing that the bride would shortly follow. As she walked up the aisle on Michael's arm, she smiled at the faces who turned towards her, clearly admiring her outfit, their warm glances wishing her well.

Before she knew it, she was alongside Jay and Frank, who winked broadly at her. Jay grabbed her hand and squeezed it.

'Oh, Carrie,' she murmured, 'you look absolutely stunning.'

Then Carrie caught sight of Babs, lovely in her coffee and

cream chiffon, her unruly hair for once coiffed into submission by the visiting hairdresser, lying obediently beneath an elegant cream hat. She gave Carrie the thumbs-up.

Then Carrie slipped into her pew, on the left-hand side of the church.

As the organ played softly, she had time for a quick look round. Across the aisle, Stuart stood with his best man. He smiled at her now, seeming somewhat relieved, although he was clearly still anxious. He looked well, Carrie thought. He had lost quite a bit of weight and had obviously been in the sun. He was a handsome young man – and would be a good husband to Ali, Carrie knew it. His parents sat behind him, his mother in a deep blue silk suit, his father in tails. They smiled at her and waved discreetly.

The church was magnificent, fragrant, bedecked with flowers on every pew and every available surface. B'stardo had done a wonderful job, Carrie acknowledged, and was thankful he had advised against the flowered arches Ali had wanted. He had shuddered with horror at the idea, proclaiming them far too American. As usual, he had been right.

Then the organ stopped, making way for the trumpet player, who took his place to the left of the altar. As the strains of the triumphant march from *Aida* filled the church, making the hairs on people's necks stand on end, Carrie, along with everyone else, turned to the back of the church.

It was Stephanie and Hope she saw first, as they stepped forward, Hope smiling, Stephanie grinning broadly, both looking gorgeous. Then, behind them, illuminated by a sudden shaft of sunlight that filled the doorway, there was Rob with a radiant Ali. They paused for a second, Rob patted her hand, smiled reassuringly, and as if answering an unspoken question, Ali smiled back up at him. Then they began their measured walk up to the top of the aisle.

Of course Carrie cried. How could she not? Unstoppable

tears poured from her eyes, but she was relieved to see that almost every other woman in the church was crying too. Her make-up would be ruined, she thought, sniffing, but she didn't care. Her heart was being squeezed so tightly she thought she would keel over at any minute. Behind her Babs was blowing her nose loudly.

And then, they were beside her. Stuart had stepped out of his pew, looking as if he would burst with pride. In a poignant gesture, Rob lifted Ali's hand and kissed it before handing her over to her waiting groom. Then he slipped into the pew beside Carrie and squeezed her hand tightly. His eyes, she noticed, like hers were bright with tears.

The ceremony went beautifully. Hymns were sung, lessons were read, vows were exchanged, and the choir filled the church with heavenly singing. Communion was distributed, enabling everyone to get a really good look at everyone else as they filed up, one after the other, to receive. Never, thought Carrie, had she seen so many beautiful people gathered in one place, although it was the sight of their well-loved friends from home that brought the warmest joy.

And then it was over. The choir were singing a final hymn and Ali, veil thrown back from her beautiful face, floated down the aisle on the arm of her new husband, followed by the bridesmaids, ushers, both sets of parents and smiling guests. One by one, everybody stepped into the sunlight.

From his vantage-point in the small café in the square, Igor watched the furore as a plethora of flashbulbs caught Ali emerging from the church, guests exclaiming over the ceremony and the mega-party to follow.

Hidden behind his newspaper, he allowed himself a grin. He had almost, but not quite, finished with the ridiculous Irishman, Frank Farrelly. Sure, he had done well out of the deal financially. He and Ivanka were well-equipped to begin a prosperous new life back in Moscow, but Igor wasn't a man to go quietly. He wanted to leave the Farrellys with something to remember him by. And the party on the yacht was the perfect opportunity. He'd be reading about it for days, he thought.

It'd be the party of the decade, all right – one that would go with a real bang. He hadn't mentioned anything to Ivanka, of course – she would have been too worried about Frank, and that stupid prick Lola had been so enamoured with, Rudi. Well, this would wake them up a bit. It would teach them that *nobody* messed with Igor Vladerewski.

Getting onto the boat earlier had been a breeze. All the crew had been getting everything ready for the wedding, and he had gained entry to the kitchens as a member of the catering team. From there, he had gone below deck to the engine room. A boat was a boat, and even that floating gin palace wasn't so different in the essentials from a Russian submarine.

Igor had left his calling card. He glanced now at his watch. It was seven thirty. Any time after midnight, the fun should begin.

Frank Farrelly had been as good as his word. The security was top notch. The bridal car and wedding coaches for the two hundred and fifty guests were accompanied by a police escort all the way to the port, although Carrie suspected that this was to avoid traffic chaos rather than a breach of security. Sitting in the car with Rob, Hope and Stephanie, she felt relieved that the ceremony was over, that they could relax and enjoy what promised to be a fabulous evening.

Excalibur and her crew had risen to the occasion. All the backbreaking hours of cleaning and planning had paid off. Now, she shone in the late evening sun, a legend in her own right, and guests gasped in awe and admiration as they were ferried out to her on two smaller boats from the port. Even Enrique B'stardo had to admit that it was possibly his finest achievement – in the entertainment stakes, at any rate.

The small orchestra played a medley of hits as guests were greeted on board with champagne, or any other drink they fancied, and since a large number of those invited were Irish, it wasn't long before everyone was gearing up to have a very good night indeed.

The bride and groom were last to arrive, having completed the requisite photo sessions on land, and were greeted with terrific cheers and applause.

Dinner was a series of buffets, each more delicious than the last, and then there were the speeches, which were respectively witty, emotional and uproariously entertaining.

Rob's was masterly and very funny, particularly when he related how the family had discovered Ali's sense of drama when she had insisted, at five, on wearing her ballet tutu, complete with pumps, to Mass for four consecutive weeks. She had been deterred only when the parish priest had told her gently that she was a distraction in church. 'But,' Rob warned Stuart, 'don't be deceived by appearances. That same girl, aged ten, on a dare that left even the local boys well behind her, climbed the highest tree on the road and got up onto a neighbour's roof. We had to call the fire brigade to bring her down.'

Then moving everyone to tears, he said how happy and privileged he was to give away his precious daughter to Stuart, whom he welcomed with open arms to the family, knowing he had what every father dreamed of: the unique qualities that would make his daughter the happy, cherished wife she deserved to be.

Finally, in a tribute that brought everyone to their feet even before the traditional toast was proffered, he turned to Carrie, sitting beside him. 'I have been, I remain and always will be amazed and bemused by my darling daughters. I shall also be eternally grateful for them. But without this incredible woman, who has been at my side for the better part of my life, neither they nor I would be the fortunate family we are. Carrie, we would be nothing without you.' He raised his glass. 'To the bride and groom, to my family, and to enduring love.'

More than one person listening noted that it didn't sound quite like the old, macho Rob Armstrong, rather more like a man genuinely moved and touched by the overpowering love he felt for his family.

As the sun went down, the orchestra gave way to a swing band and everyone made their way unsteadily to the main dining room, which had been turned into a ballroom. The bride and groom took to the floor, followed by Stuart's parents. Carrie was deep in conversation with Jay when she heard a familiar voice.

'May I?' said Rob, holding out his hand. She took it and then they were on the floor, to more rapturous applause from their friends.

She had not anticipated, thought Carrie, how natural it would feel, how easily they moved together, Rob holding her as he always had, she slipping easily into his arms, the way only thirty years of living with and loving someone could teach you.

The band was playing 'It Had to Be You', one of her all-time favourites, and she relaxed, determined not to let anything spoil a moment of this fabulous night.

'Well, we got one thing right, didn't we?' Rob was looking at their girls, all dancing. Ali, of course, with Stuart, Stephanie with an exotic fashionista, and Hope with one of Stuart's groomsmen. Rudi, unfortunately, was on duty.

'Yes, we certainly did,' Carrie agreed warmly.

'Carrie?' Rob looked into her eyes and held her just a tiny bit tighter.

For a moment, looking into his eyes, she was hypnotised, as always, helpless, locked in the grip of memories and promises that held equal delight and heartache. And then, mercifully, before she had time to do or say something she would regret, she was saved.

'Ah, now, enough of that carry-on,' boomed Frank. 'A man can't be hogging the most glamorous woman in the room, even if she is his wife.' And Carrie was swept away, the band segueing effortlessly into a considerably more upbeat number.

'I'll catch you later, then,' said Rob, reluctantly letting her go as Frank pulled her into an energetic jive.

As the party gathered momentum and everyone drank late into the night, an unexpected guest trotted back and forth along the mostly deserted deck. Having escaped his attendant crew member, whom Stephanie had bribed heavily to take care of him, Toby, still resplendent in his white silk wedding bow, searched in vain for his mistress, who was nowhere to be seen.

He knew she was below, with the other people, but try as he might, he hadn't been able to get into the ballroom. The door was manned by two or more crew members and they had shooed him away.

Something was wrong. He had sensed it long before the sinister vibrations, which had nothing to do with the music or the heaving of the crowds of humans below, had infiltrated his canine consciousness.

He had to get to Stephanie, had to warn her she was in danger, protect her. He started to run back and forth, increasingly agitated, sniffing the air and whining. Suddenly he saw a familiar figure approaching.

'What the—' exclaimed Rudi.

Toby ran to him, shivering and barking.

'Toby!' Rudi caught him by his bow. 'Who on earth let you on board?'

Toby stood stock still and tried, a last valiant attempt, to warn of impending disaster. He threw back his head and gave a long, harrowing howl. But his warning was drowned in the beginnings of a sinister rumble, then an ear-splitting explosion.

It was as if they had been plunged into the bowels of hell. Darkness reigned, smoke billowed and sirens shrieked as the yacht reared at a freakish angle, her stern blown clean off.

Then came the sound that every sailor dreaded as water, gushing, rushing torrents, poured in.

Everywhere, people were screaming, scrambling, struggling, stumbling over debris and each other to get on deck, to escape this unimaginable, terrifying watery grave.

Excalibur and those aboard her were sinking fast.

Rudi came to with smoke in his lungs and coughed. His years in the toughest Merchant Navy in the world, and his close brush with death on more than one occasion, served him well now as he hauled himself upright and cleared his head.

His crew were the best, and they turned to him now, calm in the face of collective panic, following without question his every order. Bulkheads were closed, life-rafts were lowered and inflated, maydays were sounded and, as the enormity of the disaster became evident to onlookers from the port, a full-scale emergency rescue service immediately went into operation.

Women were lowered first, panic stricken and sobbing with relief, to scramble into the waiting life-rafts, while overhead, the reassuring sound of helicopters was greeted with relief.

The men followed, those who had waited: some of the braver or more panic-stricken had jumped in and were now swimming towards the boats speeding out from the port.

Rudi waited until the last possible moment.

Finally, exhausted but certain that everyone was safely off *Excalibur*, there remained only Rudi and Rory. They were shaken, but relatively unscathed.

'Quite a wedding, eh, Captain?' quipped Rory as *Excalibur* floundered, only her bow remaining above water.

'I said it was a bad idea.' Rudi wiped his brow. 'It bloody breaks my heart – she was a stupid excuse of a boat, and she rolled like a pig out at sea, but we're watching a piece of history go down. I loved her.' His voice caught in the wind.

'We all did. You did her proud, Rudi.' He put his arm round Rudi's shoulders, showing as much support as he could in what was the most heartbreaking moment for any skipper – relinquishing a beloved boat to the sea. 'Ready, Captain?'

'After you, mate.'

And Rudi, patting what remained of *Excalibur*, followed Rory, diving into the chilling cold of the late night water that, moments later, would swallow up the most famous yacht of them all.

'M-M-Mum,' Stephanie was sobbing as she, Carrie, Hope and Ali huddled in one of the boats that were heading for the harbour.

'What, darling?' Carrie held her youngest daughter close, trying to rub some warmth into her.

'Toby, my darling Toby, he – he's drowned,' she sobbed, 'and it's all my stupid fault.'

'What?'

'Toby,' she gulped. 'He was on the boat and he'll have drowned. Salukis aren't good swimmers,' she sobbed.

'I don't believe it!' Ali shivered uncontrollably. 'My wedding and the biggest yacht in the Med have been blown to bits and you're worried about a *dog*! My *husband* could be dead, for Christ's sake!' she shrieked.

'He's *not* a stupid dog. You don't understand – you never would.'

'Shh,' said Carrie, her teeth chattering. 'All that matters is that we're safe, thank God.' She hugged them. 'We're all safe and everything will be all right. Just hold on, Stephanie, we're almost there now. Ali, darling, Stuart's an athlete, he'll be fine. He's probably in at shore already.'

'Stop! Stop!' shrieked Jay as she leaned out of the life-raft, trying feverishly to paddle backwards as she pulled something from the water.

'What the f—' a crewman mumbled. 'Quick! That woman at the end! Pull her back in – she'll capsize the bloody raft at this rate.'

And they had pulled her in. Kicking, screaming, unhinged with grief, she waved something damp and furry in their faces, clutching it to her and sobbing incoherently.

'Oh Frank, oh Frank, you stupid bollix. You shouldn't even be on the water – he can't swim!' she roared at the uncomprehending faces around her. 'Don't you see? Can't you understand? He can't swim – Frank's gone and drowned on me.' She waved the furry thing in the air. 'This is all of him that's left to me!' She rocked back and forth as a few women tried to calm her.

'It's the shock,' one woman said to another, 'and the drink. She's not making any sense.'

Stephanie was right. Salukis are not good swimmers, their long delicate legs made for running great distances over desert sands, not for struggling in cold, murky water. Toby was tired and terrified. Blown off the boat by the force of the explosion, he had struggled to keep afloat and for a while he had clung to a piece of floating wood. But that had been swept away, and now he was gasping for air, his white silk bow catching in his legs. He wanted now more than anything to hear his beloved mistress's voice and feel the sun warm upon his back as he snuggled beside her. He let out a last desperate yelp.

'Look! It's a bloody dog.' Rory bumped against him first. 'Christ, I thought it was a seal!'

'Toby!' Rudi swam alongside. 'Have you got nine lives or what? Grab him, Rory, and we'll take him in. I know at least one person who'll be very glad to see him.'

'Over here!' yelled Rory, waving to the last of the rescue boats. 'The captain, the first mate and the ship's dog coming on board!'

Back at the port, mayhem ensued. TV crews were fighting to get a piece of the action and interview guests who were giddy with relief to be back on *terra firma*. Ambulances and police cars were on hand to ferry people to the local hospital, where they would be treated for minor injuries but mostly for shock. Thankfully, as far as anyone could make out, it seemed that there had been no fatalities.

Carrie and her girls waited as the boats came in bearing the menfolk. One by one, couples were reunited.

Jay ran to a very shaken Frank and flung her arms round him. He held her to him tightly. 'Oh, Frank!' she sobbed, overwhelmed with relief. 'When I found this,' she held up his bedraggled toupèe, 'I thought – I thought—' She broke down. 'And you can't even swim!' She hit him with it. 'Don't you ever, ever put one of these things on your head again.'

'Shh, pet,' Frank smiled. 'It's all right. Sure, aren't I here and we're both together now. I promise you anything, whatever you want, Jay, anything at all.'

When Rudi and Rory came in with a shivering Toby, both

Hope and Stephanie let out delighted shrieks. As Stephanie clung to Toby and Hope to Rudi, it was then with the sudden dread of certainty, that Carrie knew something was terribly amiss.

'Where's Dad?' said Ali tremulously in Stuart's arms, her voice seeming to come from very far away. 'Dad? Where's Dad?'

'Oh my God,' gasped Carrie. 'Rob?' Her voice rang out in the suddenly still night. 'Rob!' she screamed. 'Where's Rob?'

Carrie would never forget a moment of the hour that followed – the longest hour of her life. She and her girls sat on the beach, wrapped in blankets, waiting and praying.

Suddenly a shout went up. They had found a man. They were bringing him in now. 'Is – is it Rob?' Carrie called hoarsely as she ran to the shore, then waded waist-deep into the water, where they were lifting him from a boat.

'He's all right, isn't he?' she gasped, recognising every fibre of the man she had loved and reached out to stroke his tranquil face, the mouth relaxed, his hair damp.

There was silence, a menacing silence – harbinger of the unspeakable.

'He's all right!' she shouted. 'He is – he's all right, I know he is.' But she was crying now, gasping for breath, shuddering at the chill she had felt on his face, his beautiful, beloved face. She doubled over and felt hands round her, helping her, supporting her, guiding her out of the water.

Somehow she got through the mind-numbing awfulness of what followed, moving as if in slow motion through a fog as the formalities were undertaken.

Identifying his body, following him to the morgue and gazing at him, lifeless, but so perfect he might have only been asleep. Wanting to scream at him, to shake him awake – to put an end to this horrific, unspeakable nightmare.

Then the infinite kindness – of Babs, her daughters, Stuart, all shattered but frightened for what this would do to her.

And Emilio, discreet and considerate, orchestrating behind the scenes, using his considerable influence to bypass much of the ghastly red tape so that they could take Rob home without delay.

Frank and Jay were her rock, insisting on accompanying her and the girls as they flew him home on Frank's jet.

Epilogue

Carrie had never seen the Sacred Heart Church so full. It was overflowing – crowds of people stood outside, even. It was as if everyone Rob and she had ever known had come to say goodbye.

Now she and her girls had to do the same. Carrie steeled herself. Shattered though she was, she was aware of a sense of calm, aware that without realising it she had already gone through the worst stages of bereavement in losing Rob Armstrong. In that way, she understood, he had set her free already. She had loved him – and always would. He was part of her. But she had let him go while he was still alive, and that made bearable what she had to go through now.

Now she had to be strong for her girls, her darling girls who had been her reason for living and laughing through the times when she had felt like giving up. Now, it was they who needed her.

Ali, sobbing before they had entered the church, had Stuart at her side.

Rudi was with Hope, beside her at every step, strong, silent and intuitive enough to know that Hope's calm, pale exterior was no more than a façade, knowing as Carrie did that underneath it, Hope was grieving desperately.

But it was Stephanie who worried Carrie most. Stephanie, whom she put her arm round now. Stephanie who trembled and huddled close to her, her eyes red, swollen and larger than ever in her woebegone face. She had to be strong for

Stephanie – she had to be strong for them all. And then they began, together, Carrie leading, the long, slow procession to the front of the church. She felt him now, close by her, urging her on in this final battle. She wouldn't have been able to do it otherwise. That was Rob's last gift to her.

Everybody said the funeral was beautiful. For Carrie, it was poignant, tragic, unreal. It passed like a bad movie. The church, friends, tributes, hymns, music, tears and more tears, and finally laying him to rest, throwing in a last red rose and leaving him in his final resting place. Then with the girls, heading back to the funeral car, to Fairways, where the celebration of Rob's life would be held.

It was at home, among her closest friends, relatives and other friends she hadn't seen in years, that Carrie came slowly to grasp how very much she was loved.

It was, she thought later, as if it had taken this tragedy for her to understand that. It gave her strength to go on, to pick up the pieces of her old life and turn it into something new.

(Six months later)

Babs headed for home in her brand new Nissan Micra. It was one of the few things she had treated herself to after the generous, but shocking, amount of money Rob had bequeathed to her in his will. The rest went into a rock-solid equity fund with the financial advisers he had recommended. And her investment was doing very nicely, thank you. That was Rob to a T, she thought fondly. He'd looked after his friends to the end. She patted her freshly blow-dried hair and smiled. Since the wedding, she had taken to having her hair done once a week. She had been delighted with the transformation of her unruly tresses at the determined hands of the hairdresser.

Endings and beginnings – weren't they what life was about? she reasoned. She still came in to do for Carrie twice a week in the new penthouse apartment, but it was more about maintaining a meaningful friendship than any serious work.

Fairways had been sold two months ago for a staggering amount of money. A couple in their forties with young children had bought it.

Babs had been pleased about that. It was a beautiful house and needed a family in it. There was nothing like a few children and teenagers, maybe a pet or two, to make a house a home. That's what they were meant to be, she reflected, however many bedrooms they came with.

Soon she would be off to visit her own daughter in America. Then, come September, she had enrolled on a college course for mature students in counselling. She had given it a great deal of thought and everyone agreed it was a terrific idea.

After all, there had to be some career where age and experience counted for something, didn't there?

She was nearly home now. Traffic permitting, she would have time to make a cup of tea before she sat down to watch Dr Phil on her new wide-screen TV. He was the only man on the planet with a vestige of sense.

Jay marched up the steps to the Merrion Hotel and shivered as a cold breeze whipped through the golden autumnal day. It was her birthday and she was heading to Guilbaud's, where Frank was meeting her for lunch. She checked her watch, and saw she was a good ten minutes early. Perfect. She would sit down and have a glass of champagne while she waited for him. She handed her coat to the attendant, then went to the anteroom and sat on one of the plush sofas. She nodded politely at a few people she knew and sensed, rather than saw, others, watching her covertly and whispering to each other. Since the tragic events on *Excalibur*, she and Frank had become reluctant celebrities. They had been shattered by Rob's untimely death, not to mention the series of bizarre events that had led up to it. Frank had lost not only a business partner, but a dear friend and still blamed himself for what had happened. The only positive thing to come out of it was that at least she and Frank had been given a second chance – a chance to reflect on the important things in life and, most of all, each other and their family. These days, they kept a decidedly lower profile.

After Rob's funeral, when things had settled down a bit, Frank had taken her on a surprise holiday, a real second honeymoon. They had resolved to wipe the slate clean and work on rediscovering their marriage and each other. Hearing Frank's distinctive voice now in the hallway, greeting the attendant, Jay smiled. Life was so fragile that she would never, she vowed, as long as she lived, take anyone for granted again.

Once more, Carrie went over the contents of her two suitcases and closed them – for better or worse. What on earth did you bring on a round-the-world trip? Probably too much, but whatever she had forgotten, and there was bound to be something, she could buy it if and when.

She looked around her brand new penthouse apartment. It was closer to town than Fairways and she loved it. It was bright, airy, overlooked a beautiful park in an exclusive area of Dublin, and she was still near her friends and family.

In a moment, Jay would be arriving to take her to the airport.

She glanced round the spacious sitting room, allowing her eyes to rest on the much-loved photographs in silver frames from which her nearest and dearest smiled out at her. There was Rob, of course, many of him, of them both, with his wicked grin.

The children: Ali settled happily with Stuart and expecting

her first baby. Hope, travelling with Rudi, taking photographs and embarking on a documentary they were making about South Africa. She would see them, thought Carrie with a rush of excitement – all of the family were meeting there for Christmas – when she and Emilio were on that leg of their trip.

And darling Stephanie had turned into quite the business-woman. She was running a trendy and apparently successful catering company in Dublin. She had been devastated by the loss of her father, but she seemed to be coping by throwing herself into her new business. Although her holiday romance had not survived, she had a new and, in Carrie's opinion, far more suitable boyfriend who had qualified as a vet and was about to go into practice. Toby approved of him too, which kept everybody happy.

And Emilio, dear Emilio. Carrie stroked the handsome face that gazed out at her from a photo of them together on his visit to her here. She would never have gotten through the last six months without him – kind, considerate, supportive Emilio, who understood better than anyone about loss and what it could do to you.

The doorbell sounded. She gathered up her bags and headed for the lift. Downstairs, Jay was behind the wheel of a hired people-carrier. 'I thought this would be safest, Carrie. My Merc will barely hold an overnight bag, and Frank's new Bugatti – now that the yacht's gone he had to buy something else ridiculous – wouldn't have been any good either.'

'Jay,' said Carrie, hugging her and laughing, 'I'm so glad you're seeing me off. I'm feeling a bit jittery, to be honest.'

'Nonsense. Nobody deserves a round-the-world trip more than you. If I didn't think I'd be playing gooseberry, I'd have invited myself along. I'm mad jealous. Now, fasten your seatbelt – it could be a bumpy ride, but nothing we won't handle, girl!'

'I'm going to miss you, Carrie,' said Jay, hugging her tightly, having insisted on coming in to see Carrie off.

'I'll phone, promise, from everywhere.' Carrie gave her best friend a squeeze. 'You know I hate goodbyes, Jay.' Carrie felt tears threatening again.

'Go on, get outta here.' Jay waved to her as she went through departures.

After a stroll through the shops, Carrie made her way to the premier class lounge, where she settled with a celebratory glass of champagne. Soon she would be in London, where Emilio would meet her and they would spend the weekend. Then they would fly out of Heathrow on the first leg of a long and exciting journey. She picked up a glossy magazine and flicked through it, but her mind was wandering in an all-too-familiar direction. Looking up, she caught sight of a young couple giggling, obviously off on a special trip – maybe their honeymoon. Her gaze then wandered to the television set in the corner of the room; Sky News was on. Suddenly a familiar face appeared on screen. It was Olwen. The news clip was obviously a repeat, referring to a political item Olwen had reported on earlier in the year. Carrie sighed. It was another sign. She'd been getting them for weeks and trying, without success, to shut them out.

She left her seat and approached the woman behind the desk.

'Yes?' she smiled at her. 'Can I help you?'

'I hope so,' said Carrie. 'Do you by any chance have any notepaper and an envelope?'

'Yes, of course. Just a moment . . . here you are. Will this be enough?' She handed her a sheet and an envelope.

'Great,' said Carrie. 'Thank you. If I leave a letter with you, will you'll see that it's posted?'

'Absolutely.'

Sitting back down, Carrie sighed and chewed her pen, just like she had when she was at school. On every previous occasion she had tried to do this, she had given up, torn by conflicting feelings of self-pity, exasperation, rage and, yes, good old-fashioned jealousy. Quite a cocktail of emotions.

But then she would think of her own good fortune. Her blessings. She had her beautiful girls, all happy and healthy, she had her memories, she had been spared a painful and probably drawn-out divorce – and now she had Emilio.

Then she would think of *her*, and wonder what it must have been like to lose someone you loved, desperately perhaps, and be excluded from all comfort, from closure. Not to be able to attend the funeral. To have to grieve alone.

Now she gave it a final go, and kept it simple, knowing somewhere, deep inside, that it was the last thing she could do for Rob, and the last that would perhaps help her, Carrie, to move on with her life. Rob would want that for her – and for Olwen. She took a deep breath and began.

I know you loved him, Olwen, and I know these last few months must have been hard for you. I wondered if maybe you would like to meet and talk sometime . . . not just yet, but perhaps one day. It might help us both. I'll be travelling for the next few months and will probably be in New York around the autumn. If you'd like to talk, here's my mobile number. I'll leave it up to you.

For what it's worth – and here Carrie took a very deep breath – *I know he loved you.*

With every good wish,
   Sincerely,
   Carrie Armstrong

Before she could change her mind, she put it quickly into

the envelope, sealed it and addressed it to the house where she had visited that day, which seemed so long ago. Just to be sure, she marked it 'Private and Confidential'. Wherever Olwen was, it would find its way to her.

Just as she handed it to the ground hostess, her flight was called.

Moments later, Carrie was on the plane, looking out of her window, saying a silent goodbye as the aircraft taxied along the runway, gathered speed and soared into the sky. She was leaving the past behind, taking only the good times with her. Moving forward, slowly but surely, confident and secure in the knowledge that she was – and had been – loved. That, she reflected, was the most important thing any woman could ask for.

The End

ACKNOWLEDGMENTS

Grateful thanks are due to the following people:

To Breda Purdue and everyone at Hachette Books Ireland here in Dublin and Hodder in the UK. Editors, Ciara Doorley and Sue Fletcher, respectively, for unstinting support, guidance and wisdom; to Hazel Orme for razor-sharp copy-editing. Their vision and experience contributed to making *None of my Affair* a better book. To Antigone Konstantinidou for a beautiful cover – every book should have one. To my wonderful agent, Vivienne Schuster – every author should be so lucky. To my friends and family who are unfailingly tolerant when I disappear for months on end and re-emerge expecting them to remember me. Last, and most importantly, to you, dear reader: I hope *None of my Affair* makes you laugh and cry as much as it did me – although not, perhaps, for the same reasons!